Burning the Sea

Burning the Sea

A Novel

Sarah Pemberton Strong

alyson books
los angeles | new york

MANUFACTURED IN THE UNITED STATES OF AMERICA.

THIS TRADE PAPERBACK ORIGINAL IS PUBLISHED BY ALYSON PUBLICATIONS,
P.O. BOX 4371, LOS ANGELES, CA 90078-4371.
DISTRIBUTION IN THE UNITED KINGDOM BY
TURNAROUND PUBLISHER SERVICES LTD.,
UNIT 3, OLYMPIA TRADING ESTATE, COBURG ROAD, WOOD GREEN,
LONDON N22 6TZ ENGLAND.

FIRST EDITION: MAY 2002

02 03 04 05 06 **a** 10 9 8 7 6 5 4 3 2 1

ISBN 1-55583-644-5

COVER DESIGN BY MATT SAMS.
COVER ILLUSTRATION BY MYRIAM MATEUS.

for Jaem—muse and traveling partner

PROSPERO: Can'st thou remember
A time before we came into this cell?
I do not think thou can'st...

MIRANDA: Certainly, sir, I can.

—Shakespeare, *The Tempest*

November 12
9°45'N 80°05'W

The sea is a flat sheet of blue today, blue without waves; the wind has died. If I were on a sailboat, a day like this would be cause for worry. The vastness of the sea becomes overwhelming when you don't have the power to move through it. On windless mornings like this one, I wake anxious and don't know why at first. I still carry this with me, an internal sense of the weather, a sense born in the islands. On islands the only times the wind dies are at sunset and right before a storm.

Without wind, the freighter moves forward. By this time tomorrow I will be in Santo Domingo. I will arrive as I have arrived so many places, stringing each port of entry like a colored bead on a piece of fishing line, each bead lengthening the distance between myself and the island I once called home. Yet I find myself here, traversing the same sea I swam in as a boy, the same sea that swallowed my mother, the same sea that seven weeks ago rose and swept that island clean of every leaf on every tree, uprooted palms that had stood a hundred years or more, tore houses apart from their foundations, and, in the cemetery, knocked over a headstone I have never seen.

Part One

November 12
New York

Sometimes they have to touch my arm or shoulder before I realize it's me they're addressing. I know how it looks—it looks odd, my sitting all by myself on the floor in the airport. I can see how it looks as if I'm someone else, someone hurrying through the terminal who happens to look down and notice the young woman—girl, really—sitting there on the floor with her back against the empty check-in counter. She has a bag with her; she must be waiting for a plane, but she doesn't look as if she's waiting. She doesn't have anything to read. She isn't scanning the departures screen. She doesn't look bored. She's just sitting there, a tall, skinny girl with her knees drawn up under her chin as if she were sitting on a hillside somewhere and not in an airport at all. I know how it looks: the broad but somehow distant smile; the pale, shapeless clothes. Clothes too large for me, too faded, holes. Clothes belonging to other people, clothes borrowed or found.

People notice, they just do; it's not the clothes, it's the way I sit there watching the spill of movement through the terminal as if I were watching a sunset or an ocean. People notice, and they start talking to me. But I'm not there, I'm somewhere else, I don't hear them right away.

The flight from New York to Santo Domingo was delayed fifteen hours. I wasn't the only one sitting on the floor here. There weren't enough chairs at the gate, and after the gift shops and restaurant had closed, the other passengers clustered themselves on the hard cement tile with the resigned air of people accustomed to delays for which no explanation would be provided. They had come prepared, with bags of food and blankets. They chatted with one another, and after a while a

5

woman holding a fat earringed baby began talking to me. I played with the baby, and she told me in an English punctuated with Spanish mutterings that flights to the Dominican Republic were always this late and hadn't I brought any food?

I had bought some bread and cheese in the Frankfurt airport, but it was long gone. No, I said, I hadn't. She gave me a piece of chicken from her bag and studied me. I was the only white person at the gate. This was not a tourist airline. Everyone else who was waiting was waiting to go home.

Was my boyfriend Dominican? she asked at last.

No, I said, I didn't have a boyfriend.

Surely I wasn't going to Santo Domingo alone?

Yes, I said, I was alone. No, I had never been there before. Did I speak Spanish? Only a little. No, no relatives there.

Then why on earth are you going, she wanted to ask. I saw the question form on her face and changed the subject before she could ask it.

Why on earth?

I could not have given her the real answer then. I had no sense of my own destiny. Now I can see clearly the shape of it, the shape of my destiny. It is not separate from the shape of my life itself, and that is precisely why I missed it all these years. But I see it now. It's all around me. It's given my life a completeness I would have dreamed of, had I been able to dream of such things.

I'm not saying I wanted it.

When I was three years old I climbed from the bed in which I had been put down to nap and out of a third-story window. It was a dormer window: I climbed right onto the roof. I crawled along this slope of shingles the whole length of the house until I reached the edge. Then I stopped and just sat there like a dislodged weather vane. I stayed like that for several hours. My parents found my empty bed and after a frantic search drove to the police station to report that I had been kidnapped. When they returned, there I was on the roof. They saw me right away: I had started screaming.

I don't remember all of this firsthand. It's a family story. It happened to me, but the memory isn't mine. Most of my memories aren't mine, in fact. I know most people don't recall anything of their first years, but for me, that early blankness stretches on through my entire childhood until I was almost grown. I lived all those years like everybody else, but somehow they got away from me. Where there should be birthdays, Christmases, odd flashes of scene that somehow lodge with great significance in most people's minds—a tree branch outside a window, the print of mother's favorite dress—there is nothing. I have nothing. I've always been careless with my possessions. Memory is just one of the things I've lost.

This story of me on the roof, though, there is one thing about it I do recall, something no one else knows: When I began screaming it was because I realized that the distance between the roof I was on and the neighbors' roof was too great and there was no way for me to continue my journey.

I was screaming because I could not get away.

I remember a few other things besides this, and I view them over and over like a closed loop of film. It doesn't take long to go around once. The parts I remember best, that I see most clearly, happened at night. You'd think the days, with all their activity, would contain something remarkable enough to stick in my mind, but no. It was the nights. The first time it happened I was very young, seven, maybe, or six. It goes like this: I have been asleep. I wake up. It's the moment right before I open my eyes, and I have no idea where I am.

The bed I fell asleep in has dissolved under my back. It is gone, and nothing is there in its place, only air. The blankets are gone. My feet are intensely cold, the soles of my feet flat against something hard. My left hand too is icy cold. I move my fingers and discover they are closed around a cold metal sphere.

I open my eyes. Nothing, only darkness, and then I see a slab of wood a few inches from my nose. One crystal moment of panic, clean as a knife edge, and then I know where I am.

I am standing in the hallway of our house in the middle of the night, clutching the knob of the front door.

This happened again and again. Not every night, but from then on I never knew where I would be when I woke up. Any continuity between where I was when I closed my eyes and where I would be

7

when I opened them was severed forever. The logic of time and space did not apply to me. I could have been anywhere.

Sometimes I imagined whole landscapes, entire countries, in the moment before I opened my eyes.

During the day my body did what I told it. I'd say sit and it sat, I'd say "Run," and it ran, and when I opened my mouth to speak, words did come out. But during the day I took another kind of journey without moving my body an inch. It was my mind that left. I'd be sitting at the dinner table and in the blink of an eye my mind would depart, leaving my body behind.

"Michelle? Michelle! What are you thinking?"

My mother's voice, worried; my father's, annoyed.

"Nothing," I'd say, startled. I never knew when I was doing it. I tried to be my own jailer, but my mind was too quick for me. It slipped out between breaths, and I never knew it had gone until someone called to me from far away to come back and answer for my mind's behavior.

"Nothing," I'd say. I couldn't say anything else. I never knew where my mind had gone. It disappeared like a ship over the horizon.

"Nothing," I'd say. "I wasn't thinking about anything."

And then I'd smile and focus my eyes on the frayed edge of the tablecloth or the uneaten food on my plate. I chained myself to the objects of this world as sailors lash themselves to the mast when their ship passes the sirens.

What was I afraid of?

About the world of my mind I know only this: It has never been explored. Like all unexplored worlds it is flat, like a pancake. Bordered by edges. If my mind were allowed, it would go and go until it had gone too far and dropped beyond the horizon once and for all, the stern of the ship upending before it plunged over the waterfall at the end of the world to fall and keep falling forever through empty and infinite space.

When I was twenty I left home. I wanted to go around the world. The world is round, like an orange; there are no ledges to fall off of.

When I left home my sleepwalking stopped. I still never knew where I would wake up but now it was because I moved around so much. In all the hotel rooms, pensions, cabins, tents, grass huts, empty stretches of beach, motels, forest clearings, bedrooms of friends, bedrooms of strangers, sofas, bare floors, train stations, bus depots, airports, and city parks I slept in, I opened my eyes in the same place I closed them. My body stayed with me all night and stopped deserting me. I moved so fast it was all my body could do to keep up.

And I did what I set out to do: I went around the world, the world that is round like an orange. I went all over. I went around backward and forward, through everywhere twice, and I always left by a different road than the one on which I had arrived. Every house I went into, if I came in through the front door, I left by the back. Superstition, you may say, but I covered a lot of ground.

In a land far from where I began, I heard a story.

One day in the streets of the oldest city in the world a young man named Ali was sitting in a café. He had his whole life before him, spread out in such a magnificent fashion that he did not contemplate his tea on the table or the rhythm of his own heart but instead looked all about him in the manner of one waiting for a parade. While craning his neck this way and that, he happened to notice two men sitting at a small table across from his own. After eavesdropping on their conversation for some minutes, in case he should overhear something beneficial, he divined that one of the men was none other than Death himself.

Upon realizing this, Ali became quite pale and fled from the café at once without finishing his tea, for he knew Death travels to claim those whose lives are deemed finished, and he was afraid his own name might appear on Death's itinerary. He ran straight home, where he gathered a few possessions into a sack and hired the fastest horse he could find to take him out of Baghdad to a city on the other side of the country, across a great river and a great desert to the very edge of a sea, for there surely he would be safe from Death. Day and night he rode, and the farther he left the city of Baghdad behind, the more the color returned to his cheeks, and at last his fear was replaced with visions of the town of Baku, where he could live his life in all its glory with no worry of Death coming to call.

Several weeks later, Death was still wandering around Baghdad seeing the sights when he came upon an old man standing in the street.

The two of them fell to talking about this and that, and presently Ali's name was mentioned.

"Ali?" said the old man. "Yes, I know him. His house is just across the square from mine, and if you are looking for him he is usually home at this time of day."

"Really?" said Death. "How peculiar! For I'm due to meet him tomorrow—but hundreds of miles from here, in a place called Baku."

It's an old story, of course. Destiny is the story whose ink is dry on the page before you ever pick up the pen. Destiny is the path that bears your footprint before it bears your foot. With destiny everything is in the past tense.

But suppose you have no past? Suppose your past is an erased slate? Will destiny not find you? Will destiny arrive at your house and find no one home?

It's in the eyes of the man in the porkpie hat who chooses a path I will walk down almost half a century later. It's in his hands, my destiny, as he picks up a pen to sign his name on a dotted line. He doesn't know what he's doing. He is my mother's father, my grandfather, and he's standing in a hot office on the ground floor of a building in New York City. He's going to be a rich man—that's what he's been hearing for the last hour and a half. So he is promising to pay two thousand dollars in exchange for the deed to three square acres of beachfront property on the most beautiful island in the Caribbean. He's never seen it himself, but that's what the agent tells him.

"They call this island the land Columbus loved best," says the agent, "because it was the most beautiful place he'd ever seen, and he ought to know. He got around, Columbus did."

The land already has a house on it; the pictures are attached to the deed with a paper clip. They're out of focus and overexposed, but that makes it all the more perfect, mysterious. The house is made of wood and painted white, it has two stories, and those trees beside it are definitely palms. That's really all that's visible, but it's enough for my grandfather.

"You can walk out your front door and be on the beach," says the agent. "You can squeeze rum out of the sugarcane in the front yard and mix it with coconut milk from those trees in the backyard. You'll live the good life, my friend, and then, when you're old, you can sell it to any one of the hotels that will be buying up the coastline, and they'll pay you anything you ask because they've got to have your land—see, it's right in the middle of a bigger plot, they can't build their hotel around your house. Sure, there's no tourism yet, which is why it's such a wonderful place to live, but mark my words, there will be. If you wait a few more years to buy, you won't be able to afford something half this size. You're a man ahead of your time. I can tell, it takes one to know one."

My grandfather, the man ahead of his time, signs his name, and then the two of them go off to a bar and get drunk.

They drink to the land Columbus loved best. They drink to men ahead of their time. They drink to Americans and the American way of living. They drink to banana republics, places to go to live like an American when you can't afford to live like one at home.

Hours later my grandfather takes a taxi home across Central Park. It's a beautiful night, but he can't walk it: The ground is spinning. The cab turns and heads uptown, block after block, and that's when it hits him: Two grand is a lot of money. It is. The whole of this city they're driving through was bought for only twenty-four dollars.

He's signed his name, Henry Sandbourne Harth, and that night he dreams the dreams of a rich man. Later that year he and his wife pack up four steamer trunks, eleven suitcases, one guitar, and an indeterminate number of carpet bags, hat boxes, and linen chests, and they set out by ship for this magical island. They have brought from home framed pictures, tablecloths, even a rocking chair. Their cabin on board the ship looks just like home. If you stand with your back to the porthole, you're standing in a brownstone on West 81st Street. You can put your hands on the back of Grandmother's rocking chair, and beneath your feet is the living room rug.

The living room on West 81st Street steams south, and the two of them sit in their chairs and dream of sitting in their chairs in the living room on West 81st Street with the Caribbean Sea in their backyard and sugarcane in the front and palm trees all around.

When they arrive on the island, they do not find what they expected. They find the deed they hold is to a piece of property half an hour from the sea by car, and the road to the property is so bad no car can get over it. The house is there, all right, but they can't get to it. It's on top of a hill in the middle of someone else's cow pasture and there is no road up the hill at all.

There used to be a road. Now it's a forty-five degree mud slide. You can see the gravel that used to grade it lying all over the cow pasture.

What happened to the road?

"Hurricane," says the man in the army jeep who has offered to drive them out to the land.

They nod wisely. They're in the tropics now—hurricanes come with the territory. Having never been in a hurricane, they imagine it like the rainstorm at Coney Island that one summer when the carousel was hit by lightning. Everyone crowded into the arcade to wait for the storm to pass and sang songs about the first World War.

They gamely get out of the jeep and slog their way up the hill. By the time they reach the top they're covered in mud. They go into the house. It isn't locked. Half the floorboards are rotten. You can see the foundation beneath them, light seeping through the cracks. There is no electricity or water. It starts to rain and the roof leaks.

They try to stick it out, but the weather gets them. They expected sun, they expected the water to be in the ocean, not falling out of the sky. After a few days they get back in the jeep and drive back to the town on the coast, where they check in at the Hotel American and try to figure out what went wrong.

They stay there for a while, in the Hotel American, with all their luggage. My grandfather drinks himself silly. My grandmother gets diarrhea, salmonella poisoning, and amoebas. My grandfather doesn't. He's healthy as a horse. There's so much alcohol in his stomach lining that nothing can grow there.

What a mess. The palm trees in the yard were not even the kind that produce coconuts. How could this have happened?

The history of travel, of people traveling anywhere, is the history of mistakes. Columbus died still believing he'd found Asia.

My grandparents give up and make reservations on a steamship bound for New York.

When my mother is born, she grows up with the story of The Land Your Father Bought Like a Fool. She hears it from her mother, who has the sense to be amused by the whole thing since there's nothing else she can do.

My grandfather never goes anywhere again. But my mother—my mother is like a dog at the end of a rope. My mother is at the end of her rope. She begs and pleads and works nights and weekends, and at last my grandfather says, "Yes, all right already," and my mother gets to do what she's always wanted: She buys a ticket to take a trip.

She goes across the ocean on a ship, and by herself, which is unusual in those days. She comes back to the U.S. when she runs out of money, but she talks of leaving again. It's a crucial point: She comes back and things look smaller than she remembered; America, the land so big and wide on the map, now seems to be only an image reflected over and over in opposing mirrors to give the illusion of infinite space. It has the appetite of infinite space.

My mother is not hungry.

"Will you please eat something?" my grandmother says. "You must have caught some disease out there that's ruining your appetite."

But it's not a sickness of the stomach that makes bread turn to wood in my mother's mouth—it's a sickness of the heart, the eyes. It's the sickness of a woman who has tasted a life the world does not want her to live. She knows it. It scares her, the flavor of what she got away with. She holds freedom in her mouth like an illicit kiss. She tries to forget it, she does not believe she will ever taste it again.

I carry with me one photograph of my mother. Before I was born, before she was married, this picture was taken. She's standing with her back against the railing of a bridge somewhere, laughing into the mouth of the camera. The background is washed out, like fog. It's impossible to see where she is, and when I ask her she says she doesn't know; it was too long ago.

"It might be Pittsburgh," she finally says. "I think I'm in Pittsburgh."

Pittsburgh! I want to shake her. She's not in Pittsburgh. The look in her eyes is happy, wild almost, thrilled. Thrilled is the word. She thinks she's in Pittsburgh because that's where she met my father, fell in love. But she's mixing it up, the look of being in love with the look of being in motion. She forgets now, she thinks love is all there is.

She thought if she didn't get married she would just come untied, float away like a balloon from the hand of a child. My father was her anchor.

I look at my mother and see the weight that sank her.

She didn't want me to go. She never said so, but like any daughter I could read my mother's mind. The day I finally left I could tell by the pauses in her speech exactly what she was feeling. Like any mother, she was watching her life being carried away by her daughter. Not the life she was living, but the life she never had. She didn't want me to take it. It was like giving away a beautiful dress before she had a chance to wear it herself.

She clung to the hem.

I pretended not to notice and packed my bags.

It was in Berlin that the inevitable happened: I fell in love. Her name was Heike, yes, and the fact that she was a woman and not a man made it worse when it ended. All of us who come back to our own sex for the things we thought we had to leave it to find, we all have this idea in our heads that now that we're back, love will be easy, or easier. It's a beautiful illusion, and perhaps a necessary one, for without it, I don't know if I would have had the courage to begin at all. To admit who it was my eyes followed at parties, who I lost sleep over, who made me blush.

Heike lived in West Berlin, that island whose sea was concrete and barbed wire. I stayed in Berlin what was, for me, a long time. I stayed long enough to get a job: Four nights a week I tended bar in a café in Savigny Platz. I stayed long enough to find a place to live, with Heike. We moved in together, into an apartment from which we could see the Wall from six of our nine windows. It was considered a great view. Perhaps that's why I stayed so long, long enough to fall in love; the

Wall surrounded me on all sides, and I forgot I was on the side of it where you're permitted to leave.

Love, I don't know what else to call it. When I think of her I don't think of that word but of the silent space between our two languages where words could not go. When we were out in public we spoke German; at home we spoke English. When we made love we spoke neither, although weren't silent. I think of those sounds now. In that closeness, in the heart of it with her fingers inside me and our bodies moving as one, the bed vanished and there was nothing but flesh, lips, hair, and a whole different existence in the moments when our eyes met; in those few moments I was there with her and nowhere else. In those few moments we were all that existed and all I wanted in the world.

Yes, it was love. I know because I had the illusion that things would be different because of it. I mean different in the place inside me where nothing, not even love, could penetrate because that place was too far in. If anything could reach it, I believed love could. Love can't, it seems. It didn't. But at the time I believed it would, so yes, it must have been love.

The tenderness I felt for her was sometimes so overwhelming that I was crushed under the weight of it. I would have to get up out of the bed where we lay—she sleeping and me looking in agonized tenderness at the shape of her closed eyes—get out of bed in the middle of the night and walk, first in the hall and then down the stairs and into the streets, breathing too fast and overwhelmed with the feeling of being unable to breathe.

I walked around and around the blocks of nighttime Berlin in such a state. I walked in the alleys, over the canal bridges, and along the Wall, always along the Wall. I climbed the little wooden observation staircases and looked out over the black stretch of field and barbed wire on the other side of the Wall, at the silhouettes of the soldiers in their turrets in the middle of the field. My heart was always beating too hard. I was full of a feeling I could not name, though I knew it well. At last I would descend the stairs and walk again, through Mariannen Platz and along the river until exhaustion fell like curtains over my mind. Then I would return to Görlitzerstrasse and climb the stairs to our flat, exhausted, praying she was still asleep.

I watched the disaster of my own life approaching as if it were a ship coming toward me from far away. I spotted it long before it arrived. I was powerless to stop it. I didn't tell Heike what I saw. I thought if I said nothing, perhaps it would go away again, or sink. Then it would never happen. Then she would never have to know.

It happened one night at a party in Kreuzberg. We went to a lot of parties like this one, a benefit for a movie some women we knew were making. I wasn't expecting anything. At one point I walked into the kitchen to get some wine. Five or six people were there, immersed in the conversations you go into the kitchen to have: two women at the small table, heads bent toward each other, three people clustered around the refrigerator speaking in low voices. I poured the wine into my cup and took a sip, and then I saw it. I saw a woman who looked exactly like myself standing there holding a teacup of red wine. Her head was in profile, and she had just raised the cup to her mouth. The woman was me. It was myself I was looking at, but from outside, as if I were outside the window at the end of the room. I tried to move toward myself. I couldn't.

"Are you all right?" a voice was saying. One of the women at the refrigerator had turned around and was looking at the woman who was me. "Are you all right?"

As I watched from a distance, the woman who was me dropped the teacup she held. Wine splattered on the linoleum, and the other woman came forward and touched my arm. When I felt her touch, suddenly I was back in my own body; I was able to move. I moved my head and looked at the floor. There was wine on my shoes.

"What's wrong?"

I looked up at the woman. There was worry in her eyes. I didn't know her name.

"Nothing," I said. I picked up the teacup, which hadn't broken, and smiled. If the world had been ending at that moment, I still would have picked up that cup, smiled that smile.

"Nothing," I said again, and went back to the living room.

Heike was standing with her back to me, laughing at something that had just been said. I hardly recognized her. She turned to look at me and stopped laughing.

"You look sick," she said. "Michelle, are you all right?"

I shook my head. "I have to get out of here."

"Okay," she said, misunderstanding. "We'll go home."

I sat in the apartment like a drugged person. There were things in it that belonged to me: books on bookshelves, a couch, a closet full of clothes, pots and pans, posters. They were all a kind of accident happening around me. I looked at them with no feeling of ownership. I didn't know why I'd bought them, what I was thinking.

"What is it?" Heike asked.

"Let's go to bed," I told her.

She looked at me to see what I meant by this. I tried a smile, managed to keep it there. Pleased, she reached out and touched the base of my throat with her fingers. I willed myself to attend to her touch, her body. I leaned forward, fit my mouth to her mouth, pressed my tongue against the swell of her lips that I had come to know as well as my own, the faint ridges of her teeth, the taste of her, anise and rain.

I'm here, I thought, *here, here, here,* and she slid her fingers down over my sweater, wandered them toward my breasts as if we had all the time in the world. And my body flushed with heat and wanting as I waited for her hand. *It's working,* I thought, and for one long moment I believed it too—that I could stay there forever, that the spell of her body was strong enough to save me, but as her hand slid so slow and certain toward the pulse of sparks that were now my nipples, I bent my knees and took her fingers in my mouth before they could arrive. If her fingers moved any farther down my body, they would trip over the little cloth bag with the passport in it that hung from a cord around my neck, next to my skin.

I should have known; it was right there, the warning, written plain as day in that idiom of American speech, "to fall in love." I didn't pay attention to it until it was too late. It wasn't until I felt the air rushing about my head and found myself staring down, down into an endless space below me; not until then did I think about those words.

To fall in love. To fall in. To fall.

On the last day—I didn't know it was going to be the last—I wasn't the one who left. My body was testament to that; my body sat on the floor of the apartment in front of the windows in the echo of her departure and was still for a long time. It was not my body that left.

My mind, my mind. Never say it was because I was impervious to love. It was because I had come too near an edge.

After she left I sat there in a stupor for what might have been hours before I noticed the street outside. Through the windows I could see there was some sort of demonstration going on. The streets were so full of people you couldn't see the pavement. I watched for a long time before I registered what I was looking at. They were taking down the Wall. For weeks there had been talk of this happening, but in the past few days I had somehow missed the events that led up to its commencement. In the past few days my mind hadn't been in Berlin at all.

I put some things from the apartment in my knapsack and went out the door. I headed for the train station, threading my way through the crowds of East and West Berliners celebrating. I walked for hours. After sunset the streets grew even more packed. People lit bonfires and set off firecrackers, and no one in all of Berlin went to bed. In the passion of that crowd my own journey was swallowed and so it took me a whole night and a day to get from Görlitzerstrasse to the Bahnhof am Zoo. I saw Berliners with pickaxes or hammers in one hand and bottles of champagne in the other. I was given a handful of fireworks, which I put in my knapsack, and a flag, which I lost. I ate the cake that was passed to me, and I drank lots of champagne, which was everywhere, but I wasn't part of the celebration. I didn't dance on the wall or run back and forth through the center of the city that had been divided for so many years, as the Berliners did, some of them weeping with joy. I moved through the crowds like someone in a dream. When I boarded the train that would take me out of Berlin, the party was reaching its height. The coach was mobbed with East Germans drunk on schnapps and freedom, but by the time the train actually crossed the border I had fallen asleep. When I woke up I was in another country, and the compartment was empty.

I dreamed of the house, the house on the island.

I am walking up the hill to the top, where the house stands out against the sky a brilliant white against enormous blue. The world blazes with color. Emerald, fuchsia, the sky so blue it looks swollen. The air itself blue, and dizzying, tropical, hot. I stand on vibrant grass and look up at the bright whiteness of the house, so bright it is almost blurred. I squint. Through the windows I can see people. My family is inside.

My grandmother, bent like grass in the wind.

My grandfather, looming, solid. His feet shake the floor when he walks.

My mother, whose eyes follow everything and arrive nowhere.

My father, a presence in another room.

I can't see myself. I know I am in there with them, but I can't see where.

I stare at the house, trying to see, but it's too bright. Forgetting shines like a star. To look straight at it hurts my eyes.

I awoke with a start. I was on the train. Outside the dirty compartment windows, a countryside whizzed past. Autumn grass dying in a field. The sky looked as if it had been raining. I did not know how long I had been asleep.

I was alone in the train. I couldn't see the sun, but it felt like late afternoon. I couldn't remember what time of day I had boarded the train in Berlin. I couldn't remember being awakened at the border, whether we had crossed it.

I looked out the window.

Fields, dead grass, newly turned earth. The clack of the wheels, low iron-colored clouds overhead. The train ran for a few moments alongside a highway and I saw a road sign. I was no longer in East Germany.

The house, I dreamed of that house. Not of Heike, not of the hundred different ways it might have happened instead, not of her face, which I will probably never see again. Not of the city I have just left. I dreamed of that house, a house I have never even seen.

Before my grandmother died she used to tell me stories about it: the house, the adventure in the tropics that ended in a mess. I sat beside her on a sofa, the color and shape of which I have forgotten, and listened as she told me about things that had happened, her eyes alight in rare animation at relaying the scandal of it all, of her younger days.

In lush detail and gesturing with her usually silent hands, my grandmother describes for me how silly the rocking chair looked sitting in the mud of the front yard, how the storms shook the roof until she was afraid it would blow off but it didn't, how they sat drinking rum in the darkness and waiting for the house to fall down around their ears. But it didn't, she says, it didn't fall.

I ask her if it's still there and she says she expects it is.

As she speaks of it I can see it, the house. It would be a place to wander off to, a place to hide in, to slide through the bushes and make my way up wooden steps into the shade of a roof so strong that even a hurricane would not blow it away.

Things that have happened to me, the stories of my own life, have slipped through me without a trace, but the stories my grandmother told me—stories about other people, about things that happened many years before I was alive—have caught and fixed themselves inside me with perfect clarity. I have other people's memories in place of my own.

Another memory is that of my mother, hands on hips, eyes flashing, standing in the kitchen, yelling at her parents. She's younger than I am: "She'd just had a birthday," says my grandmother. "Your mother was just twenty."

She's twenty and looks like she does in the photograph I have of her, the photograph that isn't in Pittsburgh. She's angry now, furious, but like in the photograph she is full of life.

"All right," says my mother, stabbing the air with her chin, "all right, then, I'll leave. I'll go live on the island."

My grandparents, sitting at the table, look up at their furious daughter and ask her what she's talking about.

"I'll live in the house on the island," she says. "I won't need any money. You won't wonder where I am. You won't have to do anything. I have enough money for the plane ticket. I'll just go."

"No, you won't," says my grandfather. "You don't even know where it is."

"But you do," says my mother.

My grandfather says nothing.

"You mean he wouldn't tell her?" I ask.

"You have to understand," my grandmother says. "You have to understand, Michelle. Your mother was so young, barely twenty. Back then

20

girls didn't go off gallivanting around the way they do now. Besides, it wasn't as if we said she couldn't go anywhere. Just not there, not alone. If she'd been married, it would have been different. It was a strange country, a wild country, no Americans around for miles and miles. Suppose something had happened to her? You know what I mean. It wasn't safe."

I think about that word, *safe*. A safe is a box, a box of iron. I see the hinged door, the lock, the numbers. A safe is where you put things you don't want other people to know you have.

Valuables, secrets.

I have the deed to that house with me. When I was packing to leave America, I went into my parents' room for a picture of my mother. The picture I wanted she kept in a jewelry box I had never seen her open, though I had opened it many times myself. It contained things like pearls and a lock of my hair from when I was small. There were a few envelopes, one with the hair in it, another larger one containing the deed to the house. I pocketed the snapshot of my mother laughing and started to close the drawer. Then, on impulse, I took the deed. I knew she wouldn't miss them. She never opened these drawers.

I was surprised to find out I once had blond hair. At least, on the envelope it said in my mother's writing, "Michelle, age two." But my hair is brown now.

Outside the window of the train it was getting dark. I switched on the light over my seat and pulled out the little bag I carried around my neck. I took out my passport and looked at the visa stamps, the inks in different colors—blue, purple, dark red—the smudged words in foreign languages. I turned to the front of the book and looked at the photograph on the inside cover for a long time.

I took out my money and counted it and then put everything away again and slipped the bag back inside my shirt. I switched off the compartment's reading light. Outside in the world, on the fields, it had started raining.

"You could have gone anyway," I told my mother once.

"Gone where, honey?" she said, as if I were still that young.

"To the house. On the island." She wasn't listening. *"Mom."*

"Oh," she said finally. "That. Yes, but I didn't know where it was, they wouldn't tell me. It wasn't until after they'd both died that I even saw the deed. You know that."

"You could have gone anyway. You could have just gone to the island and gone to the hall of records or something. You could have found out where the land was."

She shrugged. "I don't know. It was too much of a hassle. And anyway, then I met your father." She smiled. "And if I hadn't met your father, I would never have had you, and then where would I be?"

She kept looking at me after she said this, as if she expected an answer.

The world is not so large. From Frankfurt I took a plane to New York, where I had to change airlines. After waiting all night at JFK because the pilot scheduled to fly the plane was stuck in customs in Puerto Rico, we left—it was morning by then—and five hours later the plane dropped below the clouds and I looked down and there was the island. Green hills, red and yellow earth, the sea changing from blue to green and breaking white against the edges of the land.

When the plane touched down everyone cheered. We stood jostling in the aisles while they rolled the staircase into place. A baby sat down in the aisle and cried. An old man was having trouble with the cardboard box he had jammed into the overhead compartment. The line inched forward, and then at last I stepped out of the plane into the air and the heat and light of the island. I took my first breath of island air and suddenly I was happy. The air was alive, buoyant with the humid smell of earth, of flower sap. The sea was not only in the water but in the air. When the wind blew I smelled through the hot smell of the runway a whiff of salt and seaweed.

The terminal was one stucco building at the edge of the tarmac. I walked toward it through the wavy heat, breathing. Grass. Earth. Wind, tinged with a faint sharpness: the smoke from a fire miles away. If I had arrived here walking in my sleep, I would have known by that first breath of air that I was on an island.

We straggled up a narrow walkway half-blocked by a group of musicians frantically playing accordion and drums. Past the musicians we spilled out into a room jammed with yelling people. One end of the room was open to the runway, partitioned by a dented metal ramp onto which men in green shirts were beginning to throw the luggage. I stood at the edge of the crowd and watched. Things were being thrust at me: customs forms, a paper cup half full of warm rum. "*Es gratis,*" said the girl holding the rum tray. I took a cup and we smiled at each other. She had a beautiful wide smile that was missing two teeth.

Everyone pressed forward, shouting at the baggage handlers. Bulging suitcases and taped boxes were all over the floor. I saw my knapsack being flung into the air, but I couldn't see where it landed. I drank the rum and slipped into the press of bodies.

I found my bags and lugged them toward the opposite end of the room where the long customs tables stood. People lined up—infinitely patient though the whole island was out there just on the other side of the big metal doors—and waited for their turn to greet the men in khaki uniforms and have their papers examined, their bags and carefully taped boxes opened for inspection.

When my turn came, the customs officers went through my knapsack and all at once became very excited. They took my knapsack and my tent and carried them through a metal door where I wasn't permitted to go after them. What was the matter, I asked. I hadn't been paying attention to the luggage search. I had been watching two small boys on the other side of the room trying to drag an enormous suitcase across the floor, and now my own bags had been taken away by the customs man.

They told me what was wrong in a rapid-fire Spanish I could not understand. I thought they needed a little extra money. I was prepared for this. My Spanish was clumsy, but bribery requires surprisingly few words. I leaned against the customs table and waited for the officers to come back out and explain the imaginary complication that could be resolved for a small fee. But no one came out. The people in line behind me dragged their belongings to other tables and then I stood there alone, waiting. I became aware that I was being stared at. I looked around. I was the only gringo in the airport. My feet began to hurt.

At last the metal door opened, and two men came up to me in a blur of military uniform, sunglasses, guns, and a torrent of Spanish.

Why was I carrying something, they wanted to know.

"Carrying what?" I asked.

They repeated the word, which I had never heard before. I tried to think what could be in my luggage. Tent? Camping stove? "Do I have to pay to bring them into the country?" I asked. I wanted to make it easy for them, I wanted to get out of there.

But that wasn't it. They weren't interested in money. They were getting annoyed. They repeated the word I couldn't understand. I shrugged and tried to look charming and innocent.

They repeated themselves a few more times and then gave up on words: One of them put a hand on my arm in a way I would have understood in any language.

Come with us, the hand said.

I looked at the door in the wall through which they had taken my luggage and then I dropped my shoulder bag on the floor. Everything inside spilled and scattered. I took my time picking the things up: I was afraid.

"You're having trouble with your declarations?" A voice speaking English. I looked up from collecting my crumpled napkins and Deutsche Marks and ticket stubs. Another man had joined the customs officers, a pair of feet shifting back and forth in leather sandals. I looked up all the way, and a tall Dominican peered down at me. He was dressed in a pressed cotton shirt and trousers, not a uniform. I stood up.

"They took all my luggage," I said.

"Oh?" he said. "It's possible you'll have to pay them something." His American accent was perfect, as if he had gone to great pains to make it so.

"They don't want money," I said, grateful to be speaking English again, "I tried that."

"Would you like me to ask what the trouble is?"

Before I could answer he had turned to the shorter of the officers and said casually, "*¿Hay algún problema con el pasaporte de ella?*"

"*Con el pasaporte, no,*" the officer started, but the other officer, the one who had grabbed my arm, interrupted, speaking so fast that I understood nothing. The stranger listened, nodding occasionally. He had an unusual face. His skin was light brown, but his eyes were blue. Not the hazel-green I had noticed on a few other light-skinned Dominicans, but really blue, as blue as my own. His hair was somewhere between African and Spanish: It was brown, not black, and sat close against his head in curls too loose to be called kinky, too tight to be waves. As I watched his face while he listened to the officers discussing me, his expression wasn't exactly consoling. When they finally stopped speaking, he looked quite grave. He nodded several times and turned to me.

"What is it?" I asked.

He frowned. "This man," he said carefully, as if having difficulty choosing his words, "this man says you're carrying…explosives."

"What?"

"Explosives. Some sort of bomb?"

"Of course not. Tell him to bring my luggage back."

The stranger turned and said something to the officers. I could tell it wasn't what I'd asked him to say. I wondered if I could just leave the three of them there and walk out of the airport without their noticing. I closed my eyes for a moment.

Then I remembered something. A little cold wave passed through me. I knew what all the fuss was about.

"I know what the matter is," I said.

They didn't turn around. I went up and stood right next to them. The officer who had grabbed my arm was wearing a lot of cologne. The leather on the holster for his gun was cracked.

"*Disculpe,*" I said. I couldn't think of how to say it in Spanish. "*Yo sé que, que es la problema, el problema…*" I didn't have the words. I tapped the stranger's arm. "I know what the problem is," I said in English. "I was in Berlin, and I—"

"Berlin?" He turned all the way around and gave me an odd look.

"Berlin, Germany. You know the Berlin Wall?"

He gave me a slight nod.

"They took it down—"

"I know," he said. "On Thursday."

"People were setting off firecrackers. To celebrate. Somehow I got some. They must be in my knapsack. I forgot I had them."

He looked at me and kept looking, not casually, too long. He took in my too-short hair, my dog-eared passport, my dress with the hole in it. He was trying to decide something about me, but I didn't know what it was. Then he turned to the customs officers and began to speak. I couldn't catch any of it: His Spanish was too fast, too Dominican. So I watched their bodies instead. Whatever he was saying, the officers were not impressed.

The stranger turned back to me. "They don't believe you're a tourist," he said.

"What do they think I am, a Communist spy?"

He gave me a sharp look, a shut-up-for-God's-sake look. And I saw that his hand was shaking slightly.

"They want to arrest you," he said.

I felt myself leaving. He was saying something, but I couldn't hear it; it was as if he were saying it to somebody else. As if I were very far away or watching a television with the sound turned down, I saw the stranger turning to the officers, taking out a package of cigarettes and handing it around. The cigarettes were lit, inhaled, and they began speaking again. I watched their mouths move. One of the officers took his hand off his gun. I saw the other one laugh. The stranger laughed with him. Then he turned back to me and said something.

"What?" I said.

He frowned, and touched me lightly on the arm. And then I could hear him again. "They say you can go," he said gently.

"*Pero se quedan las maletas,*" said the short officer.

I understood that. "My bags have to stay?" I asked.

"He says if you want them back you'll have to come in the morning and fill out a special form. Then they'll give them to you."

"Can't I fill out the form now?"

He turned back to the officers, and there was a brief consultation. The answer seemed to be no.

"He says he can't return anything that's been confiscated because it's not his job. The man you need to see will be here tomorrow." He lowered his voice. "If I were you," he said softly, "I would leave before they change their minds." Our eyes met then, and I suddenly wondered why he had gotten involved in this. He obviously didn't work for the airport. He didn't seem to have any luggage either. Some man out scouting for a damsel in distress? The complication, the small fee. It was time to get out of there.

"All right," I said, "I'm going."

I turned around and began walking empty-handed along the length of the room, past the other long customs tables, which were now all empty. At last I reached the metal double doors at the far wall and the guard nodded and I went out through them and then the heat and air and brightness hit me and I was outside.

I squinted and looked around. I was standing on the curb where the taxis pull up. I knew it was a long way from the airport to the city. I couldn't afford a taxi. I looked around for a bus stop and didn't see one. The concrete plaza seemed strangely deserted. The wind I had felt on the tarmac had died down, and the air smelled faintly of diesel. I thought of asking someone for help and wished I weren't wearing a dress. I looked down at the dress. It was still there.

"Hey," said a voice in English. I turned around: the stranger again. He was holding two small leather suitcases, one in either hand. "I'm driving into town," he said. "Shall I give you a lift? The taxis cost a fortune."

"No, thanks."

"If you want to catch a bus, then, it's a three-mile walk to the main road. Do you want a ride to there?"

I sighed. Traveling by myself, very by myself, I had learned by error that the words of men are of limited value. In a language you don't speak, words are useless. In a language you do speak, words are too easily used to tell lies. Who knows what is behind words? Did I want a ride to the main road? What did that mean?

"Thanks for translating in there," I told him. I wanted to hear him say something else so I could hear his voice again. Words may lie, but the tone in a man's voice always gives him away.

"Don't mention it," he said. "It completely distracted me from my own panic. I hate going through customs."

"Panic? So *you're* the Communist spy."

He laughed, and when I heard him laugh I decided to go with him. Travel requires a certain amount of recklessness; otherwise, it's just a vacation.

We jostled down the main road in a battered and dusty sedan. He told me his name was Tollomi, spelled it out for me, and before I could ask him whether it was Spanish, he changed the subject and began to talk, more rapidly than I would have guessed he could manage in English, and told me all about the area we were driving through. He told me the name of the district, that there was a very old cemetery near here, that the highway had been repaired since he was here last but he would be surprised if anything had been done with the slums, and did I see that vine there?—that was a plant that grew only on this island, nowhere else. The overly practiced manner I had noticed earlier in his speech seemed to have disappeared, as if after a few minutes of exercise, his knowledge of English had come fully awake. I knew Dominicans often went to the U.S. to work and stayed for years. When he paused for breath, I asked him how long he'd been living there.

"I don't live in the States," he said. "I flew in from Puerto Rico, but before that I was in Guatemala."

"You're from Guatemala? I thought you were Dominican. So where did you learn English?"

"I was just in Guatemala doing some work," he said. "Before that I lived in Buenos Aires. A lot of people speak English there. See those palm trees? The ones in Argentina are totally different. These are royal palms. During storms they bend almost to the ground, but they don't break. Then when the storm is over they spring right back up again, unless of course it's a hurricane. If the winds are strong enough, even a royal palm will break."

He went on talking about the trees. I stopped listening and just looked at him. He was trying to distract me from asking about his origins by simply reciting the list of places he had been. Dazzle them with the stamps in your passport, but don't show the cover. It was a trick I sometimes used myself when I didn't want to reveal my nationality. It made me curious. I was curious about anyone who played the same games as me.

He went on about the trees and the names of the plants growing wild in the ditches. He mentioned famous monuments on the island, beaches, and the view from Pico Duarte, the highest mountain in the Caribbean. I closed my eyes and tried to hear in the rise and fall of his voice some cadence or trace of pronunciation that would give him away. I wanted to guess and guess right. But I couldn't hear a thing. Except for his looks, he might have grown up in my hometown.

I opened my eyes again. The road we were driving over was a mess, and despite Tollomi's maneuverings we kept hitting potholes. He drove like someone used to driving on bad roads, with studied carelessness. We had long since passed the place I thought the bus stop would have been, but, having gotten in the car at all, I thought I would stay in it all the way to the city. I wasn't afraid of him, and I wondered why I wasn't—and if I should be. Whoever he was, he wasn't the person sitting here beside me, driving with one hand on the wheel and yammering on about some statue some dictator had built and how someone named Trujillo had cut down all the trees.

As I was thinking this, he broke off in mid sentence and glanced at me. He saw I hadn't been listening, and his face seemed to shift and drop in dismay. Then the car swerved, and I went sliding over the seat and banged into the door as he yanked hard on the wheel to keep us from going off the road.

"Sorry," he said, slowing down. "I almost hit a bird." He glanced at me again and added, "Did you see it?"

"No," I said, rubbing my arm.

"I'm sorry—I didn't see it either until it moved. Some people say it's very bad luck to hit one." His voice shook a little.

"It's certainly bad luck for the bird."

"They say, if you kill a bird by accident, it foretells the death of a person."

His hands were tight on the wheel. What had upset him? I didn't think there was any bird. Perhaps he was unsettled because he saw I wasn't interested in the personality parade he was staging for me. I began to feel nervous myself. It was obvious he was trying to hide something behind all his practiced chatter, and now he knew I knew it.

"Would you like to stop for something to eat?" he asked.

"Yes," I said, not wanting to be in the car anymore. "I haven't eaten anything since a piece of chicken on the floor of JFK Airport."

He smiled then and turned the car off the highway onto a side road. This road was a dirt strip winding through pastureland. It twisted back and forth along itself as if it had been made by cows circumnavigating boulders and then trudged up a small, extremely steep hill. He had to put the car in first gear, and as we inched over the crest I caught a whiff of salt in the air. We were nearing the sea. Houses began to appear, small houses of scrap wood built right up against the road. We had cut over from the main highway into some sort of village. The first crossroad we came to marked its center. There were more houses here, with small fenced plots of land in the dirt behind them. I saw pigs and a few skinny dogs, children standing in the slanting doorways, two men with their heads buried under the hood of a blue pickup truck.

He stopped the car and we got out. The road was full of mud, and the air smelled of it and of the pigs. "There's the restaurant," he said, pointing to a small wooden building. A sun-bleached plastic sign commanding TOME COCA COLA was nailed over the doorway. On the faded red beside the Coke logo the words RESTAURANTE LUCIA had been carefully painted. The men working on the truck stopped to watch us as we crossed the road and went in.

Inside I was blind for a moment. I shut my eyes and opened them and blinked and saw a cement floor in a shadowy room. Five tables stood empty. At the opposite end of the room a door stood ajar. On each table stood an empty Coke bottle holding a wilting flower. No one was in sight.

Tollomi stepped all the way into the room, at ease again. "¡Hola! ¿Quién vive?" he called, and waited, looking intently at the door to the kitchen. After a few moments it was pushed open by a young man who stared at my white skin as if both of us had come down out of the sky. "¿Buenas, cómo 'tá usté?" Tollomi said. The broad vowels of the Dominican accent said better than words could, *I belong here. I am one of you.*

He did not, he was not, but he fooled the waiter just as he had fooled me in the airport: "¿Bien, bien, cómo 'tá?" the waiter returned in kind, and seemed to relax. "Siéntense, siéntense," he commanded, and we sat down.

He offered the menu, which was written in magic marker on a piece of cardboard. I held it in my hands and looked at the stumbling letters, and suddenly I felt very happy. I looked around the room at the painted blue walls of scrap lumber and the rickety tables, and I slid my feet out of my shoes and along the cool, waxed cement floor. I didn't recognize anything on the menu. I looked across the table to Tollomi. He was smiling, his face perfectly confident again.

"Can you hear the sea?" he asked me.

I shut my eyes. Through the gaps in the wall, faintly, I heard the sound of movement, a movement that would never be stilled.

"I hear it," I said.

"Do you like it here?"

I opened my eyes. He was watching me. I nodded. I started to ask him how he knew about this place, and stopped myself. The best way to find out about those who keep secrets is to say nothing. If you ask and ask, you never get an answer. If you stop asking, eventually the answer slips out; it slips out to fill the space left by your silence.

The waiter brought the food and set it down before us with much flourish, waited until I tasted a bite. I was unsure what I was eating, having chosen it at random. I swallowed the strange mouthful, grinned and nodded, offered Tollomi a bite. "*Qué rica,*" he said to the waiter. Satisfied, the waiter went away. I looked at Tollomi. He was watching the waiter cross the room, and there was an attentiveness in his face that struck something inside me and resonated in a way I knew well. In the few seconds before he brought his gaze back to the table, I saw in his face one of the things he was hiding. He was gay. I saw it like an image flashed on a screen, so quickly I wasn't sure I had seen it at all. But then he looked back at me, and when our eyes met his face changed. He knew at once what I had seen, what I was thinking. And then I knew I was right. The ability to read minds like that is the skill of women and of children. No man has that kind of intuition unless he's been treated as something other than a man. It's the skill of people whose existence has been defined in terms of someone else's power. I read it on his face and he read it on mine.

Then it was awkward, as it always is when your knowledge of a person suddenly goes way beyond what they have told you with words. It happens after you've made love with someone for the first time, or if you open the wrong door at a party and find somebody crying.

He tried to speak, stammered, stopped. All his self-assurance had disappeared again. His brown skin was flushed, as though he were on the verge of breaking into a sweat, or even into tears.

"Are you all right?" I asked.

Still he said nothing. He took another forkful of food, a drink of water, and finally looked at me out of his strange blue eyes.

"I'm fine," he said. "A lot has happened to me in the last few days. That's all."

"Such as?"

He was sweating. He wiped his forehead with the napkin and took another bite of rice so as not to have to answer. And I didn't ask again. I went back to my own meal, and we finished our food in silence.

We paid the check and still he seemed upset. He didn't have a monologue to launch into, and he wasn't used to that. I watched him pull money from his wallet and saw the strain on his face, a thin veil of exhaustion blunting his features. People used to being in control are always the most easily undone. He had lost the upper hand with me, simply because I wasn't drawn in by the well-rehearsed personality he had presented. I was interested in *him,* though. So to put him at ease again, I began to talk myself. There is one conversation whose pattern every traveler knows as surely as monks know their prayers. When two travelers meet they recite it to each other. It is the litany of where we have been and where we are going: This is what I have seen and this is what I missed, this was my fortune, that was my narrow escape. Dragons slain, maidens rescued. This is our religion.

We left the restaurant and walked past the car, through the village and down a dirt road. As we walked along the road with our feet in the red-yellow dust, I recited for him this litany as others might recite a psalm or a fairy tale: to soothe with the familiar someone who is afraid. Like any religion, this one keeps to its genre; it follows a certain path from which it does not stray. I have had this conversation of traveling a thousand times, and it may climb hills and cross valleys and pass all kinds of interesting things, but it never wanders off into unknown territory; everyone knows what the boundaries are. Nobody gets lost, everyone knows the end: happily ever after, exchange of addresses, train schedules, maps, then the parting of ways. Amen. The dirt road under our feet was growing sandy. The sun was beginning to set. The sky grew red. "Red at night, sailor's delight," I said. I kept talking. I talked of cities I had been in, seas I had crossed. He listened in silence. I talked of trains caught and missed, boats taken, planes delayed. The road ended, and we walked over a field of sand and wild palms, and I talked and talked, told him of stories I had heard and people I had met. Then the field ended and then the land ended and we stood at the beginning of the sea.

And then I realized I didn't know where I was. Something had rolled away from my mouth like a stone from in front of a cave, and the words I was speaking were not the words I had meant to say. I was telling him how I had left Berlin, of the house I had come here to find because I dreamed of it on the train. I told him how I'd left home, I told him the stories about me I'd listened to since I was a child, I told him how I had left my own memory somewhere that was not on a map. I told him how I left everywhere, was always leaving, could leave without moving my body at all, and my words came out of me like the colored scarves a magician pulls from the mouth of a stranger in the crowd.

I was the stranger, and I hadn't known such words were inside me, right on the tip of my tongue.

Who was the magician? I felt a stab of fear, as if maybe he really had been in control of the interaction the whole time, had somehow tricked me into telling him all about myself. How had he done it? By now it was dark, and, though he sat right beside me on the sand, I could no longer see his face. I peered at where his face would be if I could see it and he read my thoughts and produced a lighter from somewhere in his clothes and struck the flame.

When the tiny light hit his eyes, it was myself I saw reflected there. It was myself I was talking to, the self who goes away from me at every fork and bend and who I could never catch, no matter how I tried. My teeth began to chatter. How had he pulled all this out of me? With his own silence. All my words had gone rushing in.

He let the lighter go out, and we sat for a moment in the solid darkness. The waves broke over and over, and I was dizzy, I was hot, I was shivering cold. And then the food poisoning hit and we spent the rest of the night beside each other vomiting onto the sand.

I have never been so sick. I shook and heaved and had chills and sank into a haze without time where everything swam and rocked. I was seasick without the boat. It went on and on. When at last I could raise my head, the night was gone. I looked up at the early gray sky above us and then out over the water. It was nearly sunrise and off to the east the clouds and the sea were all red. It was very beautiful. I leaned over and threw up again.

"Hey," I said. The huddled form on the ground beside me did not stir.

Tollomi, his name was. "Tollomi," I said, "look at the sunrise."

He raised his head and sat partway up, groaned, and lay down again. "Red in the morning, sailor take warning," he mumbled.

I shut my eyes.

We lay on the beach until the sun was all the way up in the sky, and then we got up and stumbled across the sand and the field to the main road. When we reached the car, we collapsed into the seats and stayed that way for a long time. We had left the windows open, and the cracked leather was wet with dew.

We were both too weak to drive.

"Are you sure you don't want a double bed?" says the woman behind the desk. She has steel-gray hair in rollers, and quick eyes, glancing first at Tollomi then at me. Wherever he's from, he looks Dominican, and I am obviously a gringa. She's suspicious of what we might be doing here together, looking anxious and dirty, in need of more than a room. But Tollomi talks to her in Spanish for a while, and then she leads us outside, across a little yard and down an open-air hallway lined with doors. She selects one and flings it open, allows us to crane our necks around her for a glimpse of two single beds and a dresser, and then addresses me. "I have other room," she says in English, "much better. This one, beds too small, you don't want to sleep on these beds here. Too small. Come look at other room, I give you for fifty pesos. You and your husband, more comfortable there. It has"—she looks at Tollomi—"*una cama matrimonial.*"

Tollomi smiles. He told her we're married: If we say we aren't, she'll insist we take separate rooms and I can't afford it. Her insistence on propriety might be due more to her need to repair the hotel generator—which is making an ominous banging sound—than to the enormous gold-plated cross around her neck, but either way, Tollomi is right: It's easier to say we're husband and wife.

I peer into the cheaper room again. It's true—it's not particularly nice, but I don't want to spend more. I have money saved up from Berlin, but only enough for a couple of months. I don't know where I'll be next week even, and things might be expensive there. I should be frugal.

"These two single beds will be fine," I say in my bad Spanish. "This room is fine."

She shrugs—her shoulders, her eyebrows, her arms. *Crazy gringa*, she is thinking.

The shrug bothers Tollomi. I know this about him already: To him every cultural miscommunication carries the faint scent of disaster, like gunpowder carries the scent of war. He can't stand the tension, he must diffuse it.

"*Doña...*" he begins, and launching into his perfect Dominican Spanish, he tells her that his wife has peculiar sleeping habits, that she insists she sleeps better if she has her own bed. His eyes twinkle with a light he wants her to think is meant for her—American women are crazy, *doña*, we have to indulge them—and is actually meant for me—straight people are crazy, Michelle, we have to indulge them.

The woman looks at me and smiles. The smile means that we're women, she and I; we know men are crazy—they want only one thing from us. Of course I would want my own bed; I must be tired, poor thing.

I smile back and so does Tollomi. Now we all understand one another. We respect one another. It's such a good feeling it's almost as if he had told her the truth.

She reaches into the desk drawer for the room key and gives it to me. Tollomi asks her what her name is.

"Isabela Sonnenberg," she says, her tongue barely arriving on the other side of the German surname.

"And your husband?"

"Felix Sonnenberg," she says, and fingering the cross around her neck she shrugs again, smiling. It's out of her hands, this shrug means, *Sólo Dios lo entiende.* Only God understands it.

"Don't worry about the price of the room," Tollomi says while he's unpacking. "It's on me."

"You don't have to do that," I tell him.

"I know I don't have to. I want to. It's fine, Michelle. I'm loaded."

"I don't even know you."

"You don't?" he asks, and then turns away quickly and pretends to look for something in his luggage. I know he's thinking about what happened the night before in the restaurant and on the beach, that sudden intimacy of talking, and of silence too, that passed through the air between us like a germ or like desire: an invisible something that enters the body before you know what it is. It's a day later now and the feeling remains, a subtle shift in the chemistry of the blood. And Tollomi's started to talk about it and stopped himself. He's afraid to bring it up, to feel exposed all over again. So he doesn't say anything more and neither do I. It's as if we're pretending nothing happened. He hunts around in his luggage, finds his cigarettes, and lights one, and I pay for my half of the room.

Later that night, just before I fall asleep, I remind myself of where I am. I do this so I won't forget during the night. I've done it ever since I first began waking up and finding myself elsewhere. It's not the elsewhere I'm afraid of: Everywhere is somewhere. It's the not knowing how I came to be where I am that frightens me. I'm not afraid of getting lost, but of lost memory. Like all fear, this fear contains within it a seed of desire. Embrace your fear, it's said, and it will yield. I wrap my arms around my body. In this darkened room where I lie, the smell of burning trash and jasmine blossoms and cut grass tells me I am here on this island in this bed and not elsewhere. It is a marvel to be here. The wind is low, the sea muffled, quiet outside the slatted wooden shutters closed against the mosquitoes. If I listen with my whole self, through the darkness I can hear Tollomi breathing on the other side of the room. I have to stop breathing to hear him: His breaths come in the same intervals as mine.

Part Two

I wake suddenly, eyes flying open to a room shrouded in darkness. In the wall to the left, the dim outlines of a shuttered window; to the right, the empty space between my bed and another bed a few feet from my own. There is a girl in this bed, a dark shape sleeping. It's the American girl from the airport, and now the whole of yesterday surges back on me in a wave higher than my head, and panic rises in my mouth like lost breath until I choke it back and wait for the wave to subside.

Breathe, Tollomi. You're here, here in this hotel room. No longer on the boat, no longer in a telephone booth in Guatemala City. And not in a cemetery a few miles outside Christiansted either, looking among the rubble for a grave whose headstone was knocked down during the storm.

What has happened? Too much in the last seventy-two hours: death, a flight, a sea crossing, and the whole of my abandoned life welling up inside me last night on the beach with this white girl, this stranger, barely more than twenty years old. Michelle her name is, Michelle. She stared at me and asked nothing, and I wanted to tell her everything. I had to bite my lips to keep from speaking. I can still taste blood on my tongue.

Perhaps I could tell her a little. Sit on the edge of her bed in the waning darkness, wake her up and say, *You want to know who I am? All right, I'll tell you, then*—but tell her just a little, enough to gain some relief from all the unspoken words welling up like tears inside me. I could tell her just the happy parts, the magical parts. Yes, there are those; they begin like a fairy tale. All I'd have to do is stop before they change into bad dreams.

I could begin like this: Once upon a time, there were two people, husband and wife, and they lived on a beautiful island called St. Croix. They lived there, but they weren't Cruzans. They weren't West Indians at all, in fact; they were Americans. Their skin was as pale as beach sand.

The husband had a big company that shipped sugar all over the world. He had an apartment in New York and an apartment in Paris, and he must have been very fond of these apartments because he spent a lot of time in each of them, away from St. Croix. But his wife preferred the island. While her husband went all over the world attending to his sugar, she stayed on St. Croix. There weren't so many white people on the island in those days, and the Cruzans used to watch her with something like amusement as she walked wherever she wanted and did as she pleased. She liked to walk on the beaches especially, and her nose was always burned.

When their son was born, the shipping magnate was away. He didn't return until Christmas, and during the months of his absence nobody ever saw the baby. The wife still went on walks from time to time, but she always left her son at home. There was a Cruzan woman she had hired as a maid.

"Keep him out of the sun," she told the maid, "at least until Mister DeHaas gets back."

"Yes, mistress," the maid said.

There was talk.

When at last the shipping magnate returned, his wife brought him into the room where the baby lay sleeping. It was afternoon and the shades were drawn.

"Look!" she said. "He has a suntan already."

And indeed the baby's skin was the color of a cup of tea. Tea sweetened with just a bit of milk but no sugar. Tea that has steeped a long time. That color. Dark. His skin was dark, and his hair was dark and covered his head in fine tight ropes that would never uncoil.

The shipping magnate stared at the sleeping boy. Then he stared at his wife. His wife smiled. She leaned over the crib and lifted the baby up and jiggled him on her shoulder. The baby woke up and began to cry.

"Look," she said to her husband. "Look at his eyes."

The shipping magnate looked at the baby's eyes, half shut with the effort of squirting out tears.

"They're blue," she said to him. "See? Blue. Just like yours."

The next thing that happened was that the two of them left for a few day's sail on the shipping magnate's yacht. "He wants to take a vacation," the wife told the maid. "A vacation alone, so would you mind watching the baby for a few nights? We'll be back by Christmas Eve, I promise. And of course we'll pay you extra."

"I watchin him now," the maid said.

"Oh, thank you," said the wife, and the husband said, "Let's go, hurry up," and off they went.

Two days later, somewhere in the deep blue northeast quadrant of the Caribbean Sea, his wife threw herself overboard.

She did it very early in the morning while her husband was still asleep. She did it very quietly; at least, he didn't wake up. Perhaps she didn't want to disturb him with whatever was bothering her so.

And so it came about that while the shipping magnate was snoring in the stern berth of the yacht and his wife was making friends with the mermaids while her lungs exploded, their son was sitting happily on the patio having mashed papaya fed to him by the Cruzan maid.

Josephine was her name.

Josephine.

After his wife's death, the shipping magnate went away again. He commanded his cargoes of sugar from other oceans and never once went back to St. Croix, and I, the son, the boy with the dark skin and light eyes, I was left in the care of Josephine. My name was written down somewhere as Bartholomew, but to Josephine and then to everyone I was Tollomi.

Josephine moved her things from the maid's room into the master bedroom and went on living there. As it was a large house, she invited her sister Etty and Etty's husband Abel and their two children, Belle and the baby Marika, to move in too.

"And what if Mistah DeHaas come back?" Etty wanted to know before she moved everything she owned halfway across the island.

"Mistah DeHaas, he so fah away, he ain' gon know if a hurricane come, sweep dis house into de sea," said Josephine. "You tink he gon care who sleepin in de empty bed?"

So the four of them moved in, and so I grew up with Josephine and her family. I went to school with her nieces and played on the beach with them and learned how to play steel pan from Abel and how to sail a boat from Josephine's boyfriend Henry. By the time I was old enough to understand that I once had a pair of American parents, I didn't much care. When Josephine showed me photographs of these two strange white people, I only laughed. The people in the picture didn't look like me at all. My skin was much darker than theirs, and my hair was of an entirely different sort. My hair was like Josephine's but more stretched out. A little more. The only thing about me that resembled them was my eyes, which were blue like theirs. But that was not how I thought of it. To me my eyes were blue like the sea.

Besides, if the people in the picture were my parents, then where were they?

"Your daddy doan come back here," Josephine said, "because he grievin so hard fuh his wife, he can't bear to be on de same sea what drown her. And she die 'cause she can't stand to be away from you a whole day and night, you know. When your daddy tell her he ain' gon go back early jus so she can see her bwoy, de mistress so mad she jump from de boat and try to swim all de way back to St. Croix. Grief make people foolish sometime, Tollie. Dass a ting."

"I nevah so foolish what I tink I gon swim from one end of de sea to de odda and doan drown in it," I said, laughing. I looked at the picture again.

"Well, now," I told Josephine, "I see fuh true, dey ain' Cruzan like me." And thus I dismissed them.

Everyone around me was Cruzan, and I was Cruzan too. There were some whites on the island, of course, the few who lived there year-round and the tourists who came at Christmas time. Etty, Josephine's sister, worked for a white family who lived in Frederiksted. But the white people had their own parties and their own school; they had their own way of talking, which was very unmusical and stiff, and their skin was pale or bright red or sometimes tan but never as dark as mine had been since the day I was born. When I met the white people on the street, I greeted them good morning and went on my way. There was never any question in my mind that I might be one of them until one day in the middle of my fourteenth year when the shipping magnate unexpectedly sailed back into port.

No, that's too far. Back up. Wake Michelle and tell her only about Henry teaching me to sail, about cracking open sea urchins to feed to bright blue fish that hid in the reef, about the adults dancing on the front porch until the sweat made rows of tiny clear pearls across their foreheads, pearls that I, as a small boy, always wanted to touch.

I was that young then, I was happy.

But I can't back up. I left home and I aged.

I'm not going to wake Michelle. I can't tell her this story at all; it doesn't stay happy, I don't stay young. I can't separate out those memories from what follows.

What follows is that the shipping magnate showed up at the house after thirteen years and announced to Josephine that he had come to see his son.

Josephine was not happy. But she let him in the house, which was still his, and sent Etty's little girl Marika out to fetch me; I was down the beach practicing steel pan with some older boys who sometimes let me play music with them. When Marika had gone, Josephine stood in the middle of the living room and watched while the shipping magnate walked around inspecting the walls for cracks and the furniture for termites. He didn't ask her anything besides what was taking that little girl so long. Josephine answered dat it not such a long time when de beach it deh so long too, you know, and the shipping magnate said he would go find the boy himself. He went out of the house and down toward the ocean. Josephine shut the door behind him and went into the kitchen and sat down at the table and cried.

The shipping magnate picked his way along the beach through the gathering dusk and got sand in his shoes. At last he came up to where we were practicing. At his approach the playing stopped. All we boys held our sticks poised in the air above our pans, and our leader asked the stranger what he wanted.

The shipping magnate didn't answer right away. He was staring hard at the group, looking for me. I didn't know it. To me he was a stateside stranger, nothing more. Marika, who had sat down on the sand to listen to the music, got up and pointed me out.

The shipping magnate went around the pans and stood over me. It was nearly dark by this time, and he couldn't see me very well. But he must have recognized the blue eyes. He said to me, "Bartholomew, don't you know who I am?"

I looked up at the stranger who had gotten my name wrong and shook my head. I fiddled with the rubber on my pan stick and wished the stranger would go away.

"Bartholomew," said the stranger, "I'm your father."

I greeted him very nicely, considering I had not seen the man since I was five months old. I put down my pan sticks and walked back to the house with him and offered to take him around the island first thing in the morning. I said I would show him where I went to school and who I played with and the reef I could swim out to without coming up for breath and the fishing boat that belonged to Josephine's boyfriend, Henry.

"Henry takin me on de boat all de time," I said. "He say I de good, he say de boat always sailin just nice fuh me, you know. An' when we reach to de place where is de fish, he say dey more fish when I dere."

The shipping magnate said nothing. We had reached the house and gone in. He turned on all the lights in the living room and looked me up and down from head to toe without saying a word. He hadn't seen me in thirteen years, so there was a lot to take in.

He took in that I had feet that no close-toed shoes would ever fit because after thirteen years of walking in the sand barefoot you could fit a lime in the space between my first and second toes. He took in that I could play steel pan as well as any musician on the island and had no intention of ever doing anything else. He took in that I spoke Cruzan instead of American English. As he looked at me, the rumors that had gone around the island after my birth must have come flooding back to him, for he took in most of all that the color of my skin, which he had hoped he could attribute to the fading light by the ocean, now showed itself a rich and irrevocable goldish brown, dark and shining in the bright light of the room.

He looked into my eyes again. They were as blue as his own. There was that.

The shipping magnate had no other children. There was only me. His only son.

I was growing nervous beneath his silent gaze. So again I asked him if he doan wan to come out round de island in de morning an' see all de ting what I tellin you.

I even called him Father, to be polite.

Then my father spoke to me. My father said no. My father said thank God he had come home in time to take matters into his own hands before it was too late, if it wasn't too late already. My father said, "Come with me. We're going."

And he took his son off to America.

The day before my father took me to the United States to enroll me in boarding school, he took me sailing on his yacht. I had planned to spend the day with Josephine; we were to go in Henry's truck to say goodbye to all the people I knew all over the island.

"Bring what you need," she said. "And make it enough. We be gone all day."

She never spoke to me like that: so pointedly, deliberately. I understood without her saying it that the idea was in both our heads that she was going to help me run away. The island was small but big enough for that; Josephine knew everyone, and the coconut radio, as we called it, was swift and explicit. Everyone knew what had happened. I could be hidden for a long time.

Josephine, all breezy in her voice, looked at me hard while my father sat unaware in the next room. "I goin down to de mahket just now. We takin some food an' ting wid us. You eatin so much, Tollie, dat if we leave an' doan take no food, you gon eat de tires off de damn truck, I know."

I grinned. I nodded at her and she saw I understood. She took the market basket and left, and I wandered into the living room where my father sat reading a stateside newspaper. I thought I would take one last look at him, this man who I wouldn't have recognized, had we passed on the street.

"There's sand all over this floor," he said without looking up.

There wasn't; Josephine made a serious distinction between indoors and out; only down-islanders and stateside sailors tracked in sand, according to her. Our floor was always immaculate. But my father didn't know this. He hadn't looked. He also didn't know that we never brought food along for us to eat when we went visiting. It's rude to go visiting and not eat the meal your hosts prepare.

I looked at the top of my father's head, and his fingers bent around the sides of the big sheet of newspaper. He knew nothing at all. I was embarrassed for him. I started to walk out of the room.

"Bartholomew!"

I was not used to that name. He had to say it again before I turned.

"Today we're going sailing," he said.

"Not me," I said. "I goin wid Josephine to say goodbye to all me friend."

"Oh, for God's sake," said my father. He put down the newspaper. "Listen: 'I'm going *with* Josephine to say goodbye to *my* friends.' Now try this one: 'I'm going sailing with my father on his yacht. He's going to show me a fine day of fishing before he flies me up to one of the best schools in the country, where I'll get an education these Cruzans can't even dream of.'" He came over to where I stood and rumpled my hair. I winced without meaning to, and he yanked his hand away. "The fish won't wait," he said angrily. "Don't you know even that? Hurry up. And put on some shoes. You're not an animal." And he stood there, looking down at me and waiting.

And I went with him. I thought he had guessed what Josephine and I were planning. This shows how naive I was then; I had no idea how impossible it would have been for him to guess what Josephine and I had not spoken aloud even in secret, no idea that intuition was utterly removed from his experience. I went with him; I thought just what his stride and his jaw and his voice and his words wanted me to think: that he was all-powerful and I had no choice. If Josephine had been there, she would have told me to hold onto the banister, kick and scream, jump out the window, spit in his eye, do anything I had never done before to save the self I would never have again. But Josephine was off in the marketplace buying fruit I would never eat, and so I went with him, I went sailing with my father.

The yacht, he informed me, was his pride and joy. He had sailed it here single-handedly from somewhere in Europe. The wind was from the north, and I moved to sit upwind of him so that I wouldn't hear what he was saying. Good sailor though he was, he didn't notice and talked on while the wind took his words and carried them away. I sat on the pimpled white deck with the voice of the wind in my ears and stared down into the blue sleek of the water slipping along below us.

Then I saw her. Her legs had cleaved together, and her hair had gone green with algae, but I knew her at once. I cried out.

"What is it?" said my father.

I didn't tell him I'd seen my mother. I thought he wouldn't believe me.

"Mermaid," I said. "I saw a mermaid in de sea."

"Bartholomew, there are no mermaids!" he screamed.

That did it. The next moment I was up the rails of his pride and joy and over the side.

My mother: All through childhood she had been a fable, a myth. I had never dreamed nor wept on her account; I thought of her and her death as one thinks of the sun's rising and setting: a natural, impersonal fact. It was my father's return that had created my mother's absence; the shadow he cast across my life was shaped like her death.

My mother, I saw her there in the sea and to be free from the shadow of my father I jumped in.

I plunged feet first into the deep blue water and the wet relief of escape. I propelled myself down through the gloriously solid moving wet. I saw the green flash of her back and her tail ahead of me as she swam down and down, and I followed. As I descended, the world above grew very small and pale and far away. I had a fleeting sensation of the humiliation of having to return to the surface and walk about on two legs. I swam farther and farther down until at last I reached the ocean floor. My mother floated before me. "This is where I live now," she said. "Do you like it?"

"Yes. Can I stay?"

"You don't want to go back?"

I thought of my father fathoms above, imprisoned in his tiny wedge of boards and canvas on the dumb surface of my mother's world. He was up there waiting to take me away from my home.

"I doan wan to go back up evah," I said.

A shadow fell across my mother's face. I looked up. The shadow was cast by the body of my father, kicking itself down to where we stood. He grabbed me by the neck. A struggle ensued, but in the end he managed to pull me up to the surface where he let go of me, for my kicking and struggling had nearly drowned him. As soon as he released me, I jackknifed over and dove again, but before I had gone two meters

I felt his arms around my legs. I kicked. I could still see the shimmer of my mother's green skin in the depths below me. But my father caught hold of my hair and pulled my head around. Everything was thrashing arms and legs. I lost my sense of which way was up. I swam away from him and found my head against the blue boat ladder. Then he was above me and hauling me up on deck, where he threw me into the cockpit like a captured fish. I lay there gasping.

He was furious. "Who raised you?" he screamed, and, "I'm taking you away from the sea none too soon—you'll never be a sailor, you can't even swim! You sank like a stone—like a stone, do you hear me? Get below, *now*..." and so forth. He hectored me into the foreberth and slammed the door shut. I lay there dripping wet on the triangular mattress and felt the boat come about and head back to shore.

That night, my last night on the island, I dreamed of my mother. It was the same as the afternoon; I dove off the boat and found her in the water, but now she was no longer a mermaid. She was a woman drowning, and I could not get her to the surface. She grew heavier and heavier until I had to let go, and then, like a glass bottle filling up with water, a thin stream of bubbles escaped from her lips and she gracefully upended and sank.

"Come back!" I cried.

My cry was only bubbles. My mother disappeared.

It was a private school in New England. A boys' school. My father the shipping magnate and his father, whose profession I never knew, had gone there once, he said.

Disgusted with me, he left me there and said he would see me in June. He said he expected that by then I would have learned to speak properly.

I didn't say goodbye.

It was January when I arrived, halfway through the school year and halfway through winter, which I had never seen. It was beautiful and unreal to me, the snow lying in drifts over everything, the trees barren of leaves, like after a hurricane, and the icy air I would not go out in. I experienced the landscape through windows, like a prisoner. I could not go out; the layers of clothes involved were like ropes binding my limbs, and the shoes I could not get on my feet without bending the joints of my toes in on themselves. At first I had tried to go outside without the clothes and shoes. It was better that way for several minutes. The snow was like sand but weightless, made of water instead of rock. It held its shape when you threw it in the air. The air was thin and had no smell, but it burned when you breathed in too fast. When you breathed out, you could see the shape of your lungs.

After several minutes of playing in this opaque sea, I saw the winter had turned my feet and fingers strange colors. But I kept playing until I was discovered and sent to the school psychologist.

After that I confined myself to experiencing the winter from behind glass.

I missed a lot of classes.

My classmates were as foreign to me as the weather. They were all my age, but their skin was pale, a deathly pale closer to snow than skin. "He has a suntan," my father said to the dean of admissions when we were introduced. "He's spent his life in the sun. Healthy, eh? It'll fade, don't worry."

I knew it wouldn't, but I kept my mouth shut. My skin was the color of St. Croix and so it stayed.

I was not one of them. They all talked like my father, the same words, the same accent with no music in it. I was not one of them, and they hated me for it and let me know it every chance they got. The dress code required a long-sleeved Oxford shirt at all times: My bruises were not visible.

There were several other boys besides myself whom the faculty considered "difficult cases." Bradford Whitcomb stole all the silverware in the dining hall and hung it from the rafters of the chapel on Easter weekend and wrote "Jesus says eat me" on the altar with a magic marker and was expelled. John-Paul Hemenway failed every class because he never went, but he was such a good lacrosse player that they couldn't expel him. Charles Stevenson was drunk all the time, every day, and during my second semester he died, fell down on the train tracks on the other side of the woods and didn't get up, he was so drunk, and later that night a train hit him.

This kind of tragedy they were versed in there. They knew what to do at the funeral of a boy such as Charles Stevenson, the kind of pain to feel, the things to say, the way to look at it, as a tragedy: He had such promise, was planning on Harvard in the fall, something should have been done, we didn't know it was that serious, it was a freak accident, there was nothing we could do.

I remember sitting in chapel in my black suit, watching the faces of my classmates watch the chaplain above the altar, the new altar whose grain didn't match the ancient oak of the rest of the furniture up there because Bradford's marker had been permanent, like Charles's death. I sat in the hard-backed pew and cried, not because Charles was dead, but because if it had been me in the coffin instead, I knew there would be no weeping; the pews would stand empty. So I cried for myself in advance in case I should die there, in that school. I was so far away from the islands and the sea, and I could not bear the thought of dying without even the salt water of tears.

The teachers seemed to hate me as much as the students did. They didn't know what to do with me at all. I don't know if they really couldn't understand my Cruzan speech or if they simply pretended not to. I still wonder about it. "You have the syntax of a cannibal dipped in Clorox" is the comment I remember best, though it was months before I gained enough familiarity with America to understand what it meant. I never tried to answer back. My sweet speech only made things worse, and most of the time the reason for my torture was beyond me, as when one evening I happened to be brushing my teeth at the row of sinks with three or four other boys. It started as always, with questions and jeering.

"Cooper, look at how he brushes his teeth."

"Didn't his parents teach him anything?"

"Maybe they couldn't afford water."

"Maybe they didn't *have* water where he grew up."

"Let's ask him. Have you ever seen water before?"

I looked at their eyes. "I deh know damn good bout wattah an' dem bettah den all you tiefen bwoys come an' meliss wid me," I heard myself say.

"*What* did he say?"

"'*Wattah?*' Can't you say it right? *Waugh-turr.* No? Well, we'll give you a closer look at it. Come here. I'm not going to hurt you, stupid. I just want to show you up close what water is. John-Paul, grab his arms…"

It was years before I understood, quite suddenly, what had provoked this incident. The boys had noticed a habit of mine essential on St. Croix where fresh water was scarce: I brushed my teeth without water and turned the taps for just a moment at the end to rinse my mouth and spit. But here the other boys at school let the taps run the whole time. With the water that went wasted down the drain while they were brushing their teeth, you could have done a whole load of dishes, taken a sponge bath, washed your hair twice.

I couldn't learn fast enough to protect myself, to understand the brilliant subtlety of these rules. That particular session in the bathroom culminated in the stalls with my head being held underwater until I almost drowned. Luckily I still had the lungs of a swimmer, a diver. Drowning might run in the family, but I hadn't spent my whole life at ease in the vast depths of the sea to die now in a few gallons of water in a porcelain bowl. I held my breath.

My eyes were open when they pushed my head in, and I saw the white porcelain change to red as time pounded in my lungs. My blood dragged to a halt, and the red became edged with black. Then the blackness was all there was as I went down, down, down and then there was nothing and then my head was yanked backward out of the bowl and fell dripping wet onto something cold and hard and full of air. I lay gasping on the floor and slowly the blackness receded, and I saw again the faces of the boys bent over me in a circle. Their faces were white with fear.

At night I lay on the dormitory bed beneath the weight of blankets and night after night dove back into the sea. It was always the same dream. In the dream I saw my mother in the sea, but she was no longer a mermaid. She was a woman drowning, a woman out of her element, a woman gasping for air and for light she would never see again. I kicked with my swimmer's legs and pulled, but I could not raise her and she drowned. Night after night I woke in the darkness with my arms flailing, my face wet and tasting of salt.

Something had to change. I didn't know what it would be. One morning I walked across the quadrangle to class knowing that when I got there I would be asked to recite a memorized speech, and that if I did, my classmates would be reciting it back at me for the rest of the week, mocking my accent. The sound of what they thought was my voice in their mouths made me sick.

I went into class and sat down. The teacher called on us by row, and there were three boys ahead of me. I looked out the window while they talked and thought of nothing.

Then it was my turn. "DeHaas?" the teacher said. A little wave of anticipatory whispers went around the room. I looked at the teacher.

"Well?" he said.

I looked at him and said nothing. And then it happened. Something changed.

I stopped speaking.

It was easy. It required no effort at all. I just stopped completely. My teachers were highly annoyed. They ridiculed me, they lectured me, they threatened to fail me. I was sent to the principal, the school psychologist, the dean. To each of them my response was the same: silence. A letter was written to my father, but it seemed he was at sea with a cargo of sugar and could not be reached. In the meantime I completed all my assignments and showed up for class and waited to see what would happen. Nothing happened. In the face of my silence, everyone was confounded. Eventually the faculty stopped bothering me; they ran out of words.

The students were more persistent. They tried in their own ways to get me to speak, and I learned what torture teaches you: Once you know you will not give in, the torturer is stripped of his power over you. Physical pain and humiliation no longer have the power to ruin your soul. They are simply something that is happening *around* you, not to you, like walking in the rain. I hate to realize that is what it came to, my thinking of torture in that way. But how much worse it would have been without that.

After a month or so the students gave up, and I was left alone. For the first time since coming to America I had achieved a kind of power: the power of silence. I had curled up like an anemone when it's attacked. But there was no way I could last in that state; I had a mind, I did not want to be cut off from everyone around me. The isolation of silence, for all its dignity, was killing me.

I needed a different way to survive. I puzzled it out logically. My mathematics teacher would have been pleased. A: Everyone there hated me, and I couldn't stand it. B: I had to get them to stop hating me. C: They would not hate me if I were somebody else. Therefore: I became somebody else. It happened by degrees. If there was an actual point when I crossed the line, as there is an actual line between life and death, it must have happened while I was asleep. I died in my sleep. I slept in the afternoons, and at night—after everyone had gone to bed— I went down to the lounge in the dormitory basement and turned on the television. The actors in old Hollywood movies became my tutors. From them, I learned how to speak and move. I talked in the dark, empty room until my throat rasped and my tongue ached. I held up a hand mirror and practiced shaping my mouth, raising one eyebrow, tightening my lips as the men did, squaring my jaw. I learned to make my face expressionless, then to change the muscles to all fluid expression, as the best of the actresses did. I learned where the women put their hands and how the men walked, with the weight in their shoulders instead of their hips. I learned to keep my voice in one register, to take out the Cruzan rhythm, the cadence, the sea, the song. I learned to speak like an American movie star, with the flat warmth of an electric fireplace. I learned all the parts: the hero, the cop, the gangster, the soldier. The gumshoe, the businessman, the thief. I learned the beloved father.

And the following semester I took my tongue and swagger and went back upstairs.

Like all transformations, this one was made out of necessity, to save me, and it did. At first I saw only the benefits. I stopped being "accident-prone." Others spoke to me as they did to each other. I became a part of whispered conversations rather than their subject. I won several scholastic prizes: Latin, English, French. I entertained the younger boys with my ability to mimic the voice of the principal, whom no one liked. I was not in truth a part of the group that the others formed, but the line separating us became blurred to a degree that through constant vigilance I managed to camouflage myself among them. Where once they had looked and seen my face, now they saw only a mirror of themselves.

Problem solved. *Quod erat demonstrandum.*

By the middle of my third year, the boys themselves considered me one of their own. What I had come to think of as the strangeness of my skin and hair could not be completely compensated for, of course. There was also the problem of my disinterest in girls, but I faked that with almost laughable ease. I had achieved my goal: My classmates looked at me and thought me one of them. A different, strange, even exotic version, but one of them nonetheless. I knew it was not true. But I thought I could undo the illusion at will if I chose. And then, as time passed, I stopped thinking about it.

I had stopped writing to Josephine. For more than a year after my last letter to her, she continued to write, and I would unlock my postal box in the basement of the dining hall and pull out those envelopes with burning fingers, my face flushed with the heat of an uncertain shame. Her awkward, unschooled handwriting loomed ragged and black on the envelope for anyone to see; in my early days at school, these letters had been snatched from my hands and read aloud while I fought desperately and without success to repossess them. Later I had only gone to my mailbox early in the morning or late at night; I neglected to answer her letters, and at last when her letters stopped coming, I felt only a quiet emptiness I could not bring myself to call relief.

The last part of myself to go was the dream of my mother. Long after I had become like the other boys while awake, the door I had shut still swung open at nighttime, and I was back and dreaming as if I had never been away. But at last this too receded and I began to sleep soundly. I had no more nightmares about my mother or about anything else. When I slept it was only sleep. I slept like a stone, I slept like she sank. Still and all. I stopped dreaming altogether.

The horror of this transformation didn't sink in for a long time. When I graduated from the school—after almost six years, having gone from seventh grade all the way through twelfth—my father did not attend the ceremonies. He did, however, send me an enormous check, a note of congratulations that I had done so well in my studies, and the instructions that I was to get myself a plane ticket to Paris, where he would meet me and we would have a long overdue reunion.

This was the first money beyond a few dollars here and there that I had ever had. I cashed the check and bought a plane ticket, but not to Paris. I had received another gift in the mail that day, a package bearing handwriting I recognized at once. I opened it in the privacy of my empty room, my luggage on the bed beside me. Josephine had sent me a wristwatch. There was no note other than her rickety signature on a card bearing the name of a jeweler's I had never heard of, whose shop, the back of the card said, was in Christiansted. I put the watch on and sat watching the sweep of the second hand. I studied the stamps on the package, blue crescents of water faced by white sand and palm trees, a background of bright blue sky. I fastened my suitcases. I went out and cashed my father's check and bought a plane ticket back to St. Croix.

If I were to list the happiest moments of my life, one of them would surely be the moment the door of the airplane opened and I breathed again the sweet blue air of the island and stepped back onto that chunk of rocky earth surrounded on all sides by sea. I was in a sort of blind ecstasy at the smell of the air and the roundness of it and the feel of it on my skin again, at the cars driving on the left side of the road, the sounds of Cruzan being shouted at a donkey: "Move dat horse, girl!"

"Eh, donkey, mon, doan jus stop in de road like a broken truck."

I hadn't told Josephine I was coming back, and when I arrived at the house she wasn't there. The door was locked, which surprised me, but I hunted around the porch until I found the key hidden in a conch shell propped against the threshold. I let myself in and stood in the center of the living room. Some of the furniture was different, but the smell of the room was exactly the same. Flowers and salt and damp plaster. I was trembling. I closed my eyes and breathed great gulps of air. I inhaled the smell of my life until I felt dizzy and had to sit down on the horsehair sofa that stood where it always had.

I could not sit still. I got up again and stood at the window. The sounds of the sea came up through the wet purple dusk as always. I went into the whitewashed bedroom that had been mine and turned on the big metal table fan, the fan whose whirring I used to fall asleep to every night, the same fan. I was too impatient to wait. I hid my bag under the bed and went out again, down into Christiansted. I went through the alleys I had played in as a boy and out to the little board-walk, where I sat down and took off my sandals and hung my feet in the sea. I walked barefoot to the marketplace where in the morning the wooden stalls would be full of fruit I had not tasted in years: pawpaw, mango, plantain. I walked past one of the Cruzan bars that stood in a little alleyway without a sign. If you didn't know it was there, you would miss it—it was not a tourist bar. I went in because I was a Cruzan, back home where I belonged. I was so happy, I felt as if I were already drunk.

The bartender was the same man I remembered. I had played at his house often as a child; he had two sons. I stepped up to the bar, and he glanced up and stopped pouring. He held the rum bottle in midair and looked at me. He did not know who I was.

I could read his gaze as clearly as if he had spoken aloud. I was a stupid tourist, he was thinking, stumbling through the wrong section of town.

"Hello, please, Wilhelm," I said. "You lookin at me like I drown down in de sea an' come back. Tell me now, wha wrong wid your eyes dat makin it so you doan know me no more?"

He knew me then, and he took me by the head and hugged me as if I were a little boy.

With my head on Wilhelm's chest and the bar cutting into my middle where I leaned across to him, I heard the echo of my own words in my ears; they sounded strange. It frightened me. The Cruzan I was speaking no longer felt like my voice, but rather someone else's voice issuing strangely from my mouth.

And then Wilhelm was asking me, "Eh, bwoy, when you reach? Wha happen? I been tinkin I nevah gon see you no more. Josephine, she talk about you, bwoy, but you doan nevah write a single lettah. Wha she did say when she see you, Tollomi?"

"She doesn't—she doan—" My tongue was caught between Cruzan and English. I took a deep breath and heard myself say, "She hasn't seen me yet. She'll be surprised—it's been almost six years."

"Eh, mon, say wha? Listen how dis bwoy here learn to speak like he tellin de news on de radio! An' look at dese fine clothes you wearin now! What odda ting dey did teach you off island den?"

"Are you gon—You gon give me a—a rum and Coke, Wilhelm? Or you jus gon stan dere an' stare in me face?" I spoke with difficulty. I had learned my lessons at school too well. Now I tried to speak my own Cruzan and felt myself flinch with each word, as if an invisible someone were dealing me unseen blows. Wilhelm frowned a little puzzled frown. It lasted only a second, then he turned away from me and mixed my drink.

That night in the bar I got my first glimpse of what had happened not only to me but to the island. I hadn't yet seen the hotels and souvenir shops on every corner; it hadn't dawned on me that the big ships I had glimpsed off Frederiksted from the plane were oil tankers. I didn't know about the dredging that had ruined the reef, and I hadn't seen the white oil workers yet, in the supermarket aisles buying rum on Friday nights, Saturdays; then Monday, Tuesday, all week for fifty cents a pint; drinking, picking fights with the Cruzans and teaching their kids to say "nigger." I hadn't heard about the Fountain Valley murders, and Josephine hadn't told me how many people she knew who had been shot. I found all that out later. But that night in the bar I caught a flash of the essence of it. It had just showed itself right in front of me; it had showed in Wilhelm's eyes in the moment before he knew who I was.

I finished my drink and left the bar quickly. I hurried down the alley back to the main street, all my pleasure in rediscovering the town having given way to a growing sense of dread. When I got back to the house, Josephine was there. She was standing in the kitchen with her back to me. When she turned around and saw me in the doorway, she screamed.

"It's Tollomi," I said.

"I tink I know who it is," she said. " I deh still got my eyesight now. I thought I nevah gon see you again, Tollie. Come here, bwoy."

She hugged me hard. For me, it was a moment in limbo, feeling around my back the arms of the woman who had raised me, whom I loved. Then we stepped apart. She looked me up and down, and her face turned solemn. Her dark eyes fell in the shadow of her frown as she looked. Then she cut her eyes away from me and sat at the kitchen table. I sat too and looked around the room. The termites had been eating the table legs. The air in the kitchen was sweet and smoky. There was a metal brazier on the stove: Josephine had been burning herbs before I came in. *Brazier:* That was a word I had learned up there. A pot: That thing was just a pot, and she burned herbs in it to keep the jumbies out of the house or to ask them a favor.

I looked at Josephine. She didn't say a word.

"Thank you for the wristwatch," I said at last. I held out my arm so she could see I was wearing it.

"Wha dat mean, Tollomi? If I had send you a watch two year ago, you would have write me a lettah or come home den?"

I took a breath to try to make some answer and burst into tears.

It had been years since I had wept. The feeling of tears on my face was strange. I brushed at my eyes and tried to stop; I couldn't. Finally, Josephine took a handkerchief from her dress and pushed it across the table.

I wiped my eyes with the handkerchief, but its smell was her smell and it made me cry harder. I hid my face in my hands.

At last Josephine said sharply, "Wha tis dis? Tollomi, stop." Those words bridged fifteen years to when I was a small child, with nothing to cry about that couldn't be resolved or forgotten by dinnertime. Hearing them now, I did begin to stop. I dried my eyes and we sat there in silence.

"Where is Henry?" I asked after a while.

"Henry workin on one of de big fishin boat wha catch fish for a company. De men gone two week each time, livin on de boat, so dey can make dem work day an' night, Henry say, even in de night dey got tree, four mon workin, takin turn. But wha tis dis? Dis fancy voice you talkin wid, Tollomi? You tink how we speak an' ting ain' good nuf fuh you now?"

"Josephine, I ain' gon—I, I—I'm not—" I stuttered and stopped. The sound of Cruzan was so completely different to what I had come to think of as my voice that speaking it now I felt as if I were mocking someone. I tried again, again I stopped. I was too self-conscious. I could no longer speak my language.

Yet I had to say something. So I switched into stateside English and started to speak. As if nothing were wrong, I told Josephine about my last year at school and the check my father had sent me with the card telling me to come to France and so forth. Once I had started in this voice I couldn't stop. If I stopped, Josephine would say something, and I was afraid to hear what it would be. So I went on and on, hating myself, and told her about the dorm I had lived in and the other students and how I had done in my classes and what the town near the campus was like and the kind of food they had at graduation, and the more I spoke, the more the wall rose between us. I could see her, but I could not reach her anymore, and she said nothing—she just sat there across the table from me. I knew what she was thinking, and I wanted to cry out, "Josephine, this isn't me!"

But I didn't, because it was.

At last she interrupted. She held up a finger in the air and I stopped talking at once. It was all she had needed when I was a boy and it was all she needed now.

"Doan meliss wid Josephine, she deh too fierce, mon," Henry used to say, shaking his head. I bit my lip, remembering. Then I looked up and looked right at her and waited. She began to examine her fingernails. A little time passed. I looked at the deep lines around her eyes and the set of her shoulders and her yellow skirt and her old broad feet in worn flip-flops. Then she looked up from her hands.

"I doan see not one hair on your head, not one lettah come from you fuh tree year now, an' den you come walk in my door an' cry in my handkerchief so? An' den you start in talkin some foolish stateside talk bout dis white people school you disappear into like mongoose disappear down his hole. Now I gon tell you a ting, an' it gon be true, so mind you listen damn good now. Listen an' maybe you gon remember wha truth soundin like, you hear me, Tollomi?"

I nodded. "Say it," I said.

She shuffled her feet in her sandals and examined her nails again. Then she looked up, not at me but at the wall behind my head. She sighed and began to speak.

"Long time ago when I still livin on King's Hill with dat no-good Theodore, Etty she come up de road an' tell me dat de white lady she workin fuh, dis lady friend have a baby, an' she lookin fuh someone wha can mind de baby an' do dis work fuh her. She say de lady she work fuh like her, an' if dis lady tell her friend I Etty sister, she gon hire me. I could sleep in de room dere an' den dat damn Theodore, he could stay at dat house, or he could go an' live with de mongoose dem, an' yell at dem all de damn day fuh what I care.

"So I ask Etty what lady is dis, an' she tell me is de one what husband gone all de time, an' when she have her baby, de baby come out lookin mos Cruzan, you know."

Here she looked at me. But unlike when I was a child, now I couldn't read her face at all.

"Etty an' me we were laughin plenty bout dat," she went on. "It was a ting all de people dem talkin about. Dey plenty outside baby on de island always, but when it de woman wha go outside, dass a ting we gon talk about, you know.

"So I go meet your maddah an' see dis brown baby wha was you. When she see how I look at you, she know what I tinkin, an' she say, 'dat baby of mine just born wid a suntan, 'cause you can see he got de blue eyes.' An' dat was true, you had de eyes you still got, an' dat make it very strange. An' I say to your maddah, 'Yes, mistress, dat baby look very fine.' An' den she hire me. An' dat all we evah say bout de way you look. But she deh tellin me keep you inside until Mistah DeHaas come back. She tellin me keep you inside away from de sun, an' den she gone all day doin only God know what. Dat was your maddah, bwoy. But I doan listen to such foolishness. Your maddah she doan needa go fret bout de sun on your skin 'cause you so dark already dat sun or no sun you ain' nevah gon be light like she."

She looked at me. Did she want me to speak? When I said nothing she continued.

"I stay two month, tree month, an' I doin de ironin, I cleanin de house, I carin fuh you. An' den de day come dat Mistah DeHaas come back. It de first time he see you from de day you born, an' he look at you five minutes, an' den he finish wid dat. He tell your maddah dat de two of dem goin sailin, an' he tell me take care of you. Which is what I doin anyway, you know, but he doan know what I doin here, an' so he stand dere tellin me mind de baby, Josephine. An' off dey go in de boat.

"An' in de middle of de night a few days later, Mistah DeHaas wake me, he come in my room an' shake me like he crazy an' tell me dat your maddah drown in de sea. An' den he leave, mon! De stone for your maddah not yet put in de cemetery when he gone again in de same damn boat wha she jump from. He ask me do I stay, he send me a check every month, an' den he gone, leave me here all alone in dis big white house wid you.

"So I tink what to do. I tell de jumbies, if you givin me dis baby, I gon make him mine, an' if you ain', you best come fetch him now. In de mornin you still in de bed, so I say okay: I got de baby, I got de house, cheese an' bread, mon!"

Her mouth moved as if she wanted to laugh, but she checked herself—my presence here, now, in front of her, checked the happy memory. She sighed and went on.

"De people always sayin dat Mistah DeHaas doan come back here no more 'cause he know de truth, dat he shame to go walk in de mahketplace, he tink people lookin at de horns wha comin outta his head 'cause you got dat brown skin. Mistah DeHaas, he coulda laid himself in de sun all day fuh a year, but he deh nevah woulda got up so dark like you dark from de first minute de sun touch your skin. You got de blue eyes, I know, but de eyes, dass a ting you must see up close. Dat skin dere you can see from a mile away.

"So all dese years, Tollomi, I tinkin dat Mistah DeHaas he can't be your faddah. I tinkin you got a daddy somewhere who name your maddah take wid her to de bottom of de sea. I tink like dat till you walk in de door dis mornin. You talkin dis stateside talk, an' you walkin like a stateside man, you sittin in dat chair dere like Mistah DeHaas used to sit in it, like he deh own de whole damn world. It like you nevah been to dis place here at all. An' I look at you now an' I see dat maybe de color of your skin just suntan after all 'cause you de spit an' image of Mistah DeHaas now. You look in dat mirror dere an' tell me if I lie, Tollomi. You his bwoy. You his bwoy fuh true."

And then she got up from her chair very fast and began moving around the kitchen with her back to me, but I still saw the tears in her eyes.

She went through the motions of cleaning up. She wiped off the counter, which was already clean. She took the brazier and threw the magic ashes into the pail with the rest of the garbage, coffee grounds, fruit pits, fishbone, and I realized I had lost this too, the ease of magic when it is not separate from the rest of life. Up there in the States, magic had become flying saucers and stories of devil worship in supermarket tabloids and miracles of statues weeping blood for tourists in Italy. Not of this world. Unreachable. Separate. That world was once intact in my heart, the world in which Josephine could burn homemade incense and the next day find the ring that had been lost all week, the world in which I saw my mother alive and happy in the waves with the tail of a fish, the world of the spirit, the world that was large enough to hold all of life and not merely that which words and numbers could explain.

"Josephine—" I began.

She wiped her eyes and turned around.

"You tink I tellin you all dis because I hate you? I love you, Tollomi. I tell you de truth of wha happen, an' I expect you to do de same fuh me. Now talk."

"Josephine, I—I tink—"

I stopped and tried again.

"I deh reach to Christiansted an' I went—I—I goin down pahs de mahket to see Wilhelm in de bar…" It was no use.

I took a deep breath and, looking at the floor, told her in tearful and perfect stateside English what had happened in Wilhelm's bar. I told her why I was wearing the clothes I had on and why I could not speak Cruzan now. I told her what had happened to me when I first arrived at boarding school; I told her about being pushed down stairs and being afraid to go into the bathrooms. I told her about my nightmares. I told her about the long weeks of silence. I told her about Clark Gable and Gary Cooper and the sounds of their voices, about the damp smell of the green rug I'd sat on in front of the television. I told her how I felt after I won my first prize in English and how I had tried to keep my inner life alive inside me. I had felt it slipping away, but I'd thought that if I came here it would come back. And I saw now that it hadn't, and I was afraid to look in a mirror now because I could not bear to see what I would see, and I was lost, I was lost, I was lost.

Josephine sat down in the chair and put her hand under my chin and raised my head as if I were still small. "Dey teach you to speak very nice," she said quietly. "I'd like to have seen de prizes dat you win. But why you doan nevah write me nottin a dat? Dese bwoys an' dem what treat you so?"

"I don't know, Josephine," I said, and she touched my cheek before she took her hand away.

"It deh too damn late at night fuh all dis agitation. You go in an' lay down on your old bed now an' sleep de night. When mornin come we gon tink what to do wid all dis confusion we makin here. You go an' sleep a nice while now. You pale wid tiredness, Tollomi. Maybe some kinda answer come to you in a dream. Go ahead an' sleep, Tollie."

She smiled then. I couldn't tell her I did not dream anymore.

I stayed on St. Croix a week, perhaps two, I don't know. I was in a sort of nightmare I was waiting to wake up from: It could not really be happening. For moments at a time I would forget and, walking down the street, imagine myself a young Cruzan at home, sauntering down the street in a battered straw hat, my voice a part of the voices of the trees, the music of the steel pans, my body a part of the island. For moments the thoughts in my head would come in Cruzan. And then, in the reflection of a gift shop window, above the mother-of-pearl bracelets displayed on driftwood and pink velvet, I'd catch sight of a tall man with too-pale skin and a straw hat. I looked like a business-man on holiday, afraid of getting his nose burned. I stared into my eyes as into the eyes of a stranger.

I wanted to visit the boys who had been my friends, but after the first attempt I gave up. I looked up a friend I had once played with daily when he lived with his parents and brothers in a little house on the beach. That house was gone now, bulldozed to make room for a hotel, and I found my old friend inland in the tiny cinder-block kitchen of a new housing project. We sat in that kitchen for half an hour or so, and he stared at the table because he could not quite look at me; he could not find his boyhood friend in this stranger, and so he was shy of me. I had shed my stateside sport shirt and khakis for less conspicuous clothes; I had tried again and again to speak like the people around me, among whom I so desperately wanted to belong. But a deeper change had taken place within me, a change that neither clothes nor accent could unmake. I had changed as much as the island itself.

Josephine, Josephine, she looked at me with the love she always had, but it was not enough. It was as if the me she had known were dead and the me now a relative who understood as no one else did the character of the departed. I reminded her of him as the island reminded me of the island I once knew, the island without housing projects and boys hold-ing guns, without sprawling hotel chains and golf courses and murders on those golf courses. The island I used to belong to, the island that for me no longer existed.

And there was nothing Josephine could say to help me. She had fore-seen what would happen to me if I left, perhaps, but she had not foreseen what would happen to the island in the years I had been away. There's no way anyone can until the machines are in place. It's not naïveté. It's that there is only so much a human being is prepared to handle. You end up handling more than that, always, but you aren't prepared for it. The first time you never see it coming. The second time it's too late.

So even then I didn't understand in full what had happened, to the island or to me. It was too big. I have spent the rest of my life running my fingers along the sides of it, looking for the corners that signify an edge, an end. But there is no end to it. Like the earth, my life has no edges. I live on a curve.

My home was gone from me forever. I understood that. It meant I had nowhere to go, and I could go anywhere.

So I left the island and I went: everywhere. But I had become the sailor in the story whose boat is bewitched so that, no matter how he sails it, he can't reach a shore. What choice does he have then? He drowns or he keeps sailing.

I'm still here—so far.

The room is still dark. It's not even false dawn yet, but I've been awake for hours, thrashing around on this bad hotel mattress, retracing the tired path of my life. In the bed across from mine, a young woman lies so deeply asleep that in the hours since I've been awake she has not turned or stirred once. And she has no past. Or rather, she cannot remember it. And so she sleeps deeply. So deeply, she says, she can even walk in her sleep and not wake up. She sleepwalks; does she dream?

Almost twenty years of traveling have followed my departure from St. Croix. I look at them and see just how well I've learned the

\ I spent in the States. I can mimic perfectly the language of any place I set foot in. I arrive in a country whose language I don't know, and after only few days I can speak the words I've learned with no trace of an accent. No one can ever guess where I'm from. If they ask, they get lies or no answer. I'm from wherever I'm standing.

I've traveled all over the world. Not as a tourist; always I was working. I was with the volunteer work brigade in San Salvador to help rebuild the city after the bombings, or I was working for World Health in North Africa vaccinating children against smallpox, or I was part of a delegation to monitor human rights abuses somewhere else. I was writing an article about popular support for guerrilla activity in the mountains. I was canvassing on this initiative, I was with that emergency relief agency, I was booked on the ship that was leaving tomorrow for some other great cause on the opposite side of the world. All this traveling managed to make a slight dent in the funds my father the shipping magnate had established for me. I didn't need his approval to draw on them; I had hardly spoken to him since high school. But I was his only son and thus privileged by his sugar fortune: The world was mine. Most of the money I withdrew went for plane fare and sea crossings. I zigzagged back and forth across the globe with sugar money, money harvested in cane fields, courtesy of cheap West Indian labor.

From perhaps fifty different cities I worked for various organizations. I conducted interviews, I wrote reports and articles, I sent out newsletters. I spent thousands of hours on the phone, searching for money and volunteers. I filed papers; I marched, carrying signs on city streets and dirt roads. I knocked on whole cites of doors and talked and persuaded and argued. I never had any problem finding work. No matter where I went, there was never a shortage of terrible acts committed and no end to the silences with which they were received. Besides, I was so good at what I did. I spoke half a dozen languages, and I could convince anyone of anything. If language is about communication, it is also about lying, giving reality a shape other than the shape it was born with. There is no easier way to mold reality than with words.

"Why are you leaving so soon? Where are you going? Where did you learn to sail like that? How did you manage to raise so much money? Are those blue contact lenses? Where are you from, anyway?"

I would say anything. I became whoever they needed me to be. Anything except the truth. In half a dozen languages I lied through my teeth.

"Say something in your real voice, Tollomi."

My real voice? That has no meaning for me. I have no real voice, not anymore. The voice I use more than others is simply the one I have practiced most, and being the voice of America it is the easiest to fall into. That does not make it mine. On the contrary, it is less mine than any other, for its cultivation has cost me the one voice that did belong to me, my Cruzan voice, the voice I had as a child.

In the eighteen years that have passed since I left St. Croix, I have gone along with my life the way people do when their true life is elsewhere. Until eight days ago when my true life caught up with me.

The hurricane that blew through the islands in September was the worst storm to hit the West Indies in more than a century. St. Croix lay in the center of its path, and the storm took hold of the island as if the island were a blanket laid out for a picnic; it yanked it up and shook it until everything—huge resort hotels and tiny shacks, trees, telephone poles—went tumbling into the wild sea like broken dishes. When the storm had finished not a speck of green was left on the island. Trees, bushes, leaves, grass, vines—all were gone. Cinder blocks and pieces of roof and tree trunks fell back to earth and lay smashed and broken on the ruined ground.

I didn't know about it. I had no idea it had happened. I was in Guatemala writing an article about media censorship, and the only papers I had been interested in were those that were not being published. When my article was finished, I reintroduced myself to current events with a battered copy of an American news magazine someone had left in a restaurant. The magazine was a month old. I sat drinking my coffee and leafed through stories of American political scandals. Buried in the center of the magazine was a photograph of a dozen cruising yachts stacked up like firewood against the remains of a house. The article was about the damage done to the coast of South Carolina. I was glancing at this when my eyes fell on the words "St. Croix."

"After braving a night of howling winds," the article said, "vacationers to this popular island emerged from their shelters to find paradise destroyed. In addition to destruction wreaked by the hurricane, there was extensive looting and rioting by armed gangs of local residents who ransacked stores and shouted 'Whitey, go home!' at tourists. Many tourists had to be evacuated by the Coast Guard before the 1,200 troops sent by President Bush could arrive to restore order. Ninety-five percent of St. Croix's native population has been left homeless…"

I ran out of the restaurant and took a taxi to the telephone exchange.

I didn't know Josephine's number. I thought I could get the Guatemalan operator to connect me with an operator in St. Croix.

"There are no lines," the operator said after a moment. I thought he meant all the lines were busy, and asked him to try again.

"There are no lines," he repeated. "There was a bad storm there, and now there are no lines. No wires. Understand?"

Only then did I see in my mind's eye the telephone poles lying across the streets of Christiansted like felled trees. What was the matter with me? I went outside and walked back and forth in front of the building in the blazing sun. Marika, Etty's younger daughter, lived in Florida. Josephine had written me about it years ago; Marika had gone to college in St. Petersburg and got married there and stayed. Could I call her? What was her husband's name? He had a name people made jokes about. I couldn't remember it.

It was Marika who had been sent down the beach to find me the night my father came back to St. Croix. Whenever there was a storm, that beach was littered with debris from the sea: old wood that had been parts of ships, dead fish, fishnets, and line entangled in huge piles of purple kelp. In town the market stalls would blow over. The sea would be rough for days, and the fishermen complained. And those were little storms.

Stiff, that was Marika's husband's name. Jimmy Stiff. I went back inside the telephone exchange and stood in line and sat in the little booth with my hands sweating. I got a Florida operator and said Stiff, St. Petersburg.

The line crackled. I could half-hear someone else's conversation. There was a distant ringing and then nothing and then in my ear a woman's voice said, "Hello?"

It was Marika. I had not seen her in eighteen years, but I knew her voice at once.

"Marika? It's Tollomi."

I heard the soft hiss of static through the phone lines, and then, a thousand miles away, I heard her catch her breath.

"Tollomi?"

"It's me," I said. "I was up in the mountains. I didn't know about the hurricane until just now. Is everyone all right? Is the house all right? What happened?"

"Tollomi," Marika said slowly, "where the hell have you been?" Her voice carried the enunciation and slightly nasal tones of the university, but her Cruzan lilt was still there.

"I'm in Guatemala," I said. "I just found out. Is Josephine all right? Are your parents all right? Where are they staying?" There was another pause and again, through all the miles of air that lay between us, I heard Marika breathing.

"You didn't get my letter," she said.

"Where did you send it? No, I didn't. What?"

"Tollie," said Marika, and I felt that name of my childhood softly pierce me, "Tollie, I thought you knew. We wrote you months ago. Josephine's dead."

The words reached my body. My brain refused them. "What?" I said. I did not breathe.

"She's dead," said Marika. "She died in August. We did write—the last address you sent Josephine—you must have moved. We wrote a letter—"

Josephine is dead, Josephine is dead: That was all I heard, over and over as if I were being beaten with it. I put the phone down in my lap for a moment, then seized it up again, as if by holding on to it I was still holding on to Josephine. Josephine is dead, Josephine is dead; she died over two months ago, and here I was in a scuffed wooden booth, talking to her niece. Josephine was dead and I was far away.

"Tollomi? Are you still there?"

"I'm here," I said. And Marika told me what happened.

On August eleventh Josephine played cards with Etty and Joanne as she did every Friday night. She won every hand for a solid hour, and then she said she didn't feel well and was going to start home. They told her she was just afraid that if she kept playing, her luck would run out, and she said, *Yah, dey too smaht fuh her,* and then she went out the door laughing with her pockets full of nickels.

"They always played for nickels," said Marika. "Remember?"

"Yes."

When Henry came back to the house later that night, he found Josephine stretched out on the bed still in her clothes. Her heart had stopped. The nickels she'd won at poker were in a little pile on the bedspread.

I remembered her bedspread. It was big and lacy. It had been a wedding present from the mother of her first husband, Theodore. He used to beat her, and after she left him to come work taking care of me, she dyed the bedspread orange by soaking it in tea and onion skins. It was always on her bed. I could see her hands on the faded orange cotton, the pale purple moons of her fingernails.

She was dead. What was I doing on August eleventh? I thought back and tried to remember a feeling I had not in fact had. The moment she left the earth, had I felt a shiver, a little wind? Had I awakened in the night, thinking of her? Had I heard her calling my name? No. Like an unattended knot, my link to her had slipped. It had come untied, and I had not even felt the line give way. I had looked up too late, and now there was nothing left to see. I had drifted too far from shore.

"I should have gone back," I said. "I should go back now. Are Etty and Abel still in the house? What about Henry?"

"Henry?" Her voice slid into Cruzan scorn, slid through me like a knife. "Henry dead some four year, Tollomi. Of cancer dey never find until one day he drop. Josephine she write you herself an' when you doan write back, we tell her to write you off, you know? You doan get dat letter either, I see."

"Marika, I—I—" I was in tears.

"What dis 'I—I,' Tollomi? You wanna know what we doin an' ting, you got to *ask*. Next ting you know you gonna be dead too an' not know it, cause you ain' got nobody to send you a telegram. You get what I mean?"

I got it, better than she knew, and I sat there dead in the phone booth, saying nothing, but the line was still live in my hand, and at last she said in her stateside voice, "You still there?"

"I'm here," I said. I took a deep breath. "Is there anything else I should know? Are Etty and Abel...?"

"They're here with us."

"In St. Petersburg?"

"I couldn't leave them down there with no place to sleep, could I?"

"What?"

"Dat storm dey name Hugo one greedy son of a bitch."

I had forgotten about the hurricane.

"I had to fly down to get them out," Marika went on. "God, Tollomi, you're lucky you didn't see it. Remember Wilhelm's bar? It's a travel agency now but it still has that big basement. Etty and Abel had to sleep in that basement for a week before I could get there. Thank God we had the money to get them out."

"How badly was the house damaged?" I asked.

"Tollomi, you hearin a damn word I tellin you? You deh talkin like de house still dere. Ain' nothin to damage, Tollomi. Ain' nothin left. I tellin you, mon, de house down in de sea."

"The house was made of cinder-block," I said numbly.

"And it's *gone*. The roof is probably in Puerto Rico—" I heard the tears in her voice now—"and, Tollomi, the horse tree is gone too."

The horse tree was a palm tree whose trunk had grown out horizontally like a horse's swayed back. When we were children, we rode it and made the whole tree creak and shake.

"But it was a palm tree," I said. "They're supposed to just bend over in a storm, then snap back up."

"All the palm trees are gone. Everything is gone. Jesus, Tollomi, haven't you seen any pictures? Don't you watch TV? The whole island is a fucking mess. You can't walk down the streets, they're so full of junk. Broken glass and upside-down washing machines and wood and all kinds of shit. I'm glad Josephine and Henry didn't have to see it. The whole island looks like it's been sucked up by a vacuum cleaner and then spit out again. There's nothing green left anywhere." Suddenly she laughed. "I gon tell you a ting. I tell you one ting fuh true, Tollomi. Green ain' de only color wha tis gone from St. Croix. Ain' no white left dere either. All de white people dem pack up an' leave quick-quick. De only color wha stay on dat island is poor an' black."

I didn't laugh with her. She stopped laughing. "I haven't seen you since I was a girl," she said. "I didn't recognize your voice. If I saw you on the street now, Tollomi, would I know you?"

"Of course you would," I lied. And then I told her that I was in the public telephone exchange in Guatemala City, and there were a lot of people waiting to use the phone. I asked her where Josephine was buried.

"Fifteen, twenty years, Tollomi, and you don't even go back at Christmas to lie on the beach. You want to go back now and look at her gravestone? You can't. The hurricane blew it away." She paused. "You hearin what I tellin you?"

I heard her. I wanted the line to go dead. When it didn't I thanked her for writing me about Josephine, even though I hadn't gotten the letter. She said it was really Etty who had dictated it, but she would tell her what I said. I said I was sorry I hadn't known Henry had died; if I had, I would have called or written.

"Uh-huh," Marika said.

I said I was glad her parents were all right, and she said she was too. Then we both said goodbye, and I hung up.

I left the telephone exchange and went back to my hotel. I packed my two bags. It was eighteen years since I had been on St. Croix, and Marika was right: There was no point in going back now. But I couldn't stay here. If I stayed still, the voices that were starting up in my head would surround me, ensnare me, drown me in accusations for which I had no answer. I checked out of the hotel, dropped off the corrected copy of the article I'd written, and left the city quietly and at once, like a man escaping the scene of a crime.

I could have gone back to St. Croix. I could have taken a plane, a different ship. And done what? Wandered in the barren, storm-bombed landscape looking for relics of a world whose loss was to me already old? Would submerging myself in such tangible grief absolve my guilt?

I did not go back. Flight, like proper English, like lying, becomes a habit.

From Guatemala City I drifted east, drawn toward the Caribbean in spite of myself. The freighter was bound for Venezuela, a slow boat with many calls en route; I had days to decide where I was going. I didn't care much where I went. I was just moving.

The second night out I stood on deck for hours, hanging my head over the rails. I wasn't seasick, but sick over Josephine, Henry; sick over St. Croix, sick of myself.

The smell of tobacco behind me made me turn from the rails. I hadn't heard anyone coming, and I knew as I turned that it was a sailor I'd see. Only a sailor can move so quietly on a ship. He had come up right behind me.

"It's late, sir. You should be in your cabin." He spoke English with a Caribbean Spanish accent.

"I couldn't sleep," I replied in the same Spanish.

He leaned against the rail beside me. "You couldn't sleep," he mused. "This is your first trip on such a big ship?"

His ship, the tone of voice said, though the uniform did not. He wanted to impress me. "Yes, it's my first trip," I said.

"And where are you going?"

"I'm on my way to Havana." It was the first place that popped into my head; it was Cuban tobacco he was smoking, I could tell by the smell.

"Havana! We don't sail to Havana."

"I mean, after Caracas."

"Are you Cuban?" he asked.

"No, but your cigarette is."

The sailor grinned and offered me one. His teeth were very white in the darkness. I thought again of Josephine. "I'm Dominican," he said. He handed me his cigarette so I could light my own.

"From what part?"

"You wouldn't have heard of it. Tenares."

"I've been there," I said.

The sailor was enchanted. "You know Tenares? What were you doing in Tenares?"

"Building a school with an international volunteer organization." Completely false: I had been in Santo Domingo about six years ago, for the better part of a month, but I had never heard of Tenares, much less been there. I listened to myself lying and stopped thinking of Josephine and began to think instead of how not to get caught.

"Building a school in Tenares," said the sailor incredulously. "Come and have a drink with me. We'll go to my cabin."

I looked at him. For a moment I thought I'd heard another invitation within his offer. I scanned his face for the flicker of sexuality that should be there. It wasn't, and I chided myself. I was only looking for further distraction. He was asking me to his cabin simply because, being in uniform, he was not allowed to drink in the passengers' lounge. I followed him down the little metal stairs, off the deck and through the hold. I watched him as he threaded his way through the ship's belly with practiced agility. He had the splendid body of a sailor, the shoulders too broad from lifting cargo, the legs slim like a boy's. Even if I had seen him on land in street clothes, I would have known he was a sailor by the way he moved.

We sat on his bed; there was nowhere else to sit. From under it, he produced a bottle and a glass, and another glass from beneath the bed opposite. He poured a heavy finger of rum in each. We drank to his country—"*¡A la República Dominicana!*"—his head thrown back, the glass held high in the air.

"It's very good rum," I said.

"*Es ron Dominicano*. You can't buy it in Miami. I've been there. Very nice place," he said, and I waited for the standard Dominican broken-English monologue on the United States: is very nice place; my cousin/brother/uncle/father he live in New York, he working, make many money.

"My brother, he live in New York. He drive a taxi."

"Oh, really?"

"Yes, the United States is a very nice place—" he switched abruptly back to Spanish. "But they have a bad record of invading us—too often for my taste."

I looked up from my rum in surprise.

"You're shocked I said that? But I know you won't mind; you're not a *norteamericano*." I was afraid he was going to ask me where I was from, but went on: "The American, he won't go anywhere with you, he's always afraid you're going to steal his wallet."

I laughed at that and then considered: Did that mean he often asked passengers to go places with him? To come here to his room? I looked over his shoulder at the cabin, but it was completely nondescript, of course: gray metal walls with a narrow bunk bed on either side, and foot lockers and a shaving mirror and that was all. No clues.

"Besides," he went on, "you said you built a school in Tenares with an international organization. So you're an international worker and you're on your way to Cuba. You're going to build another school? Or you'll do some other kind of politics, perhaps. It's a very good time to be in politics."

I made a face. I didn't want to talk politics with this man. I wanted to drink his rum and imagine how his hands would feel holding my thighs.

"It's a good time to be in politics," he persisted, "because there is a need for many people to fight."

"I'd say it was a very *bad* time to be in politics for the same reason," I said.

"And you are making this face. You are—" he broke off. "I learned this word in English—what was it?" He frowned. "*Estás*—burned out!"

"That's it," I said. "Burned out."

"And that's bad. What's the opposite of 'burned out'? 'On fire,' *¿verdad?* Yes. Well, then, I will tell you something to make you on fire again."

"I wish you would," I said. I was getting drunk.

"The political situation in my country is very interesting," he began, and seeing my expression, stopped.

"I know it is," I said grudgingly. How to change the subject gracefully? "If you're so interested in politics," I said, "what are you doing on this ship?"

The sailor spread out his hands in front of him and examined them. I knew they were callused and hard, and I knew exactly how they would feel on my skin. He folded his hands behind his head. "I am doing on this boat what I can't do in the Dominican Republic."

"And that is?"

"Staying alive."

I was silent. If all he had left was effect, well, let him use it.

"If I had not left when I did," he said, "I would have been killed. I was lucky to have been able to leave at all. I was part of a political group that the government…"

He paused. What he said next depended on my reaction. If my response wasn't right, he would not continue the story. I had to show him my papers, so to speak. For me, even if I hadn't been interested, proving myself worthy of audience was a matter of principle. But I was beginning to be interested now.

"Being a revolutionary is a strange line of work," I said. "You're allowed to keep working only if you do your job badly. If you're effective, you tend to wind up dead."

That was more than good enough; he poured me more rum. Stamp of approval, permission to enter.

We are speaking of human life, I thought absently, and making a game of what we say, how we say it. "So tell me," I said. "I'm listening."

He began to tell me about a man called Jorge Vásquez: university professor, political analyst, journalist, revolutionary; imprisoned twice under Trujillo, again under Balaguer. Released the last time with his hair completely white, a man undone, worn out, retired, and almost forgotten until he reentered politics last autumn. Six weeks later he was assassinated while sitting at his writing desk at home. Had I ever heard of him?

I told him I hadn't.

He was a brilliant man, he had written two important books. He was an inspiring professor, an important organizer of students during the 1965 revolution. After the revolution was crushed and all the U.S. Marines had gone home, Vásquez had resigned from the political arena altogether. His two sons had been killed in the fighting, and the revolution had been his child too, his hope for the future. Now that all three were dead, Vásquez lost interest in the rest of the living. He stopped teaching. He haunted the university library at all hours, reading nothing but pre-Colombian history and working on some obscure linguistic project that would never be finished. He wandered the stacks, was talked about, and both tolerated and ridiculed because of the greatness of his former self.

After twenty years of living like this, half dead, Vásquez suddenly reemerged. He announced he was going to give a talk about the research he had been doing. That was all he said, but the posters put up around the university were more specific: VÁSQUEZ: A POLITICAL AGENDA FOR THE NEXT DECADE. The lecture hall was so full, they were turning people away at the doors.

"I went to see him," said the sailor. "I had read both his books. They were by a different man than the one I'd seen wandering around the library. It was the author of the books I hoped to hear."

Students who for years had heard stories of this man's former greatness came, wanting to see what he could do. Older people who remembered clearly what he had done came wanting him to do it again. When Vásquez walked across the stage to the podium, he received a standing ovation. When this had quieted down, he cleared his throat and began speaking.

The sailor, who by now was a little drunk and well-warmed to his story, sat up on his knees on the bed and attempted to recreate the speech for me.

"My friends, the Dominican Republic is a very old land. Here in Santo Domingo we have the first cathedral built anywhere in the western hemisphere. This university is likewise the first in the Americas. The famous Columbus, as you know from your history books, is credited with discovering America, but it was here in the Caribbean islands that he first set foot. Well. This evening I wish to speak to you about our history, but a history older than the one I have just mentioned. I want to speak to you of the Tainos."

Vásquez went on to remind the audience that before the cathedrals and universities were built, before the capital city had the name of a European saint, before the Europeans arrived on these shores, the Tainos walked on this same island for more than a thousand years. "Their numbers in these islands," he continued, "were the same as ours are now, about four million. Yet how much remains now of their civilization?"

The audience shifted in their seats, and an undertone of muttering went through the hall. They had come to be rallied to action, not hear a history lesson. Vásquez took a sip of water and coughed at them, and enough of the audience remembered he had been a brilliant man once. The crowd fell silent again.

"The history of the Tainos is a footnote in the world's history books. Their language is not on the tongue of a single Dominican, and yet all across the Americas we still possess many of their words. Even in the United States, where everything is new, they use a few words of this old language."

Vásquez reached into the lectern and brought out a piece of fruit. "*Papaya*," he said. He reached into the lectern again and brought out a small wooden souvenir carved into the shape of a boat. "*Canoa*," said Vásquez, "canoe. Hurricane. Hammock. Barbecue. All Taino words." He held up a bottle of beer.

At this point the sailor abandoned his narrative to ask me if while I was building the school in Tenares I had drunk much beer.

I thought of Dominican beer. There was Presidente, the most popular. Bohemia was imported. What was the other beer? It came in a brown bottle. "Quisqueya?" I asked.

The sailor nodded. "The Taino name for our island, Quisqueya. It meant, 'The Great.' Now it means a beer that tastes like piss."

"Go on," I said.

Vásquez reminded the audience that a mere fifty years after Columbus first set foot on Hispaniola, there were no Tainos left, on this island or any other. Not one. To get rid of four million people in fifty years is quite a feat, he said. He reminded them of how it had been done. He spoke of how the Tainos had been forced into slavery and literally worked to death; how those who couldn't deliver the daily quota of gold had their hands cut off. They died on their feet with chains around their ankles, said Vásquez; they died of the diseases the Europeans brought: smallpox, syphilis, typhus, typhoid, yellow fever, bubonic plague. They were hanged from trees for insubordination; they were burned at the stake for refusing to become Christians.

"What is genocide?" Vásquez asked. "It is not simply the killing of a nauseatingly huge number of people. We will all die someday. Genocide is the killing of something that is harder to make than babies. It is the killing of a miracle greater than the miracle of human life. Four million people, an entire nation, an entire culture, completely eradicated within the space of one lifetime. Perhaps the most complete decimation of a people anywhere, ever, at any time in history. Think of that. Genocide is the killing of history."

The hall was silent. Vásquez looked out over the room with the whole island in his eyes. At last he had the audience in the palm of his hand. Then he explained his plan. It was very simple. He wanted everyone on the island to learn to speak Taino.

He wanted it taught in the schools, spoken in the streets and the shops and the bars. He wanted university graduates to join him in striking out to the most remote areas of the island to teach the inhabitants of those regions to speak Taino. In five years Santo Domingo would be mobbed with tourists celebrating the 500th anniversary of Columbus's arrival; we should meet them, he said, speaking the language his arrival destroyed.

"My friends!" he cried. "The Spanish we speak today is the language of those who murdered our ancestors. The English that more and more of us need to know just to find work is like a weed, covering everything it touches, choking the ground so that nothing else can grow in that soil. It is time we learn to speak a different language. Taino language is the only thing we have on this island that truly belongs to us, and it is ours forever if only we care to claim it. *¡Mis compañeros!* Shall we claim it?"

Jorge Vásquez was that rare thing, a great man. The room had grown utterly still toward the end of his speech, and when he had finished speaking, the silence stayed suspended in the air for nearly a minute, such was his power.

The sailor picked up his rum, which he had not touched at all while speaking, and slowly drained the glass.

I was no longer drunk. I leaned toward him, opened my mouth, and said, "Tell me—are they doing it?"

The sailor clicked his tongue against his teeth. "When the silence in that hall was finally broken," he said, "Vásquez was laughed off the stage."

He saw how my face fell.

"But what did you expect them to do, my friend? Half the population of the Dominican Republic is completely illiterate, and Vásquez, the revolutionary, the university professor, wanted to spend his time teaching them a language that hasn't been spoken in five hundred years. Not exactly practical. Besides, it wouldn't have been pure Taino anyway. Too much of the language has been lost. But Vásquez was a linguist— he used to teach linguistics, you know, as well as political science. And he had reconstructed—invented, really—his own version of the language around what little Taino was recorded by the *conquistadores*. So that made it even worse. People in the audience yelled at him, saying he was talking gibberish, and if he thought learning to speak gibberish was any kind of political agenda at all, then he had forgotten 1965 and forgotten the Party, and it was because of people like him that we were still rotting under the thumbs of Balaguer and the United States. And so on—have you had too much rum? You look sick."

I felt sick; I was thinking of my own lost Cruzan tongue. "I'm fine," I said. I made myself look fine. "Why are you telling me this?"

"I'm explaining why I'm on this boat. You don't like my story?"

"It isn't that," I said. "Go on."

Vásquez left the stage but not his project. Being booed, he said later, is nothing after you've been tortured. He often made jokes like that.

The day after the failed lecture, there were posters up around the university announcing an informal seminar the following evening at the Vásquezes' house for those interested in the proposal outlined the night before. Again the sailor went with a few of his friends from the university. It wasn't that they thought his plan was so great. They went because they were young and disgusted with the government, because Vásquez had been famous, because he was a revolutionary who was still alive. Or perhaps it was because some of his power of the night before, even if it was the power to arouse jeers, had rubbed off on them.

About thirty people came. Vásquez's wife was there too: Guadelupe Vásquez y Cruz. She had taught anthropology at the university. The students liked her: Doña Lupe, they called her. She had made some kind of punch, the sailor remembered, with rum in it. Everyone milled around on the back patio with a plastic cup of punch, and then Vásquez came out. He spoke very briefly.

The night before, Vásquez said, he had been accused of being everything from self-indulgent to antirevolutionary. He spoke of Juan Bosch, the overthrown president whom the revolution had tried to restore to power, and reminded them that Bosch himself had said there would never, ever be another revolution here because the United States would not permit it. "So what am I to do?" said Vásquez. He held up his hands in mock dismay. "I'm a revolutionary. I don't want to be out of work for the rest of my life."

Laughter. The unemployment rate in Santo Domingo was astronomical.

"I am resorting to a revolution of words," said Vásquez, "and anyone who wishes to join me can begin studying Taino with me here tomorrow afternoon."

There was a round of cheering, and then his wife stood up. It seemed she also had a project going that she wanted to explain.

She wanted to open a museum. "When tourists come to town," doña Lupe said, "they see museum after museum filled with artifacts of the *conquistadores*. They visit the cathedral with its Gothic ceilings and statues of bishops; they visit the house of Diego Columbus with its authentic furnishings from Spain. They marvel at the treasures of the kings and queens of Europe and walk through the cobblestone streets and exclaim how much like Europe everything is.

"In 1992 tourists will arrive in droves for the quincentennial. The museum I want to open will give all these tourists something else to look at." She paused, surveying the young faces in her garden. "Our museum will be a memorial to the destruction of our pre-Colombian culture in the Caribbean. A documentation of all that was destroyed. A holocaust museum, if you like."

She told them she was writing grant proposals and soliciting artists from all over the Caribbean, from Central and South America, from Africa. The artists would be invited to create historically accurate interpretations of the holocaust of the sixteenth century in any medium they chose. Their work would be placed on permanent display, together with writing and art from time of the conquest, in old Santo Domingo. When the tourists came to marvel at the discovery of America, to wander through old Spanish fortresses and stone houses filled with the art and furniture of the *conquistadores,* they would also discover another kind of museum: a museum that documented the end of a world.

When Lupe Vásquez had explained all this, the students in the garden broke into applause. She told them she was not going to announce the project publicly until she was sure of getting funding. She reminded them that it would be considered blatant criticism of the president, who was spending forty million dollars to build his own new tourist attraction, a mausoleum functioning as a lighthouse in the shape of a giant cross, inside which would be installed the remains of Columbus himself.

When Lupe Vásquez had finished speaking, Jorge Vásquez stood up again. He said there had been enough politics for one night, and now it was time for everyone to enjoy themselves. Doña Lupe brought out a radio and people started to dance. The garden was full of dancing under paper lanterns hung from a clothesline. The party broke up very late.

It turned out later that a government agent had been at the party. No one knew about it until the next day when the police appeared on Vásquez's front porch. It seemed that while the agent was in the backyard listening for conspiracy and treason, someone had been out front setting fire to the upholstery of his unmarked car.

Vásquez told the police that if they didn't have the sense to keep their agents truly undercover, it wasn't his fault. He was so old he felt he could talk to the police like this. He wasn't afraid of them anymore, he said. And the police went away.

That was the first thing that happened. For a while afterward there was nothing else. Vásquez taught Taino classes in the afternoon, and then the students would sit around and badger him until he got going on politics. He'd talk about his younger days, the revolution and all that had led up to it, what had gone wrong, what had happened afterward. He was telling old memories, that was all, but in Santo Domingo things began to happen. On the statue of Columbus that stood in front of the oldest cathedral in the hemisphere, someone had graffitied a message in red spray paint.

"You know the statue?" the sailor asked me.

"I know I've seen it. But I can't remember how it looks."

He described it: Columbus is standing on a pedestal in the middle of the cathedral square. At his feet a young Taino Indian is inscribing Columbus's name upon the pedestal's column. Below this, beginning at the tip of the Taino's feather pen, new words had been painted. The tourists who came out to visit the cathedral in the morning stared at the message but could not read it. It was in a language they had never seen before. Fortunately, a Spanish translation was sprayed below.

"The message was in Taino?" I asked. A little thrill went through me.

The sailor grinned. "It was in Taino."

"And you saw it?"

He nodded. I almost asked him if he had written it, but stopped myself. I didn't think he would tell me. And by the expression on his face I felt I knew the answer anyway.

"What did it say?" I asked instead.

"Well, there was the original engraving in the marble: CRISTÓBAL COLÓN. And under that had been added: —IS DEAD. TAINO IS ALIVE. And it was signed, LOS QUISQUEYAS. That was what the group called itself. *Los Quisqueyas.*"

"Was anyone arrested?"

"There was one arrest," the sailor said. "The graffiti was done on Saturday night; Sunday afternoon there were more police at Vásquez's door. There were no lessons on Sunday; the police found Vásquez at home playing dominoes with a neighbor. They hauled him off to the station, where they kept him all night. He sat on a hard bench and listened to them yell at him while in the front office his wife yelled at the officer on duty and demanded that they release him."

The sailor refilled our glasses, which had stood empty and forgotten during his story, then took a small sip of rum.

He went on. They finally let Vásquez out at sunrise on Monday. When he and his wife arrived home, they found that during the night their house had been ransacked. Everything was a mess except, oddly, the game of dominoes, which still stood half-played on the patio table. Vásquez started to put the dominoes away. A car drove up. Two policemen climbed out. They came up the walk and told Vásquez he was under arrest again. Sometime on Sunday night someone had broken into the construction site of the Columbus Lighthouse. The beautiful marble being laid for the plaza and the beautiful granite walls of the memorial had been covered in spray paint. Everywhere you looked, as high as a man's arm would reach, you could read the dripping words against the government—and a lot of other "nonsense in some made-up language," as the police put it.

"So I am being arrested for made-up nonsense?" Vásquez asked. One of the officers hit him in the face. Vásquez stumbled but remained standing. He coughed and reminded the officers that they themselves had provided the alibi for his activities the night before. He couldn't very well have been out orchestrating a break-in at the lighthouse; he had been in the police station all night being interrogated.

The officers looked at the balding old man clutching a domino. His left cheek was turning red.

"Why don't you try *not* arresting me," said Vásquez. "That way, if something else happens, you'll be able to pin it on me without the problem of my having been in jail at the time."

One of the police officers tongued his mouthful of tobacco and spat. The wad of leaves and saliva landed on Vásquez's shoe. Vásquez didn't flinch. The officer who had spat turned and went down the porch steps and out the gate to the street. His partner followed. They got in the car and drove off. Vásquez wiped his shoe and finished putting away the dominoes. Then he went into the house. His wife sat at the kitchen table, smoking one of his cigars to calm her nerves.

He thanked her for not coming outside.

She was angry. She wanted him to talk to his students, tell them to stop. "The police want to make an example of you," she said. "If things go on like this, they'll kill you. Tell the students they can't come for lessons anymore, Jorge. It's too dangerous."

Vásquez asked her what she thought would happen when she tried to find a building for her museum.

"That's different," she said. "That will be an international event. There will be too many artists from too many countries for the government to dare interfere."

"Perhaps," said Vásquez, "we should send word to the spray painters to take art classes. Then, you think, we'll all be safe?"

His wife did not reply. She was still angry. She was afraid for him. She kept smoking his cigar and finally asked him what he wanted for dinner. *Langostina,* he said. To celebrate. She didn't ask what they were supposed to be celebrating. She said she was going out to buy it, then. He asked her to pick up a newspaper on her way home, and that was the last thing he ever said to her; an hour later he was shot in the back of the head while sitting at his desk.

"When I found out he was dead," said the sailor, "I was drinking in a bar near the university. It was evening, the same day. A friend came in to tell me. He had just heard. The killers came in and did it while doña Lupe was out buying the lobster he'd wanted. She came back and found him with his head down on the desk in a lake of blood. I remember I had just drunk my first beer when Virgilio came in and told me. After he told me I went into the toilet and threw up."

Then he was quiet. We sat in silence for a minute, there in the ship's cabin in the middle of the sea. The sailor looked at his hands. Then he lifted them up in the air and wiggled his fingers. I looked at his fingers wiggling and suddenly felt very drunk.

"Then I left the island," he said. "I had to. I had paint on my hands."

I held up my own hands and looked through them. The sailor didn't look at me. But he kept his own hands raised. I leaned forward through the air until our hands were touching. His palms were warm and hard with calluses. He did not pull his hands away.

His bed was narrow. Later that night the ship hit rough water, and

86

our bodies banged against the metal wall while we made love. Before it got light I had to sneak out of his cabin so that the engineer he shared the room with wouldn't find us when he came off shift.

I sat on deck by myself and watched the sunrise. I had bruises all over my arms. And I had the knowledge of my next destination.

The ship did not go anywhere near Hispaniola. I had to get off in Colón and take a plane, first to San Juan and then to Santo Domingo. The Dominican Republic—as good a destination as any. I was going to Santo Domingo to find Lupe Vásquez, to volunteer my help in raising funds for the museum, to find the students who had been pupils of Vásquez, and to listen to what they had learned, to hear from their mouths the sounds of a language dead five hundred years.

I was not going to St. Croix, I was not going to put flowers on Josephine's grave. Marika was right; the time for going to see Josephine was gone and I had missed it. For all my ease with clever explanations, I had none here. No excuse to give Marika or myself, no words with which to ask pardon. The person whose forgiveness I needed lay buried under a fallen headstone in the rocky ground of the cemetery that lay a few miles from what had once been our home.

The plane banked, descending, and I averted my eyes from the sea below. I tried to keep my mind fixed on my destination. But the sound of my own lost language vibrated through me, louder than the engines of the plane.

So yesterday I arrived in Santo Domingo. I was standing in customs when three men with guns elbowed through the line in front of me and marched over to one of the tables across the room. There was a problem. Whenever I see the customs officials—striding across the echoing floor with their black boots hitting the tile in that way that lets you know their guns are loaded—I always feel it's me they're coming for. That I have done nothing wrong at that moment is irrelevant. Border crossings always upset me. It's a question of where your sympathies lie. I stood halfway out of the queue, my hands sweating and my luggage sliding out of my grip as I counted the tiles on the wall to calm myself. I knew perfectly well that I would step up to the table and give them my papers, and everything would be in order. I would pass through, and the men with their guns and sunglasses would go on to someone else. Always someone else. Never me.

Quite a few people had clustered around the officers, and at last I gave up and craned my neck over the crowd. I still couldn't see who it was they were surrounding. It might have been anyone. It might have been me. I put my suitcases down and went over to where they stood.

It was a gringa, a young American woman. It's rare for customs officers to bother whites, but I saw at once why they had stopped her. Everything about her was completely out of place. To begin with, tourists do not come here in the middle of November; it's too early in the season. She did not look like the sort of tourist the customs men were used to seeing in any case; her clothes were shabby, her hair was cut short like a boy's and rather dirty, and she was obviously alone. And young women do not come to Santo Domingo alone in any season.

Her shoulder bag had fallen to the floor, and she was on her knees picking up its contents. The customs officers watched, not helping her, waiting for her to stand up. I slipped in among them and spoke to her. When she glanced up, her expression was the most out-of-place thing of all. She wore an abstracted, almost placid look as if she were not fazed by these men in the least, as if she were floating several feet above them in the air.

I was reminded of an apparition, though I have not seen one since I was a child.

I stepped in; I spoke to them, I translated. When they finally let her go, she went off at once without her bags, without a glance backward. After I had carried my own luggage through and found a car, I went back across the plaza for cigarettes and found her sitting on the curb. She didn't appear to be waiting for anything. She looked as if she could sit there all night. I asked her if she wanted a ride into Santo Domingo and hoped she wouldn't be afraid of me. A silly thought: She didn't seem to be afraid of anything. She accepted, and we drove toward the city in the battered car I had managed to rent at half price, off the record. She sat beside me with one foot on the dashboard. "Where are you from?" she asked of course, and of course I dodged the question. I talked as I always do with strangers, on and on with God knows what coming out of my mouth, and as always, as we spoke I felt myself shifting to fill the space between us; I heard my voice change slightly, the pitch grow more like hers. It mattered not at all that she was a stranger. It never matters. A chameleon changes colors even in the dark.

I don't know how it happened: I blathered on as we drove, and everything was as usual until I looked over at her. She was not listening to a word I said. She was looking at me, at *me,* completely ignoring whatever nonsense I was telling her, and it startled me so badly I nearly ran the car off the road. Josephine, Henry, Marika, the hurricane—I had the sensation that she could see my hidden life plastered all over my face. *Of course she can't,* I told myself, but the feeling of being exposed to this young stranger was so strong that all I wanted was to get away from her, to cover myself up again.

I couldn't leave her on the side of the highway; I suggested we stop and get something to eat. She agreed, with the curious detachment that had carried her through the encounter with the customs officials, as if, regardless of what she said or did, the scene carried a predetermined outcome whose terms she would accept with aplomb.

In the restaurant I thought I had pulled myself together. We busied ourselves with the menu, and I chatted with her as if nothing had happened. But when the waiter brought the food there was a lull in the conversation, and that was when it went wrong again: I looked away a moment, watching the waiter retreat—for only a moment was I off-guard—but when I brought my gaze back to the table she grinned at me. She said nothing, but the look on her face told me as clearly as words that she knew I was gay. I had let that slip too: What was the matter with me? She saw the things I had buried, and buried well, I'd thought. Again I felt so exposed that I wanted only to get away from her, but as I was trying to work out how, another part of me began to stir and wake under her gaze. And this part of me wanted to tell her everything, was sick of lying about where I had come from and where I was going and all I had done in between; the urge to speak honestly was so strong I felt almost physically ill.

Still she remained silent. Her grin dissolved, and she kept looking at me. I opened my mouth to invent something, anything to regain control of the situation, but I couldn't think of what to say. She held my gaze across the table in perfect silence, and her silence was a flood. It swallowed everything around us, the village, the sound of the sea, the wind in the trees, and all my words in every tongue I know. I had left silence far behind in boarding school; now, suddenly, I was thrown back hard into its power. If I said anything now it would be the truth. My lies, my stories, had deserted me like rats abandoning a ship. I was sinking.

And now here I am. In a dark hotel room in the middle of the night, in a panic because until the moment Michelle looked at me in the restaurant I have never wanted to tell the truth about my life to anyone. I still don't want to, but there it is, my mouth is swollen with it. Why not just say it, then? Because it is mine; because it is the truth. It wears the shame of truth. And it's been so many years. I'm not sure I know how to voice it anymore. In the absence of truth I've just told stories. Never mentioned Josephine, never mentioned St. Croix, or Henry teaching me to sail, or my father the shipping magnate, boarding school, my mother in the sea. We cover up for our parents long after we need to, long after we should. After the fear of punishment is gone, another fear takes its place. We fear that if we tell, we will implicate ourselves in our parents' crime. We fear that if we tell, their crime will hear us and come running, attach itself to us and play itself out again through us, now that they are no longer around to be its actors.

We hope that if we never breathe a word, their crime will forget our faces and go away.

Then, we think, we'll have escaped.

So we stop breathing. But we can't change the look in our eyes.

The sun is coming up. First the darkness thinned to gray and yielded the shapes of my bags in the corner, the outline of the door, and the bed across from my own where Michelle lies asleep. In the gray early light I watched her sleeping. The whole room was the gray of an old photograph, and in this half-light she looked very pale. She's come from Germany, she's pale with the climate of a weak sun. Or perhaps it's just her coloring; even her hair seems pale, a kind of pale brown, a watercolor rendition of real brown hair. Her eyes are blue, the same color as mine, and I'm glad they are closed now. I don't want her to look at me anymore; I feel too naked. But I no longer feel the urge to get away from her either. The flickers of connection between us— frightening as they were—I am starved for more of them. I am tired, sick of being alone—no, of being unseen, unknown, estranged from myself is what I'm sick of, sick around the heart. On the beach last night she talked to me the way I had wanted to talk to her but couldn't; she told me things she had not meant to say, had never said aloud. Her lover in Berlin had asked her to leave, but she was already gone by then; did I understand? Yes, she could see that I did. She couldn't ever be in one place for very long, she had to keep moving, she even used to walk in her sleep. I could understand that too. She told me she could not remember things. Felt something was wrong with her and didn't know what it was.

Then we both became ill: extremely, violently ill. It lasted for hours. Afterward, driving to this pension, she said something about it. She said she'd never had such a bad case of food poisoning in her life. I did not reply, but she was wrong—it wasn't food poisoning. Any diver can tell you what happens to the body when you come to the surface too quickly after being in the depths too long. The body can't bear it, the drop in pressure is too great.

I've seen men die of it at sea.

We've rented a room. The landlady tried to have us to take a larger one, but Michelle didn't want it. She doesn't seem to have much money; I offered to pay for the room we did take, but she wouldn't let me. Everything was awkward between us. The intimacy of having connected on the beach was still all around us, but our communication itself had ebbed like the last night's tide, leaving us marooned in the superficiality that passes for most of life, trying to make small talk.

While I was unpacking, it rained—a sudden, intense rain that flooded the courtyard and then stopped a quarter of an hour later. Michelle, who has never been in the Caribbean, stood at the window and marveled: Had I ever seen anything like it? It was like somebody dumping buckets out there a minute ago, and now look: It's totally stopping—she talked rapidly, her voice high and bright. It struck me that she might be nervous about sharing a room with me. In the world of small talk we were still strangers; here she was, a skinny white girl in a hotel room in a foreign country with a brown-skinned man her brain knew nothing about. For all that I felt she had perceived intuitively last night, perhaps it was not enough to calm her mind today.

She stayed at the window, hands fiddling with the seam of her dress. I remembered she had no other clothes. Outside it was getting dark.

"Michelle?" I said.

She started, jumped almost. She turned from the window and looked around the room as if she wasn't sure where she was.

"You know I'm gay," I said.

She just looked at me, her eyes vague. I was about to repeat myself when she gave her head a little shake as if to recall herself to her surroundings, and then nodded at me; yes, she knew.

"You saw it last night in the restaurant," I went on, and again she nodded. She was looking at me hard now, and in the sudden focus of her eyes, I shivered and changed tack; I didn't want to talk about last night, I wasn't ready for that tide to come in again. "I just wanted to be sure you didn't think I was going to take advantage of the situation," I said. It was a line straight out of boarding school, out of some old movie on the late show. I was embarrassed, but Michelle didn't get it.

"What situation?" she asked.

"We're sharing a room. I told the woman at the desk we were married. We've just met. I just wanted to be sure you know I'm not going to try to sneak into your bed in the middle of the night."

"Into my bed?" she repeated.

"I mean, I'm not going to try anything." But she wasn't listening now. She was looking at the bed that was going to be hers and frowning. Behind the frown I saw a faint wave of fear cross her face, more like a feeling in the room than anything visual, like a breeze. I had obviously touched a sore spot.

"You've had trouble with this in the past?" I asked.

"What?" She looked back at me, not comprehending. She seemed to have completely lost the thread of the conversation. "Trouble with what?"

"With fending off unwanted advances."

She chewed her lower lip. "No," she said slowly. "No, I'm not afraid of you, if that's what you're asking."

"That's good," I said. She was still looking at the bed. Then she looked up, and I saw that indeed the fear in her face had nothing to do with me; she didn't seem to be seeing me at all. Then her eyes focused again, registered my presence. I felt something like fear in my own body then, and so I did what her eyes were begging me to do: I changed the subject. I talked about the rainstorms in this part of the world, how they begin and end so quickly, and as I talked I watched her sit down on the bed across from me, now cross-legged, now lying on her stomach, smiling, saying, "Yes, isn't it great? "

And I thought, *I'm not the only one who has a secret life inside me*. But Michelle, she doesn't know her secret, doesn't even know she has one. If you asked her, she'd say she's fine. Yes, she'd say, she's happy.

Later when we shut off the lights and went to bed she said, "I feel so happy here. Can you smell the jasmine?" and then she slept. Amnesiacs always sleep soundly; it's memory that keeps you awake. I have lain awake on this lumpy mattress for hours, going over the memories of my life I cannot share.

Now the first wedge of sunlight reaches the room. I watch it ease through the wooden shutters and spread across the floor to the opposite wall until the room is infused with the kind of light you see only in the tropics, a light that gives everything a brightness that possesses a sensory quality of its own. It's as if you could eat it, the light, make it part of your own flesh.

The sunbeam has reached Michelle's bed now. Her head on the still-shadowed pillow with that liquid light gracing the lower half of her body gives her sleeping form the phrasing of a Renaissance painting: *Repose*. Her arm flung across the sheet is less calm. The angle of the wrist says, *Broken*. I combine the two words and think of death.

When the sunlight reaches her closed eyes she stirs. I think she is going to wake up, but no, she is dreaming. Her eyelids flicker. Her head jerks once to the side and then she is still.

Suddenly the room is full of screams. I sit bolt upright, and across the room Michelle flies out of bed like a trained soldier, wide-awake with her feet on the floor in a second. The screaming goes on, the ear-splitting shrieks of a small child. It's coming from somewhere outside the window. I open the shutters all the way and look out. In a corner of the yard is a very little girl, no more than three, standing in the new cistern ditch that was being dug when we arrived yesterday. She's climbed into the hole and now she can't get out, and she's screaming so that everyone from here to La Romana will know it. Her lung capacity is amazing. She is, in fact, enjoying herself.

"Jesus Christ," says Michelle. She turns from the window and sits on the bed. Her face is dead white.

A slim woman appears on the patio of the Sonnenbergs' house and hurries down into the yard crying, "¿Greta Maria, qué van a pensar Opa Felix y Abuelita, eh? ¡No grites como si te murieras!" She scoops up the screaming child and plunks her down on the grass. The little girl's skin is dark, dark, much darker than mine, the color of water-soaked earth—but above this black cherubic face her curly hair is shockingly blond.

"What an incredible-looking child," says Michelle grudgingly. She's annoyed at how much the scream frightened her. She's still frightened. She flops down on her side and pulls the sheet up over her head, but then she sits up again at once. She can't be in bed anymore, the sheets are stained with panic. She stands in the middle of the room in the T-shirt I loaned her last night and looks at the bed, at the screen door, at the window, out the window at the little girl. She bites her lip. She is badly shaken and doesn't know why, doesn't know what to do. I have to do something. Speak. "Do you know what she is?" I say, nodding in the direction of the child.

"A little girl," says Michelle.

"Do you know why she looks like that?"

Michelle looks at me and smiles palely. "Go ahead," she says. "Tell me the story."

"What story?" I ask.

"The story you want to tell me."

"How do you know I want to tell you a story?" I say. The color is coming back to her face.

She gives me a look: She knows, she just does. She sits on my bed and looks at me. This is the story.

By the time Hitler came to power, the Jews had been in Europe long enough that you couldn't always tell by looking who was Jewish and who was not. Some of them had blue or green eyes, some had light hair, whereas some of the Aryans were as dark-haired as Hitler himself. In these years, the middle thirties, the Dominican Republic was under the dictatorship of Trujillo, who was famous for perpetrating election fraud, massacring Haitians, palling around with U.S. heads of state, and confusing himself with God. Trujillo didn't like that so many of the Dominicans he ruled over had such dark skin: More than four hundred years ago, the Spanish had brought thousands of African slaves to the island to work in place of the Tainos who by then were all dead. When Trujillo looked out over the island he commanded, he saw Africa in the faces of his Dominicans. It did not please him. He wanted to be dictator of a whiter race.

Trujillo was used to getting what he wanted. He took note of Europe, where certain Caucasians were abandoning their homelands as fast as they could. The gas chambers weren't in place yet, the Nazis were still smashing more storefront windows than skulls; it was still possible to leave if you were lucky. To some of the lucky ones Trujillo extended an invitation: Emigrate to the Dominican Republic.

Not because of what would happen to them if they stayed in Europe. Because they had pale skin and that was what he wanted.

The Jews accepted his invitation. They didn't dwell on its irony. They were running for their lives.

So more than fifty years later, here is Greta Maria de Santos y Sonnenberg, a third-generation Dominican Jew. The result of Trujillo's attempts at the genetic import business is from tip to toe as black as the gods of the old world except for her hair, which flies bright gold above her like a flag marking the site of a battle far back in history. She is too young to know it. When she stands in a ditch and screams as if she were dying, it is not to remember her ancestors, the Africans, the Tainos, the Spanish, the Jews. She screams only because she is delighted with the sound of her own lungs.

Still dressed in my underwear and banging the screen door behind her, Michelle goes barefoot out onto the patio and across the courtyard, over to the side of the ditch where Greta Maria has jumped back in. Her mother is hoisting her out again, still scolding.

"*Buenos días. ¿Como está?*" I hear Michelle say. Her voice is still crackly with sleep and fear.

"*Mira, Greta,*" says the mother in her fluid Dominican, "you have disturbed this lady's rest."

"Oh, no," says Michelle, clearing her throat and kicking into her eager, semicorrect Spanish. "*Tenía tan hambre, tenía que despertar.*" I was so hungry I had to get up, is what she means.

"Oh!" says the mother. "On Saturday you must go eat in the dining room. Señora Isabela makes a breakfast for the guests on the weekends. Señora Isabela is my mother."

"Your mother," repeats Michelle, missing the point the woman is trying to make.

"Yes," says Greta Maria's mother pointedly. "She's a very good cook. Much better than anything you'll find in a restaurant."

"Ah," says Michelle, getting it now. "*Claro. Sí.*" And she tells the woman we will come eat breakfast in her mother's dining room.

The woman smiles. Greta Maria looks up at Michelle and smiles too, then takes in her man's undershirt and short hair and says suddenly, "Are you a boy or a girl?"

Her mother glares at her. If her daughter has offended the American lady, then she and her husband won't come eat in the dining room; they'll go to some restaurant in town. She gives Greta Maria a little "go and play" shove and looks at Michelle, hoping she hasn't understood Greta Maria's question.

"Um," says Michelle, suppressing a laugh and trying to recall, no doubt, the Spanish word for "guess," which fortunately eludes her. Greta Maria's mother, interpreting Michelle's amusement as the smile people get on their faces when they don't understand what has been said to them, looks relieved.

"I promise to come for breakfast," Michelle assures her.

"And your husband?" She means me.

"And my husband," agrees Michelle.

The woman goes up the steps to the main house, and Michelle trots back across the courtyard and comes into the room grinning. The color has come back to her cheeks. Her fear is gone.

"Are you all right now?" I ask.

She gives me a puzzled look. "I'm fine," she says. "What do you mean?

I look at her hard. She seems genuinely confused. "Nothing," I say. "Forget it." But she already has.

The Sonnenbergs' pension is one of many that have sprung up outside the old quarter of the city to accommodate spreading tourism. Soon the winter season will start, and the pensions will be packed full with Americans and Canadians and Europeans. I remember how it happened on St. Croix: Christmas Day and the flesh on the beaches as white as the sand. But it's still autumn; the pensions are empty and the gringos few. When I walk through the streets with Michelle, people turn their heads and stare at us because of her. When I go walking alone, I blend in with the crowd.

Our pension lies on the outskirts of the city center, almost but not quite in Gazcue. In our first days here we fall into a routine. In the mornings I walk down to the *malecón* and buy rolls and too-sweet corn-bread and the Dominican version of *churros* from the vendor who stands with his cart and umbrella outside the big hotels. I take the pastries to our room to eat. Michelle sits on her bed and teases me about the *churros*: long, heavy, sausage-shaped doughnuts covered in crystallized sugar. She thinks they taste awful. "You only buy them for the shape," she says. I slide one in and out of my mouth and wiggle my eyebrows, and she laughs and goes up to the Sonnenbergs for coffee, which she brings back in a dented tin pitcher.

After breakfast we separate. I go off looking for Lupe Vásquez, and Michelle, who seems disinclined to search for the house she says she has come all this way to find, simply wanders around Santo Domingo. Sometimes we walk together as far as the Zona Colonial before parting, and then I stand and watch her cross the plaza, floating along in that way she has, as if she has no bones, as if there's air inside her body instead of blood, as if she could rise like a balloon.

People stare at her. I watch Dominicans turn around to look at what just went past, this tall skinny white girl with boy-short hair and a *campesina* dress, a dress a few steps away from being rags. People actually nudge together sometimes—*¡Fíjate, caballero, esa muchacha!*—but Michelle doesn't notice. If someone catches her eye, she just grins at them, says *buenos días,* and floats on, perfectly at ease. As long as she's moving she's happy; she has no map or plan, she just wanders around and sees what unfolds.

I go off every morning with a careful agenda. *University: library, anthropology department.* Or, *CODETEL: get Lupe Vásquez's phone number.* Or, *cafés: talk to students.* But as it turns out, my own days become as haphazard as Michelle's. Lupe Vásquez is not listed in the phone directory and is no longer teaching at the university. I manage to coax one of the department secretaries into giving me the address of the Vásquez home, then spend half a day trying to locate it. When I finally find the house, the man who answers the door says he's never heard of any Vásquez; yes, he's the owner, and no, he doesn't know who the previous owners were. The next day I go back to the university and badger the secretaries some more until they tell me that Lupe Vásquez left the city right after her husband's murder. "She's gone back to the village she came from," the secretary says.

"And where is that?"

North, she thinks. A safe answer, since we're on the south coast. They won't tell me anything more.

I go into cafés around the university, the cheap ones where students hang out. I spend a lot of time sitting there with the students, talking about whatever they want to talk about, patiently steering the conversation to a point at which I can let fly the names: Jorge Vásquez, Lupe Vásquez. The language, Quisqueya. "Who were Vásquez's students," I ask, "and where are they now?"

My questions all fall like badly shot arrows. No one will admit to knowing anything about them, try as I might to convince them I'm not a government spy. I find other students in other cafés and begin all over again, taking a different approach. I'm a grant writer; I say I want to volunteer my services to help raise funds for a project I've heard about, the museum Lupe Vásquez wants to open to chronicle the European invasion. It's supposed to open in time for the quincentennial—have they heard of this?

This fares a little better. "Oh, the museum," they say. They've heard of it. They say they thought the project was defunct. "Lupe Vásquez isn't still around, is she?"

"I don't know," I say patiently. "I'm trying to find out."

"She went north, didn't she? To Puerto Plata, was it?"

"No, *caballero*, it was Santiago. Have another beer?"

"She went away after they shot her husband."

"*Ay, cabrón.* Who could blame her?"

This is all they will tell me. I look at them as we sit over our beers or coffees, at their young faces, intelligent eyes. They don't know me; I'm a stranger. If they do have more information, they aren't telling.

I go to libraries and hunt for books by Jorge Vásquez. I go to museums and look at the Mercedes that Trujillo was riding in when he was assassinated, at Diego Columbus's house full of European tapestry, at the deserted Plaza de la Cultura with its cases filled with shards of pottery made by Taino hands. But I'm getting nowhere, and as the days pass I give up on these fruitless excursions earlier and earlier in the day and go back to the pension to meet Michelle.

By unspoken agreement our appointed time is late afternoon, the end of the afternoon just when the light begins to change. If I get there first I lie on the bed and smoke with the windows open, feeling the heat of the day start to subside and listening to the sounds from the court-yard: the generator, the Sonnenbergs yelling to each other, the sudden rushes of rain falling on the roof, on the street, on the trees. Then Michelle comes in, her face glowing but not from the sun; if it's been raining she comes in glowing and drenched in rain, she stands just inside the doorway shaking water out of her short hair like a wet dog, water streaming off her legs into puddles on the cement floor. Neither of us owns an umbrella.

I'll ask her what she's been doing all day.

"I went diving for oysters with some boys I met on the beach," she'll say. Or: "Isabela Sonnenberg spent the afternoon telling me everything a newly married girl should know, and according to her I need to make my husband buy me some new dresses."

We both laugh. Michelle still hasn't got her luggage back. She's been down to the airport several times, and the customs officials tell her she's come at the wrong hour, that the man she should talk to isn't there, or that she needs to fill out a form but the forms are locked up and the key is in the pocket of an employee who's on vacation. In the meantime, Michelle wears her old green dress day after day, or occasionally something she borrows from me. She's bought a few pieces of clothing in town, shirts and a pair of shorts, but she doesn't like them. "The colors are too bright," she says. "They make me look like a tourist."

"You are a tourist," I tell her.

She sticks her tongue out at me. I cross my eyes; she laughs. We are careful to be cheerful, careful not to probe too deeply into each other's smile lest the smile deflate and reveal that awkward and dangerous nakedness of an intimacy neither of us seems able to embrace. We were on the verge of it that night on the beach, when I wanted so badly to tell her about Josephine, about St. Croix, when Michelle told me all about her life, not meaning to. Whatever passed between us was too much, it made us ill, and now neither of us seems able to speak about anything really personal. Silence, too, feels dangerous. It was the intensity of her silence that night that brought me so close to telling her everything. So now I'm careful; I don't let the pauses in our conversations go on too long.

But sometimes when I get back to the pension in the afternoon, Michelle is sitting on the stone wall in the front yard, her chin on her knees. She sits with a peculiar stillness, looking not at the street, not at the sky. She looks at nothing. It's as if she's stopped breathing. Of course she hasn't, but that's how it worries me. "Michelle?" I say after too much time has passed. "Michelle?"

She starts up, shakes her head, turns toward me with unseeing eyes. Then she sees me. She smiles and says whatever comes into her head, but her voice is tired, as if she's been running for a long time.

"Michelle," I say, "what is it?" I ask her in English, I ask her in Spanish. In spite of the emotional risk, I ask her with my eyes.

"Nothing," she says. "*Nada*," she says. She looks away.

"Michelle, My Shell," I say, "Miss Hell, *¿qué pasa, chicasa?*" I turn it into a joke—then it's easier for her; it means I don't expect an answer. It means I understand she hasn't one.

Suddenly she jumps off the wall and makes an absurd little bow. "Hi," she says, and then: "HowareyouIamfineitisverynicetomeetyou." She laughs, and I laugh too, relieved, and then she says, "Let's do something, Tollomi. Let's go out."

She's back now, from wherever she was. And now that she's back, she's ready to get going. "Let's go out, let's go out"—she never tires of moving. Unlike me, who simply continues to move.

"Let's go out," says Michelle, and so we go, wandering through unfamiliar parts of the city with the practiced ease of experienced travelers. Or rather, for me it is practiced. Michelle really is at ease in the Santo Domingo streets, she who has never been in this part of the world in her life. She stops and talks to everyone: the woman selling pottery on the corner, the vendors with their carts full of lottery tickets and packets of cigarettes. She talks to them in her comical Spanish, making fun of herself, and the Dominicans think it's great that she can speak their language at all. They invite her to visit their homes, and she goes, just like that. She wants to go everywhere, even to the parts of old Santo Domingo where the streets become mazes and the white people get lost, but not Michelle; she finds the address, or she finds another one; she meets the grandmothers and the babies and eats with them; she sits on the street with the little girls and watches while they braid one another's hair.

She doesn't see the militia on every corner. Not the bored teenagers dressed in army fatigues; nor the older men, heavy, sanguine; the military police, with their badges, their sunglasses, their boots. She doesn't see the guns in the holsters, the rifles slung over their arms, the rounds of ammunition draped across their chests.

"Aren't you afraid of them?" I ask her once after we've walked past a group of soldiers. Always, always, when I pass them I flinch.

She replies, "They're just men."

"Michelle, they're dangerous."

"What makes them dangerous?" she asks "Their guns? Their badges? Their minds? Any man could be them"—she pauses—"even you."

"No, I couldn't."

She raises her eyebrows. "You," she says, "could be anybody."

I didn't know what to say to that. So I raise my head and let her look in my eyes, which she does for a long time without flinching. I don't breathe, waiting to see what will happen.

"Let's go out," she says at last, and looks away from me.

Let's go out. She always says that.

There's a body on the floor.

It's propped up against the wall like a rag doll or a sleeping child but it's not a child's body. It's mine.

Then I'm back in the body, and I can no longer see it from the outside. I just see, through my own eyes now, my lap and my legs and my hands on the floor beside me. The floor is cool, and one of my feet is asleep. Time has passed. I wiggle my toes, I raise my head and look around.

The room is small. Four whitewashed walls and a door, one window fitted with wooden louvered shutters. Two single beds, a little desk between the beds, a chair. At the foot of one of the beds, a dresser. That's all. At night the bedsprings creak when you roll over. The shutters can be turned flat to keep out the light, but we leave them open. At night when there is no light there's the far sound of the sea.

Tollomi sits at the little desk with his back to me, bent over a pile of books.

I say his name and he looks up and sees me. "Michelle," he says, "you're back."

"My back is fine," I say. "How's yours?"

He smiles. I smile. We both look away.

Tollomi, Tollomi. I watch him, he watches me. Every day we go off separately, he to look for a woman who may not even be alive anymore, and me to avoid looking for the house I have come around the world to find. In the mornings, when we part at the corner of Avenue Independencia, I look at him for a moment in the way I would look at someone I might never see again. He could leave at any moment, and I wouldn't be surprised. When I come back at the end of the day and find him here, I know it doesn't mean he'll still be here tomorrow. Or if he is here tomorrow, it doesn't mean he'll be the same person he is today.

I know nothing about him. His personality is like his clothing: Just because I never see him without it doesn't mean it's a part of him. I still don't know where he's from. He looks Dominican, but if I saw him somewhere else—Morocco, Portugal, the U.S.—he would fit in just as well. His eyes are blue, a startling blue, a blue that makes you look twice to be sure you have in fact seen it, because the color of his skin and the kink of his hair and the bones in his face are not a white man's. "Where are you from?" I ask, and he makes some sort of nonanswer. Or he answers, not laughing, that he was born at sea. I ask him where his parents are from, and he says he doesn't have parents. I ask if he ever had any, and he says, no, he dropped down from the sky. And then I don't ask anything else.

When he asks me the same questions, I answer him straight out. But it's much easier for me to tell the truth about my life. There's not as much to tell, after all.

I can tell it in three words: I don't remember.

I come back to the pension and he's there already, lying across my bed with his feet on the floor in a metal tub of water. The tub is from Isabela Sonnenberg, and the water is from last night's rain. He soaks his feet almost every day. When I ask him if they hurt, he says only when he wears shoes. He hates wearing shoes—he's always taking them off, even in the street. Several times I've come into the room at the end of the day to find him bent over his foot with a burned needle, extracting from his heel a splinter or a sliver of glass. "What did you do this morning?" he asks. I tell him I've been down at the piers on the other side of the city. "Out carousing with the sailors again?"

I say I like to watch the ships. Then he asks me about the house, if I've found out anything about it—where it is, for starters, and when I'm going to go find it; we've been here for almost three weeks, after all.

"No, we haven't," I say. "It hasn't been that long." But as I say it I realize I have no idea how long it's been. Then I just say I haven't found anything out about the house yet, and Tollomi offers to go to the airport with me again to try and get my luggage back. In my knapsack there's a copy of the papers about the house, and in his mind the two are connected. But it's not because I don't have the papers that I haven't gone to look for the house. It's because I'm afraid. I'm afraid it isn't safe, but not in the way my grandmother meant.

"Let's go out later," I say.

"All right." He means, *All right, let's go out* and also *All right, I know you're changing the subject. All right, I won't keep asking you about the house* is what he means. "You pick where," I say. Meaning, *Thank you.*

"You're welcome," he says.

Our communication feels too large for the small time we've known each other. It's made us friends, but it's stronger than our friendship and that makes us awkward. It's not the awkwardness of strangers. It's more like what you'd find between people who were very close once but not anymore or people who have been through some terrible experience together and afterward agree never to mention it.

One morning we are sitting on the Sonnenbergs' patio having break-fast. On the weekends, Isabela Sonnenberg makes breakfast for the guests. It's always the same: greasy fried eggs, white toast, bacon, and the best coffee I've ever had. It's very strong, served with boiled milk as thick as cream. This morning the other guests have already eaten and gone. Isabela comes out of the kitchen and hovers beside our table. Tollomi pulls out a chair and invites her to sit. She declines, he insists, and of course she ends up sitting. She finds him peculiar and full of charm.

She asks if we've been to the zoo yet. She told us last week that we must go—it's so beautiful, the animals. But we never went. "Not yet," I say before Tollomi can lie about it. I can tell by his face he was going to say we had. He wants to make her happy. Isabela shakes her head at us and clicks her tongue. As tourists we are a terrible disappointment.

"You must go," she says sorrowfully, but we are spared from having to reply: Isabela's husband Felix comes out of the guest building. Felix escaped from Nazi-occupied Austria when he was in his teens, and now he is an old man. When I first met him I tried to speak German with him, but he didn't want to. Nevertheless, his Spanish is still weighted down with the sound of it, a Germanness that will not go away and makes his accent throaty and full of stops. He comes stiffly across the courtyard, extends his enormous hand to me and then to Tollomi. To his wife he says in his cobblestone Spanish, "Bea is here. I thought these two could ask her about their missing luggage."

Before Isabela can answer, the screen door of the guest building bangs open. A stout white-haired woman in a shapeless dress adorned with hot-pink flowers barrels across the yard. She addresses them in, of all things, a Brooklyn accent: "Isabela, honey, how are ya? *Como estás, como estás.* So Felix, what is this? You leave me standin' there in the hallway like I wanna rent a room."

She's at least a foot shorter than he is. Her lipstick is the same violent pink as her dress. I feel Tollomi's eyes on me, willing me to look at him, but if our eyes meet I'll laugh.

Felix squints down sheepishly at the woman. "*Quiero que conozcas a la pareja aquí—*" he begins, indicating me and Tollomi with a vague, clumsy formality, "*Que han perdido—*"

The woman cuts him off. "Spanish you're speakin' with me, Felix? Who are you tryin' to impress? Speak English: I'm going back to New York next month, I gotta keep in practice." She turns to us. "Nice to meet you, kids. I'm Bea Castillo, Felix's sister. First trip here? You're gonna love it." She plunks herself down in a chair and looks more closely at Tollomi. "Oh," she says, "*¿Dominicano?*" Tollomi shakes her hand in lieu of answering. "*¿Inglés?*" asks Bea.

"I speak both," says Tollomi in English. "It's very nice to meet you."

"A pleasure. Like I said, you're gonna love it here. Fifty years I'm here, I still love it. Whenever I go back to Brooklyn I think what a fool I am—I oughta be here. And what's your name, honey?"

"Michelle," I say.

"Very nice to meet you, Michelle. My brother takin' good care of you? Of course not. It's Isabela who does everything. Right, Isabela? *Todo el trabajo tú haces sola.*"

"*Exactamente,*" says Isabela wryly. Giving Felix a look, she rises to her feet and scoops up the breakfast dishes. "*¿Quieres café?*" she says to Bea.

"No, honey, if I drink any more *café,* I'll have a coronary. *Siéntate, siéntate.*"

Isabela ignores Bea's command to sit. She starts across the patio with her arms full of dishes. Halfway to the house she stops and calls over her shoulder, "*¡Felix, ven!*" Felix turns in his chair and looks at her. "*¡Ven, Felix!*" she repeats.

Bea looks disdainfully at her brother. "Whatsamatter, Felix, you goin' deaf in your old age? *Ven,* your wife says, and you sit there like a bump on a log. Go on, whaddaya waitin' for, a drumroll? *Vete, vete.*"

Felix lumbers to his feet and follows Isabela into the house. I steal a glance at Tollomi, who's grinning madly. He's overjoyed that this woman with fluorescent lipstick on her teeth and a Brooklyn accent you couldn't cut with a chain saw has materialized before him and created this little scene.

"So what's your name again, honey?" Bea says to Tollomi. "I didn't catch it."

Tollomi shoots me a look before answering. *Watch this,* the look says. *This is going to be good.* He smiles at her. "My name is Tollomi," he says.

"Ptolemy? So what the hell are you, an Egyptian? A Spanish-speakin' Egyptian—now I seen everything. But hey, it takes all kinds, right? Am I right or am I right? I'm right. Okay, Egypt, I work in the airport up at Puerto Plata. What's this about lost bags?"

"Oh, the *air*port. Oh, *really?*" Tollomi drawls. I know what's coming. He's not ready to discuss anything so boring as confiscated luggage. He wants to be entertained. He leans forward a little. "So, Mrs. Castillo…" He pauses.

"Bea, honey. Bea."

"Bea. So you're Felix's sister—younger sister, I take it? You were born in Austria too?"

"Born in Austria, raised in Sosúa—that's on the north coast—and in Brooklyn. Back and forth, back and forth. Not like Felix here. He sets foot on the island when he's twelve years old and never leaves it. Just like my husband, may he rest in peace, you couldn't get him off the island with a barge pole. Frederico Castillo. He was full Dominican, like Isabela. Anyway, now you got your *Dominicanos* all heading up to New York like it was going out of style, and you got your New Yorkers all coming down here for a tan. Crazy world—everybody wants to be somewheres else."

"My grandparents came down here from New York," I say. "In the forties. They bought a house here."

Bea looks at me. "In the forties your people got a place here? You Jewish?"

"No," I say. "I'm not anything."

"That's all right, honey. My husband wasn't a Jew either. He was *católico. Catho-loco,* I used to call it. But Sundays I'd go to church with him, then Saturdays I made him go to synagogue with me. We got along all right. In Europe, Jews gotta marry Jews, Catholics gotta marry Catholics. Here in Santo Domingo it's whatever floats your boat. Right, Egypt? Nobody gets upset. It's too hot to get upset here—you start to sweat, you get uncomfortable." So saying, she produces a wrinkled pink handkerchief from the front of her dress and dabs at her upper lip. She stuffs the hanky back in her bra and turns to me.

"So, honey. How come you're staying at Felix's if your people got a place here? My brother's is nice, but it ain't that nice."

I open my mouth, close it again. How can I explain this? I look at Tollomi, and Tollomi turns to Bea and without missing a beat begins telling her about my grandfather, how he bought what he thought was oceanfront property, how he came down here expecting a beach house and instead found land way up in the mountains and the house falling apart and no road access, so he went back to America and never came down here again.

"No kidding," says Bea. She turns to me. "And where is this place? You seen it yet?"

"I haven't seen it," I say. "My mother never saw it either. Nobody's seen it in over forty years. I...I came down here to look for it."

"So where is it?"

"I don't know."

"What, you can't pronounce the name? Hey, Egypt—*¿en cuál provincia?*"

Tollomi laughs. "No," he says, "we really don't know where it is. Michelle had a copy of the deed in her luggage—"

"Deed!" Bea interrupts. She yells over her shoulder at the house: "Hey, Felix, you hear that? 'Deed,' she says." She turns back to us and drops her voice. "Listen kids, let me explain something. You are not in the United States here. You are not in Europe. You are in La-La Land, okay? This is the Napoleonic code! If you are standin' on your property you own it, but if someone else is standin' on your property, then they own it— especially if they've been standin' on it for the last fifty years. That deed you might as well use for toilet paper, because that's what it's worth. Ha!"

Tollomi, delighted, kicks me under the table.

"We don't have the deed anyway," I say. "It was in my luggage, but my luggage is all gone."

"Not stolen from here, I hope? My brother lets thieves on his property, I'll crack him over the head."

"It was confiscated at the airport," says Tollomi. "We haven't been able to get it back."

"Confiscated? So somebody needed some extra dough. You gotta wave a little money under their noses maybe. Don't be such tightwads."

"We tried that," I say. "It didn't work."

Bea snorts. "Whadja do, drop the money on the floor? You gotta know how to do it right."

"They confiscated it for security reasons," says Tollomi happily. "They decided she was a potential terrorist."

"And what were you, Egypt, the terrorist's husband? I never heard of such a thing. Tell you what, kids. I work at the airport up in Puerto Plata, did I tell you that? Puerto Plata is the gringo airport, so they got what's called 'Hospitality,' which means I got a little badge on my dress says HOSPITALITY, and I walk around and straighten things like this out. Sometimes I come down here to Santo Domingo, do a little work in this airport, which of course is a mess. I can't today, I have to be back in Sosúa by tonight if you can believe it, but I'll be back in a couple of weeks. I'll stop by the airport then and see if I can get your stuff back. Aright? They know me, thirty years I'm workin' there. So leave it to me. I don't want you goin' without on your honeymoon."

"How did you know it's our honeymoon?" says Tollomi coyly, delighted at this new opportunity for fabrication.

"I can tell these things, Egypt. I wasn't born yesterday. Ha!" She gives Tollomi a wink.

"What can you tell?" I ask.

"I can tell, honey, the way you look at each other—it's all over your faces—you can't fool old Bea. You're in love, you got your own secret language. So was it a nice wedding?"

"It was lovely," Tollomi says. "You should have seen the cake. We wanted something simple, but—Michelle, ow!"

"Good, good," says Bea, oblivious to my kicking Tollomi's ankle, "that's what I like to hear. Now don't worry about your luggage. Leave everything to me. No, don't thank me, I take care of my own. But now I gotta run. Here I am gabbin' away when I gotta be over at Leopoldo Navarro by one o'clock. I gotta go to the dentist, my teeth are fallin' outta my head. Well, it was very nice to meet you two. Felix! Isabela!" She yells at the house. "*¡Me voy!*" Without waiting for an answer, she addresses us again: "All right, kids, *hasta la vista,* and trust me when I tell you: Don't worry about your bags."

We thank her and follow her around the side of the house to the road to see her off. Her car is a very old Volkswagen Beetle caked with dust and dried mud. After a few false starts she gets it going and revs the engine. A cloud of diesel thick enough for a genie to step out of rises around her, then she shifts into gear and chugs away.

"Wasn't she spectacular?" Tollomi says.

His eyes are shining: This is what he loves, talking to people like Bea. He can go on and on with them and never stop. If I hadn't stopped him, he would have created a four-tiered wedding cake with figurines on top and told her every song the band played and what my dress was like.

I just say, "Yeah, she was great," and then I go back across the yard into our room and flop down on my bed.

You two are on your honeymoon, said Bea. *You're in love, I can tell.*

She can see it then, the space between us slightly electrified, like a love affair, like sexual tension. But it's not love, it's not sex, it's something else. It's the sense that he can see me when I can't see myself, the feeling that if we could just hold still for a moment and look at each other unblinking, I would see where I go when I go, see what I can't see alone by myself, and see him too, perhaps; see what he won't show me or anyone.

I don't know if he feels the same way about this or if it's all on my side only.

You have your own language, said Bea.

But we can't talk about it.

One night something wakes me. I open my eyes, groggy; I've been asleep a good while. On the other side of the room I can just make out Michelle, a dark shadow standing by the bathroom door with her hand on the knob. I roll over to fall back to sleep, but suddenly she says, "My clothes are gone."

I sit up in bed. "Michelle?"

She turns partway toward me, her hand still closed around the door-knob. "My clothes are gone," she says again.

"We can go back to the airport in the morning and get your luggage," I say, forgetting we've already tried this without success. I'm not quite awake.

"No," she says, irritated now. "Not the airport. My *clothes* are gone."

"What clothes?" I ask.

"My pajamas. Where did they go?"

I get out of bed. She's wearing the things she sleeps in, an undershirt of mine and her underwear. What is she talking about? Some pajamas in her luggage? "Where did they go?" she says again, and it dawns on me that she is sleepwalking. I don't know what to do, save take her arm and guide her back to her bed. "We'll get your pajamas back in the morning," I say. "Now go to sleep."

"All right," she says obediently, and lies down again and closes her eyes. A moment later her breathing is deep and regular. I tuck the sheet in around her and stand there a little longer looking down through the darkness at her sleeping face, feeling disturbed.

In the morning I say, "You were sleepwalking last night."

She stops yawning and frowns. "I don't sleepwalk anymore."

"You were out of bed, standing by the bathroom, and you kept saying your pajamas were gone."

"That's ridiculous," she says scornfully. "I haven't worn pajamas since I was a little kid." But I see that faint breeze of fear traverse her face, worrying the placid surface of her forehead with lines like ripples on water. She bites her lip, and I can't help it, I hear myself add: "Or maybe I was dreaming."

And since she doesn't know I don't dream anymore, and since she wants to believe me, she believes me. "Yeah," she says, "maybe you were," and then her fear is gone and her mouth relaxes into a smile.

If I mention this conversation later, she won't remember it.

Now she hops off her bed and goes into the bathroom, turns on the shower. I hear her singing, an old Elvis Presley song. She's an American; America is the land of amnesia, there's no memory of history, everyone smiles. There's nothing I can say to the face of amnesia; even if Michelle wanted to talk about it, what, really, could I say to her? What do I know myself? Only that sometimes the impression of fear, of damage, floats around her like a perfume, suggested by chance words now and again, words she never remembers later on. It wouldn't help to tell her this; it would only make her unhappy. So I call through the bathroom door that I'm going out, does she want to come along?

"You go ahead," she yells over the rush of the shower. So I go, but halfway into town I wish I had taken her with me. It makes her happy to walk through the city with me, any kind of movement makes her happy, and the feeling radiates from her into my own body so that walking beside her I feel younger, less jaded to the sights around me. I even feel happy myself, as if I'm the one with amnesia, as if I can't remember what I truly know. When I'm with Michelle, Santo Domingo is simply the city of brunch on the Sonnenbergs' patio, of meeting people like Bea Castillo, of wandering through the market on Avenida Mella, buying nuts and fruit and wedges of cheese. It's the city of sitting on broken chairs in cafés, of walking along the old wall by the river Ozama, eating greasy banana chips. When I'm out with Michelle it's her city I'm out in, the city of being caught in the rain and not bothering to duck into a doorway, the city of going dancing and getting drunk on rum and *merengue*, of walking back to the pension late at night and all the streetlights going out at once, of stumbling along through the blackout laughing and exhausted. This is the Santo Domingo I see with Michelle. It's when I'm alone that the other city appears to me.

I leave her singing in the shower and walk out alone, and the other city swallows me up. I cannot avoid seeing certain things; I cannot cross the street or look away. I see the prostitute sitting half-naked on the sidewalk beside a pile of rotting garbage, her legs open, her cunt exposed while she ties pieces of colored wire around her feet in a delusion of shoes. I see the child pissing in the street, clutching his penis and sucking on an orange rind streaked with grime. I stand at the old city walls and look out across the muddy river to the specter of the newly built Faro a Colón, the Columbus Lighthouse, looming against the horizon like the stone of an enormous tomb. Its gray slabs are stark against the debris of color that rings it; it is being erected in the midst of the city's worst slums. Hundreds of shacks have been bulldozed to make room for it, the tin and cardboard and tarpaulins that are people's homes simply swept away. When the lighthouse is finished, its beam will project on the horizon a crucifix of white light so powerful that, according to the government, people will see it as far away as Puerto Rico. This, while in the surrounding slums the blackouts last all night.

Sometimes it's too much to take in. I turn away and walk for an hour in the opposite direction and arrive in the quiet neighborhood of the embassies. I cloister myself in the national library and take down the books I have come to read, and in a straight-backed chair in the artificial indoor light I sit reading and see the same thing I have come to get away from: death. On every page I'm reading the history of death. The Spanish, the United States, the CIA, the oil companies, the sugar companies, the dictators, the presidents, the foreign investors pouring in bullets and rhetoric, all signing their claim to this chunk of rock in an ink made out of blood.

The page blurs. I close the book and walk outside, trying to imagine this dirty city as it used to be, covered in forest and walked upon so lightly by bare feet. There are no white men here, no ships with enormous sails. The sea is an endless blue. The notion that the world was a flat thing you could fall off of belonged only to the Europeans. It never occurred to the Tainos. I walk toward the sea.

The Europeans don't fall off the side of the world; they arrive on these shores and the forest becomes a battlefield. They tear up the earth, searching for gold. They cut off the hands of those who cannot bring it to them. They set fire to all the palm thatch houses. They cut down trees they later use to burn men alive. The trees don't burn well—they're too green—but the Europeans use them anyway; all the dead wood and the things made out of wood—houses and canoes and so forth—have long since become ashes.

The Tainos do not burn so easily either. The Europeans do not seem to care. They tie them to stakes and ask them if they want to be Christians. Then they set them on fire.

The Tainos who are still alive watch all this and understand that the Europeans have come into their world to burn it down. Nothing is off limits. When everything on land has been turned to ash, what will the Europeans burn then? The Tainos turn their eyes to the sea and consider its staying power.

Then there are no more Tainos left. Not one. But there is cane to be cut, gold to be discovered. What to do? The sea is still there. The Europeans set out across it and come back with their holds full of Africans packed in like corpses. I stand on what used to be beach, on the *malecón* near the old city, and I can see where the boats came ashore. Riding low in the water. The Africans who are still alive after the journey are dragged—sick, starving, half-dead—into Santo Domingo, the largest slave market in the West Indies. Some of them end up in St. Croix. From the shores of Santo Domingo, all the most coveted goods are traded and shipped. Gold. Humans. And of course sugar.

I feel dizzy. I get off the *malecón* and walk, somewhere, I don't know where I'm walking, and in a strange part of town I go into a café and sit down, order a beer, and try to get hold of myself.

All of a sudden there's a lot of noise on the street; something's happening, people are turning their heads. An army truck with slatted wooden sides above the flatbed drives into the plaza's dusty center and comes to a halt. Four soldiers jump off the back of the truck. My hand tightens around the beer bottle. A megaphone on the roof of the cab blares, static, no words yet, and I think, *This is it,* and I slide my chair back so I can get under the table if they start shooting.

A gray-haired man walking by outside stops walking. He holds a battered briefcase in one hand and, as I watch, he sets it down carefully in the gutter, straightens up, and with his shoe gives it a little shove that sends it behind the tire of a parked car. Then he turns and walks very deliberately toward the café. I glance behind me, yes, there is a back door in this place. The man is in his late fifties perhaps, and his face is set in the frozen nonexpression of someone who's had to learn that it's either the frozen face or the other one, the one you see on people who haven't made it, who've been broken so badly they can't be fixed. In the few seconds I have to notice this about him, the loud speaker on top of the truck begins working, screaming the name of a man: *Balaguer*. It screams that he must be elected.

At the sound of the word "elect," the gray-haired man stops. He's reached the café, and there he stops and holds onto the door frame and turns to look. The soldiers are pulling something down from the back of the truck—mattresses. Now there are dozens of people, fifty or eighty people crowding around the truck, teaming up to carry away the free beds while through the loudspeaker the name of the president is screeched out over and over, the syllables rising together in an ear-splitting crackle as the noise goes on and on.

The man walks back to the edge of the pavement, stoops with some difficulty, and retrieves his briefcase. Then he comes all the way into the café and sits where he can see the street, at the table beside mine. He glances around. His face betrays nothing, not even relief. He leans over and asks me for a cigarette.

I give him the packet and start to light a match, then pass him the matches. He looks at me curiously.

"Your hands are steadier than mine," I say. I nod slightly at the square outside.

He acknowledges the understanding with a flick of his chin. He smokes. "The election," he says on the exhale. "It's only the goddamn election."

"I know," I say. "I thought they were going to start shooting."

He nods.

Outside, one of the mattresses is being carried off by six small children who have hoisted it onto their skinny shoulders like pallbearers taking a coffin. As we watch, one of the soldiers gets in front of them and says something to the boys. When they try to walk around him, the soldier leans over and simply lifts the mattress off their shoulders and heaves it back against the side of the truck.

"The children are too little to reach the ballot box," the gray-haired man says. I nod, and we smoke for a moment in silence.

"It's funny," he says. "I was in prison almost twenty years ago. I nearly died. During the year I was there, all I could think about was surviving long enough to get out. When I got out I would be free: That was what I used to think." He blows smoke from his mouth and looks at me. I know he's wondering why he's telling me this.

"You think you'll be free," I say, "but it stays with you."

He nods. "Little things happen and I react. I forget where I am. The soldiers—it's nothing more than buying a few votes. But I panic. My briefcase..." He trails off and stubs out his cigarette. The waiter is walking toward us, but the man shakes his finger at him, a Dominican "no."

"Let me get you something," I say.

"No." He glances toward the street. "I'm all right now. I have an appointment, and I'm very late already. Thanks for the smoke."

I watch him walk out. He crosses the street, not too fast, anonymous, any middle-aged man tired at the end of the day. At the first corner he turns out of sight toward whatever it is he is late for, his boss or his wife or his mistress, or a meeting in a backroom behind closed doors.

When I can't see him anymore, I pay for my beer and go. It's later than I thought, and the light is getting strange in the way it sometimes does in the late afternoon. Everything looks at once too vivid and yet somehow unreal in this light, its harsh beauty, its brightness, provoking either violence or tears.

I walk as fast as I can across the plaza, which has become completely congested with people arguing over the mattresses. I'm still not sure where I am. There are soldiers everywhere. I cut through a park, and the park is full of policemen, loitering in this intense and fading light with guns protruding from their sides like dislocated hips. I want only to be out of here. Faces rise and fall away as I pass, faces blue-black, brown-skinned, *indio*, and what they call "good color"—pale, much paler than my own. Here I am, descendant of the trader and the traded, and a traitor to both worlds. Arrived with money made in the sugar trade, skimmed from the man who calls himself my father. Here I am with the dark skin of some other man whose name and race I'll never know, with the pale skin of a mother who was not so much a mother as a fairy tale, a nightmare, a dream.

Here I am thinking of Josephine, of whom I have nothing. A language I can no longer speak, an unfinished conversation, a terrible grief I cannot begin to grieve.

I cannot stay here; this city is too much, with its history seeping from its streets like blood through a bandage. Its history is everywhere, pounding at me like the pounding on a door by someone who will not go away. I came here to do something for this city, to help, but here I am walking through its streets in a half-panic, and all I want to do is get out, go somewhere else where the pounding is not so close to the one in my heart, the insistent and awful knocking of a grief and guilt that is all my own and that I cannot speak or spill or work away.

I can only bind it, too tightly. I bite my lips, wait for it to atrophy and fall.

"Michelle!"

"I'm right here," I say, though I wasn't. Just for a moment I wasn't. Tollomi has come into the room, his arms oddly empty of books and limp at his sides. "What's the matter?" I ask. His face looks like a mask put on too quickly, his face is askew. He flops down on his back across the bed the way he does every afternoon, with his bare feet hanging over the edge of the mattress. He must have studied himself doing this so as to be able to do it now as if nothing's wrong. He reaches into the breast pocket of his shirt for his cigarettes. He takes one out and sticks it between his lips without lighting it. In a moment he'll sit up, then light it and open the window. "What's the matter?" I ask again.

He rolls onto his side and looks at me. The blueness of his eyes against his brown skin startles me sometimes. "Nothing," he says, looking past me at the wall.

I smile a little. I know this "nothing," and he knows I do. "What did you do today?" I ask.

He sits up, opens the window, and lights his cigarette. He sits with his head in the window and smokes. I wait.

"I was at the library," he says after a while. "And then I went for a walk. I was sitting in a café, and then outside a truck full of soldiers drove up—" he stops. "I'm not getting anything done here," he says quickly, "and I want to find Lupe Vásquez. If her husband was killed here in Santo Domingo, it makes sense she'd stop doing her organizing from the city. She must be in one of the other big cities, Santiago, maybe, or Puerto Plata. Where she'd have a phone, a post office, access to communications, but not so dangerous as here. Somewhere touristy, maybe. That would make sense. Do you see what I mean?"

"You mean you want to get out of the city."

He looks up, startled. Then he nods. He relights his cigarette, which hasn't gone out, but he needs to compose himself. It's upset him that I said what was true. He doesn't want that truth. He wants some other version.

"I thought we could go look for the house also," he says after a moment. "Your grandparents' house. If we went and looked up the records—there must be records somewhere—we could find it. Then we could drive there. We could come back to Santo Domingo later—for your luggage."

"It doesn't matter about the luggage," I say. "The luggage is gone."

"But the house?"

One of Tollomi's leather suitcases is lying open on the floor at the foot of his bed. It's so easy to leave a place—people think it's hard; it isn't, it's the easiest thing in the world. Leaving is so easy it's almost frightening, as if once you start you won't be able to stop; you'll just keep going, you'll go until you fall over the edge. But there is no edge. It only feels that way.

"Michelle!"

"What?" I say, startled. I've done it again, I don't remember what we were just talking about, I was somewhere else. How much time has passed?

I look at Tollomi. He sees that I don't remember. Out of politeness he looks away for a moment, pretending he has seen nothing, pretending nothing is wrong. He's finished his cigarette and extinguished it on the metal window hasp. He drops the butt in his hand like a little dead bug, and then he says, "The house. You have to look for it sometime."

That's right, the house; we were talking about the house. He's offering to help me look for the house, and what this means is that he wants me to go with him. He wants to leave, and he doesn't want to leave alone. But he can't say, *Come with me.* That would be acknowledging too much. His face is stirred up, troubled by thoughts he won't share. The look on it is something I've seen before—I can't think where—and then I think maybe the mirror is where I've seen it, in my own eyes. And suddenly I feel almost happy. I sit beside him on the bed and lean against his arm. This is what Bea sees between us, the thing she calls love that feels like loss, like absence. We share it, Tollomi and I. I can't look down into its darkness—I'm too afraid—but as I sit here beside him the edge of that darkness feels as if it's only the edge of the hotel mattress, digging into our thighs, as if the whole of my life is just this room, sticky and humid, faint traces of tobacco and cut grass hanging in the air, soft and familiar, safe like someone else's life.

When we tell Isabela we're leaving for the north coast, she shakes her head. "*No pueden,*" she says resolutely: "You can't." She crosses her arms and shakes her head. "It's not permitted. I'm sorry."

She likes us and business is slow. We like her, but we have to get out of here. Or rather, Tollomi does.

"Isabela," Tollomi chides her, "you wanted us to become tourists, I thought. So we're going off to be tourists for a while. I've been working too hard. Look how tired I am!"

"*Ay, sí,*" says Isabela to me, "I told you so!" She did: Despite her fondness for Tollomi, she has been full of criticism over his behavior as my husband. I should make him take me out to dinner more, I should make him buy me new dresses. "What does he do all day?" she'll ask me, "Where does he go?" "I don't know," I answer, or: "He studies," and she'll shake her finger at me, tell me I have to watch him. "You watch him," she'll say. "He looks tired."

Now I tell Isabela she was right; my husband has been working too hard, and so we are going to drive north, go to the beaches, relax for a while. Tollomi asks her for Bea Castillo's address in Sosúa, and Isabela goes out of the room and comes back with it carefully copied on a little piece of paper. "The beach in Sosúa is very pretty," she says.

"Were you there recently?" I ask.

"No," she says, "I've never seen it. But they tell me."

"Oh," I say. "Yes. Of course."

Then she wants to know when we are coming back to Santo Domingo. We avoid answering the question. She wishes us a good trip. We thank her and tell her we'll see her soon, in a week or so, and then it is time to go, and by this time I am anxious to be away from the city and the pension and even Isabela. Unlike Tollomi I have no real facility for lying, and going on like this with her makes me sad and tired.

We're off: Tollomi drives through the city toward the highway, and I lie down in the backseat so that the city becomes a wind blowing hard and gritty through the windows above my head. He wanted us to find the hall of records on the way out of the capital, help me search for the deed to the house. The house, the house: He keeps bringing it up. "Skip it," I say. "Let's just go, let's go, come on."

He doesn't understand this. It's true, I came halfway around the world to find this house—why? Because when my mother was my age, she wanted to run away and live in it but her parents wouldn't let her? Because my grandparents spent a handful of days sitting in it nearly half a century ago, and then, beaten, went home safe home?

Perhaps it's not my destiny at all to go look for the house, perhaps it's like my memories: I've taken on other peoples' destinies in place of my own.

Lying in the back of the car, I can't see where we're going. Looking up through the windows all I can see are clouds and sky. I don't care where we're going, really—wherever Tollomi drives is fine with me. He doesn't understand this either, like he doesn't understand how I can just walk around Santo Domingo all day with no plan in mind, no agenda plotted out before starting.

"The history of travel is the history of mistakes," I tell him. "Columbus thought this place was part of Asia. Your plotting doesn't matter—you'll wind up where you wind up. It's silly to think otherwise."

"I don't believe in destiny," he says, though I haven't said that word aloud.

Beside him on the front seat is a map of the island, but after the first hour it's no good anymore. There's a road that doesn't really exist on the map, and our shortcut off the highway peters out in a dirt road that dead-ends alongside a small river. The river isn't on the map either, and Tollomi, after folding the map back and forth a few times in irritation, starts to laugh.

"All right," he says. "Mistake. You win."

We get out of the car and wade into the river and dunk our heads to cool off. It doesn't matter that we'll have to drive back over the last forty-five minutes of absurdly bumpy road in blazing heat. We're both happy to be here, on this unnamed stretch of road with our heads sopping wet and our feet painted with river mud. Tollomi's happy to be away from the city, and I'm happy just to be moving, the two of us making our blind way over this little part of the world.

We arrived in Sosúa at night. We threaded our way along half-lit streets and down a gravel drive to discover at last, behind an imposing hedge of hibiscus, what is now our new pension: a series of one-room bungalows plunked down along a long strip of green lawn.

I slept more soundly than I have in weeks and woke in the morning to find Michelle standing over me, grinning and holding a paper bag and a metal coffeepot. She had dressed and gone out and returned with some greasy pastries, which she preceded to serve me on one of my notebooks: her version of a plate. She sat on the foot of the bed, highly pleased with herself, and as we ate and I watched her sip coffee from the bathroom water glass, talking and scattering crumbs among the covers, I forgot for a moment that we were no longer in Santo Domingo. I could have taken her halfway around the world and in the morning opened my eyes in that strange city to find her just as she was now, sitting on my bed eating cinnamon buns, perfectly at ease.

Then while I was in the shower, she yelled that I should meet her at the town beach in the afternoon. When I came out of the bathroom a minute later, she had already gone. The coffeepot was still there on the dresser. It's in better shape than the one Isabela Sonnenberg had; there are fewer dents. I wonder where Michelle got it, and if I'm supposed to return it to someone.

Walking through Sosúa I realize with a bit of a shock that soon it's going to be Christmas. Gringos blanket the streets like snow. It makes me nervous walking among them; it's too easy to become them. I don't want to go into a restaurant. I buy some food in the grocery store and eat it sitting on the curb.

Sosúa is the kind of town a vacation guide would describe as "sleepy." It isn't; if it were, a vacation guide wouldn't bother to describe it. The east end of Sosúa seems to have been settled mainly by Jewish refugees; walking through it I see tendrils of Europe entwined in the roots of the town. The unpaved main street is flanked by little houses set back from the road, their reticent fronts looking quaint and weathered and unmistakably European. There is a dairy, a German bakery, a synagogue. Besides the tourists, the streets are full of Dominicans who have come over from the west end of town to sell things on the sidewalk, to work in the tourist restaurants where the menus are printed in four languages, to hawk moped rides to gringos who want to zoom up and down the little winding streets between the beach and the hotels.

"Meet me on the beach," said Michelle this morning. I wish she'd chosen some other place. I pick my way down to the sand through the maze of market stalls where the vendors are selling maracas, T-shirts, acrylic paintings, wood carvings, larimar and amber jewelry. The sand is clogged with tourists. In contrast to the faded blue and brown clothes of the Dominicans, the tourists' bright towels and fluorescent bathing suits look like the alien garb of another world.

I find a spot under a palm tree where no one else is sitting. I don't have a towel; I never do. I sit on the sand and watch a group of Dominican boys playing in the water with part of a broken surfboard. Young men in tattered gym shorts range up and down the beach offering raw oysters, lounge chairs to rent, snorkeling equipment. A Haitian woman selling peanuts from a washtub balanced on her head stamps over the sand moving only from the waist down. There's no sign of Michelle. This is the kind of place she likes; there's a parade going by, people to talk to, a crowd to get lost in. I imagine she has gotten lost.

Upwind of me someone is chanting in a singsong voice like a man outside a carnival tent, the same lilt in his voice, as if he were yelling something like, *See the tattooed lady and the sword swallower, one dollar!* Promises. I can't make out what the voice is promising, though, or in what language. I scan the stretch of sand, looking. It's a young man swinging a metal pail.

Aha: "Dringbiradringcoke…dringbiradringcoke…" The only English he knows, no doubt. Melted ice leaks from his rusted pail in a zigzag wake as he comes toward me, yelling. He swings the pail as if he hasn't been doing it all day, and as if business is good and people are buying from him. They're not. There is a line of gringos at the refreshment stand buying soda and fruit drinks and beer. No one seems to notice this boy and his dripping pail. One of the women waiting in line for a drink looks anxiously back over her shoulder at an abandoned beach towel some yards away. When she gets her beer, she hurries back to her spot and checks underneath the towel to be sure whatever she's hidden there hasn't been stolen. The beer seller walks past her without flinching, without pausing in his almost unintelligible song.

"Dringbiradringcoke!"

When I call out to him he looks around to be sure it's him I'm talking to.

"¿Tienes cerveza?" I ask him.

"Sí." He plunks his pail down beside me, squats beside it and pulls a bottle from the pail. I ask him in Spanish if he has any Quisqueya, just to hear myself say the Taino word, and he says no, only Presidente—is that all right?

I say it is, and he pries off the bottle cap with a small knife hanging from a piece of dirty string around his neck. He passes me the bottle. It's dripping wet but not cold.

"Can I buy you one?" I say, giving him the dog-eared bills. Immediately his demeanor changes. He relaxes and sits all the way down beside me. When he sits, he looks tired. He takes the money and opens a second beer for himself. "It isn't very cold anymore," he says apologetically.

"I don't mind," I say.

"It's the best kind—Presidente. You like Quisqueya? See what you think of this."

My skin prickles. Quisqueya, Quisqueya, I wish it were a code and I had cracked it. I wish I knew what to say and who to say it to so that I could find Lupe Vásquez, find the students Vásquez was teaching to speak Taino, find someone doing something in response to this scene on the beach—what scene? A bunch of tourists getting sunburned and drunk in their rented beach chairs, the natives selling soda pop and peanut brittle their grandmother made? Yes, this, exactly this. I am sitting here being part of it as if I don't see it, but I do see it, and what it stands for makes me sick. I see it everywhere and what am I doing? I am sitting here having a beer. We clink our Presidente bottles and drink. His skin is darker than mine, and his face and chest are darker than his legs, darkened by the sun. His right collarbone protrudes oddly upward, misaligned with the other. He must have broken it once and never had it set. I wonder if it hurts him; he carried the pail with his left hand.

"Where are you from?" he asks. He can't tell if I'm Dominican or not. I look like one, I talk like one, and I bought him a beer, which no tourist would do—but. But there's something about me that I haven't presented quite right, something about me that makes him ask.

"I just drove up from Santo Domingo," I tell him. "Before that I was in Guatemala."

"Oh," he says vaguely, swallowing his beer. I haven't really answered him, but he doesn't ask again. He doesn't care; he's just happy to be sitting down. He dips his hand into the bucket of melting ice and splashes his forehead.

"Have you been working all afternoon?" I ask. The drops stick to his eyelashes, a thick fringe above eyes so brown they're black.

"Since this morning," he says. "My brother's friend works at the *refrescos* bar over there. He lets me get the bottles from him and then give him the money later. My brother works in a restaurant in town. He speaks English, so he has a better job." He looks at his pail of bottles. "I should get back to work." But he doesn't move except to bring his now-empty beer bottle to his lips for an imaginary swallow.

I don't want him to go either. "How's business?" I say.

"I'm going to learn to walk on my hands and hold the pail with my feet," he says, grinning. "Then people will notice me selling and not walk all the way up to the *refrescos* stand, don't you think?"

What can I say? I smile, feeling awful. You are young, strong, intelligent, personable, and handsome, but that's not enough here, so you work all day lugging a rotting pail trying to sell drinks nobody wants to buy. And why? The gringos don't look up when you call because they can't hear you; you don't speak like them. This is your country, but if you want to make money, you have to learn to speak like a foreigner.

I don't say this. I ask him for another beer. He opens the bottle and passes it to me. I pass it back. "This one is yours," I say. "Now one for me." As he takes the bottle our fingers touch, and suddenly I want him. I'm seeing him, really seeing him now, and I want to put my hand out and touch his chest. I'm staring at the dark areolae of his nipples while he opens my beer. They are the same dark plum color as his mouth. Above his upper lip, fine dark hairs gather in hopes of someday becoming a mustache.

He turns his dark eyes up to mine and asks me my name.

"Tollomi," I say, and spell it for him. He pronounces it a few times to be sure he has it right. Now he knows I'm not a Dominican.

"Carlitos," he says, introducing himself. "*Mucho gusto.*" We clink bottles and drink. "I thought it would help if while I'm working, I yelled in English instead of Spanish," he says, wiping his mouth, "but it doesn't seem to."

I hear his "dringbiradringcoke" litany in my head. The whole situation is disgusting. How many pennies has he made today? "You know," I say, cheerfully, carefully, "*Americanos* like it when they can travel thousands of miles from the U.S. to a foreign country and then hear people speak English to them exactly the way it sounds in their hometown. They love it—it makes them throw money like flowers."

"But I don't know English," says Carlitos, "Except for—" he clears his throat and recites his litany of dringbiradringcoke and a string of almost unintelligible English phrases: "Thangyou." "Wha'sup?" "Howar jou?" and so forth. "*Y sé muchas malas palabras también,*" he adds, "but I can't go around yelling those."

"If you did, it would get their attention."

He laughs and recites his list of American obscenities. Unlike the other phrases, these he pronounces perfectly. "Let's fuck, baby," is the last one; he says it very sweetly, grinning at me over his beer. I feel my face get hot. I laugh and look away.

"Is *inglés*, no?"

"Yes," I say. "Do you know what it means?"

"*Má' o meno',*" he laughs. I wonder how old he is.

"Hey, Carlitos. Want me to teach you how to pronounce your polite phrases as clearly as you do your dirty ones?"

"You speak English?"

I nod.

"You can teach me now?"

"Sure. In half an hour you'll be speaking English like a movie star."

"And you want to?"

"Yes, I want to. Okay?"

"Okay." He grins. "How do we begin?"

I ask him for another bottle of Presidente, and we begin with the shape of the mouth.

At last I see Tollomi. He's lying on his stomach in the sand beside someone. When I get closer I see it's one of the boys who sells things up and down the beach. There's a metal pail half-buried in the sand beside them. I come up behind them and stand over their sprawled bodies. Their dark shoulders are dusted with streaks of salt drying white on their skin. They've been swimming, they've been drinking. They don't see me.

"Boo," I say. They both look up.

"Oh, here you are," says Tollomi happily, but the happiness is not because I am here. He says something in Spanish that I don't catch— he's speaking too fast.

"What? Speak English."

He hoists himself up on one elbow. "Michelle, Michelle. I said, I've been looking for you."

I look from Tollomi's bright and glassy eyes to the face of the beer seller beside him. The beer seller has rolled over on his back and is gazing at me, at Tollomi, with tipsy enjoyment.

"You've been looking for me?"

"I have," says Tollomi, laughing.

"Did you think you'd find me in this boy's bathing suit?"

Tollomi's smile changes to a glare. "Please sit down," he says in irritated, schoolbook Spanish. "I would like to present you to Carlitos. Carlitos, may I present Michelle."

The boy brushes the sand from his hand before extending it. "*Mucho gusto,*" he says warmly, and drops his eyes. "Is she yours?" he asks Tollomi.

Tollomi hesitates. Ordinarily he would simply answer, "Yes." It's easier that way; with one little word a whole set of rules is conveyed, and then I can go where I want, talk to who I want, and have this safeguard, this *off-limits* rope hung around my body. "Is she yours?" Carlitos asks, as other men here have asked it, but this time Tollomi hesitates, and I feel his eyes on me, asking, wanting something different.

"No," I answer Carlitos, "I'm not." I'm tired of lying about it anyway. I look at Carlitos to see if he's going to start giving me the once-over, sizing up the territory, but he's not looking at me at all. He's looking at Tollomi, and Tollomi is looking at me.

Why did you tell him that? Tollomi's eyes want to know.

I shrug. *Because you wanted me to.*

He makes a face. *You think he even knows I'm flirting with him, Michelle? I'm just amusing myself. It's stupid to stop pretending just for that.*

It doesn't matter, Tollomi—I look away. "Could I have a beer?" I say to Carlitos.

"*Seguro*—" Carlitos begins, then breaks off. "*¡Ay!*" he cries, grinning at Tollomi. Tollomi nods happily, and Carlitos sits up on his knees and pronounces in slow, careful English: "De sun ees bery hoat, ees'n eet? Would jou like a col...d dring? Lemme getchou ay beer."

Tollomi applauds. Carlitos beams.

"Oh, my," I say. "My, my."

"*¿Me entendiste?*" Carlitos asks worriedly.

"I understood you perfectly," I assure him in Spanish. "You said it exactly right."

"Then why are you laughing?"

"I'm not laughing at you," I say. "Tollomi taught you all that?"

"Yes. Just now."

"Very impressive. Now do I get my beer?"

"Oh!" He rummages among the bottles in his pail, then looks up sheepishly. "There is no more," he says. "We drank it all." And then he repeats in English: "Lemme getchou a beer. *Espérese.*" He starts to get up, he wants to go get me one from the refreshment stand.

"Never mind," I say. "*Tomo una Coca Cola.*"

"Beer," he insists. "*Momentito.*"

I tell him he doesn't have to, and he says he wants to anyway. He gets up and picks up his pail and runs off down the beach.

I look at Tollomi. He's carefully examining a handful of sand. "Well," I say. "Well, well, well."

"What?" he asks, as if he didn't know.

"Well, Mr. Let's-All-Speak-Taino-to-Preserve-Our-National-Heritage-and-Resist-Cultural-Imperialism, what have *you* been doing all afternoon? 'Why, Michelle, I've been teaching a Dominican teenager how to get in good with the gringos by talking like a waiter in a Hollywood movie.'" I grin at him. "That's a very unique approach."

"He's not a teenager," Tollomi says, pretending to be fascinated with the way the sand slides off his fingers.

"But he would be if you didn't want to sleep with him?"

He looks up from his sand. "Are you jealous?"

"Of course not. I already know how to speak English."

Tollomi clicks his teeth. "Michelle, look at him. He's smart, he's funny—"

"Don't forget gorgeous."

"And he marches up and down the beach in the blazing sun and earns what, thirty-five pesos a day?"

"Less, I would think."

"So wait and see what happens. He's gone to buy more beer. By the time he gets back to us, I guarantee you he'll have made that much in one trip."

"I'm sure he will," I say.

"And is that a bad thing?"

"For him to make money? Of course not. He seems to be a quick learner. If you keep on teaching him, he can go up to the States and get a job working in a bank."

"Oh, God." Suddenly Tollomi's face crumples. I wait for him to say something, but he doesn't.

"What?" I ask. I think of apologizing, but it's not my needling that's upset him. He's tougher than that.

He looks up at me. His eyes are full of a bright blue sadness I can't read at all.

"The world is a hard place, isn't it?" he says at last.

"The world," I say, "is a rock."

We sit in silence for a little while. He is caught up in some memory, some piece of the past he refuses to speak of, and I watch as he struggles to smother it again. How much easier it is to not have a past at all. I watch him fighting with himself, and I feel almost lucky.

Carlitos comes running back toward us, pail swinging wildly. He draws up breathless and excited. "Look," he says happily, "on the way back I sold every beer—every beer!—except for three. I saved these three for us."

He takes Tollomi by the shoulders and gives him an affectionate shake. Dominican men are physical with each other in a way that in the United States you see only between young girls. It is in this spirit, unselfconsciously, that Carlitos takes Tollomi's hand in his own and holds it. "I made more money than I have all day," he says happily. "Now we'll celebrate."

From across the sand the voice reaches us. Someone is yelling: "Carlitos, Carlitos!"

Carlitos looks around. There's a man standing on the ramp that leads up to the road, shouting with his hands cupped like a megaphone. Carlitos jumps up and waves and cries, "*¡José Luis! ¡Caballero! ¡Estamos aquí!*" The figure jumps down from the cracked cement ramp and sprints over the sand. "He's my brother," says Carlitos fondly.

His brother draws up beside us. He's carrying a pair of shoes in his hands, fake leather, impeccably shined. He looks like a slightly older, slightly heavier copy of Carlitos, dressed in long pants instead of torn shorts and sporting a scraggly mustache. The brothers slap each other on the back, and then José Luis says, "Carlitos, what are you doing? I've been waiting for you."

Carlitos grabs José Luis's arms. "*Ey, macho, macho,*" he says endearingly, and tugs. José Luis allows himself to be pulled off-balance, but as they tumble onto the sand beside us, he is careful to hold his fancy shoes aloft. He sits up and brushes himself off, and Tollomi and I introduce ourselves. José Luis shakes our hands and looks at me with interest, wondering, I suppose, how his little brother has managed to take up with a gringa, and then deciding I must belong to this other Dominican sitting here. He looks questioningly at Tollomi, who doesn't notice.

"Look how much money I just made," says Carlitos. He pulls the wad of carefully smoothed pesos out of his shorts. "José, look: in fifteen minutes."

José Luis stares. "What did you do, sell the beach?"

Carlitos grins.

"Did you find it?"

"He's been teaching me English," says Carlitos, nodding at Tollomi. "Listen." He clears his throat and says, "Woo jou like a beer? It's bery hoat in the sun." And he slaps Tollomi on the back.

"He learned fast," Tollomi grins.

José Luis does not return the smile. "Where are you from?" he asks, frowning. He had taken Tollomi for a Dominican.

"All over," says Tollomi easily. "Carlitos told me his big brother spoke English and that he wished he knew some as well. He's a fast learner, isn't he?"

"Very fast," says José Luis. "Carlitos, we have to go."

Carlitos gets to his feet. "Will you be here tomorrow?" he asks Tollomi.

"Of course," Tollomi answers, and smiles his most charming smile.

I go to see Carlitos the next day and the next. Michelle doesn't offer to come along, and I don't ask her to. Carlitos and I sit in the shade under the sea grape trees, and I teach him the English word for every kind of food you can buy on the beach. We swim, we practice verb conjugation. He gets up to sell things now and again and comes back in thirty or forty minutes grinning and handing me a beer. He's making money. It's not because of his newfound English that people like him and agree to pay him to bring them their rum punch in scooped-out pineapples. People like him because of his smile, his shining eyes, his half-shy, candid face. But it's his English that enables the gringos to see his face. Without English they are blind.

In the late afternoon when the crowds begin to thin he always leaves. He has to meet his brother, he says. He never elaborates. He slaps me on the back or wrings my hand or rubs my hair and takes off. He lives somewhere in Charamicos, the maze of streets up the hill at the far end of the cove, the side of Sosúa where the tourists are afraid to go.

One afternoon as he's leaving, he tells me he wants us to go dancing: me, Michelle, himself, and José Luis, his brother. He's inviting us—he can afford to invite us now—he can afford to go, buy us all a round of drinks. Because of this money he's earning. Because of his English.

"Saturday," he says. "All right? I'll come get you."

"I have a car," I tell him. "We could pick you up."

His face clouds, and I realize I shouldn't have said this. "But it would be better if you came and got us," I say quickly. "That way we can surprise Michelle. We won't tell her ahead of time. You show up and then it will be a surprise."

"O-kay!" says Carlitos, happy again.

He doesn't want me to see where he lives.

Saturday night, Carlitos appears at the pension in his dancing clothes. Slacks and a blue button-down shirt and a gold chain around his neck, hair oiled and shining. When he squeezes my arm in greeting, I get a strong whiff of enthusiastically applied cologne. On his feet he's got real shoes, made of something not unlike leather. This is the boy from the beach with torn shorts? Yes, it's always like this. All but the very poorest people have a few pieces of clothing that are special: something for weddings and funerals, and then something for dancing, clothes scrupulously mended, pressed, always kept clean, always the same ones.

"José Luis couldn't come," says Carlitos. "Maybe he'll come later. ¡Vámanos, vámanos!"

"Are we walking or driving?" I ask.

"Driving," he says, and the three of us go out to the car. Carlitos directs us, not to one of the tourist places in Sosúa, nor even one of the many discos in Charamicos. Instead we take the coastal road east for a long time, in the darkness, over potholes, until the paved road ends and we continue on dirt. At last we hear music and Carlitos says to stop the car.

"La discoteca Teraza Fenomenál," he announces. We walk past other parked cars, motorcycles, and mopeds to an enormous low building made of cinder block set on the edge of a cow pasture. When we enter, the wall of bodies and the smells of sweat and perfume hit me like a wave. The dance floor is enormous and completely packed with men and women; a metallic ball overhead scatters chips of colored light. Carlitos is yelling something I can't hear over the music. I put my head close to his and smell the smell of his body mixed with that cologne. He bawls in my ear that he will get a table and Michelle and I should go dance.

Michelle and I make our way to the dance floor. Michelle is the only gringa in the whole place, and when we begin dancing, the people around us stop mid merengue and stare. The other women on the dance floor are all dressed in their best dancing clothes; Michelle in contrast is wearing her faded, falling-apart sundress. Of course, it's not her dress people are staring at. Nobody notices her dress at all; it's her white skin, her short hair the color of wet sand. Her blue eyes.

The men ask her to dance. They ask me, really; they ask me if it would be all right with me if they danced with her. I look at Michelle, who nods, and so I say yes, and then they grab her hand and lead her off. I dance a few dances with their sisters or girlfriends, and then Michelle dances with Carlitos; then I dance with Michelle again. Michelle hugs me and laughs, says something in my ear that I can't hear over the noise. She's a good dancer; she doesn't dance as stiffly as most Americans. That floating, weightless way she has of walking spills over into her dancing. She doesn't dance like a Dominican either, but she picks up the steps quickly enough, and we dance on the waxed concrete to fast scratchy *merengue* until our knees ache, until our bodies are covered in sweat. Then we sit down panting at the tiny lopsided table and get drunk. I drink beer mixed with tomato juice and clam broth because Carlitos and the other boys who have pulled chairs up to our table are all drinking this. Michelle drinks rum, as dark as molasses and served straight up in a paper cup with half a lime bobbing in the ooze. Carlitos teases her because she can drink it so fast. I wish it were me he was teasing. I gaze at him through the safe haze of beer until Michelle kicks me under the table. *We are imposters pretending not to be: Remember this,* say her toes in my shin, as if I could forget it. But with her here, it's as if we're both imposters from the same place. It's almost as if I belong, not to this but to something. I kick her back, we grin like lunatics, we dance together again, we order more drinks.

It's after midnight when José Luis appears. He sits at our table, straddling a chair, a scowling statue out of place in this happy circus of sweat and sound. I can see he doesn't like me, though I've given him no reason not to; his coldness is so un-Dominican that even drunk I notice it. Carlitos notices too. He grows quieter with José Luis at the table; whatever we were laughing about when he joined us is forgotten. José Luis drinks a beer and dances once with Michelle and once with a woman in a yellow dress. Then he goes off somewhere past the bar, and our party resumes its lighter mood.

About an hour later a fight breaks out on the dance floor. All the dancers stop at once, like one great beast with many sets of legs. Its many heads draw back, sensing danger, and then its body surges forward, hoping for a whiff of blood. The music stops and all the lights go on.

"Time to go," says Carlitos, getting up from the table and squinting in the sudden brightness.

We follow him around the edge of the crowd and out of the club. Sure enough, that's it for the evening. In a few minutes people start emptying out after us, lingering in the road in little groups, reluctant to leave the pool of light cast by the flood lamps over the entrance. We cross the road and walk down a little way to the car. Carlitos is looking around, back toward the disco. "I don't see José Luis," he says.

"Can we give him a ride?" Michelle asks.

"No," Carlitos says distractedly. "He has a *moto.*"

Back up the road someone is yelling: "*¡Soy yo! ¡Soy yo!*"—"It's me! It's me!"

"José Luis," Carlitos says, and calls out, "over here!"

José Luis dashes across the road, whooping joyfully. "*¡Soy yo! ¡Soy yo!*"

I glance at Michelle to see if she's registering this; she's already looking at me, eyebrows raised: What has come over him? He stops short beside Carlitos, catches him in a kind of embrace that is part headlock and part hug. His face is glowing with happiness, literally glowing, radiant through a light sheen of sweat.

"Hey," says Carlitos, protesting but hugging his brother back, and then: "*Mira,* you're bleeding."

José Luis releases Carlitos and brings his hand up to his cheek. There's a thin gash just below his cheekbone.

"What happened?"

"It's me! It's me!" José Luis yells again.

"*What* is you?" asks Carlitos.

"The champion!"

Michelle nudges me. "The fight," she whispers.

"That was you fighting?" I say.

"That was me *winning,*" José Luis corrects. He is joyful, his transformation chemical; you can almost see the endorphins sparking off his skin.

"The other guy had a knife?" asks Carlitos worriedly.

"Bah," says José Luis, as if knives were nothing against his prowess. But then he adds, "No, his ring cut me. His fist didn't even get to my face. You should see his nose. *¡Coño! Está aplastada.*"

"Let's go." I turn away from José Luis and unlock the car. This kind of thing disgusts me. "Carlitos, are you coming?"

Carlitos doesn't hear me; he's examining his brother's cheekbone.

"Carlitos," says Michelle loudly, so I won't have to.

He looks up. "Are you coming?" I repeat.

"I'll go home with José Luis. He has a motorcycle he borrowed from a friend," says Carlitos, suddenly nervous. "That way you won't have to drive me home. See you tomorrow at the beach?"

"*Sí, nos vemos mañana,*" I reply, not wanting to argue, looking from Carlitos's uneasy face to his brother's happy one. José Luis's wild grin bears no relation to the staunch frown of only an hour before. I watch as they cross the road to where José Luis has parked the bike, watch while he tries to kick-start it, and find myself hoping he won't be able to. But the motor comes to life, and Carlitos climbs up behind him. He throws his arms around his brother's waist, and then they're gone, zooming past us, eyes half-shut against the sting of the wind.

The next day Carlitos isn't on the beach. I sit by the tree we always meet under and wait, pondering alternately the best way of explaining the English future tense and the color of Carlitos's nipples: the ribbed brown-purple of olive pits. They would be hard like just-picked olives under my hands, and he has no idea, and I won't tell him, of course; he'll never know. But his eyes shine when he looks at me, his irises so dark they blend with the pupils, as if his pupils have had to dilate completely to exude all the warmth he carries within him like a small private sun.

Carlitos's chest, Carlitos's eyes. The angle of his collarbone, off-kilter from breaking it the summer before last when he fell off a *moto,* he told me one afternoon, and I wanted to trace the badly set clavicle with the tip of my tongue. Now I think of him climbing onto the borrowed motorcycle last night, José Luis driving drunk on the rush of having broken another man's nose. He might have driven right off the road. It's one o'clock now. Usually I never know exactly what time it is, but today I know. I walk back up the road into Sosúa and peer into the restaurant José Luis works in. Through the back door I get a glimpse of José Luis, the champion himself, at the sink rinsing dishes. They didn't smash up the bike, then, so Carlitos is bound to appear soon; I jog back to the beach and wait.

Another half hour passes. Still no Carlitos. At two o'clock I go back to the pension feeling stupid and annoyed with myself. I sit on the bed reading Juan Bosch's book about the revolution, a book about U.S. economic intervention, and *Apology for the Destruction of the Indies* all at the same time. I make a list of the things I should do to find Lupe Vásquez.

When Michelle comes in a few hours later, I'm still in the midst of this, papers and books spread around me and the ashtray on the windowsill full of cigarette butts.

"What are you doing?" she asks.

"I don't know," I say. "I come to Santo Domingo to find out about an indigenous political movement and wind up teaching English to a soda-pop vendor in Tourist Town. You tell me. What am I doing?"

She sits on the edge of my bed and looks at me but doesn't answer.

"Have I found out where Lupe Vásquez is? No. Have I found out anything about this museum project? No. Have I met a single one of Vásquez's former students? No. But look at my tan."

"You do have a tan," says Michelle. "Your skin is much darker. It makes your eyes look even more blue."

"Stupendous. Magnificent. Sublime."

"Grouchy," she says, and twists her head around to read the list I've made:

- *go to Puerto Plata: look up leftist political groups*
- *go back to Santo Domingo: check for national anthropological society—she might have been a member*
- *go to the university in Santiago*

"Why don't you ask Felix's sister?" Michelle says. "You know, who works at the airport. Isabela gave us her address here, remember?"

"Bea Castillo. Ask her what?"

"If she knows where your Lupe Vásquez is. She said she knew everybody, remember? 'Fifty years I been heah—'" Michelle attempts a Brooklyn accent— "'I know everybody and their brutha—' What?"

"Nothing," I say, closing the notebook and smiling at her.

"Why are you laughing?"

"Because I'm so fond of you."

"Yeah, yeah," she says happily. She takes off her straw hat and throws it at me.

"What shall we do now?" I ask her. I put the hat on my head.

"You're done with all this?" She means the books.

"I'm done."

She smiles and hops off the bed and does a ballerina twirl in the middle of the floor. "Let's go out," she says.

We go to Cabarete and spend a lot of money eating dinner in one of the new restaurants. It has tablecloths and a view of the beach, and I drink too much wine. Michelle starts to giggle and can't stop. She knocks her fork halfway across the room, and a terribly sunburned German couple glares at us.

"Let's walk on the beach," she says when I've paid, and we walk a long way down the empty beach, away from the hotel lights and into the darkness. The only noise is the wind and the pound of the surf.

"It's nice out here," says Michelle. "If you face this way, you can't see any buildings at all."

"By this time next year, there'll be a new hotel right on this very spot. I guarantee it."

She doesn't answer. Then she catches my arm. "Tollomi. Can you smell it?"

"What?" I say, and breathe in and join her in answering: "Smoke."

It's sudden and bitter in the air. We wade out a little way into the water to see if we can see what's burning, but all down the coast there's no sign of fire, the darkness is broken only by a distant string of winking lights that mark the hotels along the far end of the cove. The sight reminds me of St. Croix and I turn away from it and wade back ashore. The smell of smoke grows harsher.

"Maybe it's just garbage burning," Michelle says.

Nobody burns garbage at night. But I answer, "Maybe."

By the time we've walked back to where the car is, we can no longer smell it. We drive slowly out of Cabarete, looking for fire, but there's nothing to see.

The next day I go again to the town beach for Carlitos. I walk up and down the beach looking for him, but for the second day in a row he isn't there. This time I don't sit waiting. I go back to the pension in hopes of catching Michelle before she wanders off.

She's still there, sitting on my bed repairing her sandal with a needle threaded with dental floss. I ask her if she wants to drive back to Cabarete to see if we can find out what it was we smelled burning the night before.

"What are you, an ambulance chaser?"

"I have to chase something," I say lightly. His dark eyes, his bony hips, his plum-colored lips, his smile.

"I see." She pokes the needle through her sandal. "Have you asked José Luis where Carlitos is?"

I'm taken aback; I haven't mentioned Carlitos at all. She's reading my mind again. She, who doesn't even know what's going on inside her own.

"Well, have you?"

"Of course I haven't," I say.

"So why don't you ask him?"

"What am I going to do, Michelle, show up at the back door of the restaurant and say, 'José Luis, please, where's your brother, I just can't rest till I teach him a new verb conjugation?'"

"All right," Michelle laughs, "have it your way." She snips off the end of the dental floss with my nail scissors and holds up her shoe for me to see. "Good as new," she announces. She puts it on and off we go looking for damage.

We find it just beyond Cabarete, on the inland side of the road at the brand new stucco sprawl called Hotel Parasol. I've seen advertisements posted around Sosúa announcing "Hotel Parasol—Grand Opening Dinner Christmas Eve." It will not be opening now. The new stucco walls are blackened with soot, and the long *cana* awning over the entrance has been completely burned. Hunks of charred palm fronds lie scattered across the grounds amidst a fine dusting of black ash that has fallen like snow over the green lawn, the landscaped shrubbery, the bright white gravel that borders the driveway.

Michelle and I stand by the front gate and watch the workers. Already a dozen men are digging out burned bushes, ripping down the burned poles of the awning, spraying water against the walls in an effort to clean off the soot.

Michelle nudges me. "See the white guy?"

Standing in the shadow of the truck parked in front of the hotel is a sole gringo who from time to time says something to a Dominican standing near him, who in turn shouts to others in Spanish.

"You think he's the owner?" I say.

"Yeah. I've seen him around Sosúa."

The damage looks worse than it really is. Except for the *cana* awning and some of the shrubbery, all that's needed is a heavy rain and a new coat of paint. Being made of concrete, the hotel itself is virtually indestructible. Still, between the painting and the hauling and getting *cana* for a new hand-tied awning, the crew will be fixing it for at least a week.

A full week of work for twelve men.

We drive back to Sosúa, where I drop Michelle off at the pension. After wasting another hour on the beach, I take her advice and look up Bea Castillo.

A maid answers the door and tells me in a bored voice that Bea isn't home but that I can find her at the Sans Souci. I ask her what the Sans Souci is; she says it's the restaurant with the balcony; a Canadian owns it, down the street. Bea goes there every afternoon to eat lunch and play cards.

I thank her.

"Do you play cards?" the maid asks me.

I say I know how, and she looks up at me through her eyelashes. "Bea keeps saying she'll teach me, but she never does," she says. "Maybe you'll teach me sometime?"

I realize now that it wasn't boredom I heard in her voice; she's flirting with me. I tell her I'm not a very good player at all really, thank her again, and hurriedly leave.

I find Bea on the first floor of the Sans Souci eating a fruit salad at a table near the sidewalk.

"Egypt! What a surprise."

I lean over to kiss her cheek. "Hello, Bea."

"How ya been? Siddown, order something."

I sit. The waiter is nowhere in sight.

"I went to your house," I say. "The woman who answered the door told me you'd be here."

"What woman? Oh, my maid. Well, here I am."

"I wanted to ask you something."

"I know, I know. Your wife's luggage. You thought I forgot, didn't you? I didn't forget. Tomorrow I'm going to Santo Domingo on account of the holidays. Not that I celebrate Christmas, understand, but Felix is the only family I got left here. My sons ain't flyin' down this year, and Felix does the *Feliz Navidad* thing on account of Isabela. I said to him, 'Felix,' I said, 'you're a Jew. You wanna invite me for dinner, you invite me for dinner. You wanna give me a present—great, I love presents. And if you wanna celebrate Christmas, you go right ahead, but I ain't celebratin' it.' Felix says 'Okay, just come,' so I'm goin'. I'll stop by Las Americas and see if I can locate Michelle's bags."

"Actually," I say, "I think she's given them up for lost. But I was wondering—"

"Lost? They ain't lost, Egypt. They're sittin' in some room in Las Americas gatherin' dust. Thirty years I'm workin' for these bozos—I know what I'm talkin' about. You leave it to me. Aright?"

"Aright," I repeat, slipping into her intonation without meaning to. "We place ourselves entirely in your hands."

She beams at me.

"Bea, I want to ask you a question."

"So ask me already. Don't ask me if you can ask me, just ask me, eh, Egypt?" She cackles and holds out her hands. "Ask."

"Jorge and Lupe Vásquez," I say.

"That is not a question, Egypt, that is a name. Two names. What about them?"

"Have you ever heard of them?"

"Vásquez, Vásquez. You know how many people we got on this island named Vásquez?"

"He was a professor at the University—"

"I know who he was. Did I say I didn't know who he was? No, I said Vásquez is a popular name. He got shot a couple a years ago; he used to be in politics. What about him?"

"I wanted to see his wife," I say.

"His wife? You got a wife of your own, whaddaya want his for?" She laughs. "A joke, Egypt. Smile."

I smile.

"So really. You wanna see Lupe Vásquez?"

I tell her as simply as I can about the plans for the creation of the museum, and she nods. "I heard about that," she says. "It was a good idea. That's what her husband got shot for: too many good ideas. I heard she went a little crazy after he died, and who could blame her? My late husband, may he rest in peace, went in his sleep, thank God."

"Do you have any idea where she is now?"

"She lives in whatchamacallit. Little village in the mountains near Las Nubes."

"You know where, Bea?" Michelle, you are a genius.

"He asks me, do I know where. No, I don't have her exact address—it's a big island, Egypt. Besides, you don't *have* an address in Las Nubes. We're not talkin' major metropolitan area here. Look, I tell you what: You really want to see her, you go to Las Nubes and ask at the hairdresser."

"The hairdresser?"

"I saw her a few times with her husband in the airport. They spent a couple a years in Mexico one time, and there was some problem with them leavin' the country. They couldn't leave from Santo Domingo so they left from up here. I helped them out, that's how I know. Anyway, she had quite a head of hair on her, la señora Vásquez. Up to here she wore it." She chops at the air a foot above her head. "She couldn't do it like that herself, I'm tellin' you. If she's livin' there, up there in wherever, she's still gotta get her hair done. Right? Right. Maybe you don't know from women's hair, so you wouldn't think of it, but trust me when I tell you. Try the hairdresser."

I thank her profusely and kiss her on both cheeks.

"Aah, ah, ah." She waggles her finger at me, delighted. "Now where's the waiter? I'm going upstairs to the bar. Got a date for gin rummy. You know Ruthie? No? You should. Very nice lady, older than God and twice as strong. Come on upstairs, we'll play a few hands."

"I'd love to," I say, "but I can't."

"Whaddaya mean, you can't? You're on vacation, right? So stop tearin' around—you'll give yourself asthma."

I laugh. "Michelle's expecting me."

"Aright, that's different. You tell Michelle not to worry about her luggage. Lemme know if you find Lupe Vásquez."

Past Puerto Plata I turn inland, and after an hour of driving and asking I find Las Nubes. It's simply a cluster of houses and a few stores. I drive through it without seeing a beauty parlor, turn around, and crawl the car back. This time I notice a wooden shack set back from the road on whose outer wall is painted in mostly peeled-off pink paint: SAL MA ÍA.

I walk down the path and look in.

The beautician of Salón María is putting a towel around the shoulders of a young woman sitting in the customer's chair.

In my best *acento campesino* I greet them and say I'm looking for Lupe Vásquez, and that I thought she might be getting her hair done today.

"Today?" asks the hairdresser. "No. She should come down, but she doesn't."

My heart pounds. She knows Lupe Vásquez.

"*¿Qué Lupe?*" says the young woman in the chair.

"Lupita," says the hairdresser. She slips a plastic bag over each hand and dips one hand into a jar of white cream. "From Pata de Pavo, right?"

"Yes," I say, wondering what Pata de Pavo is. The name means "turkey foot." The hairdresser massages cream into the young woman's scalp.

"Put a lot on," says the woman. "I want my hair really straight."

"Why is it called Pata de Pavo?" I ask and immediately wish I hadn't; I don't want to sound like an outsider.

"The road splits three ways like the foot of a turkey," says the hairdresser. "So it's called Pata de Pavo."

"*Ay, sí,*" says the young woman, wincing a little from the sting of the chemicals, "that's why."

I thank them and start to leave. I don't want to be asked who I am or why I want to see Lupe Vásquez.

"Tell Lupita to come for her hair," the hairdresser calls after me. "She never comes anymore!"

"*Sí, sí, no' vemo',*" I yell back, and hurry down the path to the road.

Half a mile or so past Las Nubes, the road splits. Two of the forks are unpaved dirt. I get out of the car and walk up the first one.

Pata de Pavo is dotted with little square houses, the poorer ones made of scrap and palm wood, the richer ones of cinder block and tin. The air smells of wood smoke. I walk past the general store. It's closed and locked; this is the hottest part of the day.

A young woman comes down the road with two children behind her, all of them balancing cans of water on their heads.

I ask her if she knows where I can find the house of Lupe Vásquez.

She stares at me a moment then points back the way she came. "She's in the house up there."

"Where?"

"Up there."

"In that house?" I point.

"*No*," she says, amused at my ignorance, "in the little house on the hill. Come on, I'll show you."

"Oh, that house," I say quickly. "Thank you."

"*A su orden*," she says graciously, and I walk up the road in the direction she pointed.

The road banks sharply upward in a small hill. At the top of it two houses stand across from each other, one of cinder block, the other of unpainted wood. The cinder-block house is closed up. I walk across to the wooden house since the door is open. No one is inside, but I hear voices coming from behind it. I go around back. Under the cooking shed, two old women are seated in wooden chairs. I look from one to the other. They're wearing tent-like, shapeless dresses, and their bare feet are feet that have always gone barefoot, callused and spread, with hard cracked heels and ragged nails. One of them is smoking a cigar.

"*¿Como 'tan u'tedes?*" I say, and they look up and return the greeting, staring at me with the frank curiosity afforded strangers in a small village. What do I want, what am I doing here?

I tell them I'm looking for Lupe Vásquez; do they know where I can find her? The woman with the cigar takes it out of her mouth. Her wrinkled face has a faded look, as if when her hair changed from dark to gray, her skin, too, lost its color.

"*¿A Lupita?*" she asks.

"Yes, Lupita—Lupe Vásquez. Does she live in this village?"

The other woman laughs. "This is Lupita," she says, and pats the faded woman on the arm.

The names of saints are always popular. How many women are called Lupe? Probably almost as many as have the last name Vásquez. Stupid of me. I've tracked down the wrong person.

"I'm sorry," I say. "I was looking for a woman who was a professor at the University of Santo Domingo. Her husband—"

"I am Lupe Vásquez," says the faded woman sharply, "the one you're looking for."

My face grows hot, and my eyes fall away from hers. Stupid, Tollomi, stupid! You with your feet just as bare and hardened as hers. This gray old woman in the torn dress is the anthropology professor with the fancy hair. As you are the blue-eyed Cruzan wharf rat of Christiansted.

Not are. Were. And she?

"Doña Vásquez," I begin, "my name is Tollomi DeHaas. I've been wanting to meet you for quite a while. I've been in Santo Domingo researching the work of—" I break off. The look on her face stops me. I'm saying the wrong thing.

Lupe Vásquez turns to her friend. "A student of my husband's," she says carefully.

"¿*Sí?*" The old woman gets up and holds out her chair. "Sit down," she commands.

I sit.

"You're very far from Santo Domingo," says Lupe Vásquez conversationally. But her hands are clenched in bony knots.

"Yes," I agree, "but the buses aren't so bad if you leave early."

"*Ay, sí,*" she says. "It's always so crowded in the capital. So much noise, so many people…"

"Not like here," says the other woman. She goes over to the whitewashed clay stove. I know she's going to add sticks to the fire and boil river water and make coffee for me, which she'll serve me black with four or five spoonfuls of sugar in her best cup.

"No," says Lupe Vásquez after a long pause as if there's been no pause at all, "not like here."

"The girl down at Salón María was asking for you," I venture. "She wants you to come see her. She says you never come down these days."

It's the right thing to say. I've followed her lead in setting the tone; I'm behaving as if I've come here to visit, to make small talk. She rewards me with a flicker of acknowledgment in her eyes before she answers, "*Ay*, that María, always the same thing from her: '*¡Lupita, ven, ven acá!*' Eh, Chucha?"

"Just like that," says Chucha, laughing. She turns around from the stove and hands me my coffee.

I drink it down and thank her and hand back the cup. Lupe Vásquez slips her feet into a pair of rubber sandals and gets to her feet. She looks at me and I stand up too.

"*Bueno, Chucha*," she says. "*Nos vemos.*" We're making an exit; she's taking me with her.

"Goodbye, doña," I say to Chucha. I shake her hardened hand. "*No' vemo'.*"

"*Si Dios quiere*," she replies.

"*Si Dios quiere*," echoes Lupe.

We go out of the cooking shed, and I follow her across the yard to the dirt road.

"I'm sorry I burst in on you," I say. "I asked where I could find you and I was told—"

"Not here," she interrupts. "We'll go to my house."

I follow her along a narrow footpath that leads up a hill alongside a barbed-wire fence. She's frail-looking, thin the way some women start to be when they get older, but wiry; her step on the hillside is quick, her fingers gripping the butt of her extinguished cigar might conceal iron beneath the skin: a cross between a birdcage and a bird.

We make our way through a stile and into a thicket of guava trees, following a path that snakes around bushes and boulders until we come out in a clearing and I am looking at a garden. Cucumber vines and tomatoes and eggplant grow alongside a cloud of flowering bushes, hibiscus and *coralillo* and almond trees. Beyond the garden a clean-swept dirt path leads up to a little house covered in peeling green paint and flanked by gangly rose bushes.

"That's my house," she says.

We enter a small room with a cement floor almost entirely taken up by furniture. There are four rocking chairs set face-to-face, and two straight chairs by a small table. On the table sits a gas burner attached to a rusted propane tank wedged in beside the table and the front wall. On the wall over the table hangs a garish print of a thorn-crowned Christ gazing heavenward into an eerily green sky. What is this woman doing here, this university professor living like a poor *campesina*? If she needed a place to organize in secret, this would be it. She has the scenery down pat; there's nothing in the room to suggest that its occupant has ever ventured out of the village.

"*Siéntese,*" she says, pointing, and I squeeze in between the rocking chairs and sit down in one. She sits down opposite me, and our knees almost touch. On the wall beside us hangs the only other picture in the room: an old wedding photograph of a bride and groom, so heavily retouched that it resembles a painting. Her skin has been made to look lighter, and her eyes wider, but it's still her face. Her young husband has the large ears and piercing eyes I recognize from a photograph on the dust jacket of one of his books.

"It's a beautiful picture," I say, looking back at Lupe Vásquez.

"So tell me," she says, as if I hadn't spoken, "what is it you want to know?"

"I wasn't a student of your husband's," I start.

"I know you weren't," she says. "You're not Dominican either, are you? I don't want my neighbors to think strangers are coming around here looking for me. It's better if Chucha thinks I know you."

"I'm sorry I burst in on you like that. I asked at the hairdresser's where I could find you, and then a girl in the road pointed me here. When I saw you, I didn't realize…" I stop.

"You thought you'd come to the wrong place," she finishes. "No, you've found me. Now, tell me why you've come all this way."

I tell her I've done political work in many countries and that while traveling, I'd heard of the Taino language project and of her efforts to establish a museum to protest the upcoming quincentennial celebrations. I say that as her husband's murder showed, the work is obviously dangerous for the Dominican organizers. A more international group of volunteers would mean a greater degree of safety for everyone, and so I want to volunteer to work in whatever capacity I'm needed.

"Where are you from?" she asks.

"My passport says U.S."

She laughs. "That little blue book—the bulletproof vest. I'm sorry, I would have been happy to have you work with us, but there is no work. The museum project has been abandoned. It's over."

"What do you mean?"

"Look." She sweeps her hand around the tiny room. "You don't suppose I could organize an international exhibition of political art from here, do you? I gave it up."

"You gave it up?" I say stupidly. "Then who's in charge of it now?"

"No one. There is no project anymore."

I look into her eyes. "Doña, I know you don't know me. I could be an informer. I could have a gun in my back pocket. But I'm not, and I don't. I've been a political activist for a long time, and when I heard about the idea of creating the museum, I felt in my heart that I wanted to come here. Look at my skin. It isn't white. I'm a part of the world they're trying to erase. I was born in the Virgin Islands. I have my own lost language." My voice is shaking a little. I don't know if she's noticed.

She sighs. "You think I must be organizing in secret and won't tell you," she says, more to herself than to me. "You think this place is a cover for some secret project because there is no other reason why I, the professor, the wife of Jorge Vásquez, the—yes, I had such nice clothes, such beautiful hair. Why would I come to a place like this? In this village, no one else my age can even read. So I must be carrying out some kind of clandestine operation—that must be why I'm here? I'm sorry, but no. I know you're not an informer. If I thought you were, you wouldn't be sitting here in my house. But there's nothing to tell you. After Jorge was killed, I had to get out of Santo Domingo. I came here because I had nowhere else to go."

"They wouldn't let you leave the country?"

"I didn't try," she says. "There was no point."

"Have they tried to find you here?"

She looks puzzled. "Who? The military? *Ay, santo.*" She rocks back in her chair and sighs. "I didn't come here to hide. *You* found me, didn't you? And I trust you have fewer resources than the army. I came here because my whole life was woven together with Jorge's. We had been married for forty-five years. I was fifteen when I met him." She looks up at the wedding portrait. "He was older. He was going through the countryside with some other people from the Party making speeches. I was fifteen then. When I met him I hadn't even gone to high school. When we married, it was such a scandal with his family that he wanted to marry *una niña del campo*. They were rich, you know." Her voice is low and slightly hoarse, whether from emotion or from smoking cigars I can't tell. She looks back at me.

"After they shot him, I couldn't stay in Santo Domingo. I wasn't afraid they would kill me. They've already killed me. But I'm lucky; I had another life once, here. You met Chucha. She's my cousin. We used to play together and do the laundry when we were children."

"You never had any children of your own?" I ask.

"I had three," she says. "My daughter is married and lives in New York. Both my sons died in the war."

"I'm sorry."

"So you see why I live here now? This is the only place I can still live. What's wrong?"

I've been losing my composure, but I thought she wouldn't notice. "Don't you feel—" I blurt, then stop.

"What?"

Why not just ask her, after all? I take a breath. "Doña, do you ever feel, living here, when for so long you had another life elsewhere—do you ever feel now like an imposter?"

She runs a hand over her gray hair and is silent a moment, frowning. Then she sits up a little straighter in her chair and for the first time I can imagine her behind a lectern. "I'd like to tell you a story," she says. "It's a story about the Tainos."

"Please do."

She coughs and pats her hair again. "One of the first *conquistadores*, Juan de Esquivel, spent a lot of time talking to the Taino *cacique* Cotubanama. Cotubanama became very fond of him, and the two swore an oath of eternal friendship. To cement the bond, Cotubanama suggested they switch names. Esquivel agreed and went away with the name Cotubanama, and Cotubanama went away with the name of Esquivel." She rocks back and forth in her chair a moment before going on. "Only a few weeks had gone by when the Spanish captain betrayed the *cacique;* he sent his soldiers out to kill him. When Cotubanama heard the troops approaching, he ran out into the open crying: 'MAYAN-IMACANAAA! JUAN DE ESQUIVEL DACA!' Which means in Taino: 'Wait! Don't kill me! I am Juan de Esquivel!'" She smiles.

"So the soldiers didn't kill him?" I ask.

She gives a short laugh. "Of course they killed him. He was Cotubanama. That he called himself something different meant nothing at all."

We rock in our chairs in silence. Outside, the wind begins to blow.

"It's going to rain," says Lupe Vásquez.

"I should go," I tell her.

"You must come back again and see me. I know it's a long way from Santo Domingo—"

"I'm not staying in Santo Domingo," I say. "I'm in Sosúa."

"In Sosúa! *Ay,* I didn't know. What are you doing there?"

"I came to the north coast looking for you."

She shakes her head in mock disbelief. "Then you must come back. I've enjoyed talking to you. Are you here alone?"

"I'm here with a friend."

"Bring your friend with you. I'll make you both a typical Dominican meal."

"Thank you," I say. "I'd love to come back. But I wanted to ask you—after you came up here, wasn't there anyone who could have taken over the museum project? You weren't working on it alone, were you?"

"No, but there are a thousand projects to work on. People don't have enough to eat, their roofs are made of cardboard, they sleep six to a room. Their homes are being bulldozed to make room for the Faro a Colón. And the elections are coming. You could work on the election."

"The election's fixed," I say. "Balaguer's going to win, no matter what."

She makes an irritated sound in her throat. "Of course he is," she says. "But the more people who support Bosch, the more blatantly fraudulent Balaguer's victory will appear." She pauses, and says indulgently, as if talking to a child, "If success only meant winning, *hijo mío,* by now we would all be dead from grief."

"Do you still have the papers about the museum?" I ask. "Grant proposals, or a mission statement, or anything?"

"All right," she says sharply, "enough. I'll tell you exactly what happened. You know how Jorge died, I take it? He was shot at his desk. I was out when they did it. When I came home and found him, there was so much blood everywhere; the entire desk was covered with papers, and the papers were soaked with his blood. It was his linguistic work on Taino and all our work on the museum. There was so much blood on the papers that I couldn't get them lit to burn them. I didn't want to bury them. So I had to leave them in a pail in the sun for two days until they were dry enough to catch fire."

I can't look at her. "Doña, I'm sorry," I say at last. I force my eyes to her face. It is completely expressionless. "I'm sorry," I say again. "I didn't know. I shouldn't have asked you. I—"

"It doesn't matter," she says, and stands up. "I'm glad you thought so highly of our ideas. Jorge would have appreciated it. Come, I'll cut you some flowers to take back to your hotel."

"I'm thinking of going back down to Santo Domingo," I tell Michelle that evening. She's just taken a shower and is sitting on the edge of my bed drying her hair. She doesn't make any sign that she's heard me. "Michelle?"

She peers out from under the towel.

"I saw Lupe Vásquez today. She suggested I do some work on the election, so I'm thinking of going back to Santo Domingo."

She keeps rubbing her head; I can't see her face. "To stay, you mean?" she asks. Her voice is very careful. She's afraid I'm leaving for good, that just like that, I'm saying goodbye.

"No," I say, "not to stay, Michelle—of course not. Just for a few days. I thought I'd leave tomorrow morning and spend Monday seeing people and figuring out what I should do. I'd be back by Wednesday or so." Against my will I find myself wondering whether Carlitos might reappear by then.

"You want to leave tomorrow?" Michelle asks. She takes the towel off her head and looks at me, puzzled. "Tomorrow?" she repeats as if the word makes no sense to her. Now I'm confused.

152

"Yes," I say, fumbling for the right answer, "I thought I'd go tomorrow morning. Do you want to come? I'd love to have you come with me."

She gives a little impatient snort. "It's not that," she says. "There's just no point in going tomorrow. Tomorrow's Christmas Eve."

"It is?"

"Monday's Christmas. Did you forget?"

"I suppose I did."

She gives me an odd smile. "You're getting like me," she says.

Later that night when we're both falling asleep, her voice comes through the darkness: "Tollomi."

"Michelle," I whisper back, and she giggles and falls silent. "What is it?" I ask after a while. She takes a long time answering.

"Tollomi, remember when you asked if I wanted to go back to Santo Domingo with you? You thought I thought you were leaving for good."

"No," I say, although as usual she's right.

"That wasn't it," she says. Her voice is thin and wavery in the darkness. "I knew you weren't leaving, but you know that if you want to leave, you can. I mean, of course you can, but I mean it's all right. I mean, I don't want you to, but if you do, it's fine. Do you understand?"

It's my turn to be silent. She's said it badly, but there's no need to say it well. I know what she means: It's fine if you go, and it's fine even if you decide not to return, ever. It can't be anything other than fine. There's an unspoken law among travelers that when someone wants to leave, you let them, no matter what's happened between you. You don't ask how long they'll be gone. You don't try to make them come back.

As usual, she falls right to sleep, and I lie awake restless on the lumpy mattress, thinking about what she said. All I've done with my life is to leave things. I left Josephine, the person I loved best in the world, and never came back to her again. I've left my home, my language. I've left myself. Not on purpose but left them all, all the same. Left countless lovers and one-night stands in cities around the world, left one great cause for another, as interchangeable as destinations, as currencies. What would it take for me to stay in one place?

I honestly don't know. I think about it as I wander on the beach the next morning, looking for Carlitos; I think about it, listening to the tourists yell "Merry Christmas" to each other. At the end of their eight-days-seven-nights vacations, they'll pack up their beach gear and go back to their homes. All of them, every last one, has a home to go back to.

So Christmas Eve Michelle and I are sitting together in a bar in Los Charamicos. It's the one built right on the edge of the cliff that hangs over the west end of the town beach. We sit at the railing, looking out over the darkening sea. The sun has gone down, and the beach has become invisible below us. Only its sounds reveal it: the hiss of wind blowing up the cliff, the boom of surf on the rocks. Behind us from the street outside come the sounds of Charamicos: mopeds without mufflers zooming in from the highway, *merengue* coming out of a hundred radios, voices rising and falling under the weak orange streetlight.

We've been sitting at this table for hours, drinking slowly and eating fried *plátanos*. The memory and half-memory of all other Christmases rattle inside me like the ice cubes in Michelle's glass.

Michelle is watching me. Looking at her face I don't know how long I have known it, or when it was that I did not know it; it strikes something old within me, much older than the little time we have been together on this island. Yet this face of hers, I still do not know it. I do not know her, not really. How could I, when she doesn't know herself? In the absence of her story, my own rises inside me, begging to fill the silence that hers leaves. How long can we go on like this? In the uneven candlelight I see something pass like clouds behind her eyes. Something is gathering. Like a storm. Something is going to break. I can sense it, but I don't know what it is and neither does she.

This is what is happening as we sit here at the table, but it isn't what we are speaking of. We are talking of anything, of nothing: We're talking the way people do at the end of a day that they've spent together in a foreign city. We're talking like travelers, a vague mindless conversation whose only function is to cover up these other unspoken words. With Michelle it hurts to talk like this; we are capable of so much more. These languages we utter—English, Spanish, a little German now and then—is this what they were made for, to babble about nothing? On and on we talk, obscuring the real meanings that lie mute between us. Mute, but their presence makes the air heavy, urgent.

I'm in the middle of saying something about the lyrics of the song playing in the background, when all at once I see Michelle isn't listening to me. She's listening instead to the conversation we aren't having. Her head is tilted a little to one side, straining in an effort to hear. Fear rises in my chest, but I talk on. I want to tell her that I know, that I want to have this other conversation, the real one, but I don't know how to start. I don't know the words. There are no words. I speak six languages and none of them has a single word for what's really going on.

I know she feels it. I see it seeping through the lines of her forehead; I feel it in the rhythm of her fingers drumming idly on the table. Our eyes meet and she sees it in me too, reflected in my eyes like a mirror.

We're still talking. She's saying something about suntan lotion now, but, separate from the sounds her mouth is making, this other thing is growing; its weight becoming unbearable. But what is it? I look in her eyes, trying to see behind them to whatever is so desperately trying to speak.

Her eyes fix on mine, and I'm looking into that other place, the place she goes when she leaves this one, a little at a time like light leaving the sky until suddenly there is nothing at all, a body left behind like a shadow. Where does she go? What tongue is spoken there?

I look at her, trying to see. She's giving me her face to read; it is a gift, but one I can't decipher. She sees that I can't and wants to cry. She wants to, but she won't; she doesn't anymore, she hasn't cried in years.

"I wonder how deep is the deepest part of the ocean," she is saying. "I wonder what the name of that bird is, calling like that—hey, let's get a couple more beers. And a—" she breaks off in mid sentence. "Tollomi," she says gravely, "you're crying."

I?

She puts her hand on my face and shows me the tears.

We pay our check in gestures, as if neither of us speaks the language of this place. We walk down the stairs to the beach and over the sand and through the alleys of the town back to the pension in silence.

Words may be magic, but the magic of one world is no good in another.

Our tongues have cleaved to the roofs of our mouths. It's as if a spell has been cast. We've been turned into enchanted beasts. Words rise inside me, but I don't know what they are, can't speak them. If I tried to speak, what would come out of my mouth? Grunts, neighs, barking.

What else is there? Flags, smoke signals. Pictures drawn with sticks in the sand.

Back in the pension we sit on our beds and sit there very still in the darkness like statues. We sit for so long without moving or saying anything, it's as if we're already sleeping. But neither of us lies down for a long time. Across the room from me, I feel her wide-awake in the darkness, tense, as if waiting for something.

Not sleep.

Later that night Tollomi came over to my bed. His footfalls entered my sleep, and I felt him standing above me looking down. Even in the darkness I could tell there was something wrong.

He touched my arm. "I'm going out to look for her," he said.

"What?" I struggled to wake up. "For who?"

"I don't know where she is," he said as if he hadn't heard me.

"Where who is?"

He turned away, and I realized I'd been answering aloud only in my mind. I tried to wake myself fully. I heard the screen door close, and with great effort I dragged open my eyes. Too late. I was alone in the room. I sat up. His bed was empty. I got up and opened the door and looked out. He wasn't on the patio. The sky was still completely black. There was a little wind, and I could hear the hibiscus blossoms hissing. I stepped off the patio and went across the wet lawn and looked up and down the dirt road that leads into the center of town. At the top of the hill I saw Tollomi's shadow. He was running.

I started after him, but I was barefoot. I had to pick my way over the gravel carefully, wincing with each step, while he ran easily on his hardened feet. I couldn't catch up with him. But I reached the main road in time to see him disappearing down the road to the town beach.

When I reached the boat ramp I stopped and scanned the cove. Against the pale sand I saw in sharp outline the dark pile of beach chairs, folded up and chained to the trunk of a palm tree. I saw the huts where during the day they sell souvenirs and drinks. But Tollomi was not there. All the way down the beach nothing stirred except the sea. I looked out over the black table of water. Something flickered, a shadow separate from the other darkness. I listened for the sound that would go with it: a faint irregular splashing. There was a head, an arm, the pale wake of his feet.

I ran down the ramp to the water's edge.

"Tollomi! Tollomi!"

He was already farther out than where we swim in the daytime. The outline of his head appeared again and vanished, and then his feet flashed against the water for an instant like the tail of a fish. He had dived. I waited for him to resurface, and when he didn't I waded in and swam. The water was warmer than the air.

Swimming blind is nothing like swimming during the day. The sea and the sky are one at night, and both are endless. You can't see how far you've gone; you might have moved five yards or fifty. Even close to shore it makes your heart beat faster. My heart pounded. I couldn't see him. He was an idiot, a lunatic—even a child knows not to go swimming alone, not at night, not so far. The pounding in my chest pushed closer to panic, the closer to him and the farther from shore I swam.

His head burst out before me and bobbed in the water.

"It's my mother," he gasped.

"Tollomi—"

He tried to dive again, but I caught his shoulders.

"Tollomi, stop."

"She's drowning, for God's sake!" He pushed my arms away, and I grabbed at him again.

"Michelle, let go of me!"

I tread water with one arm and tried to get my breath. "Your mother's not down there. You're dreaming, Tollomi. Look at me."

He looked, wild eyed, unseeing. "Help me," he said hoarsely. "Pull her—" The last word was cut off by his dive.

I took a breath and dove after him.

Underwater there was no difference between closed eyes and open. I felt the water he pushed back against me as he swam downward, but I could not see at all, nor catch hold of even his heel.

I swam back to the surface and gulped air with the dark all around me. I tread water and counted the seconds that turned into minutes, and still he did not resurface. Below my lower lip the solid darkness stretched down and down, and above my head the darkness of the sky stretched infinitely farther. A picture came into my head that seemed to belong to some other lifetime: a color drawing of lifesaving instructions taped to the wall of an indoor swimming pool. The water stirred beneath me. When Tollomi's head shot out, I had my arms under his before he could draw a breath. But his body was slippery as a fish, and he slid away from me. I flung my arms through the water and sunk my nails into his sides. He dove anyway, and holding on I went down too.

Down, down, lower than light, amidst sharks or eels or sunken ships invisible in the darkness, down where the water is saltier than tears, heavier than flesh, we struggled; I to pull him to the surface and he to sink faster, to become lead and fall to the floor of what called him, the dream netted over his heart hauling him in. We wrestled blindly in this blind world too heavy for a body's gravity, our limbs moving in the water as if in slow motion through air, and I forgot my own flesh, my own tears.

Then all at once he stopped fighting. His body went slack beneath me. He had found his weight, and he sank like a stone. There was no more air in his lungs. I held an anchor in my arms.

I let go.

I let go of his body, and then I was back in my own but too late. Back in my own body I found I had started drowning.

What went through my head? Hanging there in the water like a jellyfish with my head full of blood and my lungs full of sea, I thought there must have been a moment, one secret moment, just passed, when my body whispered: Now. Now you must choose. This moment, choose to save yourself or not. This moment, the moment right before what might have been.

There must have been this moment and I missed it. I did not choose—I wasn't paying attention, for God's sake—I was trying to save a life; there were no bells and whistles, no shove on the arm, no waving flag; it wasn't fair, and the sea did not care one bit.

I thrashed my arms and legs furiously. I didn't know which way to swim to get back to the surface.

The sea offered no help and no resistance. The sea did not bat an eye.

I had awakened in the deepest part of the night. It was the time when even the crickets have grown quiet, when the birds are still asleep, when the bartenders have gone to bed but the fishermen have not yet awakened. I woke all at once and stared in the darkness. Something had awakened me; I didn't know what. There was no moonlight in the room; I couldn't see. In the darkness I listened. There was nothing to hear.

"Michelle?" I whispered. No answer. I listened again. I couldn't even hear her breathing. I climbed out of my bed and went over to hers: empty. She wasn't in the bathroom. I sat on my own bed again and looked at the door. It was ajar.

All at once I saw it; I saw her getting out of bed, drifting through the room like one who has been drugged, one who travels even in her sleep. She was sleepwalking. I jumped up and ran out after her.

I don't know how long she was in the water. With my arm around her neck I swam both of us back in and dragged her ashore and made her spit the sea out of her lungs. The body never wants to give it back. The body wants that time of no breathing, of blood-warm saltwater, of heartbeats in darkness. I pulled my fist in her chest and forced out the fountain. She doubled over, vomiting water until she was really breathing again with no loose gurgling underneath. Then she sat on the sand and looked up at me, blinking.

"Tollomi. How did you make it back to shore?" At the sound of her voice, which I feared I might not hear again, the feel of the deep water came in all around me, and I started to shake. She touched my arm, watching her own hand as she did it. Her fingers were icy cold.

"Michelle," I said as gently as I could, "you were sleepwalking. You walked into the sea."

She looked at me, not understanding, and I wondered for a moment if she were even now still asleep. Then I saw in her eyes the slow development of my words into meaning, like a photographic image emerging on paper.

"Sleepwalking?"

The picture was printed and she burst into tears.

I sat with her, her knees in her mouth and her wet clothes plastered around her while she cried. It went on and on. I put my arm around her shoulders, and my arm shook with sobs.

What has happened to her that she can cry so hard? I don't mean what terrible thing has filled her with so much grief; there is no end to the number of terrible things one can collect, no end to the space for them inside a human heart. I mean what has happened to her that keeps it all so close to the surface, yet still unknown? I felt that if I took her face between my hands and looked hard into the windows of her eyes I would see it, I would know the name of the fountain that poured forth such tears.

"I don't understand what's happening," she wept. "What's happened to me to make me this way?"

Did she want an answer? "Michelle," I said, "look at me."

She buried her head in her hands.

When at last she ran out of tears, the sky was light. She dried her eyes with her fingers and looked at her hands. They were shaking. She sat on them. She looked at the sand, at her knee, at the horizon. She looked at the horizon. "I have to go now," she said. There could be no mistaking her meaning.

"What do you mean?" I asked.

She stood up and rocked back and forth on her heels in the sand.

"Come on, then," I said, fighting to keep my voice gentle. "We'll go back to the hotel." I put my arm around her, and she allowed me to lead her up the beach. She moved slowly, as if she were still in a dream.

Inside our room she went straight to the closet and took out her shoulder bag. Her hair was still wet from the sea. "What are you doing?" I said.

She didn't seem to hear me. She pulled off her wet shirt and slid her dress on. She picked up her sandals.

"Michelle, it's not safe to go off by yourself. Suppose this happens again? If I hadn't been there, you would have drowned."

She turned around with her shoes in her hand and looked at me. A wave passed over her face. "If you hadn't been here, I wouldn't have gone in the water in the first place," she said.

"What?"

She shook her head and opened up her shoulder bag. "Nothing. It doesn't matter, I'm going away."

"Then tell me."

She shrugged. "In the middle of the night, I heard you at my bed. You woke me up and ran out of here. I followed you, up the road, through town, and all the way down to the beach and into the sea. When I caught up to you, way out in the water, you were diving over and over. I asked you why and you said, to save your mother. Your mother was drowning, you said, and you were trying to save her. That's what I dreamed."

Words. *Your mother. Drowning. Dream.* She said those words, and my whole life stopped for a second.

She was telling me what she did not, could not know. That was my dream and she had found it. Where? Not in this world. She had brought it back from that other place; it had slipped inside her as she passed through the door that separates there from here, the door I had locked and lost the way to so long ago. And now the door was right in front of me. It was ajar; if I put out my hand, it would swing open and I could pass into my old life again. How to touch it? The air between us crackled.

"Michelle," I said, "I have to tell you something."

She stayed where she was, standing vaguely in the middle of the room with her hair wet and her bag in her hand.

"What?" Her voice was unsteady with fear.

I was shaking. That dream had been the last thing to keep me who I was, and the last thing I lost the night I crossed that invisible line in my sleep and became someone else. And now she had found it. All I had to do was reach out and take it, and it would be mine again.

"Sit down," I said.

Still holding her purse, she sat on the bed beside me.

"I was born on St. Croix," I said. "Do you know where that is?"

She nodded, watching me.

"My mother died when I was still a baby. She was white. I was raised by a woman who—" the words caught in my throat and I stopped. The word *Josephine* welled up in my throat like tears. I choked back the name. If I spoke her name, I would speak everything that had ever happened; I would tell how, in boarding school, I had refused to answer her letters because I was ashamed; I would tell what she had said to me when I returned to St. Croix, and I would tell how I had left the island a second time and then gone on leaving until she died, by which time I was so far gone that I didn't even know her death had come.

I couldn't do it. I couldn't speak her name. I sat there dumb on the bed, and at last Michelle looked away from me and started to get up. I caught her wrist. "I'm trying to tell you," I said. "Wait." She sat down again.

And then I did tell her, the part about my mother and her husband, and how my mother had drowned and how, the last day I spent on St. Croix, I had seen her as a mermaid in the sea. I told how I carried that image with me for years, in a dream that my mother was drowning, a nightmare I had managed to hold onto even when nothing else of my old life was left, and how, when at last I lost even the dream, my life became so much easier because it ceased to be mine.

As I talked I felt the relief that comes only with speaking, even speaking incompletely, and when I was done there was a very long silence. I took a breath and listened to myself exhale. I was all right. I had not exploded or vanished. Then I looked at Michelle sitting motionless beside me on the bed, and with a sickening jolt I realized that though her face was turned toward me, she was not seeing me at all. "Michelle," I said, "for God's sake, say something."

She bit her lip. "I don't believe you," she said.

"Look at me, Michelle, look at my face. You can see it, you can see this is the truth, this is who I am, that dream is mine—"

She was not listening. She would not look at me.

I shook her. "Do you know what I'm saying to you?"

She began to cry. "Stop shaking me. I don't know anything. I don't even know—" Her voice gave way to sobs. I stopped shaking her. I put my arm around her shoulders. "Tell me," I said.

"I don't even know if I'm awake," she wept.

I took her hands in mine. "You are awake. You feel this?"

She looked down at our entangled fingers. "Of course I feel it," she said. "It feels just as real as it did in my dream."

"But you aren't dreaming now. You have to believe me."

She didn't answer.

After a while she pulled her hands away and wiped her eyes. "I never knew why you aren't supposed to wake up people who are sleepwalking," she said. She drew a deep shuddering breath. "This is why: I don't feel like I'm awake."

"But you *are* awake—" I started, and she jumped up off the bed.

"You don't see," she said angrily. "Any minute now, I might wake up for real and find I was never in the water at all, that I haven't even left this room. Or maybe there is no room? I might wake up and find I was never here. That I've just been dreaming. You don't know what it's like, Tollomi, not to be able to tell. You could pinch me until I was black and blue, and I still wouldn't know."

Her eyes moved over the room and back to me.

"What you say doesn't matter," she said simply. "I might even wake up and find out you don't exist at all." She turned away from me and began moving about the room, collecting her few possessions.

I watched her in silence. The space between us was wider than all the earth. I watched her and then I closed my eyes.

The sounds of her leaving: her toothbrush being lifted off the little sink, the scrape of the nightstand drawer—behind it, we had taped our passports. The rip of tape. The sound of her buckling up her sandals. The inaudible sound of tears.

"Michelle, I love you," I said.

No answer.

The sound of the door slamming shut.

I sat alone in the room and looked at her bed: empty. The sheets were twisted; in the pillow, the depression left by her head. The bed talked to me. *It's not my fault,* says the bed. *It just happened on top of me.*

In Michelle's life there have been so many hours of interrupted rest, hours lost. They cling to her like bad dreams, they wrinkle the sheets. You can feel it in the fabric: She never finished her sleep.

I smoothed down the sheets with my hands and looked around the room for other signs of her presence. There weren't any: no indication she had ever been here at all. I lay down on her bed myself. It faced the door.

I was surrounded by silence, the only thing she had left behind.

All morning I lay there. The room grew hot, and I lay there sweating. I hadn't eaten and I wasn't hungry.

When the knock came on the door I didn't move. I could tell by the weight of the hand that it wasn't Michelle. It would never be Michelle. Another knock, loud and insistent, and then a familiar voice: "Hey, Egypt! Michelle! You two in there, or what? It's Bea Castillo. Open up, I got your bags."

The door seemed very far away. I watched myself walk to it and turn the knob and pull. I felt like broken glass.

"*Feliz Navidad,*" said Bea. "What gives? For what you're sittin' here all by yourself with the shutters closed? You two have a fight? Where's Michelle? I got her bags."

"You got her bags?" I repeated stupidly. My voice cracked a bit.

"Whatsamatter, Egypt, you got a hangover? Where's Michelle?"

I cleared my throat. "She went out for a bit. Come in."

"I can't stay," said Bea. "Come out here on the porch where I can see you."

I followed her out. The air was terribly bright. I squinted down at her.

"You look like hell," she said. "But it's none of my business, right? Right. So Merry Christmas, I got you a present: Michelle's bags are out in my car."

Pull yourself together, Tollomi. Smile. Talk. "That's wonderful, Bea." *Smile, come on, Bartholomew:* "Thank you so much. I can't believe you found them. Where were they?"

"They were right where I said they'd be: sittin' in the airport collectin' dust. I was down there yesterday, before dinner with Felix and Isabela. Isabela's a good cook, not as good as me, but does she want my help? No. When Isabela gets in the kitchen, I stay outta the way. So yesterday I go down to the airport, and I talk to Enrique Palanco. I tell you no lie, Egypt, they got a room down there the size of Puerto Rico filled with lost bags. So I say to Enrique, 'Enrique, *what* do you think you're doin'? Gringos are walkin' around the streets of Sosúa in their underwear because of you people.' And Enrique says to me, 'It's all for Government inspection.' 'Inspect *this*,' I tell him, and I pick up your wife's bags and walk outta there."

She beamed at me, and in some far-off place inside myself I wished I were properly enjoying this. "That's wonderful," I said woodenly. "They didn't try to stop you?"

"Of course they tried to stop me. Head of *migración* shows up and tries to stop me. 'You can't do that,' he says. So I say to him, 'Señor Peña—' thirty years I work there, I know them all— 'Señor Peña,' I say, 'I did not barely survive gettin' shoved in an oven by the Nazis to come halfway around the world to this chunk of rock and be told by the likes of you that I'm not gonna do what I tell you I *am* gonna do.' Ha!" She laughed.

Laugh, Tollomi. I laughed with her.

"Thirty years I work there, Egypt. They're used to me."

"Thank you so much," I said again.

"So where's Michelle?"

"She's out shopping."

"Whaddaya mean, 'shoppin'?' It's Christmas Day; she was supposed to have her shoppin' done yesterday. She get you a present?"

"She gave it to me already."

"That right?" Bea frowned. "Don't worry, Egypt, she won't stay mad.

166

Now, come help me get the bags outta the limo. It's my chauffeur's day off."

I followed her across the lawn and out to the lane where she'd left her old VW.

"Aright, Egypt. There they are in the backseat. Go ahead, don't be shy. Take 'em out." I sprung the front seat forward and lifted out a dirty canvas knapsack and a nylon tent duffel. I set them on the ground. So this was Michelle's luggage.

"Open it up, honey. Be sure it's all there."

"I wouldn't know if it's all there or not," I said.

"You don't know what your own wife has in her luggage? What kind of husband are you? Open it up. If things are missin', you better tell me now."

"I know she had a tent and a stove," I said. *Michelle, Michelle, you're gone, and they're bringing me your clothes.*

"That's obviously the tent there," said Bea. "Go on, check for the stove."

To pacify her I unbuckled the knapsack and opened it up. Everything inside was wadded into a tangle of fabric. Whether this was Michelle's style of packing or the result of the customs officers' search, I didn't know.

I poked around inside it. "I think the stove is gone," I said.

"Figures. You know how many people around here would like to have one of those little stoves instead of cooking everything over kindling and ashes? I hope she keeps her jewelry on her person."

"Oh, she does," I assured her. Jewelry?

"What's a stove anyway, right, Egypt? You got each other, that's what's important. Aright, I gotta run. Don't thank me, I do this for my health."

I thanked her again. She got in the car, blew me a kiss, and chugged away.

And now I sit on the floor between our beds, Michelle's knapsack in front of me. The clothes inside are all rumpled and faded with age: blue jeans, a few shirts, another dress, all looking ready to rip. A pair of leather walking shoes with their laces completely snarled.

In the side pockets I find socks, a Swiss Army knife, a tube of German toothpaste, and a fat white envelope. Inside the envelope is another envelope, yellowed with age. Inside that, a folded piece of paper. I unfold it carefully. It's the title to a half acre of land and the house standing on it in the community of Las Piedras, province of Espaillat, Dominican Republic. Signed by one Henry something Harth, 11 April 1946.

I close my eyes.

Michelle. Come back.

I open my eyes. The clothes, the shoes, the knife. She bought these things, or found them, and carried them around with her. Now I have them and she isn't here. I must do something. Something, anything.

I pick up one of her shoes and begin trying to unknot the tangled laces.

In the evening I walk up to the hotel office and tell the proprietor's nephew, a man named Tony, that I want to pay the bill. He adds it up and doesn't ask me any questions. There's a little television set somewhere behind the counter, and he's trying to keep an eye on his program. He hands me the bill and I pay it. He thanks me and wishes me a Merry Christmas. I repeat it back to him and go outside and walk through the streets of Sosúa like a stray dog.

I go to Amigo's bar and order a drink I don't finish. I walk past the restaurant where José Luis works: closed. I buy a pack of cigarettes and lose them by the time I get back to the pension.

Her clothes and her shoes and the tent are lying all over the floor where I left them. I should have put them back in her bag, I don't want to keep seeing them, these parts of her that without her have no purpose. I sit on the floor amidst the wreck of her luggage and consider. Has she gone back to Berlin? Will she stop in San Juan? She said once that she wanted to take a train across Russia.

There's no point in guessing, even. I won't see her again. It's as if she's died, and what am I going to do with all her things?

I consider dumping them into the sea.

I'm headed for the harbor. This is a day for journey—I've already been to the bottom of the sea. My hair stinks of seaweed, my feet leave wet prints that don't dry.

If I were dead now, would I know it? If I were a ghost, people on the street wouldn't even see me. But no, the street is empty.

Michelle, he said, *you are awake. That dream you dreamed is mine.* And I stared at him, the light in his eyes growing like a fire. I feel him somewhere behind me, a star I would navigate by if I were traveling toward him. But I am going away.

It's the truth, he said. *I'm telling you the truth.*

But there is more than one truth. The truth is that I almost drowned. The truth is that I am still asleep and there is no island, no dream, no sea. The truth is that I am leaving. I have my passport in my hand.

The streets by the harbor smell of dead fish and drains. There are steamships here, freighters. There should be offices around here somewhere, the shipping offices. Sometimes they take passengers. It's a cheap way to travel. I go up the street, away from the water, looking. Everything is closed. Is it still so early? It can't be. I look for the sun, but I don't see where it is.

Far away I hear bells. And then I remember. It's Christmas Day. The offices won't be open.

I turn and go down another empty street toward the sound of the bells. At the corner of the street there's a bar, and the bar is open: Inside bars there is no time. I go in.

There are only two customers. They're sitting at the bar playing dominoes. I sit down one stool away from them and ask the bartender about the ships in the harbor. "Do any of the freighters take passengers?" I ask.

"You don't want a passenger freighter," says the bartender. "You want somebody to take you on a cruise, eh?"

"The cruise ships don't dock there," I tell him.

The man beside me looks up from his domino tiles. "She's very smart," he says. "Buy her a drink."

They look like businessmen. The one who spoke, a Dominican, has a neat pile of bills on the bar in front of him. The other man is a European with the face of someone who's losing badly.

"I have to get off the island today," I say to the bartender.

He thinks I'm joking. "What's the rush? Look at *el tipo* here." He nods at the European. "He has a plane to catch in an hour—you don't see him rushing. Right now he should be at the airport."

"Then why is he here?"

"He took a wrong turn," the bartender says, and laughs.

"I'm leaving," the European says grimly, "as soon as I win."

"You don't have anything left to bet," says the other man.

The European fingers his wallet, opens it, and looks inside it. I see from his expression that it's empty. He takes the ring off his little finger.

"Don't be stupid," says the Dominican. "Put it back on. We'll quit."

"You have to give me a chance to win back what I lost," says the European. "It's the rules."

"I don't want your ring." The Dominican turns and looks at me. "I take cash or nothing," he says, and winks.

I slide off my stool and stand by the European. "Sell me your plane ticket," I say softly. "I'll give you a thousand pesos right now."

The European looks up from his tiles. He looks at me for a while and tries to decide whether I'm serious. I wait. At last he says, "It's worth four times that."

"The banks won't be open until tomorrow," I say. "If you run out of money now, you won't be able to stay in the game to win back your losses." Out of the corner of my eye I see the Dominican and the bartender raise their eyebrows at each other. The European looks at the bills the Dominican has stacked beside him. I pull out my wallet.

"You're not serious," the bartender says suddenly. "You don't even know where his plane is going."

"It doesn't matter," I tell him.

The European reaches inside his blazer and takes his plane ticket out of a blue envelope. I take out my money and lay it on the bar. He counts it.

"Fine," he says without looking at me. His eyes return to the game.

"*Qué tigrita*," the bartender whispers.

I take the ticket and leave.

When I step onto the brown tiles of the airport plaza, I can feel my body again, my skin, the light wind. I cross the plaza and feel my feet, solid on the ground, walking.

The truth is in my hand, this ticket. I'm moving. I can go anywhere, take any path I choose; my life is my own. My destiny is mine.

At the counter when they ask for my luggage, I say I have none. When they ask for my passport, I reach into my shirt and pull out the pouch I keep it in. I hand it to the man behind the counter. He takes it from me, opens it, and starts to laugh. He tosses the passport back at me. It lands on the floor.

"What is it?" I ask. My voice comes out a whisper. I must be dreaming.

"Very funny," he says. "Now get out of here."

I bend down and pick up my passport. I open it up as he did. The picture inside is not my picture. The face looking at up me is not my face.

It's Tollomi's.

Then I am sitting alone in a plastic chair near the gift shop.

It's not my face. It's not my passport. I can't leave. But I'm afraid to go back. I would go anywhere in the world, but where my mind goes is not on any map and it is too much for me.

You opened a door, he said. I do not want it opened. Open the door and anything can come through. Anything at all could show up and look me in the eyes and be mine. And once I see it, there will be nothing I can do about it. At all.

Michelle, I love you, he said as I was leaving.

It doesn't matter whether he loves me. Love has nothing to do with it. Love is not the thing I feel anchored inside me, pulled and turned by a rope that cannot be untied or broken, no matter how far away I go. If I ran to the ends of the earth, I would still feel it, the tug and pull of that rope whose other end is somehow attached to him.

Wherever I go, it does not matter, because when I get there I will have escaped nothing. Destiny can always run faster. Destiny has already arrived.

I put the passport with Tollomi's face in it back in the sack around my neck. And because I cannot leave, I do something I have never done before, ever.

I go back.

And this is how it is: I open the door to the pension—it's not locked. There, laid out like a dinner planned to surprise me, is my lost luggage, spread out on the floor and waiting only for me to arrive.

On the table between the beds is a piece of paper I recognize from the doorway: the deed to the house.

On my bed is Tollomi, who has fallen asleep.

I wonder if he said certain words and conjured it all out of thin air. Or if he pulled it like a rabbit from a hat, if he had it with him all the time.

He wakes up.

"I'm back," I say.

He stares at me and rubs his eyes. He doesn't know what to say. *Are you staying?* he wants to ask, but he can't ask that. Without a word I step over my clothes to the night table. I pull out the drawer and untape the remaining passport from its back. I hand it to him and he opens it up.

"It's yours," he says thoughtfully, turning it over in his hands. He's quiet a minute and then offers it to me as if it were a snake. He can't say to me, *Don't go.*

So I tell him I'm staying.

"You can keep my passport," I say, "for now."

He starts to put it back behind the drawer, but the tape won't stick anymore. He looks at the little sack around my neck with his passport inside. Then he puts my passport in the pocket of his shirt. I watch as he buttons the button.

"Now what?" he says. Not looking at me. We do not hug or gush at each other or even touch hands. Between us is a minefield. What step would make everything explode? A minefield, but he is happy. "Michelle," he says, "Michelle."

"Now we look for the house," I say.

"All right," he says. Smiles.

"We have to tell them up at the office that we're leaving," I say.

Says Tollomi, "I already did."

We left late that afternoon. It had all the certainty of a ritual; there was no need to speak aloud. I drove east and Michelle sat beside me with one bare foot resting on the open window. No one looking at us would know, I thought. You can't tell by looking what's happened to us.

By the time we had passed Cabarete, it was nearly sunset. She sat up a little in the seat and looked at me and smiled. I shivered. I felt her thoughts so keenly, like a current running between us. I felt it almost humming in the air, this link, this lock, this strange and invisible line. I stopped the car, and she nodded, yes, she'd wanted me to stop. She wanted to stand on the beach. We went across the road and walked through the palms and the scrub. There were no houses here, no hotels, nothing but an empty stretch of sand, a low reef and the breaking waves turning silver in the waning light. The evening was very warm. She sat down on the sand and I sat beside her. We sat and watched the stars come out over the water, the same water she had nearly drowned in, the water she had gone into, dreaming that she would pull me from it. The dream I had dreamed so long ago, the same dream of this same sea.

Here I am on a poisoned planet, sitting by the ocean in a beautiful place that will no longer exist when I am old. With me is another human being who is looking up at the same stars and out at the same world that I am seeing. To be understood produces a peace like no other. The sea was at our feet, but I felt it breaking inside me.

"Michelle—" I started, and stopped. It was not words that I wanted. It was something else—I did not know what—but this was not a time for speaking. She was still looking out at the water, but her hand moved and found my hand and squeezed it. And then I knew I wanted to hold her. We had moved into that place where language means the language of the body. Everything in the world that was Michelle was right here in this body, and it was this that I wanted to wrap my arms around, to hold onto, to kiss.

"Michelle—" I said again, and she looked up and moved her face closer to mine.

In the dark pull of her arms and the sudden strangeness of her mouth against my mouth, her body spoke that in this place nothing mattered save that we were here, that at odd and joyful moments the world grows big enough to hold all worlds inside it, that everything that had ever happened to us was with us, between us, here.

And then it stopped and we disentangled ourselves and were once again separate sets of arms and legs and eyes looking away. We lay back on the sand, a few inches apart. But I still felt her pulse in my fingertips. The veil that separated us from each other had grown so slight: a murmur of the sea, or a dream even, could stir it and blow it aside.

Part Three

I opened my eyes to the light. The sun was coming up. We had fallen asleep on the beach and slept all night. I sat up, shivering in the dew. Michelle was asleep on the sand beside me with her arm flung over her face.

I watched her sleeping and felt very nervous. Last night we'd gone somewhere too different and strange to stay in, but I wasn't sure if we'd come all the way back. And if we hadn't, then I didn't know what would happen, or what I would do, or where we were at all.

When she awoke she didn't say much, except, rather crankily, that she was hungry. We walked back to where we had left the car and ate eggs and coffee in Cabarete, and she asked me, "Are you ready to go look for the house?"

The confidence in her voice surprised me. I'd never heard her speak of the house with anything but hesitation.

Yes, I said hesitantly, I was ready. We set out, armed only with a name on a faded piece of paper: Las Piedras, province of Espaillat.

All day we drove, crisscrossing the roads leading inland from the coast, winding up into the hills and down again. Twice it rained so hard that we had to pull over and wait; one of the windshield wipers was broken. When we stopped to eat—fried plantains and horribly sweet red sodas—or to buy the bright pink gasoline men sold in dirty plastic bottles at the side of the road, we asked if anyone had heard of a place called Las Piedras. The men would confer among themselves, stare at Michelle, and shake their heads no. Once we got a yes—an old man had heard of it, but he couldn't tell us where it was. A discussion ensued: It's near Arroyo de Peña. No, it's not; it's near Gaspar Hernandez. No, it's in Moca.

It wasn't on our map. We thanked them and went on.

The sun climbed high in the sky and began to descend again. Neither of us was tired. Our purpose was clear: to proceed. Each mile we drove and each word we spoke was heavy with the weight of its own direction: We are moving this way and not that, we are doing this and not that, we are laying down a path like the laying of rail across unbroken countryside. Irrevocable. I felt a little frightened. Whatever happened now would happen all the way.

We found the village at sunset. The deed to the house had listed the wrong province; we'd been looking too far afield. Las Piedras was off the Sabaneta road, less than twenty minutes inland, but unmarked by any government sign. Above the doorway of the cinder-block general store someone had painted its name with red paint: COLMADO PEÑA, and under that as an afterthought: LAS PIEDRAS.

Las Piedras: the stones. It was a crossroad of mud. We drove up the narrow road that led into the village, and the sound of our car in the muddy ruts brought people to their doorways. "Is there a very old house near here?" I asked. "A house that belongs to gringos?" They stared at me; a woman said something to a child, and the child ran out of the house; other children followed. "*Ven,*" one called over her shoulder, and they ran up the road ahead of us, climbing a hill, racing down the other side dodging mud puddles and stones. I drove slowly behind them.

They led us over a second muddy hill, and then the children stopped and surged back around the car, looking in. I shut off the engine, and Michelle and I climbed out. The sky was a deep soaked blue. Soon it would be dark. We were at the edge of a cow pasture that sloped up a grassy hill strewn with rocks. At the top of the hill, black against the setting sun behind it, stood the remains of a house.

The foundation and part of the wooden frame and the roof beam were all that was left, a broken skeleton.

I looked at Michelle. All the children in the village were staring at her. It might have been the first time they'd seen a white woman up close. There she was in their midst, feet apart, hands clasped behind her back, the children staring as if she'd come down from the sky. Her face was turned up toward the glowing hills. The expression on her face, that absence, you might easily mistake it for calm.

"Michelle," I said, "Michelle—" and watched as she brought herself back. She gave me a blank look. "Let's climb the hill," I said.

There was a low ditch between the road we stood on and what looked like the remains of a graded road leading up the hill. If it had once been graveled, the gravel had long since washed into the meadow; I stepped over the ditch and sank up to my ankles in mud on the other side. The children laughed. Michelle giggled and bent over to undo her sandals.

We started up the hill, and one of the children called after us, "*¡Muchacha!*"

Michelle turned around. A skinny girl—they were all skinny—was twisting her finger in her hair and looking up at us.

"*Es que, pa'allá es una casa grimosa.*"

"*¿Cómo?*" asked Michelle.

The girl repeated herself.

"Tollomi, what's '*grimosa*?'"

"She means the house is haunted," I said.

Michelle looked up at the house and down at the girl. "My grandparents used to live up there," she said in Spanish.

"But they don't now," the child said warily. "Nobody does."

"It was a long time ago," said Michelle. She looked up at the house again.

"Ghosts live up there now," the girl insisted.

Michelle squatted down so that her eyes were on the same level as the child's. "Look," she said, "have you seen these ghosts?"

"I don't have to see them."

"You haven't seen them because they only come out at night," said Michelle patiently. "During the day they're afraid of everything. So you don't have to worry."

"But it's almost dark." The girl twisted her hair in her fingers.

Michelle looked at me.

"We'll only stay a few minutes," I said to the child. "We'll come back and get in the car when it gets dark. Don't worry."

The girl raised her eyebrows and shrugged, and I thought I could see exactly how she would look when she was old.

"Don't worry," said Michelle cheerily. "The ghosts won't get us. See you later. Tollomi, come on."

We started through the mud, up the hill into the dusk. The children stood at the base of the road and watched us go.

The house stood on the crest of the hill beside an enormous mango tree. The foundation was of stone and cement, cracked but not badly. The corner poles were made of wood, but it was impossible to tell what kind; they'd been completely covered over the years by some kind of climbing vine. The roof beam was still there, held up by dangerously few supports. The walls themselves were long gone: Ghosts or no ghosts, people need wood, and the island has been so badly deforested that it's illegal to cut down trees; all wood is wildly expensive. The walls, and whatever the roof had been made of, had probably been carried off years ago, to use in building houses down in the village.

I pulled the vines away from one of the corner posts and thumped on the beam. It was soft with rot. The roof beam would be rotten too, then. I climbed up onto the foundation and walked to the far edge and looked down. The hill fell away steeply below me. Far below, at the bottom of the hill, almost lost in the dusk, the ground was shining. It was a river, a broad, splendid river winding like a fat snake around the cut of the hillside. I followed it with my eyes between the hills, across the lowlands, a bright strip of silver in the darkening plain.

"Michelle!" I yelled. "Michelle, come up here!"

She climbed up beside me and looked down at the river. "It's beautiful," she said. "Do you think they knew about it?"

"Who?"

"My grandparents."

"They must have. How could anyone miss it? Look there, on the far side. That's all banana groves."

She frowned. "Nobody ever said anything about a river."

"You think this isn't the right place?"

"Oh, no," she said quickly, "this is it. Can't you feel it?"

It was a serious question, so I closed my eyes and tried. I felt the soft wind of evening. I felt the cool slab of cement underfoot. I felt Michelle beside me, anxious that I should perceive it as she did and feel that slight electrical pulse in the air, that shiver, that sense of presence—I knew what it was, but I didn't feel it at all. I couldn't. I opened my eyes.

"Don't you feel it?" she asked.

"Yes," I lied, and Michelle slapped me hard on the arm.

"Mosquito," she said, and wiped her hand on her jeans.

"Caught," I said, and she laughed.

"Tollomi. Let's spend the night up here."

"And wait for the ghosts?"

She smiled and gave a slow nod.

So we went back down the hill to get her tent out of the car. It was almost completely dark now, and the children were nowhere to be seen.

We pitched the tent and found branches to use for the missing stakes. Then we walked back into the village and bought some fried chicken at the cafeteria. Everyone stared, but no one asked us anything, silenced by the utter strangeness of a gringa in their midst. If I'd been alone, they would have asked. We took the chicken to go and climbed back up the hill and ate inside the tent. We didn't talk. Just yesterday morning I had pulled her drowning from the water. She had left, she had come back, and I had touched and lost my childhood world again. A day and a half wasn't enough time to hold all that. I was exhausted.

We went to bed soon after, lying side by side on her open sleeping bag with the soft walls of the tent arched above us.

"Tollomi?"

It was completely dark inside the tent; I couldn't see her at all. "Yes?"

"It's true, then? What you told me about the dream I had. Your mother really drowned?"

"Yes."

She was silent for so long, I wondered if she'd fallen asleep.

"So did he push her, or didn't he?" she said suddenly.

"What? Did who push who?"

"Your father, or whatever you call him. The shipping magnate. Did he push your mother overboard?"

Everything stopped—the frogs, the wind, my heartbeat. Everything froze motionless while her question stumbled and echoed its way into my heart and took hold.

"I don't know," I said. "I don't know if he pushed her. I never thought about it before."

"But you said—" She fell silent.

"What did I say?"

"Tollomi, I'm sorry, I didn't mean to ask something that would upset you. I just—the way you told it, I thought you thought he did."

"What did I say?"

She coughed. "I don't remember now."

"Try."

"I don't know. Maybe you didn't say anything. I don't know why I asked you in the first place. I'm sorry, Tollomi, really. I'm sorry, I—"

"It's all right," I said. "Forget it."

"I don't even know why I thought that. I don't think I was even listening when you were telling me."

"Michelle, it's all right. Forget it, okay?"

She sighed. "Okay." She rolled over, and then in a little while I knew from her breathing that she had fallen asleep. But for me the night was just beginning. I lay there replaying the story I had told her that morning in the hotel, my own story. What had I said without knowing it? What had she dreamed? I thought of my father the shipping magnate, now an old man in a house somewhere in France. What did he dream of? I thought of Josephine, who must have known what had really happened; she could have told me before she died. She might have told me, had I not disappeared so completely from her life. Josephine who lay buried in the earth in a grave that had lost its marker to the storm, Josephine whom I would never see or speak to or dream of even, ever again.

I must have fallen asleep at last, for some time later I woke to Michelle shaking my arm. "What?" I said. "What's wrong?" My heart was pounding hard.

"Tollomi?"

"Michelle, what's wrong?"

"Tollomi. We have to fix the house." Her voice was blurry with sleep.

"Fix it?" I was relieved and annoyed. She was half-dreaming.

The sleeping bag rustled as she turned toward me and sat up. "Build it. I want to make it a house again."

"All right, Michelle, fine."

"I'm awake," she said. "Listen." She poked me in the ribs. "I'm serious, Tollomi."

"Build it out of what? Mud? *Cana* leaves?"

"Out of wood. The way it used to be."

"All right," I said, "we'll do it," and then she lay down again. In a moment she was back to sleep. I thought she wouldn't remember it in the morning.

In the morning came the problem of breakfast. There were no mangos on the mango tree; it was the wrong time of year. Michelle had a few packages of broken saltines in her satchel; she'd gotten them in the airport, she said, so we ate those, sitting on the edge of the cement foundation.

As we finished the crackers, the children from the village began to appear along the crest of the hill. "There were no ghosts," I called out, but they all hung back along an invisible circumference known only to themselves and stood there and stared as Michelle wandered around and around the foundation of the house, looking up at the rotten wood and running her hands along the edge of the cement. After a while she came back to where I was sitting.

"The foundation is good," she said. "We could lay floorboards right on top of it and sink poles for the corner posts. We could make the roof out of palm thatch—*cana*."

" 'We?' You and me?"

"We could hire people to help us. We can start as soon as we get the wood." She was waving her hands in the air.

"And where do we get the wood from? You can't just waltz over that hill and chop down a tree." And I started to tell her how most of the island had been deforested under Trujillo. She nodded impatiently, not listening. "All the wood has to be ordered from overseas now," I said, "and it costs a fortune. You can't make a house out of wood here."

"We could buy the wood on the black market, then."

I didn't bother to reply to that. I asked her if there were any more crackers.

"Tollomi, we can. I know who we can talk to."

"Come on, Michelle. How would you know that?"

"It's somebody I met on the beach. Why are you laughing?"

"Michelle, the black marketeer. Michelle, the French connection…"

"Yeah, yeah. Well, this guy is some friend of José Luis's."

"José Luis has friends? I thought he just had fistfight partners."

"Tollomi, listen. We were all sitting on the oyster-diving rocks one day when you were off somewhere with Carlitos, and this guy was telling me how sometimes lumber gets washed ashore. Not broken stuff, good wood. The oil tankers coming up from South America use wooden boards to keep the oil barrels from rolling around. When they get to wherever they're going, they just dump the lumber overboard. Some of it washes ashore here. Then these guys get it off the beach and hide it until it dries out. Then they sell it."

"All right," I said, "look. Suppose there is all this lumber that's been washed ashore from God knows where, and some boy who's running for the black market is going to sell it to you. Where are we getting the money to pay for all this wood? From me?"

"Of course not." She smiled beatifically. "I'll get a job."

"Doing what?"

"Anything. It's the tourist season, isn't it?"

"There's no work even for the Dominicans."

"I'm an American. Besides, if anyone can go off and come back with a job, I can." She looked at me and frowned. "Besides, Tollomi, what are you so afraid of?"

It was an odd thing to say. I was about to tell her so when I did feel it, a cold finger of fear sliding down my chest.

But it's not my fear, I thought. It's yours, Michelle, it's your fear I have inside me. You don't know it.

So this is what I dreamed of, this is the house.

This strange ruin the children will not come near, this vine-covered rotting wreck overlooking a cow pasture. This is where they were, my grandparents. When the house had walls they sat within them and drank rum while outside the wind shook the mango tree and the rain came in through the roof. And now I'm here. Two days ago I thought I was leaving this island forever. I had a plane ticket, I had it in my hand. Now I'm sitting up in the mango tree and looking out through the leaves at this house. And I see I was completely wrong about leaving. Leaving is impossible. I was meant to be here. If you step off the path, everything you were meant to encounter steps off too. I have Tollomi's passport in the sling around my neck. It's the same color as mine, blue— blue: color of eyes, ocean, sky, and America. It's an American passport. Born on St. Croix, largest of the U.S. Virgin Islands, thus a U.S. citizen. Mother—American, father—debatable. On paper it would say his father, too, is American, meaning white, from the States. Not Cruzan, not Puerto Rican, not African. Not black. But there is another possible father somewhere. Nobody knows who he is. As nobody knows who Tollomi is. As Tollomi makes himself incognito, seems to belong every-where, belongs to nowhere, feels himself nowhere, feels that his real self is in a place that is no longer real.

He refused to speak of it, and it howled in his thoughts. What he banished from his thoughts appeared in his dreams. When he stopped dreaming, the dream went somewhere else. And I woke up in the sea.

"I don't believe you," I said when he told me. I do believe him. That other place is real. My whole life is there. Everything I know but cannot remember is in that place, waiting, restless or gathering dust, waiting to come into this world and inhabit a form, a shape, a name. But I don't know where, I don't know what. I can't think about it beyond a certain point—beyond that point everything gets foggy like a picture going out of focus.

I look at the ruined house before me, at the banana groves on the other side of the river. I look toward the sea. When I look into Tollomi's eyes, my skin prickles. It's the same feeling as before a storm, when the light turns wrong, dark and bright at the same time, and you look up and see the seabirds flying inland, and in the air itself you can feel the pressure drop.

Weather, this is where I start talking about the weather. I get to a certain point and change the subject.

"Tell me about your grandparents," Tollomi says. He wants to know what kind of people—young, just married, supposed to be settling down and having babies—would pack everything up to move to a remote house in a tiny country they couldn't have found on a map even, before beginning the adventure.

"What were they like?" he asks.

So I tell him again what he already knows, that they had money in the thirties and forties and then lost it: My grandfather had drunk it away by the time my mother was in her teens. By the time she got married they were already old. When I was born they moved in with us.

"No," Tollomi says. "I mean, what do you remember about them?" As soon as he's said it, he wishes he hadn't. He keeps forgetting it's not a good question to ask me.

"Sorry," he says. "I meant—"

I shush him and pretend to think. I cast down a hall of locked doors, looking for one ajar, for a sliver of light between the door and the frame. There was a photo of my grandfather that hung in that house somewhere, by the stairs maybe. He was a big man, not fat but weighty, like a large animal. I can imagine that photo of him better than the man himself. He had very striking hair, he wasn't at all bald, he had beautiful thick hair that was pure white. He'd run his hands through it, and it stood up around his face like a mane. Yes, I remember him doing that. Not from the photo—he wasn't doing that in the photo, I really remember it. He used to run his fingers through his hair, I remember this, a single, animated gesture, a real memory. It's not something anyone would have told me. It's something I know, his white hair, his hands: well-kept nails, fingers solid, knotted, his palms as smooth as a child's. Supple, eternally strong.

"I remember his hands," I say aloud. "He had beautiful hands."

I thought she would forget about building the house. I thought she would wander into the village and get involved in something, get invited for lunch at the home of some of the children maybe, and then spend the day sitting in a straight-backed chair in someone's yard, drinking coffee and watching the chickens run around. The time would pass like air, unnoticed, and she'd promise to go back the next day for lunch, and then the day after; she'd stay all afternoon, meet other people, let the village envelop her like warm water and forget all about building the house.

I was wrong.

In the morning she goes off looking for a job. She takes the car and drives to Cabarete, Sosúa, Puerto Plata. At the end of the day she comes back and asks if I need the car tomorrow, because if I don't, she wants it; she's heard about another place where she should try to get hired—a travel agency, this one is, or a new restaurant.

"Take the car," I say. "I don't need it. Just let me ride with you as far as Sosúa."

Making the drive from Las Piedras to Sosúa is like watching a time-lapse film on the history of modernization. We start in Las Piedras, a village bisected by one dirt road. When we turn onto the paved road and pick up speed, suddenly time speeds up with us. First the local stores spring into view, wooden stands selling liquor and soda and fried chicken. Then we hit Cabarete and a frenzy of construction: hotels, restaurants, gift boutiques. Years of development compress into moments as we whiz by, and then at last we reach Sosúa: pavement, telephone poles, indoor plumbing. We have arrived at the present. It's perhaps forty minutes from Las Piedras to Sosúa. History happens so fast.

I make my way through a sea of pale-skinned bodies down the road to the town beach. I haven't seen Carlitos since the night we went dancing and José Luis got into a fight, but today Carlitos will be here, I feel certain of it. The beach is packed. This is the busiest week of the year, the week between Christmas and New Year's; he could make a lot of money off this crowd.

He's here. I see him far off, standing in the sand with his pail at his feet, talking to some people sitting in beach chairs. He's too far away for me to see his face, but I know it's him. The blurry shape bending down and lifting the pail has a quality of movement I recognize. My blood speeds up. I can't just walk up to him. I don't know if he wants to see me. I start down the beach, walking toward him but closer to the water, with the little flat waves breaking over my ankles. I'll let him see me, but give him the option of pretending not to.

"Tollomi! Tollomi!"

He runs after me, catches my arms so hard I nearly fall over. Carlitos!

"Where have you been?" he asks. He's laughing, patting me on the back. His hands are warm.

"Where have *you* been?" I say. "I haven't seen you since the night we went dancing. The next day you weren't here. I was beginning to think you'd found another English teacher."

"No." His brown eyes show relief and hurt. "I went to the hotel where you were staying, and they said you'd gone."

I tell him about finding the ruins of the house in Las Piedras and Michelle wanting to camp there.

"Michelle," says Carlitos, shaking his head ruefully. "*Ay ay ay.*"

I tell him Michelle is out looking for a job, that she has this idea she's going to fix the house up.

"There is a house?" Carlitos asks.

"A ruin. She wants to build a new house on top of it."

"*Build* a house?" He laughs. He's not making fun of her. He just doesn't know what to make of this at all.

"It's a fantasy," I say. "She's just having fun. It's a game, something to think about. She won't really do it. The house is nothing more than a bunch of rotten beams. But it's right on a river, on a hill by a river, and the river's beautiful. Do you want to see it? Why don't you come back with us?"

I'm nervous. He's making me nervous. "Come back with us and see it. We've bought a new stove, and Michelle and I spent yesterday in Gaspar Hernandez getting things for camping—pots and dishes and mattresses. We'll cook you dinner on it—on the stove, I mean."

He smiles at me, the smile disappears. He presses his lips together. "I can't," he says. "José Luis—I can't."

"What about José Luis? He'll survive a few hours without you. Just come for dinner. I'll drive you back after."

"No," says Carlitos, "tonight is no good. I'll come another night. I'll cook for you, you and Michelle, spaghetti. I make good spaghetti. All right?"

"All right," I repeat, wondering what is going on.

"Good," he says, picking up his pail. "Let me sell the rest of this beer. Don't go anywhere. I'll be right back. Then we can swim, all right?"

"Yes," I say. "*Claro.* Fine."

We swim a long time, we sit on the sand and have an English lesson, we go swimming again. When we get out of the water I feel light-headed.

In English Carlitos says, "When you come here again?"

"Will you be here tomorrow?"

"If no—¿*cómo se dice llover?*"

"Rain," I say, pulling on my shirt.

"If no rain…I am come here…*todos los días, caballero, ya sabes.*" He's here every day unless it's raining, I should know that by now.

I put out my hand and rub his head. His crown of wiry hair feels like my own. The hairs all over my body stand up as if in recognition.

"Hey," he protests, ducking out from under my hand. He jumps to one side and lunges for my head as if we're going to wrestle, which in my sudden state of arousal is not a good idea.

"See you soon," I say hurriedly, walking backward, away from him, nearly tripping over a girl lying facedown on a towel, "*Chau, no' vemo'*— Excuse me, I'm sorry, I didn't see you there—¡*Carlitos, NOS VEMOS!*" and I turn around and run. I have no idea what time it is, but it's late; I'm late for meeting Michelle.

We fall into a new pattern, Michelle and I. She goes job hunting, and I go to Sosúa to see Carlitos. I don't want to think about what I'm doing, coming to the beach day after day, as years ago when I was younger I could take myself again and again to men's bodies and not think about what I was doing or what it meant. In those days I could make love with every nerve and pore violently awake, but all the time keeping my mind shut off, hanging onto that blankness like an exhausted man hanging onto sleep, unwilling to wake into an awareness of my surroundings and what they might mean.

Now, of course, I know exactly what they mean: I am gay and I want Carlitos. I could trick him into it; I've tricked people into far more than going to bed with me. I could get him drunk but not too drunk, start talking about sex, keep talking, watch his trousers bulge, suggest something, and somehow it would happen. He would do it with his mind shut off, not thinking, and afterward my mouth would taste like metal, and he would never speak to me again. Not worth it.

So I lock this want inside myself, I swallow it. Day after day we spend the whole afternoon together, and I never let anything slip. We swim at the town beach; we walk through Sosúa and out to the oyster-diving rocks, and if no one's there we lie in the sun, our bodies maddeningly close, Carlitos asking me what this or that is called in English, asking how do you say this, singing snatches of songs popular at the moment. His hands linger on my shoulder, my arm, my knee, when he touches me, to make a point or simply out of affection. There exists in this country a habit of touch between men, so for Carlitos, his touch means nothing; he'd never imagine that for me these gestures are heavy with innuendo. I receive each caress of his fingers as the sand receives water. I soak them up and they vanish. I swallow hard. I manage to grin at him while inside I feel myself bursting and desire riots up and down my loins.

At sunset he goes home. He still hasn't showed me where he lives, the room somewhere in Charamicos that he shares with José Luis in the house of relatives. He hasn't taken me to meet his mother, who lives somewhere outside Charamicos, farther down the coast. That he has not even invited me to his house for dinner would be considered almost unspeakably rude under normal circumstances, but the dynamic of our friendship has quietly slipped over into a murky tension that is in itself unspeakable. Carlitos feels it, perhaps without knowing it;

he can't even name the thing that's developing between us, but he's ashamed of its existence. And so he's afraid to bring me among his family, his friends.

I see José Luis when he comes for Carlitos, but this is not often. Usually, Carlitos takes care to leave me before José Luis finishes work. But now and again Carlitos loses track of the time, and then his brother comes down the beach looking for him. Instantly, Carlitos is nervous, awkward, digs his toe in the sand. José Luis rarely speaks more than the curt "Carlitos, we have to go." It almost amuses me, his dislike of me, because he himself does not know what it is founded on. His jealousy of me for somehow usurping the role of big brother is perhaps clear to him, but still hidden from his mind is the way Carlitos looks at me, the way I, if I'm not careful, look at Carlitos. Though nothing more than looks have passed between us, they have acquired a faint electricity that starts deep within us and ignites when it reaches our eyes. And José Luis sees this without knowing what it is he's looking at. He only knows that he dislikes me, that I bother him.

I say it *almost* amuses me; my own dislike of him keeps me from enjoying the situation. It's an effort to be sociable toward him; I can do it, of course, but I have to think about it.

"An extra-long English lesson?" he asks now, not too snidely. He's being generous today; half the time he doesn't speak to me at all.

"No," I say easily, "Carlitos is too good a student." I glance at Carlitos, who looks away. "He learned everything I planned to teach in the first half-hour, so afterward we went swimming. Pretty soon he'll be speaking English better than I do."

"Oh, yeah?" says José Luis in English, his mustache rising above a curled lip. "And then what?"

"How do you mean?"

"There's a saying here," says José Luis. "Have you heard it? *'Él que no va a los Estados Unidos muere inocente.'*"

He who does not go to the United States dies innocent. "I've heard it," I answer, and the emotion in my voice surprises me; I didn't mean for it to be there. José Luis hears it too; he looks at me for a moment as if he'd never seen me before, his dark eyes suddenly soft the way his brother's always are. Then he blinks and looks away.

"Nobody's talking about going to the United States," Carlitos says nervously. "How would you know anyway, José? You've never been there."

"*Inocente* doesn't mean stupid," says José Luis. "Let's go, Carlitos. We're late."

I found a job. Bea Castillo told me where to go. It's a bar in Puerto Plata, a gringo bar but not really a tourist one. It's in the center of town, and the gringos who go there are all locals, Americans and Canadians and Europeans who live here year round.

The owner is an American named Sam Johnson. When we met, he extended his hand and said, "Call me Sam." In the States he would have said, "I'm Mr. Johnson," but here in Puerto Plata he sees us as intimates: We're both white. So we belong to the same club. He's that kind of man.

He doesn't have the pallid nocturnal complexion of most bar owners. Weekends he spends at the harbor working on his boat—his nose and his cheeks are permanently sunburned. The scorched pink and the peeling skin distract from the broken capillaries beginning to cluster on his nose. When he first appears for the day, his graying blond hair is impeccably combed. By the time he's given me the money for the register and had a drink and talked with the first customers of the day, his hair has gone limp in the heat. It's fallen over one eye by mid afternoon.

There's only one Dominican who comes in here: Sonya, the girl who comes in every morning to clean. She's young, not more than twelve or thirteen. While I set up the bar, she mops the floor and bleaches the toilets. She works gravely, silently, her child's hands skating the scrub brush over the floor with the deft, automatic movements of an adult. When she finishes she goes upstairs to collect her money from Sam, and then I don't see her again until the next day. She leaves by some other door. The floor Sonya scrubs, the bar floor, is the first wooden floor I've seen on the island. The whole building is wood, both the bar and the apartments upstairs. It must have been built a long time ago when there were more trees. The walls in the bar are wood also, and every available inch of space is decorated. The front walls are draped with fishing nets and glass floats, wooden ship's pulleys, rope, and anchor chains. On the bar itself two little iron anchors sit, one at either corner. They're too small to be real—they're propped up on little iron stands like bookends. The varnish on the bar top around them is chipped from when the anchors get knocked down.

Toward the rear of the bar, the nautical motif peters out and a dusty collection of American license plates takes over the back wall. Hung amidst the license plates are thumbtacked posters of bikini-clad women, arching their backs and drinking various brands of beer. Out front above the tables several old wooden ceiling fans are suspended. When I come in in the morning I turn these on.

"You do it, not Sonya," Sam said when he was showing me around. He also told me not to feed the bird, which lives in a cage that hangs from the ceiling behind the bar. I don't know what kind of bird it is. It's very big, with a bill like a parrot's, but it's pure white and doesn't talk. It doesn't sing either, or even croak. Its eyes follow me as I move up and down the bar working. It's too large for its cage.

When I ask Sonya how long the bird's been hanging there, in her ancient child's voice she answers, "*Siempre.*" It's been there forever.

I picture my grandparents here, fifty years ago, sitting in a bar like this one. A bar where time is like dust, gathering on everything and changing nothing. What would they do here in this bar? My grandfather would pick out "his" table and sit there with my grandmother and begin getting drunk. And my grandmother? After an hour or so of straight drinking my grandmother might get bored just sitting. She'd excuse herself, maybe say she was going to the ladies' room. She'd disappear in there for a while, and then when she came out she wouldn't go back to the table—she'd sit at the bar and talk to the bartender. She'd order gin and tonic and tell the bartender she was only drinking it for the quinine. "I don't want to catch malaria down here," she'd say. Something like that.

Looking around this bar, at the tables filling and emptying with people, at the liquor bottles growing lighter in my hands as the shift wears on, it occurs to me that my grandparents could in fact have been here in this very bar. When they were here in the forties, this could have been a bar and they could have sat in it. It looks old enough. I mean to ask Sam when it was built, but I keep forgetting.

I have two night shifts and two day shifts. At the end of my first week, with surplus money in my pockets for the first time in quite a while, I go to the hardware store in Puerto Plata. I look at nails, hand-saws, bags of cement. I look at them in the same way I would look at train schedules, at the prices of airplane tickets. Such options, there for anyone who has the cash. And it occurs to me that perhaps building a house is not some big mystery that only certain people have the skill to master—it isn't that at all. It's like traveling: Only certain people have the will to start.

The hard part is starting. Once you start, then you're doing it, you're moving, you're on your way. What happens out there? You don't know in advance. Even if you have a map, blueprints, a plan.

The man behind the counter in the hardware store is watching me. He asks if I need help. I buy a hammer. I don't have the car with me, so I can't buy anything heavy or big. But a hammer is enough for now. It's the start.

He takes my money, wondering what this gringa could possibly want with a hammer, but he doesn't ask and I don't tell him.

I like how it feels in my hand. The swing of it: solid, heavy.

I want Tollomi to see where I work. I tell him what it's like, about Sam, about the customers, about how I'm getting a reputation for making cocktails that no one drinks down here, things like old-fashioneds, Manhattans, Rob Roys. The regulars like it; they say they're sick of all this "froufrou shit with umbrellas," meaning margaritas and chi-chis and piña coladas and so forth. Fine, I say, there's your martini, straight up, two olives, breath of vermouth, just the way you like it.

Whatever faults my memory has, I'll say this for it: It never forgets a drink. I used to make them for my father and my grandfather when I was young. They showed me how and then I did it myself and it became a joke, how well I could do it, being so young and all. I don't remember doing it, of course. My grandmother told me. But I remember the drinks.

I ask Tollomi to come pick me up at work some evening when I get off early. We'll have a drink at Sam's and then we'll go out somewhere, I say.

He says he'll give me the car, and then I can drive myself back; that way I won't have to wait for him.

I don't want a ride, I say, I want you to see the bar. You could come during the day and bring Carlitos. Shake things up a little. These guys are in the Dominican Republic, after all—they ought to sit next to a Dominican once in a while.

"No," says Tollomi. "Definitely not. No scenes."

"So come alone, then."

He doesn't say anything. I ask him what's the matter.

"Nothing's the matter, Michelle."

"Don't want to see where I work?"

"Of course—it isn't that."

"What is it, then?"

"All right," he says tiredly. "You work the day shift tomorrow? I'll come in with you in the morning. I'll be your first customer. All right?"

"All right," I say, feeling confused.

When we get to the bar and I pull out the keys, Tollomi looks surprised. "You've only been here a week and he's given you the keys?" he asks.

"Just to the front door. Not the liquor room." I open the padlock and unlock the deadbolt, and we go in. We must have just missed Sonya; the floor is still wet from her mopping, as if it had rained inside during the night. I pull the stools off the bar and tell Tollomi to sit. He perches, taking in the fishnets, the little iron anchors on top of the bar, the girly beer ads, the feel of trashy Americana the whole place subtly exudes. He frowns, makes a sucking sound with his teeth.

"It's a job," I say.

"I know," he says quickly. "I know, it's fine. Make me a drink?"

"I have to get the ice first."

I come back lugging the ice bucket in time to see Sam thump down the stairs in flip-flops and freshly combed hair. He doesn't see me, and he stops on the bottom stair and stares at Tollomi. I can see the words forming on his reddening face: *What the hell is this Dominican doing in here?*

"Sam," I say loudly, "this is Tollomi."

He frowns at me. "The bar's not open yet. I don't want you letting customers in early."

Tollomi clears his throat and slides rather stiffly off the stool. In two strides he's standing before Sam, extending his hand and saying, "Tollomi DeHaas," in a slightly nasal voice I've never heard before.

Sam's hand comes out as if of its own accord and lets Tollomi shake it.

"So you're the boss," Tollomi says heartily, "Sam, it is? Michelle's told me about your place here."

"Sam Johnson," says Sam, flustered for only a second before switching gears: "Good to meet you, ah…"

"Bartholomew DeHaas," Tollomi says.

"DeHaas. Siddown, siddown. A fellow American? Good, good. Siddown. What are you drinking?"

I see a flash of something cross Tollomi's face. He's trying to remember something. "Scotch and soda, twist," he says.

"Well, whaddaya know. Whaddaya know! That's my drink. Did Michelle tell you that?"

"It's all I ever drink," says Tollomi.

He never drinks Scotch. At least I've never seen him drink it. Did I tell him it's what Sam drinks? I don't remember.

"Michelle," says Sam pointedly.

"Coming up," I answer. I make the drinks and notice I feel a little ill.

"Cheers," says Tollomi, and raises his glass.

I turn away from them and concentrate on setting up the bar. I can half-hear Tollomi going on in this odd voice, a flattened-out voice that isn't his. Is this the voice of boarding school in New England? It makes me feel cold. I pull the bottles, I start cutting the limes, I don't listen, and then after a while I don't hear them anymore, I'm somewhere else.

When I find myself back again, I'm standing at the sinks with a jar of cocktail onions in my hand. The bar is all set up now and their voices are back in my ears.

"What kind of boat?" says one of the voices. It's Tollomi's but not the Tollomi I know.

"Old Sparkman & Stephens thirty-two footer," says Sam's voice, "all oak and mahogany. A beautiful, beautiful boat. She's a sloop I had yawl-rigged so I could sail her more easily single-handed. She's really a beaut. You should come down and see her sometime."

"I'd love to," says Tollomi, sounding genuinely excited. "Where's she moored?"

"Right down the street at Port Authority. There's a yacht club at Luperón, but it's too far away. I like to keep her right where I can see her."

"In Port Authority with the freighters?"

"They got a little dock there too, DeHaas. I'm the only yachtsman they let tie up there. I know people. All the other yachtsmen have to go to Luperón—hey, Michelle. Two more, eh?"

"Not for me," says Tollomi. "I've got to go. Turn a glass upside down for me, will you, Michelle? A rain check. All right?"

"Anytime," says Sam happily.

I glare at Tollomi. He smiles, not at me, a dull flat fixed smile with his eyes looking past my face. "See you tonight then," he says dully. "Thanks for the drink."

He shakes hands with Sam, who tells him to come back anytime. He walks stiffly to the door as if he were wearing shoes and the shoes were too small.

"Swell guy you got there, hon," Sam says to me. "I gotta say, though, when I first saw him, I thought he was Dominican."

I ignore this. I pick up their two empty glasses and jam them onto the scrubbers. On the bar next to one of the cocktail napkins is an American dollar. Tollomi's left me a tip.

That evening when the relief bartender comes on and I'm ready to go, Sam comes downstairs again. He has my pay in an airmail envelope. When he gives it to me, he says, "I didn't know you were building a house."

"Tollomi—Bartholomew told you that?" I ask.

"A house. Never would have thought it to look at you. A woman of many talents, eh?"

I give an unamused laugh. I'm polite enough to make some sort of response, not so polite that I pretend to enjoy it. He's oblivious anyway.

He goes on, "I stuck a little something in with your pay. For materials."

"What?"

"Michelle, when I started here, what I had was guts. Not money, guts. I built this business up from nothing. You see yourself it's a success. In a few months I'm opening another place in Cabarete, another bar, but with a restaurant attached. I still have guts, but now I've got money too. Now you're starting out and I'm doing all right. So I'll help you a little. Besides, you're a good bartender."

He takes my hand and lifts it up and puts the envelope in it. My fingers close over the money. He has it, I need it.

"Thanks, " I say. I put the envelope in my pocket.

"Don't mention it," says Sam. "You're a good bartender." He smiles.

I get out of the bar fast. I don't know what just happened. I don't feel like I've been given something.

I feel like I gave something away.

"Then why did you take it?" says Tollomi when I tell him about it that evening.

"It's money. He just gave it to me. Because you told him about the house."

"Three thousand pesos? No strings?" He raises an eyebrow.

"I'm not the one who was the prostitute this morning," I say. It just slips out.

"No," he says, "you're the one who got paid." And then almost immediately, "Michelle, I'm sorry."

"Don't apologize. The tip you left was more than generous."

"I told you I didn't want to go in there."

"No, you didn't, Tollomi. I asked you why you didn't want to see the bar, and you told me you did."

"Well, what did you think would happen?" he asks. "Did you bother to think about it?" He folds his arms and raises an eyebrow at me, as if it's my fault that he spent half an hour pretending to be the kind of man I know he despises.

I have nothing to say to that man, so I don't answer.

Later that night while I'm brushing my teeth, he crawls out of the tent and stands beside me. I pass him the toothpaste, but he shakes his head and takes something out of his pocket. "This is yours," he says, grinning, putting it in my hand.

It's a saltshaker.

"I stole it from the bar," he says. "While Sam was talking to me."

"Tollomi, what if he'd seen you? Do you want me to get fired?"

"If he'd seen me, I wouldn't have taken it. But I thought you might want it back. You might be making some guy a Bloody Mary and you might be looking around for the salt—"

I hand it back to him. "Keep it," I say. "Use it to salt your plantains."

Even in the darkness I see him smile. He shakes some salt into the palm of his hand and tosses it over his shoulder. "Thanks," he says.

"Tollomi?"

"Hm."

"Don't come visit me at work anymore. Okay?"

His face turns serious. "I won't," he says. "I promise."

I did go to see Sam's boat. His words stayed in my head—*Sparkman & Stephens, oak and mahogany, original hull*—and I couldn't shake them. I already had a mental picture of what the boat looked like, and despite myself I wanted very much to see it. So before noon, when I knew Sam would still be at the bar having Michelle feed him his morning Scotch, I went down through the alleys crammed with depressing corner stores and dimly lit furniture shops to the dock at the Port Authority. The soldiers in the guard house at the dock's entrance stared as I approached. I forced myself to keep walking, to raise a hand in greeting as I passed. I knew they wouldn't stop me; people could walk on the piers if they liked. Still, my skin prickled cold, and I felt their eyes on my back as I passed.

Then I saw the boat. I forgot about the soldiers. The pounding sun and the smell of diesel and dirty harbor water all faded as my eyes fell on the boat and I stared.

It was easily the most beautiful boat I had ever seen. The mast and the deck and even the hull were of old dark mahogany. The line of the hull was a strong, graceful sweep from high stem to stern, with the cabin seeming to rise naturally from the plane of the deck as if the whole boat had been sculpted from a single block of perfect wood. It had a radiance that only old, well-loved boats ever achieve.

The boat I'd learned to sail on had it too, a sort of living glow. Josephine's boyfriend Henry had a small sloop he fished from, and every moment he wasn't actually sailing, he spent coaxing the boat into staying seaworthy a little longer. The *Lilah* was just an open cat-boat barely half the size of Sam's yawl, with a badly made fiberglass hull that required constant patching. When we sailed her she didn't point high enough, and when we motored, the motor was extremely temperamental. But when I was a child I didn't think of the *Lilah* in terms of her faults. When I was a child the *Lilah* was *the* boat, the image that the word *boat* meant, the standard against which all other boats were measured.

Sam's boat, this beautiful boat before me, would have fallen short in those days, as would have any boat that was not Henry's. I stood now looking at the beautiful thing floating before me that was beautiful not simply because someone had loved it and taken care of it but because it had been built that way, with mahogany and oak and copper and brass, with the long graceful lines that showed an artist's hand. It was a boat for rich people, people who could appreciate such things, people who knew how to enjoy them, who didn't need to make their living catching fish. White people, people who could recognize a Sparkman & Stephens from all the way across the harbor.

I could. I could appreciate it, and I wanted Sam's boat. I wanted to sail it and feel it slice through the water and heel up with almost impossibly perfect grace. I didn't want to want it. I didn't want to be able to recognize it from a distance. I didn't want to know how it would feel under my hands. But I already knew. It was a knowledge almost sexual in its precision. I crouched on the dock and ran my hands over the glossy mahogany deck. Then, without meaning to, I actually stepped aboard and sat in the cockpit. My fingers closed around the tiller and moved it just a little, and I felt the rudder shift, I felt the water pushing back against my hand. I wanted to sail this boat as much as I had ever wanted any lover. I looked down at my brown hand holding the fine smooth wood of the tiller and felt a rush of shame. I had betrayed Henry's old beloved boat with my desire to sail this rich man's toy. Henry dead four years of cancer never caught. Henry who had taught me to sail. Henry whom I hadn't seen since I was thirteen.

I walked back across the asphalt lot, letting it burn my feet. I went across the road out of the Port Authority and down to the *malecón,* where I stood at the rusting rails and looked out at the sea. The long strip of cement and the sliver of pebbled beach below it were deserted. I climbed over the railing and up onto the rocks by the old fort. I left my clothes on the rocks and fell into the water and swam far out, out to where the sea turned dark, and there I dove, surfaced, dove, surfaced, dove for a long time.

"You should set that bird free," Tollomi tells me.

"What bird?" I ask.

"Sam's bird, in the cage over the bar. It must be miserable."

"Yeah, set it free and say what? That it escaped?"

"You should. Tell Sam he must have left the cage door open, and that when you arrived in the morning, the bird just flew out the front door."

"What if it can't fly? He might have clipped its wings."

"It'll fly. Why should he clip its wings when he's got it in a cage?"

So I arrive in Puerto Plata a little early and let myself in. The bird stares at me out of one eye as I climb up on top of the bar. From up there I can see all the dust on the tops of the glass floats and the license plates.

I reach up and turn the brass handle that opens the door of the cage. It's stuck. I jiggle the handle and try to work my fingers through to the other side, but I still can't get it open.

"He always keeps it locked," says a voice behind me, and I almost fall off the bar. It's Sonya. She's come in without making a sound. I feel my face flush hot, but before I can think of what to say she comes around the bar and starts filling the metal bucket with water, as if my standing on top of the bar with my fingers in the birdcage is the most natural thing in the world. I stay where I am and watch the top of her head. She gets the soap, the mop, the scrub brush, and dumps them all in the bucket and lugs it back out front.

"He always keeps it locked?" I hear myself say.

She looks up at me briefly and nods, expressionless.

"Why does he always keep it locked?" I sound like a four-year-old.

"So no one will let the bird out," she says, and for the first time ever I see her smile. She knows she's caught me. I smile back, then. I know she won't tell.

She mops the floor, I set up the bar. Carrying in the ice, I whistle. We're partners in an uncommitted crime. The bird watches.

"I know where the key is," says Sonya after a while.

"Where?" I say, nonchalant. I could steal it, perhaps.

She says it's on a string around Sam's neck.

Sometimes Sonya is there when I arrive and sometimes she isn't. If she has a regular schedule, I can't figure it out. One day, a day that she isn't there, I run out of gin. This happens fairly often: I'll run out of something, and then Sam has to come downstairs and open the liquor room. He makes a great show of getting out the bottles.

I stand at the foot of the stairs that lead up to his apartment and yell: "Sam! There's no more gin. I need the keys. Sa-am!"

But it's Sonya who appears on the top step. She descends cautiously, first knobby knees, then too-large shorts and faded halter top, and last her smooth inscrutable face comes level with mine.

"Sonya, what are you doing up there?"

"I clean his house too," she says, scratching her arm and looking with interest at the customers behind me, "every Saturday."

"Is he up there now?"

"Si—pero está durmiendo."

"He's asleep? It's four in the afternoon."

She shrugs.

I take a few steps up the stairs. "Sam! It's four o'clock! The sun is over the yardarm. Arise!"

The man who ordered the gin—a retired businessman from Miami and owner of the under-construction Hotel Hacienda—laughs.

"Sam's asleep," says Sonya again, meaningfully.

This time I get it. "He's drunk?"

She nods.

I don't know how to say "passed out" in Spanish. "He won't wake up?" I ask.

She shakes her head. Then she says that if he doesn't wake up he won't pay her and her mother is coming to pick her up and she won't have any money.

"When is your mother coming?" I ask.

She says she doesn't know; her mother is cleaning a house in Sosúa, and then she'll take a guagua here to pick her up. Her mother won't let her take the *guagua* alone, Sonya tells me, and so she has to wait. Sometimes her mother gets here on time but sometimes she comes very late. Sometimes she can't come at all because she has to take care of Sonya's father, and then Sonya stays here.

"Here in the bar?" I ask. This is the longest speech I've ever heard her make.

"No," she says, impatient at this detour from the issue of her pay, "upstairs. On a sofa, a big sofa, with pillows." Her mouth lingers over the word "pillows," and I wonder what she sleeps on at home.

"What's wrong with your father?" I ask.

She says her father is in a hospital in another city.

"Santiago?"

She shrugs. I ask her why he's in the hospital. I don't understand her explanation, but from the places she points to on her body it seems to be his lungs.

"So your mother goes away and you stay here all night?"

"Yes," she says. "*¿Y mi pago?*"

"Sonya," I say, "When you're done cleaning upstairs, come back down here. If Sam isn't awake by then, I'll pay you out of the cash register."

Sonya thanks me with a barely audible "*Gracias*" and vanishes back up the stairs like some long-legged bird taking flight.

Mr. Miami yells, "Hey, Michelle, is there gin or what?"

"Or what," I say, going back to the bar. "It's a new drink called 'or what.' One taste and you'll forget gin ever existed. My specialty."

"Lady, I like the way you talk," says Mr. Miami with an unnecessary wink.

Under the lip of the bar, where he can't see, I pour white tequila and white vermouth and peppermint schnapps into a glass. I squirt in tonic water, add a lime, and hand it to him with a flourish.

"It looks like gin and tonic," he says dubiously.

"Trust me," I say, "it isn't."

Michelle talks incessantly of building the house. She drops me off at the beach in Sosúa and then goes to the hardware store to look at tools for an hour before going to work at Sam's. She hangs around construction sites and watches the workers. She doodles equations on scraps of paper, on cocktail napkins that have found their way into her pockets, calculating the cost of building materials. She works at the bar and comes back late at night and crawls into the tent smelling of cigarettes and spilled liquor. In the morning I find a pile of crumpled peso notes on the sheet beside her head.

"We're going to build the house," she says over and over. "Next week," she says, "I'll have some money, I'll get the wood."

She goes to the hardware store, Spanish dictionary in hand, and discusses cement and handsaws with the owner. We're going to build the house, Tollomi. The house.

One day she says, "I did it."

"What did you do?"

"I gave him the money, the guy in town. You know, the black marketeer, the French connection. He says he'll bring the wood up here when he gets it." She folds her arms and smiles regally. Queen Michelle. To her mind, the possibility does not exist that the wood will never be delivered. I can see her talking to this character, the "black marketeer" whose name she says she forgets. I can see her waving her hands around, drawing a map to Las Piedras on a cocktail napkin, explaining where she wants him to deliver the wood. She gives him the cash, just like that, and he goes off shaking his head.

A few nights later we're getting ready for bed when through the din of the frogs comes a man's voice shouting from the hill. I'm in the tent, and Michelle is outside with the flashlight, brushing her teeth. The beam of light sweeps over me as she crosses the yard to see who is there.

I climb out of the tent. Two men—no, three—the third leading a donkey, make their way toward us. Michelle aims the flashlight waist-high to light their way, and the beam makes a bright flash on the metal of the gun protruding from the donkey owner's hip pocket.

"It's all right," Michelle says to me, "it's the guys with the wood."

The men look at her, at me, at one another. The one with the gun in his pocket shifts his feet and announces that they wanted to bring the wood tonight but can't.

"Why not?" Michelle asks.

"*Los tigres*," they tell her.

"Tigers?" repeats Michelle incredulously. "Oh, please."

The men look at her strangely.

"It's Dominican slang for thieves," I tell her.

"All right then: What thieves?"

The men frown at her. They are not used to being questioned, certainly not by a skinny barefoot gringa. Then one of them tells her they'll need more money before they can deliver the wood. They have to pay someone else, they don't have the wood, someone else has it, they have to protect it from *los tigres*, they need more money—*¿Entiende, muchacha?*

Michelle makes a face. "Just tell us where the wood is," she says, "and we'll get it ourselves."

The men look at one another. The one with the donkey lets go of it and takes a step forward. He puts his hand in his hip pocket where the gun is and looks at me.

"Michelle," I say in English, "we have to give them the money."

"I already did," she says. "I don't see why—"

"He has a gun," I say. "We're being mugged. Don't you get it?"

"Oh, for God's sake," she says. "This is ridiculous."

My hands are shaking. I make myself look at the men, and then I close my eyes a moment, trying to understand and become whatever is needed here. There is some money in the tent, and our gear, and there is the tent itself. How the transaction is going to take place is another matter. Not only do they have to win and leave here with what they came for, they have to feel that they won as well, they have to look tough. Waving a gun around is one way of looking tough. There are others too, and I don't know how to get out of this.

"*Señores,*" says Michelle, "we can't do anything now, it's the middle of the night. So why don't you come back in the morning? I don't want to talk about it now."

I open my eyes and stare at her. The men stare at her as well; they can't believe she's saying this. The one with the gun looks at me, and I shrug and hold up my hands: I can't believe it either, pal. And suddenly we are mirrors, this man and I; we have the same expression on our faces.

Like a change in the wind, without warning, the hostility shifts. It blows off in another direction. The man takes his hand off the gun. He shrugs back at me, a "women—what can you do?" shrug.

"Hey," says Michelle suddenly, "your burro is getting away." They all turn around. The donkey has disappeared down the hillside, in search of the short grass where the cows graze, probably.

"*¡Coño!*" says the donkey's owner with great feeling, and starts after it.

"Wait," I say. I take the flashlight from Michelle and hand it to him.

He nods briefly and turns and goes after the donkey, and the four of us stand there watching the beam dart down the hill. After a moment he gives a shout. "*¡Lo tengo! Vámanos.*" The two men nod at us, then turn and go, making their way down the hill toward the light at the bottom. Michelle and I stand there in the darkness.

"Sorry about your flashlight," she says. And then she goes back to brushing her teeth as if nothing happened.

Two days later they're back with the lumber. It's hardwood, of a kind I've never seen before, warped from the sea but not badly. It's all sound. But some of the beams are stained black with oil, and I point this out to Michelle.

"Good," she says simply, "it will keep the termites away."

The earth around the sides of the foundation must be cleared, new cement must be poured, poles sunk, lumber sawed. We work: Michelle, myself, and sometimes Eligio from the village. He's an older man, a carpenter. He can build without power tools or prefabricated ladders, without squares, even. He does own a level, his most cherished possession, which he keeps in his back pocket where it's held in place by the rum bottle he also carries there. Michelle, who has never built anything in her life, watches everything Eligio does, how he mixes the cement, how he digs—first with a pickax, then with a shovel—how he holds the saw. She watches and then she copies him, and then the next morning I'll wake up and find her hard at work, going on with whatever was begun the day before.

"It's not even seven o'clock," I'll tell her.

"I like to start early," she says through a mouthful of nails.

It's hard work; besides our inexperience and lack of power tools there is the sun to contend with. I'm used to working in such heat, as is Eligio, but Michelle gets dizzy by early afternoon. Yet when Eligio goes home for lunch, she wants to keep working. "This is the hottest part of the day," I tell her. "Stop for a while." She does stop, but grudgingly.

"I want to do this," she says. "I want to get this going. How much do you think we can have done by the end of the week?"

Not as much as she'd like; we get two days of heavy rain, which prevents us from making cement, and then she has her two day shifts at Sam's. The next week brings more rain and then a day when Eligio gets drunk and doesn't come. Michelle wants to work anyway; together we saw a pile of boards.

Her hands grow rough from swinging tools all day and red from washing glasses and cutting limes at the bar. I tell her to take a break, relax a little. She ignores me. I tell her I'll cut the boards while she's at work, not to worry about it. She just shrugs. I buy her a pair of work gloves in Puerto Plata. She loses them.

She comes home exhausted and wakes up exhausted but insisting: We have to build, we have to keep building.

Michelle, I'll say, Let's take today off, let's go swimming in Cabarete. Let's go see Lupe Vásquez, I promised her I'd come back and I haven't. Let's go see Bea Castillo, let's go down to the river and swim. Come with me to see Carlitos—

"No," she always answers, "not now, Tollomi. I just want to finish digging this." Hammering this. Cutting this board.

"But you need a day off. You look exhausted."

"Tomorrow," she says. "I just want to get this one thing done."

I offer to stay and help her.

"No," she says, "go on. Tell Carlitos I said hi."

Carlitos and I swim at the town beach, or at the hidden beach, at beaches without names that he knows about, where we have the whole wide stretch of sand and hard surf to ourselves.

There's an easiness about him that pulls me. It's something I once had, an ease in one's surroundings; it's something that can neither be learned nor assumed, nor found once you've lost it. The trees we lie under, the water we swim in, the rice and beans we order from the cafeteria on the beach—he's a part of all of it. It isn't separate from him; his life isn't separate from him; he is all the way in. His skin glows in the sun, his eyes shine with light. I stare at him over my plate of rice and beans and lose track of time.

I get back to Las Piedras late. The sun is setting. Michelle sits by herself up on the far edge of the foundation, leaning against the new corner pole, the first one, sunk yesterday. The old pole is still there beside it, rotten, an old shadow waiting to be cut down. She doesn't hear the car, doesn't see me cross the yard until I'm almost beside her. Then she looks down at me and smiles. There is a smudge of dirt on her cheek. She nods at the stack of newly sawed boards under the mango tree, put there, I suppose, under pretense of keeping them dry. We don't have enough tarpaulins.

"You and Eligio cut all that today?" I ask.

"No," says Michelle, "I cut it myself."

In the morning I wake to the sound of her sawing boards.

"You don't have to help, you know, if you don't want to," she says when I join her.

I tell her not to be silly, of course I'll help.

"I want to get both these corner poles sunk today," she says, "but I don't know if we'll have time. I hope it doesn't rain again. I have to stop at four to get ready to go to the bar."

Watching her makes me uneasy. It's the tone in her voice perhaps, or the way she moves, her habitual vagueness suddenly transformed into an energy so focused it is somehow disturbing, the single-mindedness with which she saws wood, board after board. She eats when I remind her to, goes down to the river and bathes distractedly, her mind on lumber and angles and the price of *cana,* and then in the evening she gets into the car and goes off to work the night shift at Sam's.

"Be careful," I say as she's leaving. Of what I don't know, and she doesn't ask, or answer.

At night I lie by myself in the tent, unable to sleep, trying to pinpoint the apprehension I feel on her behalf. I imagine her in the bar after closing time, sitting there drinking rum after rum. Will she get behind the wheel drunk and try driving home? Along the potholed coastal road that has neither light nor line to mark it, nothing would be easier than to swerve into an oncoming car, a tree.

I lie in the tent imagining car wrecks until at last I hear the sound of the car approaching, breaking through the chorus of frogs. She cuts the engine at the bottom of the hill, and then in a few minutes I hear her moving around outside the tent, stepping out of her shoes, unhurt. Why am I so worried? It's true, every night when she comes in, her skin reeks of the bar, of booze. "Kiss me good night," I say once, my voice blurry with feigned sleep, and she gives me a kiss as a child might, immediate and sweet, and flops down exhausted. There's no liquor on her breath; she hasn't been drinking. So it's not that after all. It's something else.

"Michelle," I say finally, "you have to take a day off. No building. No bar. No work at all. Let's go out and do something. We'll all go out and spend the day together, all right? I insist."

"Who's 'all'?" she asks.

"You and me and Carlitos. Tomorrow."

"I can't tomorrow. If it's sunny, Eligio is coming up to work."

"Saturday, then."

"Saturday I have to work at Sam's."

"Sunday."

She frowns at the house. "You said you'd help me cut the rest of the wood for the frame, remember?"

I hold up my hands, blistered from sawing, and wiggle my fingers.

"I remember," I say. "Michelle, look. I'll cut all of it if you'll come out with us on Sunday."

She gives me a puzzled look, failing to understand why I'm being so insistent. "All right," she shrugs. "I'll come."

That afternoon, on the beach in Sosúa, I tell Carlitos I want the three of us to take a day trip: I want to drive inland, up into the mountains.

"What's there?" he asks, as though it were outer space; though Charamicos is less than a mile wide, it's made him a city boy of sorts.

"Lupe Vásquez," I say. "The woman I told you about. I want us to go see her."

"All right," says Carlitos agreeably. *"Un día en el campo. Sunday? Está bien."*

When I see him Saturday, he tells me José Luis wants to come with us, which surprises me.

"I'd love to have him along," I say carefully, "but usually he's so busy. Why the exception?"

"He wants to meet her. Lupe Vásquez."

"He knows who she is?"

"He wants to meet her," repeats Carlitos. "I guess he heard about her when he was at the university."

"José Luis was at the university?"

"Only a year."

"In Santo Domingo?"

"Yes. He wanted to study political science."

"Why didn't you tell me?"

Carlitos grins and says in English, "You never ask."

He's developed the habit of switching into English when he doesn't want to answer a question. Now he frowns. "Is right? 'You never ask?' "

"Asked," I say. "Past tense. Why didn't he graduate?"

"I guess is lazy," says Carlitos, and then he jumps up and runs into the surf.

On Saturday night Tollomi and I are sitting in the car at the foot of the first hill in Las Piedras. It's raining, hard, and the ground is too wet and muddy to get the car up the rest of the road to the house. So we're just sitting there watching the rain stream over the windshield. It's getting dark, and the sight of all that water is being replaced by its sound, a steady drumming everywhere, tinny on the car roof like millions of small nails being dropped.

"Look at this," says Tollomi, meaning the sky. "It won't blow over by tomorrow. You won't be able to build anyway."

"I already said I'd come with you," I tell him. Though in fact the sky could very possibly be clear tomorrow and he knows it. But I said I'd come. I don't know what's wrong with Tollomi. He seems afraid to go without me, or afraid to let me out of his sight. Afraid of something.

"Michelle," says Tollomi sharply.

"What?"

"You're not listening," he says. Not angry. Worried.

"What's the matter?"

He shakes his head and asks if I want to walk back out to the main road, even though it's raining, and have a Coke. There's a sort of café there with a few tables. You can sit there and drink Coke or beer with ice in plastic glasses.

I say I want to, not because I do; in fact, I drank Cokes all day at the bar. But I want to make him happy, so I say a Coke would be good and then he smiles.

There are some empty garbage bags in the car that we use for umbrellas. Holding these over our heads we step out into the evening rain and the cold mud of the road.

The next morning it's still raining, but on the way to Charamicos it starts to slack off. By the time we pick up Carlitos and José Luis, the sun is shining. I think of my lumber waiting for me under the mango tree. Three of the corner poles are sunk, and I've begun building the frame between them. If the weather stays dry, I'll mix the cement for the fourth one this afternoon. Once the frame is in place, we can start making the roof. I was right about building—the hard part was the getting-started. I've started; now it's simply a matter of movement, movement forward. I'm building a house.

The sun is shining, why did I say I'd go with them? I don't even want to meet this Lupe Vásquez. If we get back to Las Piedras by three, I should have enough time to sink the last corner pole before dark. I drive a little faster.

"Michelle, slow down," Tollomi says, and turns all the way around in his seat and addresses José Luis. "Carlitos says you were at the University of Santo Domingo," he starts.

"For a year." José Luis mumbles.

"And you studied with Jorge Vásquez?"

"He wasn't teaching anymore when I was there."

"But you knew him?"

"I just told you," says José Luis, irritated. "He wasn't—"

"I thought you might have studied Taino with him," says Tollomi.

"Taino? How do you know about that?"

I glance in the rearview mirror. José Luis's habitual bored scowl has changed to a look of surprise.

Tollomi tells him some story about a man on a ship, a sailor he met somewhere.

"Who was it?" says José Luis, and when Tollomi tells him a name he mutters, "Sí, el maricón."

The word means "faggot," and I flinch. But Tollomi doesn't move a muscle. "You knew him, then?" he asks.

"I met him. He was in my class."

"The one Vásquez taught?"

"I told you, I didn't study with Vásquez. I went to hear him speak once. He was very good. It was right before they shot him. He was an important man, so I want to meet his wife. Okay?"

"Okay," says Tollomi, grinning because José Luis is annoyed but trying to hide it, "delighted to have you along."

"Tollomi." I nudge him to make him turn around and stop bothering José Luis. "Tollomi, where am I supposed to turn?"

"Not yet," he says absently. "José, why didn't you stay to graduate?"

José Luis holds up his hand and rubs his thumb and fingers together. "Money," he says softly in English. "¿*Dinero. Comprendes, señor?*"

"Of course," Tollomi says, and then turns back around.

We leave the coastal road and head inland. The terrain rises. We're somewhere south of Puerto Plata, I'm not sure where exactly, running alongside a small river, passing through clusters of houses made of palm wood, and all the time traveling uphill. We are driving into the mountains.

When at last Tollomi says to pull over, we're at the edge of a dirt road that leads off the main road and up through a village. "We can walk from here," he says.

We follow him through the village, skirting lakes of rain that have filled up the ruts in the road. We climb a grassy hill, following a path that runs alongside someone's fence. We could be in Las Piedras. Everything there looks the same as it does here, the wire fence, the wild guava trees, the uneven yellow earth covered with patchy grass and stones. It's as if we haven't gone anywhere, as if we've driven in a circle. I stop walking.

"Go," says José Luis, who's had to stop behind me on the path. In front of me Tollomi turns around. He says something to Carlitos and comes back to where I stand.

"We're almost there," he says in English. "Miss Hell, I'm so glad you came."

"What?" I say. If he's trying to tell me something, I don't know what it is.

"What's the matter?" Carlitos yells back at us.

"*Nothing,*" I say, giving Tollomi a push. "I'm fine. I just stopped for a second."

At last we come out of the trees and into a clearing that is someone's yard. The ground is swept clean and level. There's a small wooden house, a cooking shed, and bushes covered with red flowers. Tollomi calls out, "¿*Quién vive?*" and an elderly woman in a faded purple dress comes out of the door.

"¡Ay, Santo, qué milagro!" she cries, as if we're all long-lost friends. Her feet are bare, and her hair is so gray it is nearly white. Is this Lupe Vásquez? I imagined her differently, younger, for one thing. And with shoes. This woman looks like she's lived in this village her whole life. She's old and bony and strong-looking, and when she takes my arm I get a whiff of what smells like cigars. She herds us around the house and sits me down in a chair parked under a lime tree. She makes everyone else—the men, I suppose—follow her into the house, and they emerge a moment later carrying more chairs. They set the chairs up in a circle, and then we all sit there in the hot still air and look at one another. The woman, it must be Lupe Vásquez, says something about how there's more of a breeze in this part of the yard. José Luis explains that he and Carlitos are brothers, that they met Tollomi on the beach, that he used to go to the University in Santo Domingo. She nods politely, as if she herself had no connection there, and it occurs to me that this story about her being a professor is just another thing Tollomi made up.

She makes us coffee and we sit there rocking back in the chairs and they talk about how hot it is, about Los Charamicos, and how many more tourists there are in Sosúa than there were last year. I sit there half-listening and look at the bright blue sky and think of my lumber. It's stacked up under the mango tree, almost all cut now, waiting. Tollomi nudges me with his toe.

"Yes?" I ask. Everyone laughs. Someone's asked me something and I didn't know it.

"Do you like chicken soup?" Lupe says to me.

"Yes," I say again, and then she says she wants to make us some. The best *sopa de pollo* we've ever had, she assures us, with rice and cilantro.

I force a smile. I've watched Eligio's wife make chicken soup, and it takes hours. The chicken has to be killed, and then plucked, and then cut up and boiled over a wood fire. And we don't even have the chicken yet: I'll never get back to Las Piedras in time to build.

Lupe explains to José Luis where to get the chicken, and José Luis nods and tells Carlitos to come on. Carlitos doesn't hear. He's listening to Tollomi, who's telling him something so quietly I can't hear the words, only the soft cadences of Spanish meant for Carlitos's ears alone. Carlitos is listening with his whole body.

"*Carlitos,*" says José Luis.

Carlitos's body jumps the way mine does sometimes when I'm caught being absent, being away.

"Are you ready?" José Luis asks.

"Ready," says Carlitos cheerfully. "Eh, José, why don't we drive?" He turns to Tollomi and says in his best beach English, "Can...we go...on the car?" Tollomi gives Carlitos a big smile.

"Of course not," says José Luis. He glares at Tollomi. "I suppose you're teaching him to drive too?"

"I already know how to drive," says Carlitos. "José Murray and Lobo and Ramón and I, we learned to drive last year when—-"

"We'll walk," says José Luis. "It's just at the crossroads. Come on." And without waiting he starts across the yard and disappears around the side of the house. Carlitos looks uncomfortably at the ground for a moment, then raises his head and rotates his finger around his ear to show us José Luis is crazy. Then he turns and runs after him.

"Isn't it beautiful here?" Tollomi says to me when Carlitos has gone.

"Yes," I say, still irritated because I'll be stuck here all day. Lupe looks at me and asks if I would like to see a typical Dominican kitchen. I've seen a hundred of them, but I say yes, I would. She must think we're tourists from Sosúa. I don't know what she thinks, actually. I wonder what Tollomi told her.

I follow her into the cooking shed. She tells me how the stove is made, out of a special kind of earth that dries like clay. I look up into the smoke-blackened *yagua* leaves that are the ceiling. I can see sky through the spaces between them. This roof will leak when it rains. I have to start thinking about how I'm going to make the roof at Las Piedras. I have the roof beam cut, and I know how to nail the frame together, but the roof itself, the covering, will be difficult because according to Eligio it's very hard to get *cana* now—it's all being used up by the hotels.

"You like the quiet?" says Lupe abruptly in English.

"What?" I ask. The surprise of hearing words in English has over-whelmed their meaning.

"You talk very little, I think. You like the quiet?"

Her English is heavily accented but enunciated perfectly. To hear it spoken in this setting gives it an almost unreal sound, as if it were a language occurring in a dream. I smile at her and nod.

"Lots of talking all the time is not for me either," she says. "*¿Es más tranquilo aquí en el campo, verdad?*"

Yes, I agree, it is more relaxing in the country, and then José Luis's voice calls out that they're back with the chicken. We go out to meet them.

He's holding the bird under his arm. Its muffled little voice protests into his T-shirt.

"Do you want me to do it?" he asks.

"No," says Lupe, "pass it here. If you scare it too much, you'll make the meat tough. Here—" she takes the bird from him and holds it against her chest. She strokes the chicken's feathered head a moment. I watch. Gracefully, as if giving the bird its freedom, she tosses it into the air, but her hand stays tight around its neck. The body is jerked back, the neck broken at once.

"You see?" says Lupe. "You have to be quick."

"*Profesora, profesora,*" says José Luis, teasing her as if they were old friends, smiling one of his rare smiles. Lupe smiles back and takes the dead bird back into the cooking shed.

"Carlitos," says Tollomi, "come look at the river. You can see it from behind the house."

Carlitos glances around to see if José Luis is listening, but José Luis has followed Lupe. "All right," Carlitos agrees.

"Coming, Michelle?"

I shake my head, and the two of them disappear around the far side of the house.

José Luis goes all the way into the cooking shed. I suppose I should be social and join them, but I don't feel like it. I sit in my chair and watch a highway of ants make their way across the bare earth toward the house.

After what might be a long time, José Luis comes back. "How's the soup coming?" I ask.

"Fine, fine." He sits in the chair Carlitos was sitting in and glances around the yard.

"She speaks English," I say, just to say something.

"And so do you, and so does Tollomi, and so do I. And now even Carlitos is learning it. So maybe we should all just speak English from now on, eh?"

His tone is light enough, but it's costing him an effort. "Oh, come on," I say. "I just meant I was surprised."

"Why should you be surprised? She was a professor. At the oldest university in Santo Domingo."

"You were in the kitchen a long time, José," I say to change the subject. "Was she teaching you to cook?"

"Bah," says José Luis. But then he looks up and smiles again. His smile is just like Carlitos's. "I was talking to her about Santo Domingo," he says, leaning forward in the chair. "She and Vásquez were important people. Not just at the university but everywhere. You've heard of the revolution we had here in '65? Vásquez was a big organizer. They were both in prison, and they were both tortured. I heard he wrote a book about being in prison but no one would publish it."

"Um," I say. I don't want to hear about torture and prison. José Luis has moved his foot into the line of ants. Most of them have rerouted around the toe of his shoe, but a few climb frantically up the buckle.

"I guess after they shot her husband she was afraid to stay in Santo Domingo," he goes on eagerly, "so she came up here, but they won't even bother with her now because she's not doing anything worth noticing anymore."

"Well, she's old," I say. "Besides, if they shot her husband…" A few of the ants have discovered his sock. I watch, waiting for him to feel the tickle.

"You don't spend your whole life working for something and then just stop," says José Luis. "You don't just say, 'Oh, I'm scared, I'm leaving.' She just needs someone to motivate her again—hey, Carlitos!"

They come around the side of the house, Carlitos and Tollomi, a little out of breath. Not grinning, but they might as well be. Carlitos is carrying in his hand a large branch covered with little round pods. "*Limoncillos,*" he announces. "Take some, Michelle. It's a fruit. You eat it."

I pull off a few of them and throw one at José Luis to distract him from glaring at Tollomi. It doesn't work.

"Where were you two?" José Luis demands.

"Getting *limoncillos,*" says Tollomi brightly. "What's the matter, José, you don't like them?"

"Stop," I say in English.

"Stop what?" says Tollomi innocently. "José Luis, there are ants all over your shoes."

José Luis looks down. He picks the ants off his ankles one by one and crushes them between his fingers before flicking them away. "These ants," he says, looking up at me and shaking his head, "they bite."

Tollomi drags his chair closer to José Luis's, and the scrape of wood on the bare earth sends a faint shudder of tension through the air that only Tollomi seems oblivious to. He and José Luis are going to get into it again—it seems neither of them can resist baiting the other. Carlitos half rises from his chair, wanting to get away, and sinks back again, having no excuse for an exit.

"Hey, Carlitos," I say, "pass me some more *limoncillos,* will you?"

"*Sí,*" he says gratefully, and walks the branch over to me, smiling his beautiful smile. When he smiles his eyes shine so warmly that what his mouth does seems almost like an afterthought. He squats down beside my chair and looks up at me.

"What's it like where you come from?" he says softly.

"You mean the United States?"

"*¿Sí. Cómo es?*"

"I don't know," I say. "My family was always trying to get away from it. To come here. First my grandparents came, and then later my mother always wanted to come here too, but she never did, and now *I'm* here. Funny, huh?"

"But what's it like *there*?" Carlitos persists.

How can I answer that, really? I wouldn't know where to begin.

"*¡No me digas eso!*" Tollomi's voice rises in annoyance from across the yard. "Don't tell me there was no political ideology behind it!" They're deep into their argument now. I look at Carlitos's face and catch the wince. I have to keep our own conversation going.

"The United States is big," I tell him. "Everything is bigger. You can drive for thousands of miles without reaching the ocean."

"But Nueva York is near the ocean?" he asks.

I think of distant names: East River, Long Island Sound. "Yes," I answer, "but it's not an ocean like here."

"Is cold?" This in English.

"Yeah, it's cold. And *el agua es color de café.*"

"*Ay ay ay,*" says Carlitos. Then Lupe sticks her head out the doorway of the cooking shed and tells Carlitos to go pick her some cilantro from the back of the garden.

"*Con permiso,*" he says graciously, excusing himself to me before racing off, out of earshot of Tollomi and José Luis.

"Rotting away in prison, for God's sake," I hear José Luis say. Then I tune them both out entirely. I don't have to go anywhere; I just let my mind go and then their argument and Carlitos's nervousness and the ants on the ground and the chair against my back all recede and then I don't see or hear any of them, I'm not there anymore, I'm somewhere else, I'm away.

Chicken, yucca, rice, fresh cilantro. We bring our chairs together in a circle and eat with the bowls in our laps. The soup is delicious, but one of the chicken's feet is floating around in the pot, clutched and tipped with claws. Maybe it's supposed to be good luck to put it in, I don't know. I worry that I'll be served it on second helpings, but the thing winds up in Carlitos's bowl.

In the car on the way back, Tollomi resumes his argument with José Luis, who rises to the challenge at once. Carlitos and I sit in the backseat, listening.

"Vásquez made bad decisions," says José Luis. "You don't spend all your time teaching your students some half-invented version of a language nobody speaks anymore and then look surprised when they try to do something a little more relevant."

"You mean breaking into the lighthouse?" Tollomi asks. He must mean the lighthouse in Santo Domingo, the expensive one they're building in honor of Columbus.

"I suppose your *maricón* friend the sailor told you about that too?" José Luis asks.

"As a matter of fact, he did," says Tollomi, quite unruffled. "But you

can't say studying Taino was irrelevant. It was what inspired them."
His coolness annoys José Luis far more than anger would.

"It wasn't studying Taino that inspired them," José Luis says fiercely.
"It's being hungry. It's watching your parents work all their lives and still
not have enough to buy toilet paper. It's living in a slum with no water
or light and then seeing it bulldozed—*that's* what inspires people.
Vásquez should have been teaching them to organize, to plan an action,
to protect ourselves—"

"He was a professor, not an instructor in guerrilla warfare," says
Tollomi airily. I can tell from his voice that he's needling José Luis on
purpose.

"Yes, but—" José Luis breaks off and grunts in frustration. "Why am
I talking to you about this? What do you know about it? You lie around
in the sun all day teaching Carlitos English. Why don't you just buy
him a plane ticket to New York and send *him* to college?"

I look over at Carlitos. He's leaning his head against the half-open
window as if he feels sick.

"Oh, believe me, José," says Tollomi, "New York is the *last* place I'd
like to take Carlitos."

"What's that supposed to mean?" snarls José Luis.

"What is what supposed to mean? I hate New York as much as you
think you hate it. I *know* I hate it. I've been there." Tollomi's coolness
has turned cold, his voice full of icy edges. Beside me I hear Carlitos's
breath come out in a shudder.

"Tollomi!" I say it so loudly that even Carlitos raises his head and
looks at me. "Stop the car a minute."

"What's wrong?" He slows down a little.

"I feel sick," I say, looking at Carlitos. "I need some air."

He pulls the car off the road, and I jump out. We're beside a field
of sugarcane taller than I am. The air smells like molasses.

Tollomi comes up beside me. "Are you going to throw up?" he asks.

"No," I say in a voice that means, *Don't be stupid.*

"What's wrong?" He sounds genuinely puzzled. When I don't
answer he says, "Michelle, I can't read your mind."

"Or anyone else's either, it seems." I want to go on, but José Luis
and Carlitos have gotten out of the car.

"Are you all right?" José Luis asks. When I nod he says, "Good. Carlitos and I will walk the rest of the way home."

"What?" says Tollomi. "Don't be silly."

"We're almost there," says Carlitos. "If Michelle doesn't feel well…"

I look down the highway. We're not almost there, not really. The turnoff for Charamicos is about another mile up the road.

"We want to stop and see a friend on the way home," José Luis explains. "We just passed the road to his house, back there. So we'll see you later."

"Okay," I say before Tollomi can say anything, "see you later, then."

"*Nos vemos,*" says Carlitos gratefully as I pull Tollomi back to the car.

"What was all that about?" he asks after we've driven a few minutes in silence.

"Don't tell me you don't know."

"I don't."

"You have to stop baiting José Luis. Don't you see what it's doing to Carlitos?"

"I'm not baiting him. Is that why you had me stop the car? Michelle, I was trying to have an intelligent discussion."

"No, you were trying to get a rise out of him so you could look superior."

Tollomi sucks his teeth at me. "Michelle, that's ridiculous. If José Luis isn't capable of being civil to me for one afternoon, it's not my problem."

"But you're making Carlitos miserable, and that *is* your problem."

"I am not making him miserable. He's doing it to himself. Whenever he's around José Luis, he turns into a spineless jellyfish."

"Well, what do you want him to do," I say, "throw everything aside and hop in the sack with you?"

Tollomi laughs. "Yes," he says, "I do. That's exactly what I want." He grins at how wonderful it would be. And he turns his grin toward me like a peace offering.

"Well, it will never happen," I say. "You know it won't." I'm still annoyed with him.

Tollomi stops grinning. "Are you sure?" he says sharply. "Do you see the way Carlitos looks at me? When you see him look at me, Michelle, what do you see?"

I think of Carlitos's eyes, very dark eyes, eyes you can look into. I think of how they light up from within when he smiles. When he turns his eyes to Tollomi they radiate an even deeper warmth, a sudden stillness. A faint quiver of surprise at the strength of their own gaze. It's there—Tollomi is right.

"But Carlitos isn't like you," I say. "He's not used to pretending."

"Pretending what?"

"Tollomi, look at his life here. Where are the gay bars in Charamicos? If you lead him out of there, he'll never be able to get back in."

"He's leading himself out," Tollomi says. "I haven't so much as touched him. Besides, it's not as if he has to stay in Charamicos the rest of his life. He could go to Santo Domingo. There are some gay bars there. So it's not Amsterdam, it's not San Francisco—"

"Tollomi, what are you talking about? This is *Carlitos.*"

"And Carlitos feels the way he feels. You can see it. It's there whether I do anything or not. Are you saying it's better he should never know?"

"I—" I stop. *Is* that what I'm saying? That he should never know what it is that is taking up so much space in his heart? That he should never know what it is to realize desire? He could shut his heart in a box and have a life half-lived, and his heart would stop speaking to him. Then he would never even know what that lost half of his life was. He might never even know it was lost at all.

"No," I say, "I'm not saying that."

"Well, then?"

We're almost to Las Piedras.

"I don't know," I tell him. "I don't want to talk about it anymore."

"I'm sorry," says Michelle the next morning. "Do whatever you want. It's fine."

"What's fine?" I ask.

"About Carlitos. The whole thing driving back from Lupe's—I wasn't saying you should leave him alone. I just meant…" she trails off.

"Don't bring José Luis on any more picnics?"

"Yeah." She grins and considers the matter dropped. But I don't go into Sosúa that day or the next. I stay in Las Piedras and help Michelle work on the house. In two days we get nearly half the frame in place; on the third day, when she has to leave to go to work at the bar, I tell her I'll stay and finish nailing in the side braces.

"You can't," she says absently. "It needs two people."

"I'll do the verticals then."

She stops studying the woodpile and frowns at me. "Don't you want a ride into Sosúa?"

"Not today. Do we have enough nails?"

"*Tollomi.*"

"What?"

"What's going on?"

"Nothing."

"Something is—you haven't been to Sosúa in three days."

"So?"

"So don't tell me you aren't going to see Carlitos at all now."

"Of course I am. But I was there almost every day last week. Maybe he wants a break. After all," I roll my eyes at her suggestively, "I wouldn't want to lead him into anything, right, Michelle?"

She spins away from me and looks at the pile of lumber. "All right," she says flatly. "Do the verticals, then. It would be a big help."

When she turns around again I'm sorry I teased her. Her mouth is all wrong. "I didn't mean it," I say.

"I know. It isn't that. Do you have the car keys?"

"They're in your pocket." She draws out the keys and fidgets them between her fingers. "Then what *is* the matter?" I ask.

She sighed. "I don't know what you're doing. You say things, and I don't know what you mean. I'm not saying I expect to. But then things happen, and I don't know if you planned it that way or what."

"Planned what? I'm not planning anything," I say truthfully.

She shoves the keys back in her pocket. "I'm going to be late," she says. It seems she's about to cry.

"Would you rather I came with you?"

"No," she says quickly. "No, stay. If you want to. I'll see you tonight."

"Michelle, look: On Sunday you didn't build because you spent the whole day at Lupe's—because I asked you to. So I thought today I'd stay here and build. That's really all I meant. I'm not planning anything, whatever that means. Okay?"

Her mouth works itself into a smile.

"Okay," she says. "Thanks."

After she leaves I begin building at once. The sky stays clear, and when the sun reaches its zenith, I take a break and go down to the river. The banks are always empty at noon. It's too hot to wash clothes, and the cows are all out grazing. In a few more hours, when the day will have cooled down, people will appear again to bathe, bringing pails to fill or leading their animals down to drink. I swim awhile, fill the water jugs, and start back up the hill. When I reach the crest, I see someone sitting on the stack of wood under the mango tree. I'm too far away to perceive more than the blur of a body, but I recognize whose blur it is, and as I look at it, I feel myself sigh as if I've been holding my breath. Without knowing it I've been waiting for something to happen, and now it has. As slowly as I can bear, I walk toward the tree. Carlitos sees me and jumps up.

"Where have you been?" he demands.

"Carlitos, how did you get here? I was down at the river."

"For three days?"

If he didn't looked so panicked I would laugh with delight; it has happened. It has happened!—but he doesn't know it yet. His face is tight with nervous anticipation. He's in the kind of pain that comes when you believe yourself to be on the verge of taking some long-pondered and dangerous action, some great leap, but in truth the leap has already been made. He made it by coming here, by deciding to come. He made it the moment he left his house this morning. He doesn't know that yet. But I can see it in his body as he stands before me, his skin sleek with a light film of sweat. We are going to make love.

I stay calm. There's no need to hurry now, no fear of making a false step.

"I'm sorry I haven't been to see you," I say. "I've been helping Michelle build. I've missed you," I add, which makes him look away. He doesn't want to hear that. He hasn't come to talk. He stands there miserably, pretending to scrutinize the bark of the tree trunk and wondering why he's come all the way out here. What for? His mind feels dumb, drowned.

"Do you want to take a walk?" I say, to put him at ease. He agrees at once, relieved to be in motion. "We'll go swimming. Why don't you leave your shirt here?"

Mechanically he pulls it off. He folds it carefully and lays it on the woodpile. We set off across the pasture. There's a steep path cut by the cows that leads down to the river through a dense slope of trees. At the end of the path, there's a cluster of rocks broad enough to sit on, and on the far side of the river, a narrow stretch of beach.

We sit on the rocks. He doesn't want to swim. I try to talk to him, make him relax. He doesn't want to talk. So I hang my legs over the ledge and stretch out on the warm stone and close my eyes.

I feel the sun on my body and the cooler air from the river around my feet. For a long time Carlitos sits very still beside me, and then at last I hear him lie down. More time passes. I wait.

At last it comes. I feel his fingers brush my arm. That's all. A sweet and frightened touch fine with desire. I open my eyes and turn toward him. He lies on his side staring at me. His eyes are weighted to mine, wide and unblinking and intensely still. I move my hand and touch his mouth. His lips are hot and dry. His mouth closes over my finger, his staring eyes never leaving mine. I draw my finger out and slide it damp over his chin, along his broken collarbone and down at last to his chest and the hard areola of each nipple, to the smooth skin tight over his stomach muscles, to the hem of his shorts. Down over his shorts. His cock hard under my hand at last with only a thin layer of cotton between us. His heart is pounding so hard, I can feel its pulse even in my hand. And then our eyes close, and his mouth and the heat of his mouth open into mine. His hands fumble a moment against my stomach, and then our bodies find a rhythm and rise, like a bird that after a seemingly hopeless beating of wings suddenly lifts, ascends, and becomes pure flight.

Sex is purer than anything else I know. We make love without speaking. In sex I never lie.

I stand behind the bar, I walk up and down, I pour drinks, pour drinks, chat the customers up. I'm so good at it: I can do it without paying attention, without listening or thinking, even. I just watch their lips move and their glasses grow empty, then I nod and pour refills.

When I first began to tend bar in Berlin, I was afraid what would happen if people began to notice that a part of me was frequently absent. That I was not quite all there, as they say. I needn't have worried. No one ever noticed, not ever.

"Mm-hmm," I'd say, one elbow on the bar, my head turned toward some customer who believed we were actually engaged in conversation. "Really? Sure. Ready for another drink? Thanks. Go on, you were saying…"

It's the same here at Sam's. In this way a bar is the perfect place for me. No one notices anything. I never have to answer, nobody asks.

Mr. Miami bangs in yelling. The fishing hat he usually wears is crumpled in his hand.

"Goddamn it to hell, I need a drink," he yells. "Michelle, where the hell is Sam?"

I mix him his gin and tonic and try to remember his real name. "It's only noon," I say. "Sam's not down yet. Relax yourself." I point at a stool. Sit, boy.

He picks up his drink and swallows half of it in one smooth motion. He hasn't sat down yet. "Hit me again, Michelle. Goddamn sonofabitches."

I refill his glass. Drake, Sam calls him, Peter Drake, that's it. He always tips well. "What's the matter, Drake," I say, "you fall on a nest of sea urchins?"

"Some sonofabitches set fire to my hotel," he says. "That's what's the fucking matter." Then he sits down on the stool and looks at me.

"That's terrible," I say, though in fact I can't even remember which hotel is his. It's one of the new ones being built in Cabarete, but I can't think which. They're all sprawling and ugly. I get into my listening pose with my elbow up on the bar and ask him what happened.

While he talks, slamming his glass on the bar each time he sets it down, I remember the other hotel that burned in Cabarete. It must have been before Christmas that it happened—the night Tollomi and I were walking on the beach and smelled smoke.

"All over the goddamn driveways," Drake is saying. "And you know that gazebo I told you I was having put in? For the outdoor bar, by the pool. I had them make one of those native roofs for it, those palm tree ones. It's completely torched. You know how much that alone is going to cost me?"

"How much?" I ask, interested now because a *cana* roof is what I want to put on the house in Las Piedras, but he doesn't answer this; he blathers on about all the ruined shrubbery, the paint job, the slowness of the workers. I stop listening. He doesn't notice. I don't know what I'm doing here, serving alcohol to these men who spit on whatever they touch and think they own whatever they spit on. I'm making money, that's what I'm doing here. I can make more money in an hour than plenty of Dominicans make in a day.

I want to talk to Tollomi about this, about how it feels to stand between rows of bottles and nod at these men, waiting for their money and pretending to listen to their words, but when I get back to Las Piedras that evening Tollomi isn't there. This is unusual—he's always back before me—but I make dinner and the stars come out and still he doesn't come. I take a lantern and the pot of rice and beans and climb up on the foundation and lean against the last corner pole and wait a little longer. He doesn't come and I sit there waiting, and finally I just eat everything, cold now, by myself.

From the hill I can see our lanterns burning through the darkness.
Michelle must have taken them up on the foundation with her. I call
out, and one of the lanterns is raised in the air.

I clamber up onto the foundation and sit beside her. "We should
build some steps," I say.

"Where have you been?"

"In Cabarete. Michelle, guess what happened."

"Another hotel burned down."

"No. After you left, Carlitos showed up."

"Here?" She sits upright and looks at me. "Tollomi!"

"Yes?"

"You did it."

"How can you tell?"

"By the neon sign flashing SEX over your head. I don't believe it."

"Believe it, Miss Hell." She's right about the neon sign; I feel myself
radiating pheromones, lit up from within.

"I don't believe it," she says again.

"What don't you believe?"

"I never thought Carlitos would really do it. Is he all right?"

"Of course he's all right. He's glorious."

"He didn't freak out on you afterward?"

"No, why would he?"

"Tollomi, just think for a minute. Think about what's going to happen to his life."

"Michelle, his life has just been immeasurably enriched because he's
experienced for the first time one of the most joyous parts of being alive.
Don't you remember the first time you had sex with a woman? After years
of not knowing why you didn't want a boyfriend? Wasn't it like a light
being switched on and suddenly you saw what all the fuss was about?"

She doesn't say anything.

"Well?" I persist.

"I don't remember the first time," she says.

"Oh, Michelle—sorry."

"Don't be. It doesn't matter. You're right, it's good what happened. You can see in Carlitos's face how he feels about you. I'm happy for you."

But she sounds so sad. I change the subject. "How was work?"

"Oh! I started to tell you." She sits up straight, animated again. "Did you see the hotel that caught fire?"

"The one that burned down a few weeks ago?"

"No, somebody set fire to another one right near it, last night. Peter Drake, the guy who owns it, was in Sam's all day having a fit. It was due to open next week."

It gives me a little physical thrill, a shiver through my chest, to think of someone setting fire to the growing sprawl of hotels that's beginning to eat away at the coastline. "How bad is the damage?" I ask.

"Awful, to hear Drake tell it, but I looked from the *guagua* on the way back here, and it looked all right to me."

Of course. "That's the beauty of cinder block," I say. "He'll probably open up right on schedule."

She shrugs. "He had some outdoor bar thing that was made of wood and *cana*. He'll have to rebuild that."

"So he gets ten men in there and does it in five days."

"While it's taking us forever." She looks up at the new roof beam. "Well, if he has to hire ten workers, at least *they'll* be happy. Hey, Tollomi. Do you think that's who's setting the fires?"

"The construction crews? No, I think it's some kind of political group."

"Why do you think it's political?"

She's serious; she really can't see why I'd think that. I feel annoyed with her. She should see it, everyone should see it, should see what I've seen happen to St. Croix, the developers breaking ground for new golf courses and resort hotels, breaking up the land the Cruzans have lived on for generations, breaking the Cruzans into their new housing-project homes like breaking in a pair of too-tight shoes, like breaking a wild horse. The oil companies broke up the reef with dredging. The whole island wound up broken.

"So why do you think it's political?" she repeats.

"If you don't see it, you don't see it."

"What's that supposed to mean?"

"Setting fire to the hotels is a political statement," I tell her, "especially since they don't even burn down—"

"But for all we know, it could just be some arsonist who likes to make trouble."

"Well, if the police catch whoever's doing it, we'll go and interview them about their motives, all right, Michelle?"

"You don't have to be sarcastic." She hops off the foundation.

"I'm sorry," I say. "Don't leave."

"Who put such a bug up your ass?"

"I'm sorry, I didn't mean to be snide." I cast around for something to keep her from going. "What does Sam think about all this?"

She leans against the foundation and looks up at me. "Sam Johnson doesn't think anything beyond whether he should go ahead and put a *cana* roof on his new restaurant like he was planning. He doesn't care who's doing it or why. He just wants his money."

"What about the guy whose hotel got burned? What does he think?"

"Let's talk about something else," she says abruptly. "I had to hear every stupid detail of this all day at work."

"Anything you like," I say, but we lapse into silence and after a moment Michelle says she's going to bed.

I stay where I am, sitting on the edge of the foundation. Only after she's disappeared into the tent do I remember our conversation of that morning.

You say things, and I don't know what you mean. And then things happen.

She thought I'd wanted to stay in Las Piedras today because I'd known Carlitos would come? But I hadn't known. Had she, somehow, foreseen it? I hop off the foundation and go across the yard to ask her. She's lying on top of her sleeping bag with her eyes closed and her limbs flung out as if she's fallen.

"Michelle?"

I know she's not asleep, but she doesn't respond. I speak her name once more and get no answer.

All week at work, Peter Drake's burned hotel is the talk of the bar. The other expatriate gringos who own bars or hotels all come into Sam's to commiserate and scheme. Who will the arsonists target next? What can the white people do to protect their buildings? Sam, who is opening a second bar in Cabarete, wants the police to put sentries on all the new developments from sunset to morning. "After all," he says, "it's in the government's interest. You know what percent of the Dominican economy depends on gringo money? Forty percent, that's how much. If foreign developers get scared and start to pull out, the country's whole economy collapses."

He asks me how my house is coming along. "She's building a house," he announces. "This girl right here, my A-1 bartender. She's building a house way up in the hills."

The men lined up at the bar all like this idea, me building a house, me with my skinny arms and ragged haircut. They peel off peso notes and slide them toward me like telephone numbers.

"Better watch out," says Drake, "they could torch your house next." The others nod in agreement, trying to draw me into their circle.

"Be careful of suspicious characters," Sam says.

"I don't have to be careful," I tell him. "My house is haunted—the village kids say so. It's true, the ghosts scare everyone away."

They all look at me the way I look at them when they've had too much to drink. And because they don't know what else to do, they laugh and drink some more.

That evening Sam gives me another five hundred pesos. It's not my salary. He just gives it to me.

"Take it, honey," he says when I hesitate. "Use it for fire insurance."

Tollomi's gone all hours. When I have to work at Sam's, he gives me the car, but even with no car he starts staying later and later in Sosúa, with Carlitos until well after dark, after the *guaguas* stop running. When he does return, he comes whistling up the hill in the darkness, happy in a happiness that surrounds him like mist, that I cannot get near. At night in the tent he falls asleep at once—after he's been with Carlitos he sleeps differently. He gives himself up to sleep entirely, as if sleep itself were his lover's arms.

I lie in the tent beside him, exhausted and awake. I lie thinking about the house, weighing how much money I have against the price of materials. The frame is almost finished. The roof beam is up, and most of the side braces. I still have to nail up the rafters. With the five hundred pesos Sam gave me, I'll have almost enough to buy the *cana*. And I'm adding another shift at work.

"Are you sure you want to work Saturday night, then drive all the way back here and work Sunday morning?" Sam said when I asked him for the hours.

"I'm sure," I told him.

"You could stay in town," he said dubiously, pushing his hair off his forehead. "There's some cheap hotels here I could get you a deal in. Rick's Place, for example. Want me to ask?"

"No," I said. "I like the drive."

"Hell, you could just stay upstairs here and not pay a cent. I'll put you in the guestroom with Sonya. Maybe I should open up a hotel, eh?"

"Ha ha," I said, though I wasn't sure he was joking.

On Sunday morning when I come back for the day shift, Sonya is just finishing the floors.

"Michelle!" She stops mopping and stares up at me with her ancient child's gaze.

"¿Sí?"

"Michelle, are you going to sleep here on Saturday nights now?"

"No. Did Sam tell you I was?"

The corners of her mouth twitch, a conspiratorial almost-smile.

"Yes," she says, nodding, "but he was drunk."

I ride through Cabarete at least twice a day, going to and from
Carlitos. At night, or in the very early hours of the morning along the
Cabarete coast, the hotels burn. One, then another, yet another a
fortnight later. Small fires appear on moonless nights, flame up and
lick brick and cinder block, devour the *cana* thatch of veranda roofs
and outdoor bars just built. When morning comes, someone discovers
the damage, the new walls black with smoke, the landscaped driveway
littered with tongues of ash, and so the workers are rehired. They come
in and paint, replant. The roofmakers come with their ladders and loads
of green palm branches and make a new roof. A guard is posted. And
then a week or ten days later the hotel looks new and safe again, and the
first guests arrive, pale and unknowing and fresh from the plane. And
then, a little farther down the coast, another fire is set.

Each time I hear that a hotel has been targeted, I feel a small yelp
of victory; a small animal inside me escapes from its cage: Someone is
protesting what's happening here, someone can see it. Someone doesn't
care how much money tourists bring into the local economy, or how
many new jobs the hotels create. Someone thinks the price is too high.

I wait for news that some political group has claimed responsibility
for the arson; I scan the pages of *El Listin Diario* to see if anything's
been written up. But no group comes forward; the entire north coast is
awash with tourists, and news of the fires never reaches the newspaper
offices of Santo Domingo. And in truth, as a media event, the orgy of
new construction far outweighs these little fires. Piles of burned *cana*
and ruined paint jobs do not make headlines; the papers boast instead
of the wonderful housing projects the great president Balaguer has had
erected for the indigent masses. The elections are drawing near. I quit
reading the papers altogether, only partly out of disgust. I rush to Sosúa
as early as possible most mornings, hurrying to the town beach and

Carlitos. I forget to stop to buy anything as mundane as a newspaper; the world is brilliant with the colors of new passion; monochromatic newsprint is lost in the swirl.

The fire that happens between us is more skillfully set than any arsonist's: It burns everything, every time. It immolates down to the core. Since the day we first made love, every time I arrive at the beach Carlitos is waiting for me. Anxious. We don't stay at the beach; he hurries me away from his friends, back to the road, where if I don't have the car we'll catch another *guagua* somewhere else, someplace empty, shielded, hard to find. He wants to be alone with me, to make love, but no matter how hidden we are, as long as it's daylight Carlitos can't relax. He's afraid we'll be discovered, no matter how empty the road or how far from Charamicos we go. So he no longer leaves me at sunset. He stays with me until the safety of the night has descended, and then, in a dark field, in the darkened car, under cover of darkness, Carlitos opens like a flower.

He's happiest when I have the car. Then no one has to see us together. He doesn't have to worry about what the passengers beside him in the *guagua* are thinking, if maybe they can tell just by looking at him what he's done with me, what he's about to do again.

"I have the car today," I'll say, and watch his whole face relax for an instant before tensing again in anticipation of what is to come. We walk with measured steps across the sand, up to the highway where I've parked. It's an effort to walk slowly, to pretend we are ordinary humans and not pure energy temporarily confined to solid form. Just looking at him sideways while he walks along the edge of the cracked asphalt makes my fingers twitch with the effort of not touching him. The car keys jump in my hand.

Sex in the car: The taste of Carlitos, the taste in my mouth of sweat and semen, occasionally mixed with mosquito repellent. The pressure of his thighs, the way his thighs jump and tremble against my shoulders, under my hands. The gearshift digging into my side melts away. The next morning, mosquito bites on my thighs. Strange bruises, but no memory of pain. Our smell becomes part of the car. Now that he's begun loving me he can't stop; he's like a man getting enough to eat after a lifetime of going hungry: He kisses and sucks and holds me greedily, as if somewhere deep in his body he's still starved.

Finally, we make love right on the town beach: It's very late, and we can't go anywhere else. I don't have the car, and Carlitos refuses to get into a taxi with me; people will talk, he says. So we wade out into the water up to our waists. It's very dark, and the night has no moon. The water pulls and laps against us, first cold and then holding us up, and Carlitos moves behind me and his chest slips tight against my back, his hands come round me and then I am swept out, away, drowned. I give myself over, I sink in the exhale of pleasure. I come up gasping. He lifts me from the sea and pulls me to him. He pulls my mouth to his and holds my head, his lips hot, his chest pounding, as if he cannot breathe save through my lungs.

One morning I arrive at the beach, much earlier than usual, to find Carlitos deep in conversation with his friends, the boys who rent beach chairs to tourists.

"Hi," I say, coming up behind him, and Carlitos jumps, startled, and tries to cover himself by saying boredly, "Oh, hi," and to his friends: *"Es mi maestro de inglés."*

The boys already know I've been teaching him English; to my ears the needless "He's my English teacher" carries an implicit denial in its echo: *He's my teacher, not my lover.*

"Okay, Tollomi, less go," Carlitos says, getting up, and without waiting for my answer he turns and walks off, leaving an awkward silence in his wake. He thinks I'll follow him, and he's right, but even as my skin flushes in anticipation of his touch, another part of my desire is the desire to stay here, sitting on the sand beside the beach chairs with Carlitos and his friends. I want simply to sit and watch them, listen to them talk and make jokes, feel their happiness at one another's company work itself into my skin like oil.

But Carlitos is halfway down the beach now. *"Chau,"* I say to the boys. *"¿Nos vemos?"*

"Nos vemos," they agree, *"Oquey,* bye-bye."

And I start up the beach after Carlitos, pausing to look back when I hear a whoop of laughter. One of the boys is pointing toward the water, and now all of them are looking that way, laughing at whatever they see there. I look too, but see only the bathers and the waves. I start off again, Carlitos's friends still laughing behind me, their voices rising together and joining in appreciation, not of the joke, but of their camaraderie with one another. A thing that, like the joke itself, I will never share or know.

Despite Carlitos's *"Es mi maestro de inglés,"* lately I've been his English teacher in name only. He doesn't want to talk much these days; all he wants to do is make love. Our bodies speak a tongue of their own, and by comparison speech seems imprecise, outdated. But it's more than this; he's afraid of talking, afraid of the thinking that goes with it. He doesn't want to think about what we're doing. If the words appear in his mind—*I'm making love with another man*—all the other words will follow: *maricón, mariposa, mariquita, faggot,* and he'll freeze and be unable to continue, and he couldn't bear that. So he continues, the fire of his body melting metal to chain his thoughts closed.

I want to tell him there is more. That not all words are painful, that there are other words for what happens between us in the moments we touch each other. Words he won't allow to penetrate his mind. *Pleasure. Love.*

"You know," I say casually, "there's an organization in Santo Domingo. *Grupo de los derechos homosex—*" But whenever I start to talk like this, he stops me. He doesn't want to hear it, he stops me from speaking: He covers my mouth with his own.

I'm up on the ladder nailing rafters. It's a job for two people, but Tollomi is off somewhere with Carlitos, and Eligio has gone home. There's a little daylight left, and I want to use it. The moon was new last night, so once the sun sets I'll have to stop working until morning. On nights when the moon is full I wait for it to rise, and then if the sky is clear I can go on working for hours more.

When I come down from the ladder for more nails, I notice my hands are shaking. Not badly. But bad enough that I notice. I sit down. I forgot to eat lunch. My body feels made of rubber. I sit there a moment resting, then tell my body to get up. The daylight is almost gone.

My body doesn't move. "Get up," I say aloud.

But it lays itself down on the foundation. Something is wrong.

"Get *up*." My body refuses to budge.

"Michelle," says a voice, almost in my ear, and I jump. My body sits right up then. It would know that voice anywhere. Down to the bone that voice goes. It belongs to my mother.

I turn my head. Not all the way. Just enough to see the white canvas sneakers and the hems of the pedal-pushers over bare calves. It's my mother. She's here. I raise my head the rest of the way, and there she is, standing on the cement, looking down at me, my mother. Her blue eyes.

"So," she says, "here you are."

"Here I am," I say.

Here she is. She's found me. As if I never left. I don't know who I thought I was fooling. She's here. I haven't gone anywhere at all.

She looks around like someone who's just stepped off a plane; she looks at the house. She squats beside me and pushes her gray-blond hair behind her ears. "Ye gods," she says, "this is quite a project."

"I'm doing it," I say. "I'm building this house."

"But what for?" Her voice is the same as always. "You have a house, honey. Back with us."

"Mom, that's your house." How did she find me?

She looks at the beams overhead, at the patched cement foundation. "But this house belongs to your grandparents."

"They're dead," I say.

She looks at me strangely, and I see there's something wrong. I wonder if she's forgotten they're dead, if like me whole chunks of her life are just lost.

"They're dead, Ma," I say again. "They don't want the house."

My mother starts to cry.

"I always knew you'd come here," she says, crying, and suddenly I remember something. Without the slightest warning something cracks open, and there inside it I discover quite intact a memory: my mother standing in the grocery store crying. She pushes me in the cart up and down the aisles without taking any food off the shelves, without buying anything at all, and I sit in the cart and look up at her face almost serene in its silent flow of tears.

And I was used to this, her crying. I'd find her crying in the morning, standing by the washing machine. When I came home from school, I'd walk into the kitchen and find her leaning against the kitchen sink with tears everywhere. She wouldn't hear me come in. When I called to her, she'd look up and stare at me with eyes like wet glass.

I never knew why she was crying. I never thought to ask. It was unknowable: She was an adult, she lived in a world apart. I'm an adult now. I'm in that world. And I still don't know. I still don't ask her. "Ma," I say, "Ma, don't cry."

She wipes her eyes, wipes her wet hand on her pants and gives me her smile, that smile so terribly weighted with sadness and love. I must have seen her do this a thousand times, these same movements, this same smile, and each time forgotten it.

"What are you doing here?" I ask.

She wipes her eyes again and sighs. "I just want you to be happy."

"I am happy," I tell her. "Look." I stand up and lead her to the edge of the foundation and look out over the wide valley. I look down at the curling silver of the river below and the darkening banana groves beyond. The sun has ripened the clouds in the western sky to the red-orange of mangoes and edged them with light. Beneath them, the high green hills look gold.

"Look," I say, "look at the world."

I turn to be sure she's looking, but she's no longer there.

I'm alone in the house. My mother has disappeared.

I sit absolutely still on the concrete. The sun sets and I sit in the darkness. I am alone. This is my house. Not my grandparents'. Mine. *It's mine,* I say silently, over and over, *mine, it's mine, it's mine.*

But it doesn't feel like it.

Much later, Tollomi comes back. The beam of the flashlight floats up the hill, crosses the yard, stops by the water sack. I can't hear him over the cheeping of the frogs. I watch the light bob over to the tent and switch off. He must think I'm asleep in there. A moment of darkness passes while he crawls inside, and then the light snaps on again and he comes out and waves the beam all over the yard and yells my name.

"I'm up here," I answer. My voice comes out in a croak.

Then he's sitting beside me. His hands are on my shoulders. My arms are cold.

"Michelle, what are you doing up here? I didn't see you. Are you all right?"

How can I answer this? But he doesn't wait for an answer.

"You weren't waiting up for me, were you? I'm sorry it's so late. We went to Río San Juan, Carlitos and I."

"I wasn't waiting," I say. "I lost track of time."

"So did I," he says. He grins. His teeth flash white in the darkness. He hasn't noticed anything is wrong. He just wants to tell me about Carlitos.

"How was it?" I say. "Where you went, Río San Juan." Speaking is an effort. He starts to tell me. They were in some town; they ate *mondongo*. He wanted to rent a hotel for the afternoon, but Carlitos was too embarrassed. So they stayed on the beach in Río San Juan. They did it on the beach, out in the water. In the dark.

I try to keep Tollomi's face in focus, but the words recede. His mouth keeps moving but silently. His hands flutter through the lamplight, making gestures from very far away, semaphores, a secret language. They're not for me. What is? I see my mother's face, my mother who spills tears in the grocery store, at the kitchen sink, for no knowable reason—this same mother looks down at me on the day of my grandfather's funeral. Her eyes are stone dry. I look up at her face, startled because she's not crying. Not a tear. It's a funeral, you're supposed to cry—I'm young, but I know that much. And yet my mother's eyes are as dry as my own. I don't expect myself to be crying: Unlike my mother, I never do.

I don't know if I wanted to weep. I don't know if I understood death, even. I didn't not understand it. At that age it wouldn't have occurred to me that death was something to be understood any more than a stone lying in the road needed to be understood. You could leave it where it lay and never think of it again. Or you could pick it up, feel it cold in your palm; you could take it home in your pocket.

"Michelle!"

He's shaking my shoulder. Tollomi. Peering anxiously at my face. I've done it again, I've gone away—I don't know what he's been saying or if he was talking at all.

"Yes," I say. "Go on, I'm listening."

"Michelle, what is it? What's wrong?"

"I was just sitting here," I say, and I realize I'm going to tell him what's happened after all. He asks and I answer. He's asked for it.

"Michelle, tell me," he says, so I tell him. That I heard my mother's voice, that I looked up and there she was, right where he's sitting now. I tell him she was crying. I tell him she was wearing tennis shoes.

He just looks at me. A soft, unhappy look. He doesn't move a muscle. I shouldn't have said anything. He's thinking: *To see her dancing, to see her laugh, you wouldn't think there's this other thing she carries with her, this thing she holds in her arms like a dead child—she can't save it, she can't put it down. And it's growing heavier.*

He wants to take it from me, he wants to do something for me. He hates to be helpless. I hate to see him hating it. I try to think of something that will sound normal, something to reassure him.

"Want to go down to the village and have a beer?" I say. "I've been up here all day. I could use the walk."

"Oh, Michelle," he says sadly. "The cantina's been closed for hours. It must be two o'clock in the morning."

I've been sitting here for hours and hours, then. I shouldn't have said anything.

"Michelle, have you eaten at all today?" he goes on.

"I had breakfast. With you, if you remember. It was eggs."

"I mean since then, Miss Hell."

"I wasn't hungry."

He sighs. "I'll make you something now."

"I don't want anything now. I'm fine, Tollomi. Let's just go to bed."

"Michelle, if you aren't getting enough sleep and you forget to eat and then you work outdoors in ninety-degree weather and don't drink enough water, sooner or later you're going to start hallucinating. It's that simple."

"It wasn't a hallucination."

"You still have to eat. Mother says."

"That's *not* what she said, as a matter of fact. I told you, she said—"

"All right, Michelle, let's just—"

"Would you like to know what she did say, Tollomi? She said this house I'm building isn't mine at all. She said it belongs to my grandparents. What do you think of that?"

He doesn't answer. I jump off the foundation and start across the yard.

"Where are you going?" he yells after me.

"To bed."

He follows me across the prickly grass, and at the door of the tent he catches my arm. He puts his hands on my shoulders and turns me around.

"Just look for a minute," he says, so I do. He stands behind me with his arms around me, holding me while we look at the house. It's black and bony in the moonlight, darker than the dark blue-black of the sky, dark as the trees. "It's your house," Tollomi says into my hair. "You built it, My Shell. Every board and every nail in every board is there because of you."

"But the foundation isn't," I say.

He sighs. "All right," he says. "Let's just go to bed."

I didn't sleep much that night. The deep and sweet exhaustion I usually felt after making love with Carlitos deserted me. In its place I felt all the unexamined disquiet that seemed to emanate like heat from Michelle's body lying asleep a little distance from mine. When it got light outside, I got up and cooked breakfast. I brought it to her in the tent and tried to chat while she pretended to eat. At last I said, "Should I stay here today and build?"

"You don't have to." She picked at her eggs.

"I know I don't have to. I'm offering."

"What about Carlitos?" she asked.

"What about him? Eat."

"He won't be expecting you in Sosúa?"

"I didn't say I'd go. Eat. At least finish the plantain."

It was true, I reasoned, I hadn't told Carlitos I'd be there. But I hadn't said it because there had been no need to say it; since the day we'd first made love I had looked for him on the beach daily, and each day found him there, waiting for me. But here was Michelle, her eyes vague with the hallucination of last night and her breakfast uneaten before her. I was afraid to leave her here alone. I thought that if I stayed, my presence might keep her safely on this side of whatever line she was in danger of crossing.

"Is the *cana* coming today?" I asked.

"Supposedly."

"Then we ought to get the rafters finished. Will Eligio be here?"

"Uh-huh," she said.

"Well, the three of us ought to be able to get all the rafters in place. Then, when they deliver the *cana,* they can start tying it on and then the roof will be done, Miss Hell. After all this time we'll be able to take down the tent and sleep in the house."

She did not reply. She was still thinking about her mother. I wanted her to turn toward me as she used to: full of excitement over even some small thing, a new alley she had found to wander in, or the sight of a ship leaving the harbor for the open sea; she would look at me with her face full of smile and wind: *I love this, and here I am watching it with you.*

Now she turned toward me, looking at me over her bowl of half-eaten plantain and untouched eggs and smiled, but the smile was full of apology.

"We can sleep in the house," she echoed. What she meant was, *I'm sorry, Tollomi. There's nothing you can do.*

"You're not trying," I said, and then suddenly she was angry.

"All right, fine. Nothing happened last night. No one was here. My mother wasn't here. I was dreaming. And today, everything is fine too." She jumped to her feet. "Here comes Eligio. *Eligio! Ven acá.*"

"Michelle—"

"Get up. We have the whole side of a roof to finish. Are there any more plantains? I want to give Eligio some."

So I got up and doggedly followed her into the realm of right angles and bent nails and planing saplings. Work seemed to make things better. Once she had turned her attention to the problems of building, she lost the look of trouble that had shrouded her eyes since last night. When Eligio went home to have lunch and look out for the *cana* delivery, she kept working; I watched her straddle the roof beam, her mouth full of nails, hammering in strong, easy strokes, and I decided I would go to see Carlitos after all. In the afternoon, once the *cana* had arrived.

But when Eligio came back at two he was alone.

"Where's the *cana*?" I asked.

Michelle looked up from the water sack. "Don't tell me it's not here."

Eligio grinned a silver-toothed grin, amused at her impatience. "Not today. It will definitely be here tomorrow or the day after. But the price has gone up."

"What do you mean, the price has gone up? What is this, *cana* inflation? We agreed on the price last week."

"Manuel says the price has gone up," Eligio repeated. "It's all the new hotels. They're taking all the *cana*. And then somebody sets a hotel on fire and—*¡bueno!* They buy even more *cana* to repair it. So you see the problem."

"How much more is it going to cost me?"

"*No sé.*" Eligio put his hand to his back pocket and touched the rum bottle he kept there, as if for reassurance.

"Well, tell Manuel he can't just deliver all this *cana* here without telling me what he's charging. And if I can't afford it, we'll just have to wait."

"Michelle, just get the *cana*," I said in English. "If it's too expensive, I'll give you the money."

She shook her head no and started up the ladder.

"Why not? When the roof is done, I'll be sleeping under it."

She didn't answer.

"Or do you have other ideas?"

She turned around and came down two rungs. "Of course I don't. But you don't have to give me the money. I'll get it from Sam."

"He's just going to give it to you?"

She sighed. "I'm adding another shift at work."

"Michelle, no. You can't."

"I already did. I worked it on Sunday. You didn't notice."

I would have argued this with her, but we were interrupted by a shout from the road. Michelle climbed back up the ladder and squinted. "It's Carlitos," she said. "You made him come all the way out from Charamicos?"

"I didn't know he was coming," I said, and she made a face with her mouth. "Michelle, I didn't."

Carlitos sprinted across the yard and came up beside me, out of breath. I smelled the sweat on his body. But he wasn't looking at me, he was looking up the ladder at Michelle.

"I come…for help you with the house," he said in English.

"Carlitos, I'm so glad." She came down and hugged him. There was nothing but welcome in her voice, but I was careful not to catch her eye. I could not look at Carlitos either; the nearness of his body was charging the air between us. If our eyes locked, our bodies would assume command, and we'd find ourselves running off toward the guava trees, or scrambling down the cliff, or worse, simply stepping toward each other right there at the foot of the ladder with Michelle and Eligio looking on.

"Hello," I said simply, and turned away from him, and told Michelle that we should get back to work at once. I turned the full burden of my desire to the task of building, and with the blood pounding hard in my veins from my loins to my temples, I hoisted and hammered and hauled and tried to become as acutely aware of the wood under my hands as I was of Carlitos who stood just three yards away, hammering nails and pausing every so often to wipe the sweat from his face.

When we stopped for a break, the tension became nearly unbearable. We sat on the beach chairs under the mango tree, and Carlitos, not daring to speak or even look at me, pretended to be fascinated by the droplets of water condensing on the base of the water sack.

I couldn't look at Michelle; she was too well aware of what was happening. Only Eligio was cheerful, having uncapped his rum at last.

"She's getting a roof made of *cana*," he said heartily, addressing Carlitos. "What do you think of that?"

"Oh, very elegant," said Carlitos unhappily.

"The roof should be done by next week," Eligio continued, "unless another hotel catches fire, eh, *caballero*?"

"I don't know," Carlitos said. "Politics doesn't interest me."

"And what does politics have to do with it?" Eligio leaned forward.

Carlitos began to say something, stopped, and forgetting himself, looked at me. It was a flicker of contact, no more, but it was enough; our gazes had caught and snagged, tangled, pulled us taut. He turned his whole head away from me, but it was too late—his body was pulling hard at mine, and I felt the pull grow stronger as I leaned away from it; we were both hooked. My thoughts of what I would do with him later flew from my eyes to his body, and when they arrived, his body jumped. We were reeling each other in.

No one said a word. Even the wind seemed to have stopped. Were the other two staring at us? Or did I feel only the intensity of my own gaze?

"I have to go to the hardware store," Michelle said abruptly. "We're almost out of nails again. Eligio, would you come with me?"

I looked over at her. She was already standing up. *Michelle, you don't have to do that,* I thought at her. But she wouldn't look at me.

"We'll be back later," she called over her shoulder. Eligio was still getting to his feet. Later? She'd drop Eligio off at his house, she'd go in for coffee, she'd start talking to his wife and end up staying for dinner. Later meant Carlitos and I would be alone here for hours.

As soon as they were out of earshot, Carlitos turned to me. "Why didn't you come to the beach today?" he asked. He was still sitting there looking at the condensation on the water bag.

"I had to stay here," I said. "I'm sorry. I didn't say I'd come, though."

"I know," he said wonderingly, picking up a hammer, not seeing it, thinking, *How did I get here? How did I get to this point?*

I stood up. "Carlitos? Put the hammer down."

He did.

"Come here." He got up and took two steps toward me and stopped.

"Not here," he said. "Someone will see us."

"Who? The cows?"

"Let's go swimming."

"You came all the way out here for a swim?" I asked, and he twisted away from me and kicked at the ground with one foot. He was exquisite. I grinned at him. "What was wrong with the water in Sosúa?"

Without answering, he turned and started across the pasture toward the river. I followed him across the grass and down through the trees, along the slick mud trail until we had reached the point downstream where the water was shallow and flowed fast and hard over a meadow of stones.

He took off his shoes and waded across. I was already barefoot. I followed. He clambered up the bank on the far side, and ran up through the long grass into the banana groves. Only then did he stop. We were hidden in the green light of the leaves. He dropped his shirt in the sandy yellow earth and began to touch me.

I was lost for what might have been a long time in the weight and taste of his body. I lost my sense of time. Afterward it came back slowly, with the awareness of the ground under my back and a change in the quality of light filtering through the leaves. I looked up for the sun, to see what time it was, but all I saw was green.

Carlitos rolled away from me and sat up. He reached for his shirt. "What are you doing?" I asked.

"I have to go."

I got to my knees and fell against him, pushing him back down. "You can't," I said. I pinned his arms and kissed him again.

"I have to," he said through the kiss. "Tollomi, get up."

"Wait until Michelle comes back with the car. I'll drive you home."

"You should stay and help her build," he said. "I'll take a *guagua* back."

"So what should I tell Michelle? That you just left?"

"Don't tell her anything," he said forcefully.

"Carlitos, Michelle knows we're together."

"You told her?"

"Of course I told her." He looked so astonished that I laughed. "Carlitos, we have to get you out of this *pueblito* mindset. Let's go to Santo Domingo, just for the weekend. The *three* of us," I added when he gave me a sour look. "We'll all sleep in separate rooms, all right?"

"*Ay ay ay*," groaned Carlitos.

"Can I take that as a 'yes'?"

"Stop," he said. "I can't go away with you. Now, come on. I have to go." He stood up and put on his shirt.

"Why? What could be more important than lying here under the trees letting me lick ripe banana off your chest?"

"Cut it out."

"I'm serious, why do you have to leave all of a sudden? The way you keep running off as soon as we've had sex, you'd think you had to get back to your wife. You aren't secretly married, are you, Carlitos?"

"All right," he said angrily, "I'll tell you why: Ramón and Lobo and I are going to Ramón's cousin's house to watch TV. There's a movie on tonight. Satisfied?" Without waiting for an answer he turned and started back toward the river. I followed him and we waded across in silence.

"I'll go this way," he said, nodding at the trail along the bank. It led downstream to a place where the river went under a bridge at the main road. You could climb out there and in this way avoid walking through the village. He didn't want to be seen here, I knew.

"All right," I said, "goodbye," and I turned as if to go. Carlitos remained standing where he was.

"When do I see you again?" he asked.

"You see me now."

"I have to go now, I told you."

But he didn't move. He was waiting for me to kiss him.

"You could have invited me along, to watch the movie," I said.

"*Anda,* Tollomi—"

"Carlitos, what do you think I'd do? Grab you and stick my tongue down your throat in front of all your friends? I won't even *talk* to you if you don't want me to—I'll talk to them."

"If you don't even want to talk to me, then why would you want to go?"

"I didn't say I don't want to—Carlitos, look, I'm tired of sneaking around with you. I want to just go dancing again, you and me and Michelle, or go sit on the beach with you and your friends. Is that so much to ask?"

"Yes," he said simply, "it is."

"All right, then. Goodbye." I started up the path to the house.

"Tollomi!"

"What?"

"Will I see you tomorrow?"

"I don't know. Michelle might want to go to Santo Domingo, even if you don't. We might leave for the weekend."

He frowned. "You're not going away. Michelle has to work."

"You're right," I said, "I lied. Come here."

He came toward me and kissed me hard on the mouth. Every muscle of his body held itself taut against mine.

"Tomorrow?" he said in my mouth.

"In the afternoon," I answered, and felt him sigh against me. He opened his mouth for another kiss. I pushed him back. "Hadn't you better go, Carlitos? You don't want to be late for your engagement."

He frowned. "You wouldn't like the movie anyway," he said. "It's from the United States. About the boxing champion. *Rocky.*" He held up his fists and threw a jab at my shoulder that landed a little too hard to be playful. I stepped away from him.

"See?" he said. "I told you you wouldn't like it." And then he was gone, one step, five steps away from me, following the narrow bank of the river toward the village, pushing up a curtain of branches that were bent low with the weight of vines, and then the branches fell back, and I couldn't see him anymore.

I stood there a while longer, looking at the trees as if I could see his afterimage glowing against them. Then I turned and began the climb back up the hill.

Michelle had come back from the hardware store. She was sitting by herself on the edge of the foundation. I felt a rush of fear—this was just how I had found her the night before when she had insisted she'd seen her mother. And here I had left her alone yet again.

"Michelle?"

She turned her head at once and my stomach relaxed. I climbed up beside her.

"Where's Carlitos?" she asked.

"He went home."

She regarded me with that soft, searching gaze I always found unnerving. "You had a fight, didn't you?"

There was no need to answer; she rested her head on my shoulder in what might have been a gesture meant to comfort me. We sat in silence, looking out over the river toward the banana groves where Carlitos and I had just been. The light was beginning to deepen and intensify, the way it does in the hour before twilight, the hour of radiance before the inevitable fade. The valley was on fire with color: green, brown, blue, silver, and brilliant white where the sun struck the round stones that covered the far side of the river bank. I had been inside all that color just a short while ago, under the broad leaves full of light, and Carlitos had had a streak of dirt on his cheek, and his eyelids fluttered when he came—and then we had argued, and now he was gone again; he'd be halfway to Sabaneta by now. When Michelle spoke I jumped.

"What did you say?" I asked.

"That sometimes when I'm with you, I feel so sad."

Her face was turned away from me, down toward where the river slipped round the glowing hills.

"Sad because of me?" I asked.

"I don't know," she said thoughtfully. "I feel like I'm on a mountain, far away from everyone. When you're here I feel it more. But it isn't you."

She raised her head, and I followed her gaze past the green blur of the banana groves, out over the lowlands. Far in the distance lay the hard blue spill of the sea.

"Do you want me to go?" I said at last.

She knocked her head gently against my shoulder in reproof. "Tollomi, you know I don't. Besides, it wouldn't make any difference if you did. Don't you know that?"

I remembered the morning she had tried to leave the island. When she came back, holding my passport, I had felt the line between us pulled tight, as if a knot had been made fast. Lately I had been so caught up with Carlitos that I had not felt that line at all. What would happen to it if I left? Would the line tangle like kite string? Would I lose the wind and fall? Would I notice it at all?

"You don't believe me," she said. "You think if you left, or if I did, that would change things. But it wouldn't. Whatever's going to happen to me, or to you, is bound to happen. We can't change it…" she trailed off.

"I don't believe in destiny," I said. "We can do whatever we want. If you think you can't, Michelle, it's only because you're afraid of what you might do."

She shook her head. "That isn't it," she said. "No. You don't believe in destiny because you think you don't have one. You think you can just slip out the back and go somewhere else and become someone else and start all over. That's what you believe."

"It's what's always happened." I didn't look at her.

"That's not lack of destiny," she said. "That's just a mess."

Tollomi sleeps as if nothing can wake him, nothing except Carlitos perhaps. I can't sleep at all. I'm thinking about my mother, thinking about the house, about whether it's mine or not. I'm thinking about that word, *mine*. A thing that explodes.

I watch the dark shape of Tollomi's body sleeping, and the whole concept of sleep seems strange, foreign, impossible. His body can do it; for me sleep is an animal that cannot be caught.

When the sky begins to lighten, I watch Tollomi's face emerge from the darkness, his closed eyes, the way his nostrils move slightly as he breathes. I watch his face until I don't really see it anymore, I'm just looking. But it doesn't work, I'm still here, still awake, still thinking. At last I slide out of my sleeping bag and climb over him and step out of the tent.

Everything is wet. There's a chill on the wind. In the early light the house stands gray and silent. The beams and poles as pale as the cement.

I have built a house; out of a pile of black-market wood and a family story I have built it. Out of my grandfather's whim and my mother's thwarted journey. It is mine. The muscles in my arms and across my back have turned to rock, the palms of my hands are sandpaper. The *cana* should be here any day. Soon we'll be able to pack up the tent and sleep under a roof again. We'll be able to sleep in the house. My house. My nose is permanently sunburned. My lips are blistered and cracked.

One of the beach chairs Tollomi stole from Sosúa is lying overturned on the grass. I hoist it up on the foundation. I'll sit on the edge of the foundation that overlooks the valley and watch the sun rise—that will be a good thing to do, a normal thing. Tollomi would approve. I start to sit down, but if I stand up I can see the river too, a curling line of silver beginning to show through the mist. Soon the sky will color. This is my house. I have the calluses to prove it, the muscles. I have enough money to pay for the *cana*. I've done it, this house is real.

I turn to sit in the beach chair. There in the chair is my grandfather, scarcely a foot away from me, sitting in our stolen blue beach chair as if he's been sitting there forever. It's not a hallucination. I don't remember him clearly enough to hallucinate a whole person. It's not a memory. It's him.

His white hair is luminous, a shining mane above his light blue eyes. He smells faintly of aftershave, aftershave and juniper and wool. The smell goes through me like electricity through water. I remember it now, it's him, it's him.

He doesn't speak. He doesn't have to. *Come here,* say his eyes. He stretches out his hand, and of its own volition my hand rises too. His hand slides into mine and his perfectly manicured nails cover my own dirty ones. My grandfather's hand is warm.

"It's all right," he says. "It's a big house. No one will even know I'm here."

"But it's *my* house," I say. "It's *mine*." Even as I say the words I know they're not true—they're ridiculous, the words of a temper tantrum, a five-year old: mine, mine, mine. So instead I say, "You're dead." Isn't that what you're supposed to do with ghosts? Remind them they're supposed to cross the river to the nonliving side and stay there? Give them a little shove toward the opposite bank?

I yank my hand free. "You have to leave," I say. "You're dead."

"Not to you," says my grandfather gently. He shakes his lion's head and smiles.

When I come out of the tent, I find Michelle sitting motionless on the edge of the foundation. Something has happened; I'd have known that at once even if I had never laid eyes on her before. Her shoulders say it: the slight but unmistakable angles of distress. I hop up and sit beside her but jump down again at once. "The cement's all wet," I tell her, now feeling nothing but annoyed; I just put on my last pair of clean trousers. Michelle looks up at me.

"I think I made a mistake," she says. "I shouldn't have built this house after all."

"It's a little late for that, isn't it, Michelle? Get up, the cement's all wet."

"It *is* a little late," she says. "A lot late." Her teeth are chattering.

"Get up, you're cold. What's the matter?"

Her lopsided mouth curves into an unhappy smile.

"I don't know what to do. Tollomi, what am I going to do? Am I going crazy? Tell me. Look at me and tell me what you see."

"What, for God's sake? What's wrong now?"

"Yes, *now,* I know, it's one thing after another, isn't it? And now this. Well, I can't help it. Forget it, then."

"Michelle, I'm asking you to tell me: What do you want me to say?"

We go back and forth like this for a while, and I sit down beside her on the soaking concrete, and at last she tells me. She saw her grandfather in the beach chair; she touched him, talked to him. She breaks off in the middle of telling me this and jumps up and glares at me with her mouth trembling and her teeth stuttering against each other like a handful of broken stones.

"You don't believe me," she says.

"You know I do," I tell her, and it's halfway true: I believe it for *her;* or *as her* I believe it; looking through her eyes, I can see the arrangement of her world. But regarding her with my own eyes—standing up and walking over to the chair and dragging my hand along the rubber strapping and looking with my own eyes at the newly finished rafters overhead—I feel only an uneasy sinking in my chest that spreads out through my body, that pulls at my hand and whispers *hurry* and *leave*.

I coax her off the foundation and down the path to the river, hoping that if I get her out of sight of the house it will make a difference. It doesn't: She sits beside me on the flat rock with her arms tight around her knees as if she were cold; she's shaking.

"What can I do?" I ask. Cook her some food, rock her to sleep, feed her *dulce de leche?* Tell her to close her eyes, kiss her eyelids, then tell her she's dreaming and wake her up?

"Nothing," she says miserably. "You can't do a thing."

If the man she saw was real, I could cajole him from his beach chair, out-talk him, disarm him, make him leave. If she had fallen from the ladder and been hurt, I could clean the wound or splint the bone, keep her awake in case of concussion. But there's no one to speak to and nothing to bandage. Trouble darkens her face like a circling plane.

"The world looks so solid," she says. "See?" She bangs on the rock with her knuckles.

"Don't. You'll hurt yourself."

"So wonderfully solid, Tollomi. So *here*. As if there weren't another world all around us every moment. As if there were no chance that at any moment everything could just give way."

Again she brings her fist down on the rock.

"Michelle, stop it." I put my hand over hers, and she looks up at me, then away. And I realize that if she lets me, if she lets me look into her eyes now, I'll see what's there. I'll know what it is that she keeps hidden from herself. I'll know what makes her leave, what she runs from, what's wrong. I won't know it with words, perhaps. But I'll know.

I don't want to look. I don't want to be privy to a secret she's still excluded from. But as I think this, I feel the secret anyway, not as a shock or anything sudden, but with the quiet dull certainty of something I've already known for a long time. It's part of her sleepwalking and her forgetting and part of her vision of this man who even from the far side of death can reach out and grab hold of her hand.

And she thinks she remembers nothing. She thinks that to forget a thing is to make it as if it never happened. She can't remember what he did to her, so she thinks nothing was done. How young was she when it started? How old at the end? If such a thing can be said to be ended. She is living and breathing her past with every moment, unaware. In, out. Like air.

It happens to so many women, so many girls—why should I be surprised? You can always see it if you look. I hadn't wanted to be looking. Some women wear the damage like clothes that don't fit right. The shoulder straps keep slipping, as if their bodies want to be a different size. Sometimes the damage shows in their faces; it signals from their eyes like someone leaning from a window, calling for help. Some women hold the damage in their hands like a knife, turn it inward against the wrists and press hard. And a few women hold the knife outward, hack a trail where no trail is, cut a path out; some women get away.

But Michelle? She loses her clothes. She leaves her home. She is indifferent to weapons of every kind. And you look in her eyes and see nothing, no one signals from the window, she isn't there at all. The room is empty.

"Michelle, I think we should leave here," I say.

Her expression changes. An odd little smile flickers at her mouth and vanishes.

"Leave here?" she echoes. "Leave where?"

"The house. We could go to Santo Domingo. Or east somewhere. Just away from Las Piedras."

"And what would that accomplish?" She sounds almost amused. "What does Las Piedras have to do with this? Tollomi, I can't leave. There's nowhere to go. Don't you see what I've done? I've covered thousands of miles. I've gone so far away. I haven't been home in what—three years? I've gone all the way around the world and come to this spot and built a house—a whole *house,* Tollomi, and who's in it? My parents. My grandparents. Look at all the shoe leather I've wasted. You'd think death, at least, would have made a wall between us, but it doesn't. The door opens and everything is right here, just as I left it. The door opens and anything at all could come through." She pauses for breath. "Tollomi. Am I'm going crazy?"

"You know you're not crazy," I tell her.

"I *don't* know—that's why I'm asking you. Tell me. Look at my eyes and tell me. I'll know if you're lying. Tell me what you see." But she keeps her eyes on the river. She doesn't want to know.

"Now, listen," I say, "I want us to leave here for a while. I'm not talking about a major exodus. I'm saying we should get in the car, drive a few hours, spend a few nights in a hotel away from this place."

"Who's 'we'?"

"You and me. And Carlitos."

"What makes you think he'd come? Anyway, I can't. I have to work at Sam's."

"You can't go to work. Tell Sam you need a few days off. He'll give them to you."

"But it won't make any difference, Tollomi. There isn't any point. If we go somewhere else, everything will still be just the same."

"Then will you come simply as a favor to me?"

She sighs. But she doesn't say no.

"Ask Sam today. I'll drive you over there later on and then we can—"

"Oh, no." She jumps up.

"What?"

"I have to go. I have to go to work. I told Sam I'd be in early today. He has some meeting in Cabarete about his new restaurant, and I said I'd cover."

"Michelle, you *cannot* go to work."

She looks down at me.

"Why not?" She's serious.

"Because of what's happening to you—what do you mean, 'why not?' You can't just go in there and pour drinks for eight hours and make small talk. Not now."

She shakes her head. "You think they'll notice? You think they'll say, 'Look at Michelle, what's wrong with her, she's coming unglued?' I could walk in there with no *head*, Tollomi, and no one would notice. It's a *bar.* No one's going to notice a goddamn thing."

She starts up the muddy path, and I get up and follow her. When we reach the top of the pasture, we both stop: Between the house and the mango tree are four men—Eligio and Manuel and two others—all unloading piles of newly cut palm from the backs of two donkeys. The *cana* has arrived.

Eligio sees us and waves. "*¡Carpintora!* Your roof is here at last! We'll have the house finished in no time!"

Michelle and I just stand there.

"What timing," she says at last. "It's really very funny if you think about it."

"Go ahead and laugh, then."

She gives me an empty look and walks off toward the tent.

One of her sandals is lying in the grass outside the tent fly. She works her foot into it and stands there in one shoe, still watching the men unload the *cana* I go over to the tent myself and find her other sandal and hand it to her. She puts it on without noticing it.

"You're really going to work, then?" I ask.

"Apparently."

"I'll ride in with you."

"You can if you want, but hurry up. I'm late."

Michelle drives. When we reach the road that leads down into Sosúa, she pulls off the main road and stops.

"I'm coming with you to Puerto Plata," I say.

"What for?"

"To be sure you're okay."

"I'm okay. Get out." She taps her fingers on the steering wheel. "Tollomi, go. Carlitos will be waiting."

She reaches across me and opens the passenger door. She looks me in the eye. "Go," she says, and I get out of the car and stand barefoot on the burning pavement. I shut the door and lean in through the window.

"Promise me you'll ask Sam for some time off."

"I promise. Now will you go? I'm late."

"You're sure you're all right?"

"Don't ask me that," she says angrily, and jams the car in gear.

She's right; it's a stupid question. And if she won't let me tell her what I feel I know, then there's nothing else I can say. I feel the unspoken words swollen in my throat so that no other words, not even lies, can get by. So I watch her drive away, and then I walk down the road to the beach.

Carlitos must have been waiting for me. I've only just stepped onto the sand when he appears from beside a cluster of trees. I wave. He comes toward me but with his head turned toward the sea as if he hasn't seen me at all, just in case anyone's watching.

"Where's your car?" he asks, still looking at the water.

"I don't have it today."

"You didn't bring it?" The tense anticipation in his face shifts toward something like José Luis's habitual scowl.

"Michelle has it," I say. "Look, let's take a *guagua* to Playa Long Beach. We can get out by the park and then go say hi to her at work." I don't want to leave her in the bar unattended.

"There are too many people on Long Beach," says Carlitos.

"Too many people to just sit on the sand for a while and go swimming?"

"Cut it out," he says irritably. "You know what I mean."

Of course I know. He wants to go off and have sex; I can feel the energy of it pulsing around his body, reaching me even through my layers of worry about Michelle like a strong sun piercing through haze.

"I can't believe you don't have the car," he says. He looks up and down the beach as if he expects to see it parked on the sand.

"Come on," I say. "Let's go see Michelle, and then we'll get a hotel room in Puerto Plata."

He takes a half step away from me and mumbles a string of curses under his breath. "I don't have *time*, Tollomi. I have to meet José Luis when he gets off work."

"So be late." He doesn't answer. "Carlitos, what do you want me to say? Let's stay here, then. That would make me perfectly happy. Let's sit right here on the sand for an hour and just talk to each other."

He picks up a handful of sand and throws it at the water. He looks up and down the beach again.

"*Coño,*" he mutters. "All right, come on."

"Where?"

"To my house."

"Your house?" I'm genuinely surprised. "After all this time?"

Instead of replying, he turns and walks quickly down to where the sand is still wet from the outgoing tide. Down by the water he can cross the beach without having to stop and meet the gaze of anyone he knows. To make him happy, I don't run to catch up with him. I walk up the sand to where the vendors are and cross the full length of the beach by myself.

He's waiting for me at the stone steps. He hurries me through the streets, an arm's length of space between us, lest any passersby think we're together. But we are together; Carlitos himself isn't fooled. By the time we stop in front of a small two-story building deep in Charamicos, he looks as miserable and angry as if we'd been arguing all the way.

It's a cinder-block house with faded yellow paint and a lopsided iron balcony. That's all I have time to notice before he unlocks the padlock, pushes me through the door, and shuts it behind us. The room's windows are shuttered, and I blink in the dimness. There's a double mattress on the floor with no bedding save for a rumpled sheet. Two wooden chairs and a small dresser are pushed against the wall. Some toothpaste and a few jars sit on top of the dresser. Other than this, the room shows no signs of actually being lived in.

"Where do you cook?" I ask.

"Upstairs," he says shortly. "My aunt."

He kicks off his shoes and unbuttons his jeans.

We make love too fast, on the bare mattress. It's the first time we've ever lain down on a bed together, but his hands on my body are as hurried and impersonal as if we were strangers.

Afterward, he sits up again almost at once. I reach out to pull him back onto the mattress; he resists. I slip my hand under his shirt, which he hasn't bothered to take off, and trace lines across his shoulder blades.

"We have to go," he says.

"Carlitos, relax."

"Shh—what was that?"

"What?"

"Listen."

I listen: On the other side of the walls the sounds of the street pass all around us. I hear motorcycles, snatches of music, voices calling and other voices answering, a door being slammed. Then, in the apartment above our heads, a radio begins to play.

Carlitos jumps as if the musicians themselves had burst in on us. "My cousin's home," he says hoarsely.

"Your cousin? Let's go meet him."

"It's not funny, Tollomi. Get dressed."

"I'm not being funny," I say. "I want to meet him. Don't *worry*, Carlitos. He's not going to know unless you tell him."

"Will you please get dressed? Come *on*."

"Your voice sounds just like José Luis's right now."

"You know something? I wish the rest of me were just like him too."

"You don't mean that," I say.

"How do you know what I mean? If I were José Luis—"

"It's not José Luis I'm in love with."

He stares at me. I've said the forbidden word. I look straight into his eyes, but he can't hold the gaze. He looks down.

"Just put your clothes on," he says.

I don't move.

"Will you put them *on*?" He picks up my trousers and throws them at me. "My cousin comes down here sometimes. We have to go *now*." There's an edge of panic in his voice. I put on my trousers.

"Where are your shoes?" he asks.

"I wasn't wearing any." He should have known that.

Carlitos goes to the door and opens it. He'll never bring me here again, I realize, and glance back at the bed to remember what it looks like. Then we are out in the street and Carlitos is locking the door.

We walk together as far as the road that leads to the highway, but though I match my strides to his, I might as well be walking alone. When we part he says goodbye to me as if I were anyone, as if he were someone else, as if the taste of my cock were not still on his tongue.

After he leaves, I turn and walk a little way back into Charamicos and sit at a sidewalk bar. I drink beer and watch a man across the street fixing his motorcycle, and a dog nosing in a pile of rotting orange rinds. A boy calls to a woman hanging laundry on an upper balcony. For Carlitos, this is the whole world: this street, these people. Once upon a time I too woke in the morning and looked out at a world that was the only world there was. That world was made up of the smell of frangipani and plaster and ocean, the sounds of Josephine and Etty talking and banging dishes. Those were the sounds and smells of all the mornings in the world, to me, once.

I order more beer and drink until the noises from the street begin to blur a little at the edges. I drink until the street grows soft and indistinct in a wash of color just vague enough so that it might be anywhere at all.

I've seen it in his eyes: He loves me. He doesn't know how to make a space for that love, he doesn't know where to put it, now that it's here, but here it is. It's not his fault.

"Love laughs at locksmiths," goes the line, but once love has tricked the knob into turning and opened the door, what then? Where is the bed that is big enough for love to lie down on? Where is the world big enough to hold all worlds inside it? Where do you put love when the room is too small?

I have no answer. I signal the waiter and order more beer.

When I get up from the table the sun is setting. It's too late now to go into Puerta Plata; by the time I arrived, Michelle might be on the highway heading back to Las Piedras. So I go back to the house to wait for her.

The *cana* men have come and worked; they're gone now, but the entire east side of the roof is done. The still-green points of *cana* hanging over the eaves shine bright and almost golden in the sharp light of the sunset. I climb onto the foundation and look at the beach chair sitting there. This is where Michelle said she'd seen her grandfather. It doesn't matter what happened here this morning; what matters is what happened to Michelle years before. I could tell her what I sense, what I believe, but will she hear the words at all, assuming I can even say them? Or will she see my mouth move but hear only the river, the chirping frogs, the wind?

And what are we going to do with this house, now so close to completion, this thing she's built that has turned out to be just what she's spent her whole life running from?

I drag the beach chair off the foundation so Michelle won't be reminded of who she saw in it when she comes back from work. I move the two chairs across the grass, away from the house, and sit down and light a lantern and try to read. The moon is rising, and every frond in the roof's silhouette stands out sharp and black against the bright indigo sky. I'm distracted: by my own thoughts, by the presence of the strange roof overhead, by the moonlight, by listening for the sound of the car. When at last it comes, the engine straining up the hills, I feel no relief. But I jump up and wait impatiently while she parks at the bottom of the pasture and then trudges up the hill.

"Don't say anything about this morning," she says, glancing toward the new roof and, as far as I can tell, not registering it. "There's nothing to say. All right?"

"All right," I say. "How was work, then?" I want to know whether she told Sam she'll be taking a vacation.

"Ixnay on that too," she says.

"What?"

She flops down in one of the beach chairs. "Ix-nay. Ig-pay atin-lay. I don't want to talk about work either."

I sit down in the other chair. "Did you tell Sam you need some time off?"

"I—no, I didn't. I got there late and he was in a bad mood, and then when he came back from Cabarete he was too drunk."

"Ask him tomorrow, Michelle, or I'll ask him myself. I'll *tell* him. So ask him tomorrow. All right?" She just sits there. "Michelle?"

"I know you want to get out of here," she says dully.

"Not for my sake. For yours."

"And Carlitos?"

"That's another subject."

She looks up quickly. "What happened?"

"Nothing," I say. "I finally saw his house."

"You had an argument."

"Why do you think so?"

"Did you?"

"We aren't talking about Carlitos," I say. "We're talking about getting away from here for a while."

She sighs. "All over the world, Tollomi, there are people who can't just leave places to get away from things. They have bad jobs or bad marriages, or someone dies or there's a war, but they just stay there and go on with their lives."

"And so what? I'm not one of those people and neither are you."

"Maybe I'm becoming one," she says.

We go to bed after that. I thought she had gone to sleep right away, but about an hour later she sits up and says in a low, clear voice, "Will you do something for me?"

"Of course. I thought you were asleep."

"Tollomi, listen, I—I know you want to leave, and if you want to, you should of course. I already told you that..."

"What is it you wanted, Michelle? Just ask."

"I—*no me dejas sola aquí con los espantos, ¿de acuerdo?*" The words come out in a rush: *Don't leave me here alone with the ghosts, okay?* She could never have said them in English; that would make the words too vulnerable, too much hers.

I draw my arm out from under the sheet and find her hand and hold it. "I won't leave you here," I say, speaking in Spanish also. "I promise."

"I promise," Tollomi said. I didn't ask him to promise. I shouldn't have asked him at all.

When I wake up the next morning, I wake alone. Tollomi isn't beside me; he isn't outside, and the car isn't there either. Where could he have gone so early? His things are still here, but when he does leave for good, this is just how it will be. He'll take the car, leave without saying anything because nothing can be said. I'll stand here alone and watch the house just as I'm watching now. I'm watching it like a door. I'm waiting to see who will come through.

The air is still heavy with mist, and the house sits sphinx-like, half-dark in its own shadows and as cold and still as the air in a well. Its voice held back like a breath but on the point of bursting, ready to burst into echoes the moment I let something fall.

I'm afraid. I go back in the tent and shut the fly. All of Tollomi's things are still here: his suitcase, the shoes he never wears, a book he stole from the library in Santo Domingo. He wants me to go with him, to leave here.

Yesterday after I told him I had seen my grandfather, he insisted we leave at once. "a vacation," he said, "Río San Juan, Santo Domingo, Samaná, even."

I would like to go, I would like nothing better than to go with him and go away and be somewhere else. But I can't go, it's not possible, I have lost the one thing absolutely vital to the undertaking of a journey. I have lost the belief that I will end up in a place different from where I started.

I couldn't explain this to Tollomi. We sat there on the flat rocks by the river, and I turned away from him, and there on my other side sat my grandfather. Again, there he was. When I looked at him, he turned his head and his eyes met mine. He nodded, *Yes, that's right, Michelle. You could go all the way around the world, Michelle, but you can't leave home simply by running away.*

My grandfather followed us off the rocks and sat behind me in the car on the way to work. Tollomi didn't feel a thing; he kept glancing at me, anxious, but he thought we were alone in the car, and I almost laughed—it was almost amusing.

My grandfather followed me into work. Other footsteps followed his. I didn't need to look to know who it was. My grandmother always wore high heels with rubber grips on the soles to keep her from slipping, a very distinctive tread. And then my mother's footsteps—I'd recognize them anywhere: sandaled, booted, in tennis shoes or barefoot I'd know them. I could distinguish her footsteps from all others, anywhere.

The three of them, my grandfather, my grandmother and my mother trooped in after me. The bar was already full of other people, and Sam was behind the bar making drinks, and Sonya was still there cleaning, wiping dust off the little iron anchors that sit on the corners of the bar.

Sam was yelling. I only half-heard the words, as if they were part of a television program I wasn't watching. *What is this you're forty minutes late I'm supposed to be in Cabarete right now since when is it Dominican time in here?*

He was yelling at me.

"What?" I raised my head.

"Michelle! You're a gringa, I'm a gringo: When I say 'noon,' I mean noon, and you know it. What am I running here? A *business*. I said *noon*." He pushed his hair out of his eyes and glared at me.

Sonya looked up from wiping the anchor and shrugged. *He's been like this all day,* the shrug said.

Neither of them had noticed my little family entourage. I felt the three of them behind me, looking around, choosing seats, deciding what they were drinking. I looked around the bar myself, at the other customers, but no one else had noticed them. A bar is a haunted place already.

"Go," I said to Sam. "Goodbye. I'll see you tonight. And leave the glass here." He had gone as far as the door with his drink still in his hand. He turned halfway around, took a swallow of melted ice, slammed the glass down on a table, and banged out.

When he had gone I turned to Sonya, who had started in on cleaning the license plates. "I'll finish the cleaning," I said. "You can go home."

"I can't," she said, wiping license plates as if her life depended on it. "My mother is still in Santiago."

I went over and took the rag out of her hands. "Sonya, stop working."

"What do you want me to do, then?"

"Anything you want. Play."

She regarded me with her great somber eyes for a long, unblinking moment, and then she nodded.

I watched her go up the stairs to Sam's apartment, and after a moment the sound of television music came faintly through the ceiling. I recognized it: American cartoons.

I stood there and mixed drinks. I made small talk. I broadcast a pre-recorded program and nobody noticed. My grandparents sat at a table near the stairs and drank gin and tonics. My mother didn't sit with them. She was restless. She wandered back and forth between their table and the bar. "That bird up there looks unhappy," she said once.

"I know," I said. "I ought to set it free."

She didn't seem to hear me. "If that were my parrot," she said, "I'd get a bigger cage."

"It isn't a parrot," I told her.

"What?"

"It's not a parrot. The bird."

My mother looked around vaguely. Her eyes came to rest on my face. "Oh," she said, no longer listening. "Well, you can ask your father when he gets here."

"Where is he?" I asked.

"Who knows?" said my mother. She rolled her eyes and gave an elaborate shrug. She waved her hands in the air and walked back to the table where my grandparents were sitting. I watched them for a moment, and then I couldn't stop watching, even though I needed to: Someone had come up to the bar and wanted a drink: Peter Drake. I heard him saying my name and me not answering to it. My mother was still talking to my grandparents. Then my grandfather pushed his chair back and stood up. He was coming toward me, coming up to the bar. I couldn't stop watching, but it stopped being me who watched. Someone else was watching them, and I became the glass in Peter Drake's hand, the lime at the bottom of the glass. I became the fan revolving overhead, the jar of maraschino cherries. I was the bottles of liquor lining the shelves, I was the shelves. I was the bucket of ice, I was the bird in the cage.

And then I was back in my own body again, and the table where they had been sitting was empty. Peter Drake was drinking a full highball I must have poured. I wished Tollomi were there, but Tollomi was off with Carlitos, and Tollomi thinks leaving means the same thing as getting away. He's wrong, he can't help me at all, and this morning I wake up and he isn't even here.

I promise, he said, and I shouldn't have asked, I know, but I was desperate. The ghosts are going to get me. I am desperate, but there's no point in going to look for him. I'm here in the house. There's nowhere else to go.

I had awakened at dawn with a headache. Michelle lay sprawled half in, half out of her sleeping bag, her arms awry, her shirt twisted around her stomach. Don't leave me alone with the ghosts, she had said, and I promised I wouldn't. *Don't leave me alone with my grandfather,* she should have said, but it's too late for that. And she still doesn't know. Without waking her I climbed out of the tent and went across the misty yard to the house. I knew I wouldn't see what I was looking for, but I looked anyway, squinting, holding myself terribly still, as if by being properly patient I could force an apparition from the air.

Los espantos, to the children.

My grandfather, to Michelle.

House, to Bartholomew, house and nothing more. If something more was there, I couldn't see it. I tried closing my eyes, and then I did feel something, a prickle of anxiety in my breath, along my fingers. Someone else was here with me.

I opened my eyes: the house was still empty. Of course it was still empty. But the feeling persisted, and the hairs on my neck stood up cold. I turned and looked out over the yard, and then I saw the person. Someone was coming up the hill, running hard.

Carlitos, I thought, and my pulse surged and then stumbled, checked itself. It was not Carlitos. It was José Luis. I watched his pounding strides up the hill, and thought dully, he's found out about us somehow; he saw us together on his bed in Charamicos. I wondered what I would do if he hit me, which he almost certainly would, and then I thought that I didn't want Michelle to wake up and see this, so I went across the grass and down the hill to meet him.

He was out of breath.

"Carlitos—" he began and broke off panting.

I waited. Would he try to hit me in the face? The stomach? Would I duck? Hit back?

"Carlitos has been hurt," he finished.

"Hurt how?"

José Luis ran his fingers through his hair in agitation. "He was lighting a stove, and the propane tank exploded."

"Is he all right?"

"No, he's not all right, he's burned. You think I'd come all the way out here if he was—"

"Where is he now?"

"Near Cabarete."

"Cabarete! You left him in Cabarete?"

"The burns are too bad to take him on the motorcycle. I came because we need your car."

We ran back down the hill to where the car was parked. As José Luis got in beside me, I noticed a man sitting on a motorcycle a little farther down the road. José Luis gave him a nod as we drove past, and the man revved his engine and pulled out behind us. I started to ask who he was but was stopped by the look on José Luis's face. He was staring straight ahead with a fixed blank expression I had never seen before. It had softened his features to such a degree that he looked quite young somehow, and I realized with a start that what I was seeing was fear. The recognition sent a wave of fear through my own body. It jumped through the air between us and grounded itself in my gut.

We reached the main road. "How did he do it?" I asked.

"I told you," said José Luis. "He was lighting a stove and the gas blew up on him."

"In his face?"

The steering wheel was slick with sweat under my hands.

"Not his face so much. His hands and arms."

"Where was the stove? There isn't one in your house." As I was saying this, I remembered dimly that José Luis wasn't supposed to know I had been in their house; I glanced at him and saw he hadn't even noticed the slip; he was too upset. "He's badly hurt, isn't he?" I asked.

"Will you just drive?" he snapped, and his familiar anger comforted me for a second. Then the second passed, and neither of us spoke until we were almost to Cabarete, when José Luis said suddenly, "Turn here." He pointed inland to a narrow dirt road.

"Carlitos is up there?"

"Yes."

The dirt road forked off into a lane barely wide enough to get the car through. Branches scraped through the open windows as I drove. The lane dead-ended at a shack made of unpainted palm wood. The door, which had been shut, opened as we drove up. A young man in blue jeans stood in the doorway. We got out of the car, and he stepped aside to let us pass.

The shack had a dirt floor. Carlitos sat on the floor leaning against the wall, his head hanging down. His hands and forearms were covered with long, mottled burns. His skin looked as though pieces of wet tissue paper had been plastered to it and then scraped away—this was his skin, too light in some places where it had been rubbed over on itself, and too dark in others, the terrible color of lifted flesh, rosy with the nearness of blood.

"My God," I said, "Carlitos?"

He did not raise his head.

"He's drunk," said José Luis. "We gave him rum to dull the pain. There was nothing else; we can't take him to the doctor."

"We can now," I said. I knelt beside Carlitos and choked on the smell of burned hair. There was another smell too, something chemical. Gasoline.

"Carlitos?" I touched his shoulder.

He raised his head. His eyebrows had burned off. His eyes stared blankly from a face that seemed frozen in a grimace of surprised pain.

"Carlitos?" I said gently. "I'm here now. We're taking you to the doctor, I have the car. Lean forward, I'm going to help you stand up."

"He can't go to the doctor," said a voice behind me, and I remembered there were other people in the room. José Luis and the man in jeans had been joined by the man I'd seen on the motorcycle. It was he who had spoken.

"Can't?" I repeated. I looked from him to José Luis, and then José

Luis squatted beside me and for the first time really looked me full in the eyes.

"Listen," he said softly, "if we take Carlitos to a doctor, we'll all be arrested."

"What do you mean?" I asked, but even as I said it I saw it. All at once, in his eyes I saw it. The fires. Not burns from an exploding stove. From fires set on purpose. The hotels. Hotel Parasol, La Hacienda, Pension Tic-Tac, the Windsurf Beach Hotel.

"It was you," I said. My voice sounded far away.

"All right," said José Luis, still very softly, "it was us. Now you know. Now come on, we have to get Carlitos to the car."

"It was you?" I heard myself say again, and this time it came out like a question. "All this time I thought whoever was burning the hotels was doing it to protest what's happening to the island, and now I find out it's just you?"

"Come on," interrupted José Luis, "We don't have time for this."

"You, whose idea of protest is getting into fights in bars with—" I broke off and looked at Carlitos. José Luis was right, this was not the time. "He still has to go to a doctor," I said. "We'll take him to Santiago. No one will know him there."

"No hospital," said the man from the motorcycle. "Understand? No hospital. No doctor."

I looked up at him. He was somewhere in his twenties, about the same age as José Luis, and his eyes held the same furious intensity. "No hospital," he repeated, and I stood and faced him.

"Because *you* don't want to get caught? Look at Carlitos's arms. You have no choice."

"Tollomi?" The voice, oddly clear, was Carlitos's. We all turned and looked at him.

"Yes," I said, "I'm right here."

"No doctor." His eyes found mine and made an effort to focus. "No doctor, Tollomi. He's right. I can't."

José Luis swore. "Come on, for God's sake. Let's get him to the car."

"And go where?" I said.

"Will you just shut up and help me move him? We're going to take him to Lupe's."

"Lupe Vásquez?"

"Yes, Lupe Vásquez."

"What for?"

"She'll take care of him, idiot."

"José, that's crazy. You can't just show up at her house and expect her to—"

"She already said she'd help us. She *offered,* Tollomi. Weeks ago, she said that if we ever got in trouble she'd help us out. Now move."

I couldn't take in what he was saying. So I stopped trying. I made my mind shut down and focus only on getting Carlitos to his feet and helping him out to the car. We managed to get him into the back seat and José Luis climbed in beside him. The other two men stood in the doorway and watched as I tried to turn the car around and realized I couldn't; the lane was too narrow. So I drove in reverse all the way down to the main road. José Luis held Carlitos's shoulders, trying to brace him against the bumps in the road, but Carlitos gasped in pain each time the wheels hit a rut.

When we turned onto the paved highway, José Luis let go of Carlitos and sat back, and I said, "Explain about Lupe."

"Explain what?"

"Damn it, José, you know what. Talk. Tell me right now."

And he did; I had to keep prodding him, but he told me, beginning with the day we had all gone to Lupe's for lunch. While Carlitos and I were down by the river eating *limoncillos,* while I threw *limoncillo* pods at the river to keep my hands occupied so I would not simply reach out and grab Carlitos by his beautiful shoulders, while we played on the riverbank, drunk on each others' presence, José Luis was up in Lupe's cooking shed, watching her pull the feathers off a chicken and telling her he had been setting fires down by the sea.

"Then she knew all this time that you were running around without any real plan, pouring gasoline over whatever suited your fancy, and she said she'd help you? Bullshit, José."

He leaned forward in the car seat until I felt his breath hot on the side of my jaw.

"Who says we had no plan?" he hissed at me. "You think you know anything about what we were doing? You know nothing! And do you know why you know nothing? Because you're too busy taking my brother and—" He fell back against the seat and the rest of it dissolved in a mumble of curses. In the rearview mirror I saw him look at Carlitos, miserable and hazy with pain beside him. He put his arm gingerly around Carlitos's shoulders again, and I dropped the subject for the moment and turned my attention back to the road; we were nearing the turnoff for Sosúa. I slowed down and pulled into the Texaco station.

"You can't stop for gas here," said José Luis, "we're too visible. You can buy some further on at—"

"I'm not stopping for gas. We need things from the pharmacy. Bandages."

"*Coño,* Tollomi, what we *need* is not to be seen. Drive, for God's sake."

I yanked the keys out of the ignition, just in case, and ran around the gas pumps to the drugstore.

Inside a normal morning was going on. There was already a line at the register. A gringa in front of me was buying suntan oil. I waited. I made myself breathe slowly. She had to count her change twice before she picked up her purse and moved out of the way.

I asked the druggist in English for amoxicillin. He gave me the strips of pills, each one wrapped in a red plastic wrapper and attached to the next like a strip of penny candies. I asked for gauze, Merthiolate, hydrogen peroxide, codeine, and a box of tampons.

"For the codeine you have a prescription?" asked the druggist in careful English. He was already getting the other things down from the shelves.

"They said I didn't need one," I replied in indignant American. "The doctor said we could just get everything over the counter, not like in the States." I scratched my chin. The panic I was keeping out of my face was burning a hole in my chest. I had no idea what I was going to say next. "My girlfriend fell off one of those rental scooters," I said. "She got banged up pretty bad. Nine stitches." I leaned on the counter and looked straight at him and waited.

The druggist coughed. "Which doctor you go to?" he asked.

"Down the road there, the one on the corner across from the supermarket." I had no idea if there was a doctor there or not, but the druggist nodded. He didn't move from the counter, though.

"Codeine is an opiate," he said. "People use it like drugs."

Two people had come into the shop behind me. I hadn't turned to look at them, but I heard them shifting impatiently in their rubber sandals. *Stay with it, Tollomi. Think—American guy.* I took a deep breath. "Well, hey, could you like, call up the doctor and check or something? Really, it's not for me. It's for my girlfriend."

The druggist sighed. He looked down at the counter, and his eyes fell on the tampons. He sucked his teeth. "I give it to you this time," he said grudgingly. "Next time you bring the prescription."

I thanked him and paid. He put everything in a bag for me. I walked slowly across the asphalt, bought a bottle of 7UP from the *refrescos* stand, and got back in the car.

"Are you crazy?" howled José Luis. "Are you fucking crazy?"

"Don't yell," I said.

"You want to fuck this up? Somebody might have seen us! You want us to wind up in jail?"

I opened the bottle of codeine and shook out two pills. "Carlitos," I said, "these are painkillers. I'll give you two now, you can wash them down with this—"

"For God's sake," said José Luis, grabbing the soda, "if you want to help him, just get us out of the busiest intersection on the whole goddamn coast. You'd like to see *me* get arrested, wouldn't you? Well, think about Carlitos. You want to see *him* lying in a filthy cell? With flies crawling over his—"

"Stop it," I said. "Carlitos, open your mouth." He did, and I gave him the pills.

"*Hijo de la gran puta, maricón,*" José Luis said to me.

I didn't contradict him on that, and then he shut up.

I parked as close to Lupe's as I could; even so, we had to walk more than a quarter of a mile uphill, and then through the guava trees. José Luis and I got on either side of Carlitos, and we walked sideways, crab-like, up the narrow path. It took more than half an hour; Carlitos kept tripping, and each time his hands banged against us he moaned. The rum had worn off.

We came through Lupe's garden three abreast, stepping on her lettuce plants. She must have heard us; she came out of the house and started across the yard. Halfway there she saw Carlitos clearly; she stopped where she was, and her hand flew up toward her mouth in a gesture she checked at once so that the hand stayed frozen for a moment in midair.

"*Santísimo*," she gasped, "what have you done?" But she did not want an answer. "Bring him inside," she commanded, now in control of herself again, and she hurried ahead of us, pushing rocking chairs out of the way, and drew back the curtain that hung over the doorway to her bedroom.

"Put him on the bed," she said. "We'll need water. José Luis: the rain barrel outside."

He disappeared without a murmur, and she turned to me.

"We'll have to cut his shirt off. Tollomi, get me the scissors. In that drawer. Carlitos? Sit up, *mi amor*."

She sat on the edge of the bed and helped Carlitos swing his feet onto the floor. Carlitos looked vaguely around the room.

"Where is José Luis?" he said thickly.

"He'll be right back. The scissors, Tollomi."

I gave them to her, and she snipped open first one of Carlitos's sleeves and then the other; then the shears opened and closed across his chest and the whole shirt fell away like the skin of a ripened fruit. And there was his body, the body that had wrestled me into ecstasy in the soft earth of the banana groves a few days before.

"Lean forward," Lupe was saying. "Here's José Luis with the water. We're going to clean your arms now, Carlitos. It will sting."

José Luis set the water down with a bang. "Put your arms in here," he said.

I said, "That water's dirty."

"It's rain water."

"It doesn't matter, José. His arms will get infected. Carlitos, wait." I fumbled in my pockets for the bottle of Merthiolate I had bought in Sosúa.

"What is that shit?" said José Luis.

"Iodine." I poured it in, and the water turned the color of the river after a rain.

"Iodine," repeated José Luis incredulously. "What do you think this is, drinking water for gringos? All right, Carlitos, go ahead. Dunk in your arms."

"Not yet," I said, "we have to wait five minutes."

"Tollomi, José—" Lupe glared at us. "Get up. Go outside. Leave Carlitos with me."

I stood, not to leave but to face her.

"Go outside," she repeated.

"Lupe, this is crazy. Carlitos should be in a hospital. Look, I'll take him clear over to the other side of the island. I'll take him to Santo Domingo."

Lupe put her hand on my arm. "Tollomi, you know that's ridiculous. Carlitos will be fine here. I've seen burns that were much worse than these—"

"I'm sure you have—who else has José Luis dragged up here with his skin half off?"

"Stop it." She dug her nails into my arm. "Stop it now. Stop. What's happened has happened and Carlitos is here. There's no sense in taking him somewhere else. Have you ever seen our hospitals, Tollomi? They're not a pretty sight. He's better off here. Now get hold of yourself."

She let go of my arm. Her nails had pressed four crescent moons into my skin. I looked at the marks in a kind of daze for a moment and then back at Lupe.

"Go home now," she said. "I'll take care of Carlitos. Come back later this evening, and you'll see, he'll be fine."

"All right, Carlitos," said José Luis behind me, "put your hands in the water."

I turned around to look at them, but Lupe caught me by the arm again. "Tollomi, *ven*," she said, and nearly dragged me out of the room. She was surprisingly strong. She led me through the tangle of rocking chairs and onto the veranda.

"If you could bring something for pain when you come back," she said in a low voice. "I don't know what you can get without a prescription, but try and find something strong. I don't think he'll be able to sleep otherwise."

I took out the codeine bottle I had bought in Sosúa and gave it to her. She read the label, then looked up at me and sighed a smile.

"You're very good," she said, "very clever. I wish I'd known you before, Tollomi—in Santo Domingo, before Jorge died. We could have used you."

"I wish I'd known you then too," I said. "I'd like to have met you when you were using your talents for something a little nobler than providing the hideout for a gang of fire-happy *machos* with no agenda other than trying to show off for each other—" I caught myself, but not in time.

Lupe blinked at me. "You would have preferred that Carlitos be left lying in that dirty shack?"

"It's not a question of that, Lupe. You knew from the beginning what they were doing; José Luis told me you knew. You know what he's like. He's just doing this because he likes to make people angry. I've seen him after fights—it's like sex for him, he doesn't care about anything but the thrill of watching things burn. Can't you see that?"

"You don't know anything about José Luis."

"And you do? Lupe Vásquez, once a great organizer, now running a safe house for the National Would-be Revolutionaries Ineffective Arson Brigade. Have you written a proposal? Are you applying for grants? Is this what your idea of being a revolutionary has come to?"

"Stop it," she said hoarsely. "*Cállete.* Shut up."

The words stopped me the way a slap in the face would have. For a moment I was too surprised to say anything, then I heard what I had been saying and felt ashamed. Not wrong, but I wasn't helping the situation.

"Go home," Lupe said. "Go away."

"Doña, I'm sorry. I just—"

"Just go."

I touched her wrinkled arm. Her skin was dry and powdery. "I'm sorry," I said again. "I'm just worried about Carlitos."

She moved away from me and stood in the doorway. "Look, Tollomi, I'm sorry Carlitos was hurt. I'm sorry Jorge was murdered, I'm sorry my sons were killed, I'm sorry that the life we have here forces us toward difficult things. But don't berate me. I'm too old to be reprimanded by anyone other than myself. Now go home, please. If you want to come back, wait until this evening, after it gets dark."

She left me standing on the veranda and went back inside.

I walked across the yard and out into the garden. The lettuce plants were broken where we had stepped on them. The bushes were full of flowers, and every flower was the color of fire: orange, yellow, red. His skin would fall from his flesh like petals.

José Luis came banging out of the house. So she had sent him out too. He crossed the yard and came toward me, pushed past me and stood at the edge of the garden yanking violently at a branch of hibiscus. He tore the branch free and looked up. "Are you satisfied now?" he asked.

"What does that mean?"

No answer. He raked the broken branch violently through the hibiscus. The whole bush shuddered and a soft shower of petals floated to the ground.

"Tell me this," I said. "Was Carlitos in on this hotel-burning scheme from the beginning? He fooled me, José—that ought to make you happy. I had no idea what was going on."

José Luis looked up from the half-shredded branch. There were beads of sweat on his upper lip.

"Do you want to know what happened?" he asked.

"I know what happened. You and your friends wanted to get your rocks off and show everybody how tough you were, so you went out with a bottle of gas—"

"*Coño,* will you shut up? You *don't* know. Carlitos had never set the fire before last night. Do you want to know why last night was different?" He threw the branch away and immediately began twisting at another. "I'll tell you," he said harshly. But his voice shook like the branch in his hands.

"Tell me, then."

He did, in a string of disjointed sentences, methodically tearing the hibiscus to shreds as he spoke. The sketch he gave me was crude and incomplete, but its few lines suggested the whole of the scene with a clarity that made it painful to imagine. As he spoke I saw exactly what had taken place, and there in the bright heat of the garden it made me cold.

Yesterday, then:

Carlitos brings me to his house in Charamicos, the room he shares with José Luis, the place he hasn't let me see. We make love on a bare mattress on the floor, the same mattress he shares with his brother. I don't think about this, but Carlitos must be painfully aware of the presence of his brother all around us in the room. Perhaps while we we're making love he's thinking that later in the evening he and José Luis will lie on this same mattress, and he, Carlitos will not be able to sleep at all. He'll have to lie there in the darkness with his brother's naked body sleeping beside him, wondering if his brother can somehow sense—through his skin, perhaps—what he, Carlitos, has been doing on this mattress hours before.

This is what Carlitos is thinking of while he is touching me. This, and the fact that he is going to be late meeting his brother, that he shouldn't have brought me to his house at all, he should have stayed on the beach—he should never have talked to me in the first place, but here he is with his mouth around my cock and his chest heaving, and he wants to be cold, inert, dead, made of metal—but he is alive and I am alive and our bodies have laws of their own.

He rushes us through sex. He jumps at some little noise from the upstairs apartment and says we have to leave. He's always in a hurry now. He can't wait to get to me, and then, afterward, he can't wait to leave.

What I don't know is where he's going once he leaves me. While I go off to a bar and sit there angry and blunting myself by getting drunk, Carlitos runs as hard as he can through Charamicos, across the highway, and up some dirt road to wherever the place is where they have their meetings. He bursts in. The men sitting there are startled, half-rise, then sink back when they see who it is. But they keep looking at him, curiously, and then with something other than curiosity. They all look at him, all except José Luis, who stares at the floor.

"What?" says Carlitos. Though he knows what. He can see it in their eyes. What he most fears is finally happening. These men have heard rumors, and now, as they look at him, they know the rumors are true: They can see it. I'm on his skin. I'm in his hair. I've dried to his body like salt water: a taste, a hue.

Carlitos strides defiantly across the room, sits down in a chair beside his brother.

"Look, look how he walks now," says one of the men.

"Does he walk like a girl?" says another. They laugh.

Carlitos looks to his brother, but his brother will not look at him, and Carlitos flushes with hurt. It fills his chest; it swells to his cheeks, his forehead.

"Eh, José, *esta niña* shouldn't be here."

Carlitos has no wish of his own to be there; he is there because of José Luis. It is José Luis who has taken care of him, who has taught him how to survive; it is José Luis who has gone through the world first and held aside the branches for Carlitos to pass. And now it is José Luis who is looking at the floor and wishing Carlitos were not his brother at all.

José Luis looks at his friends. A vein in his forehead pulses. "You think Carlitos is too young to be here?" he says, evenly enough.

"He's too something," says his friend.

José Luis rises from his chair. No one says anything. He stands there, unsure what he will do. "Carlitos stays," he says after a moment.

A chair scrapes the floor. Carlitos stands up. They turn to look at him. He meets their eyes.

"I'll set the fire," Carlitos says.

Silence. Setting the fires is José Luis's job. He has a special way he does it, a way he likes to pile the rags, soak them down with gas. He bends over his work and flicks a lighter, and when the fire leaps to life at the flame, the bitterness inside him is torched too, and for a moment he is transformed. For a moment he can relax, he can exhale; it is beautiful, everything swallowed by flames, everything consumed; it is dangerous and it makes him the best. What José Luis loves most in the world is his anger.

What Carlitos loves most in the world is José Luis. José Luis loves fire. "I'll set the fire," Carlitos says. If he sets the fire, everything will be all right again. His humiliation, his exposure, his desire, José Luis's betrayal, or perhaps it is his own betrayal—he isn't sure now—all of it will go up in flames and smoke and vanish.

Slowly, José Luis's body relaxes. His friend leans back in the chair, looks pleased. "All right," says the friend, without asking José Luis what he thinks, "you do it, Carlitos. Go ahead."

Sometime after midnight they are ready. Carlitos doesn't know where they're going—they never tell him anything really. He doesn't care anyway; it is for José Luis that he's here. They wheel the mopeds out of the bushes, and Carlitos climbs on behind his brother. José Luis leans forward and twists the handlebar, and they zoom onto the road, wobble, straighten, speed up, and fly through the darkness. The wind is hard against Carlitos's face. He wraps his arms around his brother's middle and closes his eyes.

They hiss directions in his ear and hide in the shadows. Carlitos crosses the few feet of bare earth to the edge of the building. Against the wall facing the beach he piles the rags in a long row. He's never watched how José Luis actually does it; he's only watched his face. The wild and fleeting transformation of his face. Carlitos sets his jaw like José Luis does and prepares for the same strange epiphany to grace him with its power.

He pours the gasoline on the rags. The bottle is heavy, and the liquid sloshes; it splatters and disappears into the newly-turned earth. He screws the cap back on. Then, crouching over the soaked cloth, he holds the lighter in his hand and flicks his thumb.

A rush. A dull explosion, like a balloon burst under a blanket, and then everything is alight. When he jumps back the fire jumps with him, and then he is screaming; he's shaking it from his hands like water, but it clings, and the pain is a slow bolt of lightning that goes on and on through him and he cannot stop it and then his brother is upon him, knocking him backward onto the ground; he is still screaming, and then something is stuffed into his mouth and then everything turns into nothing, silent and black.

When he comes to a few moments later, he is so overwhelmed with pain that he does not even realize he is in his brother's arms.

José Luis wiped his sweating face against his shirtsleeve and glared at me. "This is your fault, Tollomi," he said. "Do you understand that? Do you understand that this would never have happened if not for you? You could have stayed away from him. Carlitos doesn't want you. He didn't know what he was doing when he went with you."

"That's not how it seemed to me," I said.

"And now everybody knows what you two do together. How is he supposed to go back to Charamicos now? He even won't be able to walk down the street without people saying things. Everyone will know."

"You're right about that," I said. "Everyone *will* know what happened—they'll know by the scars on his hands."

"I'm not talking about the fire," he said through his teeth.

"Well, you should be. He didn't know what he was doing, and so now he'll have scars up to his elbows. You think that's my fault? You shouldn't have made him choose. But he chose you, you're thinking. Does that mean you've won? Was it worth it? Answer me, José. Was it worth the skin of your brother's hands?"

"He set the fire because of you," said José Luis.

"Answer me: Was it worth it? All this time I thought that whoever was setting the fires was somebody trying to make a genuine political statement, to protest the coast being sold off to developers, but that's not it at all, is it? You've been running around setting things on fire just because you enjoy it, because it makes you feel like a big man."

"You know that's a lie, Tollomi. Don't pretend what we're doing is nothing. You know better than most people why we're doing it. Why won't you admit it now? Because I'm the one who was behind it? Because you didn't think of it yourself?"

"Because you haven't achieved anything."

"How can you say that? How can *you* say that? You are really incredible." He was yelling now. "You come here with a lot of big words about the Tainos and colonialism and slavery and the *quincentenario,* but what do you do? You lie around sunning yourself on the beach in Sosúa, you take Carlitos and teach him to suck up to the tourists, and then you—" he broke off. He couldn't say the words.

"Yes?" I prodded. I wanted to hear him say it: *You fucked him. And he loved it.*

But he didn't say anything, and now there was a kind of fire in me too; now my whole body was charged with dizzy anger. "You've achieved nothing at all," I said, "nothing but a smoke-blackened wall that will be repainted by tomorrow night. Is there one less hotel in all Cabarete? One less gringo, even? No. In a few days the hotel will open. The tourists will check in as if nothing had happened."

"You don't know anything about it," he said furiously. "It wasn't even a hotel, it was a restaurant, and the whole roof was *cana*. If Carlitos had done it right, the whole roof would be gone. It would have taken more than a week to fix *that*."

All at once my anger gave way to an uneasy recognition. A restaurant with a *cana* roof? Why did that sound so familiar?

"What was the name of the restaurant?" I asked.

He looked at me as if I had lost my mind.

"The restaurant, José. What was it called?"

"I don't know." His mustache twitched. "Some gringo name."

"Johnson's?" I asked.

"That's the one. His whole roof would have gone up in flames—"

The look on my face made him falter.

"You're so stupid," I said. "Do you know who Sam Johnson is?"

"I don't care who he is. The restaurant owner."

"You should care: Sam Johnson owns the bar in Puerto Plata where Michelle works. Its clientele is the local American expatriate gang—other hotel owners, most of them—and they sit there drinking their weight in imported liquor every day, and Sam Johnson makes money hand over fist, and guess what, José? The whole building is made of wood. If you'd set fire to that, you would have made headlines, but you didn't even bother to find out about it, did you? You have no plan, no structure; you just like to set things on fire. You want to be effective? Stop running around trying to set fire to cement. It's useless."

José Luis started to say something, but when he opened his mouth what came out was a sigh. We just looked at each other for a moment. He started to break off another branch of the hibiscus and then changed his mind and took his hand away.

"You know what?" he said. All the bravado was gone from his voice; it sounded like the voice of a little boy. "Even if I did burn down your Sam Johnson's wooden bar—even if I burned it right down to the ground, it wouldn't change anything. You know that? It's the big resorts that are really the problem. Sam Johnson is nobody." He shook his head. "When we first got together up here, we were going to set fires at the Club Med they're building. You know Club Med? It's so big, it's like it's its own country. People inside don't even use pesos, they use dollars. But we couldn't find a way to get inside. They have guards posted day and night at those big places. We couldn't even get through the front gates—they only let in gringos." He paused for breath and saw my expression. "Don't look at me like that. We're not as inept as you think, Tollomi. We broke into the Lighthouse in Santo Domingo, all right? The Faro a Colón."

"What do you mean, you broke into the Lighthouse? When?"

"Last year. You know the real reason I left Santo Domingo?"

I stared at him. "You weren't one of the Quisqueyas."

"How do you think I knew your faggot sailor boyfriend? Why do you think doña Lupe said I could bring Carlitos here? I'm not just some illiterate waiter, you know. Yes, I was a Quisqueya."

"You can't have been." But I knew he was telling the truth. I took a step back from him as if that distance would allow me to perceive him clearly. All I saw was a thin young man with a thin mustache and impassioned black eyes, his faded yellow shirt dark with perspiration under the arms. "Then you did study with Jorge Vásquez?" I asked.

"Not that Taino bullshit. But I knew him and doña Lupe in Santo Domingo."

"You knew her already?" I was having trouble making sense of what he was telling me.

"Yes, I knew her—that's what I'm saying. I knew her, she knew me. We just didn't let on when you brought me here. ¿*Comprende?*"

"You've all been lying to me, then?"

José Luis shrugged. "So now you know the truth," he said, and a trace of satisfaction flickered at the corners of his mouth. He turned and started walking across the garden.

"Where are you going?" I asked.

"I'm going home. I have to be at work in an hour, unlike some people. And thanks for the tip about the wooden bar—we'll torch that next time. Where did you say it was?"

"Go to hell, José."

He took a few steps back toward me and looked at me, ran his tongue thoughtfully over his mustache. "You know why you hate me?" he asked.

"Because you're an asshole."

"Because you can't stand that I do something about what I believe in, and you just talk, talk, talk, and lie around on the beach. What have you accomplished for all your talk since you've been on this island? Nothing. Not one thing. At least I've done something, not like you."

"I did do one thing that made a difference," I said.

"Yeah? What's that?"

"I fucked your brother."

He looked at me for a long moment. "Bastard," he said softly, but his hard and scowling face came apart on the word; suddenly his eyes were as soft as Carlitos's eyes and just as candid; I could see the hurt. My chest contracted. Why was I fighting this man? I turned from his dark eyes, stepped over the hibiscus branches he had broken, and made my way out of the garden.

Michelle was not at the house. I climbed up the ladder and scanned the valley, but I couldn't see her in the river either. I went back down the road into the village and asked in the store if they knew where she was.

They did. She had come down to get a ride to work; Alfredo had taken her as far as Sabaneta on his motorcycle, "*Y estaba muy guapa contigo, hombre.*" This said to the accompaniment of laughter: She'd been angry with me for taking the car, and had come down and told them so.

I left the men joking at the counter and walked back up the hill. I had forgotten Michelle would be at work. I thought of driving back to Puerto Plata to get her and then decided against it: It was Sam's new restaurant they had set fire to—the bar would be full of people gossiping about it; the police might be there, even—and Michelle would be standing in the middle of it all, pouring their Scotch. So I stayed on the hill and passed a few bad hours pacing between the tent and the house, the house and the mango tree. I tried to read and could not, I tried to eat; I had no appetite. I walked down to the river and sat on the rocks until it started to rain. Then I swam awhile; when the rain stopped I climbed back up the hill. My steps were heavy. The weight was anxiety; a thousand little stones of fear piled up inside me. When I reached the house, I forced myself to be still. I dried the rain off the beach chairs and sat down to wait for Michelle.

When at last she arrived it was dusk. She came up the hill and across the grass and stood over me, looking down.

"Michelle, I'm so glad to see you," I said.

"Thanks for going off this morning and taking the car when you knew I needed it," she said nastily. "And thanks for not leaving a note saying whether you'd be back in time. I was late to work again. Sam was pissed enough as it is. Someone set fire to his new restaurant, and then I had to listen to him scream at me for being late—"

She went on; I hardly heard her. I sat in the beach chair and waited until she had run out of words. I waited.

"Well?" she said at last.

Very calmly then, I told her what had happened, beginning with how Carlitos and I had argued in Charamicos the day before. She sat down on the edge of the other beach chair and listened in silence. When I told her how he had spilled the gasoline on his hands, she interrupted.

"Is he going to die?" she asked.

"No, it's nothing like that. It's pure luck his clothes didn't catch fire, but they didn't. He has second-degree burns on his hands. They'll scar."

She turned her own hands over in her lap and looked up at me. "It was Sam's new place they set fire to."

"José Luis didn't even know Sam was the owner," I said. "He was just setting fires wherever he felt like it. I told him if he was going to risk being sent to prison, not to mention risking his brother, at least he could have chosen a worthwhile target. When I told him he should have set fire to Sam's *bar* if he'd really wanted to make an impact, he said he didn't even know Sam had a bar. He hadn't even bothered to figure out whether—"

"You told him to burn down the bar?" She was staring at me.

"I was just making a point, Michelle. José Luis sets fire to a cement restaurant, and Sam—the owner, in other words—might be angry, but fifty pesos later there will be no sign anything ever happened. At the end of the day it's a completely useless gesture. And get this—you won't believe this: He used to be a Quisqueya."

"A what?"

"The group who broke into the Columbus Lighthouse." She looked at me blankly. "Forget it, it doesn't matter. Even the Columbus Lighthouse is going to open right on schedule. That's what's so awful, Michelle.

Even when you make a statement, it's just a statement; it's just a gesture, nothing more. The Lighthouse goes up, and the hotels keep going up, and nothing anyone does makes a difference—"

"You told José Luis to burn down the bar," she said again.

"And José Luis is right—even if he'd burned it down to the ground, ultimately it wouldn't matter. There will always be more Sams."

"I can't believe you told him to do that."

"Michelle, are you listening to me? When I said that, I was just making a point."

"How do you know what you were making? You don't have any idea, Tollomi. You're so busy thinking about what you want, you don't see the effect you have on people. I knew something like this would happen to Carlitos, and so did you—or you would have, if you'd bothered to think about it for five seconds."

"What's that supposed to mean?"

She didn't answer.

"What do you mean, you knew this would happen? Michelle, don't tell me you knew it was José Luis setting the fires."

"Jesus, Tollomi, I didn't know who was setting the fires. But obviously *something* was going to happen to Carlitos. Did you think he was just going to keep on running back and forth between you José Luis forever? He was bound to get hurt. There's no point pretending you're surprised."

"You're actually saying all this is my fault?"

"It's not your *fault*. But Carlitos was in an impossible situation and you knew it."

"Yes, I knew it, Michelle—I'm the one who's been trying to get him to leave Charamicos, get away from Charamicos so he can relax a little—"

"So *you* can relax, Tollomi. It has nothing to do with what Carlitos wants."

"It has everything to do with—"

"No, it doesn't. You want him to do what *you* want, which is to go off somewhere just the two of you and screw your brains out without Carlitos saying, 'Not here, Tollomi. Be careful, someone will see us.' You want to go off with him and let the rest of the world go to hell, but Carlitos can't do that. You want him to just slip out of his own life and make himself at home in yours, but he can't. He already has a home, and he doesn't want to give it up. He's trying to go back and forth, and he can't do that either. Obviously he can't, Tollomi. You have one home, or you have none at all." She flung herself back in the beach chair. "Talk him into going away with you," she said coldly. "I'm sure you can if you keep at it long enough. But it won't be like you imagine. I'm telling you now." Her voice wavered on the last word, and she turned her head away.

"If you're so afraid I'll leave you," I said quietly, "just say so. I won't. You don't have to tear me down."

"I'm not trying to make you stay here," she said, and her voice shook. "I'm telling you to go. Take Carlitos and go to Santo Domingo if that's what you want. It's not going to be like you think, but you want to leave, so do it. Here—"

She reached into her shirt and pulled out the sleeve of cloth that held her passport. "Take it," she said, unsnapping the snaps. "You might need it there."

"What am I supposed to do with your passport in Santo Domingo?"

She sat up in surprise and stared at me, and her whole face trembled as if she were about to break into tears.

"Michelle?"

"It's *your* passport, Tollomi, I've had it ever since Sosúa. You don't remember anything!" And she threw it at me. The little book hit my arm and fell to the grass.

We stared at each other. She was breathing hard, deep halting breaths on the verge of sobs. If she really had wept, I might have been able to get up out of my chair and put my arms around her and hold her, to communicate through my body what I couldn't prove with words: that I did remember. I remembered everything that had passed between us, and even now I still felt a connection to her, that, like the dream she had dreamed of my mother, was born from an empathy more profound than could be told through speech.

But her eyes stayed dry and I didn't move from my chair, and then the moment to do it passed. Michelle took a deep breath, and then her breathing was calm again.

"Tollomi?"

"Yes?"

She swung her legs round the side of the beach chair and faced me. "It doesn't really exist, does it?" Her voice was calm. "This thing, this special link between us that we never talk about. I've been making it up to make myself feel better. Or no, not to feel better. To anchor myself here. But I've been making it up. There's no link there."

"That isn't true," I said, and suddenly I was near tears myself.

"You don't know if it's true or not, because you don't feel it either way," she said. There was no reproach in her voice. "See?" She waved her hand back and forth through the air between us. I felt the breeze in my mouth and eyes. "See, Tollomi? There's nothing between us but air." She stood up.

"Where are you going?"

She smiled then. "Only to sleep."

"Come with me to see Carlitos."

"Now?"

"I said I'd be back tonight. Come with me, Michelle." I heard the pleading in my voice.

"I'm exhausted,"she said. "I just want to lie down."

"Please, Michelle, I want you to come with me. I—"

"Tomorrow," she said, as if speaking to a very small child. And like a child, I felt certain that tomorrow was too distant, and that the thing I needed so badly now would be irretrievably lost if I gave in and waited. But I watched her walk off toward the tent.

Before she had gone five steps she stopped and turned. "Will José Luis be there?" she asked.

"At Lupe's? I doubt it. Why?"

Her mouth flashed a grin. "If you see him, you might tell him I have a job for him to do. I have a house here that needs burning down."

She laughed; I didn't. She left me sitting on the beach chair and disappeared into the darkness that had settled over the yard. After a moment I heard the tent zipper open and then shut.

My passport was still lying in the grass somewhere. I hunted between the chairs until I found it. It had fallen face-open and the pages were wet. I dried them on my shirt as I walked to the car.

I hear Tollomi start the car and drive away. I listen until I can no longer hear the motor. Then I just sit in the tent and listen to the hiss of wind against the nylon walls and the frogs chirping outside. I sit like that for a long time. At last I light the lantern. By lamplight I search through Tollomi's bags.

I'm not sure where he's put it. In the inside pocket of his suitcase there's nothing but some old maps. In the bag he uses as a toilet kit there's only what you would expect: soap, hair oil, razor blades. I go through the pockets of all his clothes, but what I'm looking for isn't there either.

I find it at last in the bottom of his writing case. I pick it up, my passport. I hold it in my hand and wait for the twinge of electricity I always feel when I touch it, a spark coursing from my fingers to my heart. But nothing happens. I press both hands against it, but I feel only the smooth blue cover and the thick edges of the paper, nothing more.

All magic charms lose their magic at last. The treasured amulet becomes simply a peculiar stone, the wishing lamp a dented piece of brass. The magic carpet to carry me out of danger becomes a little blue book with a picture of my face inside. It will no longer take me anywhere that is really away. There is no *away* now, not anymore.

I blow out the lantern and lie down on my sleeping bag. I cradle the blue book against my heart like a doll and close my eyes. But now it can't even gain me entrance into the country that is sleep, and at last I sit up again and light the lamp a second time. I put the passport away in the bag around my neck because it feels odd to have the bag hanging empty. Then I take the lantern and go outside.

The house stands there waiting. The frame I worked so hard to saw and sink in new concrete, the old cement foundation I patched and reinforced, the raw beams arching gracefully overhead, and on top of them, the brand new *cana* roof. Splayed green fingers of *cana* hang down in a heavy fringe over the eaves. The house is waiting for the one who made it. I am that one, and I'm afraid to go in. I'm afraid to go in, yet I've never left it, and I cannot leave it now.

If José Luis were to show up here suddenly, with his can of gasoline and his flashing eyes, if he came and poured gas on the corner poles, if he climbed the ladder and leaned onto the roof and soaked down the *cana,* if he struck a match and jumped back and then listened—as I too would be listening—to the suck of air and the long exhalation of flame and then the burst and splintering, if we watched as the whole house wrapped itself in a shimmer of fire and the roof crashed down and the flames rose high in the air so you could see them for miles, if the whole house burned down to the ground, then could I begin again? Could I leave this place, leaving no trace but ashes and burned grass?

I built this house out of wood because that was how it was in my grandparents' day. I had the roof made of *cana* because of some romantic image of palm fronds overhead and the sounds they would make every time the wind passed through. Tonight there is no wind. Did I build the house out of wood and *cana* because I knew that someday I would want to burn it to cinders? I don't know. I don't know what I was thinking during those early days of exuberance and rain.

I stand in the wet grass beside the foundation and lift the glass globe off the lantern. I tilt the flame against the corner pole I cut and planed myself and hold it there and wait. The smoke from the flame makes a black smear against the wood, and a little kerosene runs over my fingers, but that's all. I climb onto the foundation and stand on tiptoe and hold the lantern up to the *cana* fronds overhead.

The tips of the *cana* hiss when the flame touches them. I hold the lantern there and the fronds smoke and turn black. But they won't catch fire. I get only the sharp smell of smoke as the *cana* singes. I can't make it catch fire and burn; it's wet and too green.

My arm aches from holding the lantern over my head; my throat is knotted. If José Luis were here, I would ask him what he does with the terrible frustration he must feel when his fires fail. What does he do when he walks past a hotel the next day and sees it in all its cinder-block glory still standing, as he knows it will be, no matter how much gasoline he pours? All the new hotels are made of cinder block and rebar. They are all built to withstand anything: fire, high seas, anger of local residents. But this house is wood; if José Luis were here, perhaps he could get rid of it for me, take it down to its very foundations and then step back and let rain wash the ashes away. I cannot do it. I am trying. All my life I have been trying. But I cannot do it. The house refuses to catch fire.

I could go looking for José Luis, ask him to come back here. I could walk down to the village and pay someone to take me all the way to Charamicos. Except I don't know where he lives. He might not be at home anyway. He might still be with Carlitos at Lupe's. He might be out setting fire to some other place. Wouldn't he, just once, like to see one of his fires really burn something? Tollomi was right, Sam's bar would burn, really burn, like wooden matches; like dry leaves, the whole thing would flame. The decorations on the walls would catch fire first, the hanging fishnets falling down in webs of cinders, the horrible girly beer posters turning to sheets of flame. Then the shelves would catch—something would fall over and the liquor bottles would break and the spill would ignite at once, a soft mouthful of fire licking its way along the floor. The wooden floor would start to burn, and then the whole of the room would catch in earnest, the floor sparkling with flame and broken glass, the bird shrieking in its cage above the bar as the heat and the smoke thickened and rose. And Sam upstairs, drunk and asleep in his clothes, would know nothing, sense nothing, never open his eyes.

And Sonya, where would she be while the flames devoured everything they touched, while the smoke ate the air? Upstairs in Sam's living room watching television with the sound up too loud? Asleep on his sofa, the one with the big pillows that she told me about? Or down in the little back room, having fallen asleep on the folding cot Sam keeps there, waking up to find her entire twelve years of life going up in flames? She might. José Luis might do it. Why shouldn't he? Wouldn't the sight of high fire and billowing smoke and the sky orange and black take his mind off all the pain in Carlitos's arms?

I blow out the lantern and jump off the foundation. I run across the grass to the tent and find my shoes and a fistful of pesos, enough to make some young man with a motorcycle leave his friends to their domino game and drive me all the way to Puerto Plata at top speed at who knows what time of night it is by now. I might not even find anyone to take me, it might be well after midnight, I have no idea. I look up at the night sky and curse Tollomi, who would know in an instant what time it is simply by checking the position of the stars.

Lamplight shone through the slatted walls of Lupe's cooking shed. I stood at the edge of the yard and called out; after a moment her voice came back through the darkness, ordering me to approach. "Tollomi, *ven acá.*"

She met me at the shed door.

"I thought you weren't coming back," she said.

"I'm sorry it's so late."

"*Entra,* Tollomi, *sientese.*" She pointed to a chair and I sat down. Two oil lamps stood burning on the table. A third lantern hung over the wooden counter where she had been washing dishes in a plastic tub. She rinsed her hands and joined me at the table.

"How is he?" I asked.

"He's fine," she said curtly.

"Fine?"

The lamplight flickered over her frown. "He's not in unbearable pain. He slept a while, and when he woke up he was quite lucid."

"Did you give him more codeine?"

"He wouldn't take it. He only wanted aspirin."

Had I not been in Lupe's presence I would have cursed aloud this professed indifference to pain, undoubtedly a José Luis-influenced bit of machismo. "Is Carlitos sleeping?" I asked instead.

She shook her head. "He's awake. I just gave him something to eat." And then as an afterthought she asked, "Are you hungry?"

"No." I took a deep breath. "Doña, I'm sorry about this morning. What I said about your being a bad revolutionary. I apologize."

"It's all right," she said without expression, and I realized I would never talk politics with her again. "Go on inside, Tollomi. Carlitos must know you're here."

"Thank you for taking care of him. I don't know what we would have done otherwise."

"You'd have managed," she said evenly. And then: "I meant what I said earlier, Tollomi—I wish we'd known you in Santo Domingo, before."

"You and José Luis?"

"I meant Jorge and I. But who knows? Maybe you and José Luis would have been friends, even."

"I doubt it," I said. "He doesn't think much of me."

She nodded, that was all, but in that simple movement of her gray head was an implicit understanding, and I realized she knew Carlitos and I are lovers.

She broke the awkward silence by getting to her feet. She picked up one of the lanterns and guided me across the yard to the house. When we reached the veranda, she stepped aside and with a flick of her fingers indicated that I should go in alone. I made a weak smile of thanks and said aloud that I wouldn't be long.

"Stay as long as you like," she said. "Carlitos is wide-awake and so am I."

"I'm not going to make you sit outside in the kitchen all night, doña."

"No? *Qué pena*—I'm in the middle of such an interesting book about Cuba."

I must have stared a little: She looked up at me and laughed.

"*¿Qué tiene, Tollomi?* Did you think that when I moved here I forgot how to read?"

"The first time I came here," I said, "I was shocked that there were no books in the house."

"You didn't look under the bed," she said dryly.

"You hide your books under the bed?"

"*Ay, no*—I don't *hide* them. But around here, people don't keep books in their living rooms."

"No one around here *has* any books," I said.

"Besides, since Jorge died, I've had terrible insomnia. So at night I read. I like to have my little library handy." She smiled without a trace of irony. On impulse, I bent and kissed her cheek.

"Thank you again, doña."

"*A su orden*," she said awkwardly. She felt in the pocket of her dress and pulled out the stub of a cigar. She stuck it in her mouth without lighting it and went back across the yard to the cooking shed.

Carlitos was sitting propped up against several pillows with his eyes closed. Lupe had bandaged his arms up to the elbow in strips of blue bedsheet. He wore no shirt, and I noticed a burn on his chest that I hadn't seen earlier, a dark scorch that began below his protruding collarbone and spread down toward the base of his sternum. I came all the way into the room and he opened his eyes.

"How do you feel?" I asked.

He looked down at his bandaged hands before answering. "Better. A little sick. Burned."

"Do your arms hurt very much?"

He shrugged and the movement made him wince.

I sat on the edge of the bed. "Carlitos, I know what happened, why you set the fire. José Luis told me." When he made no reply I blurted, "You didn't have to do it. Not for them. Carlitos, it doesn't matter that they know about us."

"It doesn't matter to you," he said wearily, then glanced toward the doorway. I turned; no one was there. When I turned back to him, the mattress shifted under me, and he winced in pain.

"Sorry," I said. "It's bad, isn't it?"

"Better than it was. Just don't jostle me." His voice was clear and a little cold.

"I'll give you some more codeine." I put out my hand to touch his knee; it was a gesture of comfort that might have done as well for a small child as a lover, but his body stiffened, and he halfway winced again—in anticipation of pain, I thought. I withdrew my hand. "Your legs aren't burned too?"

"It's just that everything hurts," he said. "And talking or thinking about it makes it hurt more."

"Lupe said you wouldn't take the codeine this afternoon."

"It makes me feel sick. Then on top of everything else I want to throw up."

"It won't make you nauseated now that you've eaten."

He didn't answer. A light mist of perspiration had broken out above his upper lip and across his forehead.

"Are you feverish?" I asked. I put my hand to his forehead, and again his body tensed. This time I read the movement correctly. "For Christ's sake," I said, "I'm not trying to seduce you. I'm trying to see if you have a fever."

"Tollomi, keep your voice down."

"Lupe can't hear us."

"I heard *you* out there."

"Would you like me to sit a little farther away just in case she pokes her head in the door? I could go stand over there in the corner if you like—" I stopped myself. "I'm sorry, Carlitos. I keep saying the wrong thing—I've been doing it all day. I was really worried about you. But you might have told me what was going on."

"I couldn't, Tollomi. José Luis—" he broke off, realizing that way lay an argument. We sat in silence for a moment, my hand just a few inches from his calf, his face looking worn and suddenly years older. There was a guardedness in his eyes that had been there for weeks, I realized, perhaps longer. It had been there since we first became lovers, laid over the original openness of his expression like a veil. I was sad to recognize it, and then I did want to kiss him; I wanted to press my mouth against his dry, peeling lips that would taste of salt and Lupe's soup and adrenaline and ash. I wanted to free him from his own fear; somehow. I knew he would not let me kiss him now. I looked away from his face, and my eyes caught on the bare lightbulb hanging overhead. Its crown was speckled with the bodies of dead insects. I closed my eyes, and the afterimage of the light played red on my eyelids. Where could we go from here?

When I opened my eyes, Carlitos was looking at me. "Thank you for helping this morning," he said haltingly.

"You're welcome," I said.

He cleared his throat. "It was José Luis's idea to go get you. I was in so much pain, and then I think I was drunk also—they gave me a lot of rum. I couldn't say or do anything…"

"I know."

"If he hadn't thought to go get you, I might still be sitting in that shed." He began some gesture with his bandaged hand that was immediately curtailed by a rush of pain. He bit his lip and gingerly returned the hand to his lap.

"Carlitos, let me give you some more pills."

"I'm all right now. I must be feeling better or I wouldn't have forgotten and tried to move. I'm all right." But he was gritting his teeth.

"Now that you've eaten, the codeine won't make you sick, you know. Here—"

"Tollomi, I said no!"

"All right, I heard you." I tried to think of some way to ease the conversation. I felt worn out and dull in the head. "The pain means there's no nerve damage," I said.

Carlitos sighed. "Lupe says my hands will scar no matter what."

"They might."

"And they'll take months to heal."

"Yes."

"So I can't go back to Charamicos."

"If you did, you'd run the risk of being arrested."

"And our family would find out." He paused. "José Luis wants me to go to Santo Domingo."

"With him?"

He didn't look at me. "He never wanted to leave there in the first place. But he had to."

"The great Quisqueyas," I said bitterly.

"If he'd stayed, they'd have put him in jail."

"You might have told me. You knew I'd been looking for them."

"José Luis wants me to go to Santo Domingo with him and live there," he said tonelessly. "He wants us to live with a cousin we have who has a place near the university. He says he'll take care of me until my arms are better, and then he'll help me find a job. He wants me to live there with him and forget any of this ever happened."

"You can't," I said.

"Can't what? Can't go, or can't forget?"

"Carlitos, listen to what you're saying. You wouldn't go to Santo Domingo with me for three days even, and now you want to go there and live with José Luis? *Think,* Carlitos. You'd be miserable."

"And what is it you want me to do?" he said harshly.

I answered at once without knowing I was going to say it. "I want you to go to Santo Domingo and live with me."

As I said the words I had the sensation that I was waking up from some self-administered anesthesia that had been dulling my senses for days. I became aware of the cool of the cement floor under my feet and the texture of the sheet against the flat of my hand and the hollow place inside my chest that had opened up at last and begun to breathe. Carlitos was shaking his head. "It would work," I said. "Carlitos, just think for a minute."

"It wouldn't work, Tollomi. *You* think. Think how it would be for me. If I went to Santo Domingo and lived with you, it would be just like it is here. It would be exactly the same, but it would be worse, we'd be living together. It would be just like Charamicos."

"How can you say that, Carlitos? It would be nothing like—"

"Listen," he said hoarsely. "Every time I walk from my house to the store on the corner, I feel people staring at me. They've heard things and they look at me and I think they can see it. Even when I know they're not looking, Tollomi, I feel them looking just the same."

"But that would go away. In Santo Domingo it would go away even faster."

"No, it wouldn't. Not for me."

"How do you know? You've never lived in a big city."

With difficulty he sat up a little straighter. "Tollomi, listen. I'm not you. It's easy for you to say everything would be fine in Santo Domingo because this isn't your country. You can go anywhere and behave how you want to behave, and no one will really care what it is you're doing because you're not Dominican. You talk like us and you look like us, but you're not one of us. So you can do anything. You have nothing to lose."

"You have nothing to lose either," I said. "You've already lost it."

He looked at me and then closed his eyes. "I know I have," he said tiredly. "Do you think I don't know?"

"Then what do you think moving in with José Luis will do? Do you honestly think that if you go to Santo Domingo with him and don't see me anymore that things will go back to the way they were before you met me? Because it no longer has anything to do with me, Carlitos. You want to go off to Santo Domingo and live with your horrible brother and never see me again? Fine. Go. Fade into your brother's life and tell yourself the months with me were an accident, or a dream, or that you didn't know what you were doing, that I tricked you into it."

"It's not that at all—"

"And who knows? Maybe you'll even believe it. Maybe you'll get married and have ten children, what do I know?"

"You don't know anything, Tollomi. You don't know what it's like—"

"I'll tell you what I know: One day you'll be walking down the street, and you'll pass some man walking in the other direction. Your eyes will dart toward him, and you'll pull them back the way you always do. But after you've gone a few steps farther, you'll find yourself turning around in spite of yourself to look at him again. And you'll see that he's stopped walking too, and he's standing there on the pavement looking right at you. And then you won't even think. Your body will just move toward him all by itself. You'll follow him somewhere, into a hotel if he's rich, or the bathroom of a dark bar if he's poor. But you'll follow him, and your body will tell you that all the years you've spent trying to fool it have all been for nothing, that you haven't fooled it one bit, that the only thing you've done is wasted time. So you'll start seeing this man, or maybe you'll never see him again, but you'll start going to the bar he told you about, sneaking in just in case someone who knows your wife happens to be passing by. You'll sit there with a bunch of other men too afraid to meet each other in daylight, and if I walked into that bar ten years from now, I'd find you sitting there, still in this same panic that you'll be discovered."

Carlitos was looking past me at the curtain over the doorway—to see if Lupe had heard, I thought. "Are you listening at all?" I asked.

"You're wrong," he said. "I'll never end up in that bar."

"I wouldn't know, Carlitos. I won't be there. I'll be on the other side of the world with somebody else, and if I ever think of you it will only be—"

"Tollomi, shut up!" He thrust his head toward me. "Listen. *You* listen. You say you want me to go to Santo Domingo, but you've just finished telling me what a disgusting life I'll end up with if I do."

"If you go and move in with your brother and keep on deluding yourself like this, yes."

"You think I'm deluding myself?" He gave me an odd look that I couldn't read at all. In another context, I would have said he looked amused.

"You have to make a decision," I said. "You know what I want. You know what José Luis wants. You can't go on pretending you're not balancing on a wire between us. You know what you want, but if you're going to keep pretending you don't want it, tell me now and I'll leave and not come back. I can't stand this anymore."

For a full minute he didn't say anything. Then, very carefully, he moved his right arm off his leg to the sheet beside him. Then he moved his left arm. With his feet he pushed himself upright until he was sitting straight up in bed, not touching the pillows. "I wasn't going to tell you now," he said.

I waited.

"I talked to Lupe earlier. Before you got here. She said she would help me. She offered. I told her I'd pay her back."

"Carlitos, what are you talking about?" His eyes were bright and glassy.

"I didn't tell José Luis either."

"You still have a fever," I said. Did I know what was coming? My eyes darted to the aspirin bottle on the bedside table. I wanted to give him aspirin and hold a glass of water to his mouth and not hear what he was on the verge of saying.

But then he said it, and I did hear it.

He said he wanted to go to the United States, and there it was.

I protested. He looked at me almost in wonder, as if nothing could be more obvious; then some twinge of pain moved in him, and he grimaced and looked at his arms. "Damn this," he said, and then, "I told Lupe I'm going and she said she'd lend me some money. Now I've told you. I haven't told José Luis. Don't tell him."

"Carlitos, this is crazy."

Very gently, so as not to jostle anything, he shook his head.

I tried to talk him out of it. I spent nearly half an hour trying, and he sat quietly without interrupting. After a while he leaned back and closed his eyes again. I kept talking. Was it for my own ears that I sat there and recounted the bitter cold of snow and strangers, and myself as a boy practicing the pronunciation of his consonants in the blue flicker of late-night television in a dormitory basement? At last I fell silent. Carlitos sighed—from pain or weariness, I couldn't tell—and shifted his legs under the sheet. I knew instantly, and was angry at myself for knowing, that I would remember this simple movement afterward, over and over again: the line of his legs moving under the heavy cotton, its blue and white checkers resembling a tablecloth's. One corner of the sheet had ridden up over his ankle, and he pulled it down with his toes.

I got up then and straightened the sheet for him and tucked it in. I stayed standing. Then I said I would go. Carlitos nodded. In more than an hour of talking, neither of us had managed to speak of the farewell that had now arrived. And now it was too late.

"I'll see you tomorrow," Carlitos said helplessly, and I thought, *He's terrible at lying. That's one thing he never learned from me.* His face, in the dull harsh light from the bulb overhead, looked almost gray, but his eyes were shining. I bent over him. He raised his head to kiss me, and his lips parted. His eyes met mine, then darted sharply past me to the curtain over the doorway. I turned my head; there was no one there. I straightened up again.

"Lupe's all the way out in the kitchen," I said bitterly.

"I know. I can't help it."

We were back where we had started. I left the room quickly and went out through the jumble of rocking chairs to the open darkness beyond.

At the doorway of the cooking shed, I paused and looked in at Lupe sitting with her chair drawn close to the table, reading her book. As I watched, one of her lanterns began to smoke and then went out. I stood there in a kind of ruined daze, wiping tears out of my eyes and watching as she got up and rummaged around at the back of the shed. It must have been kerosene she wanted and did not find, for she came back to the table with a little glass jar and a bottle of cooking oil instead; she was going to make a homemade lamp. I had seen these lamps in other places, here and in St. Croix and in other countries too, made in jars or enamel cups or empty cans.

I stood in the shadows outside the doorway as if transfixed and watched as she poured a little water into the jar, and then on top of the water floated the oil. She left the table again, and I heard the back door creak. When she came back she had a rose in her hand, plucked from the bush outside. She pinched off the stem and pushed the rose into the oil. Then she found a paper bag and tore a square from the corner. She twisted the middle of the paper scrap into a point and set it atop the rose, which would hold this paper wick aloft. She poured more oil over the paper, then struck a match and held it to the wick. The small flame wavered and sprang up. Lupe watched it burn a moment and then sat down at the table and resumed reading.

Still I did not go in. She turned a page and moved the jar a little. The wavering light cast her face in upside-down shadows. Josephine used to make those lamps when there was a power outage, using small stones to hold the wick instead of a flower. I knew just how the lamp would burn, the smell of singed paper and smoky oil that would permeate the room. The paper wick would burn for hours, floating on the rose until the oil was all gone. Then it would begin to draw water, and the flame would sputter and smoke and shrink to an ember. Then with a soft hiss it would go out altogether.

Lupe read on in silence. She neither saw nor sensed me. And at last I stepped back from the door and found my way across the yard and through the garden, going out the way I had come in that first day.

His mind was made up. He would borrow money from Lupe and go through Mexico, cross the border at night into Texas. He would take a bus to New York. At first he would stay with an uncle or cousin. He'd learn the subway system, find some sort of job, begin to meet people. He would hate the winter, hate the looks people gave him on the subway, hate his boss who after six months would still not remember that he was Carlitos, not Chico or Juan or Ramón.

But one day he'd meet a man. It would be summer. He'd peel off layers of clothes and take the subway to different neighborhoods, learn where to go. Something in his body would relax. He'd move to a different part of the city, move in with a lover, or with friends. He'd have a better job now, fake papers, eventually he'd pay Lupe back. He'd send her the money from Nueva York, city of dreams.

It was very late when I reached Las Piedras; the stars said somewhere between one and three. Michelle would be asleep, had been asleep for hours, most likely. Walking up through the pasture in the darkness, I realized there was nothing I wanted more than to wake her and tell her what Carlitos had said and be comforted. But would she comfort me? I could hardly remember our conversation in the distant past of early evening—she was angry at me, she'd thrown my passport in the grass, I had ruined something for her. I had ruined something. She was desperately in need of help, and I had gone away.

She might still be up; if she was I would apologize. The tent was dark when I reached the top of the hill, but I unzipped the tent fly and poked my head in, still hopeful. And at first I thought the shadows were lying. I had to press my hands onto her sleeping bag before I was convinced that the tent was truly empty. Michelle was gone.

I found the lantern and lit it, then sat staring numbly at the wreck of my luggage spilled across her sleeping bag.

She had gone through my clothes searching for something: her passport. I had forgotten we'd traded passports until she'd thrown mine at me. I had put her passport in my writing case weeks ago, and now it was gone. She was gone, then. There were signs and I hadn't read them. There were signals, shouts; I had ignored them. I was reminded of the long-ago sensation of being awakened from a dream by faint and troublesome degrees, becoming aware of the painful reality that the dream had briefly hidden. I was awake now, and Carlitos was leaving me. He was leaving me for a lover called America, and it was I who had introduced them. And now Michelle was gone too. There were tears on my face for the second time that evening. I was awake; there was no one left to lose. I had lost them all.

The lantern beside me had begun to smoke; at last I noticed it. I burned my fingers while lifting the globe to blow it out, then sat there and cursed in every language I knew.

When I had run out of curses, I went outside and looked up at the stars. It was still several hours before sunrise. Plenty of time to get to the airport and stop her, or go with her, or at least distract her long enough to make her miss the plane.

I walked down the hill and got back in the car, and drove once again over the road I had been traversing since early this morning, searching for someone I feared I would not find.

Part Four

Michelle was not at the airport. I looked all over the open-air plaza, and outside in the badly lit parking lot, on the wet grass that bordered the asphalt square. I looked in the ladies' room—the attendant had gone for the night. Then there was nowhere else to look; the cafeteria and all the check-in counters were closed. When I felt certain she wasn't there, I got back in the car and drove on into Puerto Plata. She had keys to Sam's bar—would she have gone there to wait for daylight? Or to get money from Sam so she could leave?

No lights were on in the apartments above the bar. I banged on the front door. No answer. The windows at street level were all shuttered behind iron grilles. I went around the building looking for a side door. Down an alley I found one and banged on that. To my surprise, the door gave slightly; I pushed and it swung open.

I stepped inside and found myself at the rear of the bar, among garbage cans and folded cardboard. The room was partially illuminated by a small light over the cash register. I pushed the door shut behind me and went all the way into the room. In the shadows at the other end sat Michelle, slouched at a little round table beside the front door. Her back was to me. If she had heard me come in, she gave no sign of it.

"Michelle," I said, and my voice broke loud into the stale air. She didn't look up. I went across the floor and sat down in the chair opposite hers. Her eyes were wide open, and her head tilted at a faraway angle I knew well. I touched her hand and waited for her to reel herself in from wherever she was, impatient with relief that I had found her. In a moment she would shake her head and look up at me, blinking.

I waited, my eyes on her face. I waited. "Michelle," I said sharply, "it's me." She didn't move.

This had never happened before. I took her head between my hands and very gently raised it up and looked into her eyes. She didn't see me. Her breathing was soft and regular. But her eyes were as empty as rooms.

Water—I would get her some water. I jumped up and started around the other side of the bar and nearly fell over Sam. He lay sprawled on his back on the floor between the bar and the wall, his legs and one arm flung out in the unpleasant angles of drunken sleep. His hair had fallen over his eyes, and his shirt rode up to reveal a wedge of tanned, heavy flesh flocked with silver hairs. I stepped well over him. To pass out in any bar is pathetic; to pass out in your own bar is disgusting.

I filled a glass of water at the little sink beside the liquor well and thought of Michelle doing this simple motion day after day, here by herself without me. I had a sudden intuition that water would not help, but I took the glass and went back around the bar, stepping over Sam again. I glanced down at him—his khaki pants with the clasp unbuckled, the strip of exposed stomach. One of his feet was bare, and the other was shod in a lime-green rubber sandal.

It was the feet that did it. I took an involuntary step backward, my mind still unaware of what my body, animal-like, had already sensed. I felt the fear go through me as I squatted down and made myself push his hair out of his eyes.

His eyes were open, but he was no longer seeing or breathing. He was dead. My hand jerked back, and then I just crouched there, staring at his body, caught up in the fascination that the dead seem to engender in the still-alive.

Then my mind begin working again and thought, *He's not dead.* After all, how could I tell just by looking? I forced myself to stretch out my hand again and put my fingers against his neck. There was no movement of life there; only the strange, waxy firmness of his flesh.

Close behind me came a sudden, small noise: a human noise, a whimper. I jumped up and backed away from Sam. Was I alone here or not? Michelle had not moved. The sound came again, from the right. There was a door in the wall that I hadn't noticed, slightly ajar. I pushed it with my toe.

The room inside was a small one into which were crammed high shelves stocked with liquor, a table covered with papers, an overturned wooden chair, and, half-hidden behind the door, a narrow army cot. On the cot sat a child, a girl. Her face was stained with tears. She stared up at me with bright frightened eyes.

"What happened?" I said in Spanish.

She stared at me and said nothing.

"¿Qué pasó?" I asked again.

She made a hiccupping sob. This must be the girl Michelle had told me about, the one Sam had hired to do the cleaning. I hadn't imagined someone so young, though; she couldn't be more than eleven or twelve. Her eyes looked a hundred. Had Michelle mentioned the girl's name? I couldn't remember. "I'm a friend of Michelle's," I started.

The girl went on staring at me while I searched for words, and when I didn't produce any, she asked, "Is he dead?"

"Yes," I answered, and the expression, or lack of expression, on her face did not change. I sat on the cot beside her. "Did you see what happened?" I asked.

She nodded.

"Tell me."

She wiped her nose on the back of her hand. "Michelle did it," she said.

The words didn't quite penetrate. They hung in the air between our heads while I asked her what she meant.

"She hit him," the girl said flatly.

"Hit him where?"

"Here," she said without pointing to any part of her body.

"Where?"

"Michelle came in here, in the bar," she said. She shifted on the cot and wrapped her skinny arms round her torso in a thin brown knot.

"Why did she hit him?"

No answer.

"Was he drunk?"

The girl shrugged: What did it matter if he'd been drunk? Now he was dead.

"All right," I said, "just tell me, what did Michelle do?"

"She hit him." The girl began to cry again.

"But why?"

"She saw us," the girl said.

Us, that one word. She didn't have to say any others. I imagined the scene in ten different ways, and all of them were right: Michelle had found the door unlocked and come in quietly, or it was locked but she had a key. She saw them, Sam and this child, at one of the tables, or here on this cot, or—judging from the position of his body—just outside of this room. He with his hand up her skirt while she sat on a bar stool, or with his fly open, or he had her on her knees before him, but however it was, he had her, that was the important thing. He could do anything he wanted with this girl; that was what he'd hired her for. It was part of her job along with washing the floor and emptying dirty ashtrays, and he had made her do it so often that she was used to it now—it was just something else he made her do—and this night was a night like every other until the moment Michelle came in the door.

I looked at the girl. She just sat there, no longer crying. "Michelle saw you and Sam together?" I asked carefully.

She shrugged again, then nodded. Her T-shirt was too small for her, and the tight material showed the puffiness of her new breasts. One of her knees had a scab on it, and her dark shins were dusted with fine blond hairs. She was still a little girl, this person here on the cot beside me, and I wanted to pick her up in my arms and carry her down to the sea and wash him off her; I wanted to scream and make her scream with me; I wanted to kick his body where it lay until it burst like rotten fruit.

"I'm so sorry," I said, and I started to put my arm around her, then thought better of it. "I'm sorry," I said again helplessly, and she looked up and asked me what I was sorry for.

It was a good thing Sam was dead, I said; he was a bastard, he should never have touched you, do you understand?

She looked up at me and saw that I wanted her to say yes, so she opened her mouth and said, "Yes." That was all.

I took a deep breath. "What's your name?" I asked.

She wiped her nose again. "Sonya."

"All right, Sonya, come on."

She got to her feet at once, and we went out of the supply room. I lifted her over Sam's body as if I were lifting her over a puddle in the road. She followed me to the table where Michelle sat just as I had left her, slouched down with knees and shoulders all akimbo, her eyes looking at nothing at all. Her hands alone betrayed emotion. Her hands were balled into fists.

"She hit him with that," said Sonya, pointing.

Under the table lay a very small anchor, not a real one, no more than a foot in length from ring to crown. I picked it up. It was made of iron and had an iron foot protruding from the stem so that it could be stood upright like a bookend.

"Where was this?" I asked.

"There." She pointed to the bar.

"Will you take it and wash it off and put it back where it was?"

She nodded.

"It's not too heavy?"

"*Está bien.*" She took the anchor from me.

Sam must not have heard Michelle come in. Or if he had, he hadn't moved fast enough. It takes a fraction of a second for an image to enter the eyes; in that flash of time Michelle had seen their two bodies together, one broad and heavy, the other small, bird-boned, a brown-limbed feather pressed between the wall and her boss's suntanned hands.

Michelle saw them, and then: Did she hesitate? Did she stop, consider, doubt? No. Her mind, perhaps, paused, muttered some half-formed phrase of excuse and backed out of the room, erasing the sight as neatly as chalk words from a slate. Her mind did, perhaps. But her body did not go along. Her body rushed across the floor and tackled, hands reaching in passing for something to grab at and closing around the anchor. Her body pulled him away from Sonya and began to hit him, and though her arms had grown strong from months of building with lumber bought with his money, it was not this strength she drew on when she brought down her hands.

A body waking up for the first time is a marvelous thing. A body waking for the very first time after years of not existing, of being dragged around like a shadow beneath notice—when this body wakes up for the first time, it is flooded all at once with the miracle of its own power.

When I held Carlitos I held a body that was waking up to passion. It was not only passion for me but passion at the discovery of his own body, passion for the body itself, that invested his touch with such power. Michelle's body had just awakened to a different kind of passion. But no less powerful, it seems, is the passion of rage. And no less eager to make up for lost time: She struck him, and it was not only him she struck. It was not only him she was killing. She killed twenty years of amnesiac sleep with the same blows.

I put my hands on her shoulders, and very gently I shook her again. I touched her forehead and smoothed her hair. I knelt down and looked up into her eyes.

"Why doesn't she answer?" Sonya came up beside me and began slapping Michelle lightly on the cheek. I caught hold of her small hand to stop her, and outside the bar a motorcycle went past. Time was passing. I went to the window and turned the louvered shutter open. The sky was growing pale. It would be morning soon, and here I was standing in an empty bar with a dead man, the woman who had killed him, and a traumatized child. I turned back to Sonya. She was standing there watching me.

"Listen, Sonya. Sam is dead. And Michelle killed him, right?"

She nodded.

"And Michelle's your friend?"

"Sí."

"Then I need you to help me get her out of here."

"¿A dónde van?"

Where indeed: I hadn't got that far. We needed to get off the island, today if possible, but how far could I take her in the state she was in? I couldn't very well carry her onto an airplane.

"¿Y Sam?" Sonya asked when I didn't answer.

I half-looked toward where Sam lay. What about Sam? Sam was an American; his death would attract more police attention than the death of a Dominican. Though the police might not assume it was murder: When my mother drowned, the local cops drew the most elementary line to connect the dots: *Dat woman, she unhappy. She deh jump from de boat an' kill herself. Yah, mon.* A line of logic elegant in its simplicity. All right, then: *Dis mon here, he drinkin a lotta rum, you know. Fall down an' hit his head an' dat de end of his life. Dass de way it go. Yah, mon. Dem white people dem can't hold dere drink so well here on St. Croix.*

But this isn't St. Croix. What's the difference?

Coño, cabrón, el borracho se cayó. Shit, man, the drunk guy fell down. It would come to the same thing.

Tollomi, think. It doesn't matter what the police decide; you have to leave the body where it is and get out of here. And you don't even know where you're going.

All right: At the very least I'd have to lock Sam in. I crouched down beside the body. Keeping my eyes averted, I slid my hand inside the pockets of his pants. I could feel his thighs through the thin khaki. In the left pocket was a fat ring of keys. There were car keys, a tiny key to the cash register, and padlock and deadbolt keys for the bar and, I supposed, the apartments upstairs. It would be at least a day, maybe three or four, before anyone got suspicious enough to break the door down. But he'd start to stink.

I jumped up and moved away from the body, then stood fidgeting the keys through my fingers. One key caught my attention, and I stared at it a moment without realizing why. It was a silver key with a blue rubber ring around the head and a familiar name stamped into the rubber. Then I knew: It was the name of a nautical supply company in the States. A shiver of a thrill went through me; this was the key to the cabin of Sam's boat.

Sam's boat was just down the street, moored at the Port Authority. The oak and mahogany Sparkman & Stephens that I had gone to see in spite of myself, and coveted so intensely that I'd had to leave the harbor and purge myself in the sea—I was holding the key to that boat in my hand. I closed my fingers around it. I closed my eyes for a moment. On this boat I would sail us away.

I put the keys in my pocket and opened my eyes.

"All right," I said to Sonya, "we're going."

"Where?" she asked.

"We're leaving the island. Wait here while I get the car."

When I came back in, Sonya was standing beside Michelle again, shaking her. She stepped away when she saw me, and then it was my turn to try: I took hold of her shoulders and shook her too, more firmly this time. "Get *up*," I said, and shoved away the table and pulled her into a standing position. She stood, her arms draped heavily over my shoulders as if we were dancing, but her knees did not buckle; she supported her own weight. I guided her out to the car. She didn't stumble, but she didn't seem aware of her own movements either. She neither helped nor resisted as I pushed her head down to keep her from banging it as I maneuvered her into the backseat.

I found the key that locked the alley door. Overhead the sky was turning pale gray. The sun would be up soon. I didn't want to run into any soldiers going on duty down at the port; we'd have to hurry. Beside me on the broken pavement, Sonya burst into tears.

"What is it?" I asked. *Stupid question, Tollomi,* I thought, but her answer surprised me.

"I don't want you to take me away," she wept. "My mother won't know where I am."

Poor girl—I had not thought of taking her on the boat with us. I had not thought of her at all beyond this point, in fact. What was I going to do with her? The look that had entered her dark eyes said that I could do anything I wanted, and she would accept it like someone taking a foreseen but unavoidable blow: head down, surrendered to the belief that nothing would ever be different.

"I'm not taking you away," I said gently. "Where do you live?"

She pointed back toward the center of the city. *"Pa' alla."*

"You live near the bar?"

She shook her head no, then reconsidered. "I live *at* the bar," she said.

"You *live* there?"

"Upstairs. When my mother's away."

I couldn't keep the disgust off my face; I averted my eyes from hers and looked up at Sam's apartments. Hadn't Michelle known Sonya was sleeping there? She must have, but she had never mentioned it. Hadn't it struck her as odd that the pre-pubescent maid was spending the night in the boss's house? No, it hadn't struck her as odd at all, because when she looked at Sonya, she saw her own life. And her own life was what she couldn't see; she had erased it. In the place where memory should have been and wasn't, she saw nothing. Memory shaped like two bodies, one large, one small.

My mouth was full of acid. Sam's body was big enough to crush this girl in his sleep, to swallow her whole when he woke up starving, to drink her like scotch, to piss her away. I felt a useless anger rising in my throat, useless because he was dead and there was nothing I could do to him, useless because Sonya stood before me painfully alive, staring at me out of the darkest depths of childhood and I was not going to help her out of them, I was not going to do anything for her at all.

What had she just said to me? She lives at the bar when her mother's away. "Is your mother away now?" I asked.

She wiped her nose. "In Santiago."

"When is she coming back?"

She shrugged.

"Do you know where your house is?"

Nod.

"Can you walk there?"

She shook her head no. "We go in a *guagua*."

All right. I am standing outside a dead man's bar; his body is inside sprawled on the floor, in the car beside me is Michelle who has killed him. I am on the way down to his boat which in a matter of minutes I am going to steal. The thing to do is get down there and cast off and get the hell away from the harbor before the sun rises and the soldiers show up. Here I am standing in a garbage-strewn alley in Puerto Plata with a young girl in a too-tight red T-shirt, her face streaked with tears.

"All right, Sonya," I said. "Tell me where to go—I'll take you home."

As we drove through the city, I told her what I wanted her to say if she was asked. I made her repeat it back to me over and over: that Sam had sent her home this morning and said not to come back to work until Friday; that he'd said he was going on vacation, and she didn't know where, didn't know anything more. When she had learned her part to my satisfaction she climbed back into the backseat beside Michelle. We drove in silence until I glanced in the rearview mirror and saw she was trying to pry open Michelle's clenched hands.

"Leave her alone," I said. "She's in shock."

"She took the key to the bird," said Sonya.

"What bird?"

"Sam's bird. In the cage."

Then I remembered, that strange white creature he kept in the cage over the bar. "Did she let it out?" I asked.

"No, it's still there. But she took the key, after he fell down." She paused. "I want to let the bird out."

We were several miles down the main road by this time. "We can't go back now," I said. "It's too late."

"But no one will feed it."

"If we go back and someone sees us—forget it, Sonya. It's impossible."

"The bird will die," she said matter-of-factly, and leaned back in the seat, resigned. *It's bad luck to kill a bird,* I thought suddenly. Josephine told me that years and years ago.

An' if you drivin up de road in a car an' you hit any kinda bird an' kill it, well, dass a sign of death, you know.

"There's my house," said Sonya, "stop." She pointed to a row of sagging wooden houses built right up against the edge of the road.

I pulled over and stopped the car. Sonya whispered something to Michelle that I couldn't hear and kissed her gravely on the cheek. Then she turned to me, ducked her head in farewell, and got out.

"Wait," I said.

She turned and waited. In truth I had nothing to tell her. "Will you be all right?" I asked.

She nodded; she knew I wanted her to nod.

"And Michelle?" she asked.

"She'll be all right too," I said helplessly.

"And the bird?"

"Look, Sonya, the bird won't starve in two days. People will be looking for Sam by then." His body would be stinking by then, I thought. Someone would break down the door and find him.

"But how will they get it out of the cage? Michelle took the key, Sam had it around his neck, and she took it. I saw her."

To pacify her I leaned into the backseat and forced Michelle's fingers open. Her hands were empty, and her old green dress had no pockets. I looked on the car seat and on the floor.

"The key's not here," I said, "so she must have left it in the bar. So when they find Sam, they'll find the key too, and they'll let the bird out then."

The sky was turning pink, the sun was coming up, we were out of time. I looked into her dark eyes. "All right?" I said.

"*Sí*," she answered mechanically.

"Now, if no one comes to ask you anything, don't go back to the bar until Tuesday. That's two days from now."

She shook her head that she wouldn't.

"Promise me, Sonya."

"I swear it," she said.

"All right. We'll be long gone by tomorrow if anything goes wrong. Don't forget what to say."

"I won't."

"Tell me again."

She did; I hardly listened. I was looking at her eyes. They were heavy with secrets; they were nothing but secrets. Even if she never breathed a word of them, the secrets themselves would always be visible in her eyes, dark ciphers that would set her apart from the rest of the children around her and from the adults too; her eyes would set her apart all her life.

I watched as she turned and walked quickly up the street and disappeared round the corner of one of the houses. It looked just like every other house on the row.

It was a ten-minute drive back to the pier. While I drove, the sky began to color, deep shades of orange and pink. Red in the morning, sailor take warning: What would I do if the Port Authority guards were there already? Would there be sailors working on the freighters? I needed the dock to be absolutely empty—just one policeman, one boy on a moped, or one old woman poking through the garbage on the beach—if just one person looked up and saw us, we wouldn't be able to risk taking his boat. It was too well-known. And then what would we do? I kept thinking about the bird hanging in its cage above the bar. What I'd said was true: It wouldn't die in two days and Sam's body would probably be found by then. But Josephine's voice persisted in my head: *An' if you kill de bird, dat bad luck what you get wid your foolishness gon stick on you like jelly but ain' gon wash off, you know.*

When I moved my hand from the wheel to the gearshift, my hand shook. How many hours was it since I'd eaten, slept?

When I reached the waterfront, the guardhouse was still locked up. I left the car on the side of the road that was closer to the center of town, with the windows rolled down and the key in the ignition. With any luck someone would steal it. Sam's boat was moored just where it had been the day I visited it, at the end of the little dock that jutted out into the cove. It was at least thirty yards from the car to the boat. Would Michelle walk that far?

The sky overhead was warming into blue, the east was aflame with color. I got Michelle out of the car. As before, she stood—with my arm around her for balance. When I walked she came with me, but haltingly, with no volition of her own, the weight of her body heavy against mine as if she were asleep. It would have been easier were she really sleepwalking. But I could not wake her to bring her back; she was already awake, awake and gone.

We staggered around the chained entrance to the pier, down the crumbling dock, past the glass-bottomed tour boat and a fishing trawler whose deck was filled with rusted oil drums. Just as we reached Sam's boat Michelle tripped, and I dragged her the last few feet of the way. The boat swayed under our weight as I lifted her aboard.

I helped her into the cockpit, and she sat down at once, head drooping, shoulders down. Her hands were still balled into fists. I resisted the urge to shake her again, raised the foresail, and went forward to cast off. I was afraid to start the motor because of the noise; we would have to sail out of the harbor. I loosened the lines with trembling fingers, tightened the jib sheet, and headed away from the dock. When I straightened up I saw the sun had risen.

I was covered in a film of sweat. I took a deep breath and noticed for the first time the sharp taste of sea in the morning air. Here I was, standing barefoot on the mahogany deck of Sam's boat, raising the sails, the motion of the sea moving through me like my own relief. It was too early to be relieved; we were not yet away. Still, the garbage-strewn beach was empty of people, the guardhouse was closed, and there was no one on the wharf near enough to see us. And here I was holding the tiller of this boat, this beautiful boat I had wanted so intensely to sail.

And now I was sailing it away. For a moment I had a flash of what Michelle meant when she spoke of destiny. The whole morning had stopped and held its breath, waiting for me; now I was here.

From the north a light breeze was beginning to blow. I sailed out of the harbor, tacking back and forth. The boat responded perfectly, so finely was she tuned. And my hands on the lines and on the tiller understood perfectly in return; I did not have to think even; I had only to move my hands, my body, and we flew out, skimming whitecaps, the bow pointing high. The wind was elusive but I caught it all. I was sailing as I had never sailed before. It was like making love.

The island we were leaving slid backward through the water. I let the sails luff a moment and turned to look back. The trees on the *malecón* were indistinct swatches of gray and green, too far away to see clearly now. The Puerto Plata harbor had receded to a gray and yellow furrow scraped into the line of the coast. Back there Sonya would be sitting in one of those dark shacks by the edge of the road, her dark eyes watching everything in silence. Back there Sam's body would be cooling, growing stiff on the hard floor of his bar, blue eyes staring at nothing, filming over with death. And farther inland, Carlitos would be waking up in Lupe's bed in the hills of Las Nubes, his hands aching in torn strips of sheet, his mind on fire with future plans.

A small cloud of dark smoke was rising above the trees. I was too far away to know exactly where it was coming from. It might have been west of Puerto Plata where they sometimes burned whole fields of sugarcane to feed the soil. But no, there was the thin smudge of the harbor, and the smoke rose just to the east of that. I let the sails slacken and stared toward the rising plume, straining to see until my eyes hurt. I imagined, I think, that I heard the explosion, the bursting of all that liquor into flame. The flames themselves I could not see, but as the smoke thickened and spread, I felt something like the satisfaction José Luis must have been feeling too, the heat of the fire surpassing the heat of the new morning, expanding out into it with the bright and irrevocable power of burning. And, however small, the undeniable change.

I tightened the mainsheet, and soon the whole island became an indistinct blur of green, receding into the blue of so much sky and sea.

As I watched the long of hump of land fade and tilt away from me as the island slipped below the horizon, I thought too of the fires the Tainos watched, the fires the first Europeans set to burn away the world. On that same island.

Michelle sat beside me in the cockpit and never stirred once. I wrapped my shirt around her head to save her from the full heat of the sun. I flicked seawater on her arms and shoulders, and ran a wet hand across her forehead from time to time, but she neither moved nor raised her eyes. When the boat heeled up she braced her legs, or her legs braced themselves perhaps; I don't think she was conscious of it. I talked to her in snatches, tried to give her water, and squeezed her hand in mine now and then. In the bright blue ring of sea around me, perfect and unbroken on all sides, I felt unaccountably free of everything. The fearfulness of the situation I was in had followed the land over the horizon, out of sight, and I sailed like a man who is happy. I *was* happy, guiltlessly, foolishly happy: No one was coming after us, no one had seen us leave, and now here I was, holding the tiller of the most beautiful boat I had ever seen or sailed, whistling. A man was dead and Michelle had killed him and I whistled, though the wind flung it away, and then I sang.

I was not really thinking. There was too much going on all around me to let fear intrude: the bright windy blue, the salt-sweet air, the pleasant stinging in my palms where the tiller was beginning to rub, the sails tight and full, the feel of this exquisite boat skimming so lightly over the sea. And the hard spray of sea blowing against my face was the same sea, the same molecules of water that had blown in my face off St. Croix when I was eleven years old and Henry had let me take the *Lilah*'s tiller for the first time. The memory did not even make me sad; it did not seem a memory. I sailed as if all the empty and wasted years of my life had been cut away from the cloth of my life, and the remaining pieces—every moment I had ever spent surrounded by salt water and sails—had knit seamlessly together, and I had always been this happy, I had always been a sailor, I was living the life I was always meant to have.

Each time I moved to pull the tiller or trim the sails, I felt the perfect mechanics of the boat moving with me, as if the tiller were an extension of my own limbs. All day I sailed the fantasy of what my life might have been like and it was wonderful; it ran glorious and unchecked until sunset: At sunset the wind died, and my fantasy died with the wind.

The sails luffed and fluttered, then hung silent. I came out of my glorious daze to find myself sitting becalmed in a stolen boat whose owner lay dead in his bar, if the bar was still standing. What had I done? Beside me sat the woman who had killed him, as motionless as he. I had gotten us away, but now what? I had made no plan.

A high haze of cloud had thickened across the overhead sky. I sat beside Michelle and put my arm around her waist and watched the light ebb. The sunset was oddly colorless; some streaks of dull metallic pearl and then nothing, just a dullness that grew increasingly dark, and then darkness itself and the uneasy quiet that settles over a boat when there is no wind.

Michelle sat so utterly still beside me. For the first time all day, her condition really frightened me. Once again I put my hands on her shoulders and shook her very gently. Her body let me shake it, and the hat I had made for her out of my shirt slipped down over her eyes. I pulled it off and threw it at her feet.

"Michelle," I said, "look at me. Please."

She didn't move. She breathed, her heart was beating. Her eyes occasionally blinked. But she didn't see me. As if I were the one who had gone away.

As I sat beside her, looking for a sign of awareness that was not there, I began to be aware of my own body. My tongue felt swollen. My eyes ached from squinting in the wind, and I was terribly thirsty. I put my arms under Michelle's and pulled her to her feet.

"Stand up," I said, "we're going below." But this time her knees buckled and we both fell back against the seat. Again I tried to get her to stand on her own; she wouldn't do it now. At last I hoisted her over my shoulder. Staggering beneath her weight and accumulating half-felt bruises along the way, I squeezed us both through the hatch and carried her down the ladder to the cabin below, like a fireman saving a child. I got her into the forward berth and dumped her on the bed. I found myself lying down as well. I was out of breath. My legs felt made of rubber.

After a while I raised myself up on one elbow and thought as hard as I could at her absent eyes: *Michelle, My Shell, Miss Hell, wherever you are, turn around. Turn and walk back toward me. We are away. We are out in the middle of the sea. Every moment you have ever spent leaving your life has led you to this moment where you no longer need to. You're safe. You can come back.*

I waited. Nothing happened. All around me I felt the emptiness of the sea, the miles of nothing on all sides as empty as Michelle's blue eyes. I put my face nose to nose with hers.

"Listen," I said aloud, "you have to snap out of this. I need you to help me sail. I don't even know where we're going."

Silence.

Damn it, Michelle, say something.

She didn't. Wherever she was had nothing to do with me.

At last I got up and went into the galley. I had glanced in that morning and found drinking water and a bowl of oranges; now I opened the cupboards and discovered more water, liquor, club soda, and tins of nuts. I drank some water and ate a handful of cashews and an orange and felt a little better. I rummaged in the cabin and found Sam's charts and spread them out on the galley table. Tomorrow I could make it around the east end of the island if the wind was good. But what then? I closed my eyes and saw the whole of the Caribbean sketched there before me, its ragged edges of continents and islands. Where was I going? I got up and went back on deck.

It was completely dark now, and the haze I had seen gathering earlier blocked out the stars. This frightened me. I needed the stars to navigate, but more than that, I needed them to hang above me in the sky and give me a sense of place that had nothing to with navigation. With no stars overhead the darkness around the boat was almost palpable, heavier than normal air and expanding in all directions, above and below, as if there were nothing in the world but this darkness, no sea even, no sky.

I was overtired, that was the problem. I hadn't slept in a day and a half. I'd been sailing single-handed since this morning, and I'd hardly eaten anything at all. All right: I would lie down and sleep until the wind picked up, and when it did, I would come back on deck and sail some more; sailing would clear my head, and then I would be able to think clearly about what to do next.

Having made this plan, I tightened down the sheets and went below. I shut off the light in the galley, and then the cabin was completely dark. I felt my way into the forward berth and moved Michelle over on the mattress and lay down. She was so still. My body was trembling. I moved up close beside her and closed my eyes.

The huge, unfathomable silence of an ocean without wind hung all around me. The sounds of my own breathing, and Michelle's, and the occasional creak of wood or rigging brought on by a slow, crestless swell— all these were nothing against the larger silence of the night. Nothing could break into it. It swallowed all sounds even as they were being made.

I was exhausted but I couldn't fall asleep. I lay watching a slice of darkness through the open hatch overhead. Somewhere behind the clouds, the stars were changing position in the sky. Time was passing. But I couldn't see it pass, as if the rotation of the earth itself had stopped along with the wind.

I listened to the sounds of her breathing. I listened to my own breath. The sounds sank into the stillness around us, and the stillness went on.

The sound of lines creaking as we hit a swell, the hoisted dinghy rubbing against the block. The slap of water, then silence again.

At some point during that long night I groped my way aft and climbed on deck again and yelled as loud as I could, again and again until I was hoarse, and the silence swallowed it all. Not even my own echo came back to me.

The entire night passed without my sleeping. I lay beside Michelle and watched the dark wedge of sky through the hatch until at last it began to pale. I watched the sky lighten and made myself wait until I was sure the false dawn had passed and it was really sunrise. Then I went back on deck.

The sun was not up. The sky was all haze. I watched and watched the blur of gray through sore, wind-rubbed eyes until at last it sharpened into a line with sea above and sky below. The same blanket of cloud was still overhead. The sun rose and showed itself orange for a minute, then disappeared behind the scrim of haze.

There was still no wind. I turned on the engine and watched as the fuel gauge arrow moved to the one-eighth mark and then stopped.

Eh, Tollie, you tink you a smaht sailor mon. You forget dat story bout de jumbie what tief de wind of dat mon boat?

I shut off the engine and stood up with the idea of walking up and down the deck a few times, just to clear my head, get my legs moving, but once standing, I had to sit back down at once. I was dizzy. I sat there in the cockpit a long time. Behind the clouds, the sun climbed higher. *Get out of the sun, Tollomi.*

There is no sun. It's behind the clouds.

The heat, then. You're not drinking enough water. Go below.

I made my way below again.

The cabin was dark to my eyes. I stood gripping the ladder until I could see it. I drank some water and ate another handful of nuts. Then I poured water into a highball glass and took it in to Michelle.

She wouldn't drink. The glass knocked against her teeth, and the water ran down her chest. I carried the glass back to the galley and returned with an orange.

Josephine knew how to peel oranges so that the rind would come off in the shape of an animal. I didn't want to think of Josephine now. Feeling dazed, I fetched a knife and cut the orange into sections. I held a slice up to Michelle's mouth and pressed it against her teeth.

Please, Michelle. Look at me.

The juice dribbled over my hand.

Here is her body; here are her eyes, unseeing, open, her long arms and legs askew on the sheets. Here is her hair, which I touch, but she cannot feel me touching; you can touch this body, and she'll never feel a thing; you can sneak into her room at night and touch her anywhere you please, and she won't know it, she won't be there, she'll never tell, Michelle, but then one day she'll kill a man and then she'll disappear.

I lay on my side and ate the orange myself.

I tried to sleep. Sleep would not come.

Tollie, come here now. I gon show you a ting here. You see dis orange? Well, we gon make a picture from dis piece a fruit. Now study dis, Tollie, 'cause when Henry come back you gon show him what you learnin now.

Peel it like dis. You peel it jus nice like dis, you know…an' it make a picture fuh you. What dat dere?

Mongoose!

Now we take anodda one here an' take de peel like dis. You see?

It make a angel, Josephine.

You take de oranges dem out fuh Belle an Marika. But first I gon show you one more picture, an' dis one it deh gon be fuh you, Tollie… Dere. You see?

It make a snake.

I went on deck and threw the orange peels into the sea. They floated. I walked up and down the deck. Nine paces from bow to stern.

Long ridges of sea without whitecaps, swell of current in waves that settled back into flat water before they could break white. And no wind.

Was it noon? Was it three? I couldn't see the sun behind the clouds. The air was heavy, thick with salt and the pungent smell of my own sweat.

I have to move. I can't just sit here.

Why he tief de dead mon boat? He wan sail away from dat mess he make on de shore?

It was just another voice in my head. Not Josephine's, not my own.

Yah, mon, he tink he de good, a real smaht mon, dat Tollomi. He tell dat bwoy go burn down de bar, an' den he get dere first an' leave a dead mon dere! Flat on de floor, just to make de ting more fun. Cuz it seem like jus a fire alone, dat ain' enough fuh 'im now, you know. An' now dat bird gon burn up in de fire too. He gone bring down all kinda trouble on his head.

Say wha? Wha foolishness you tellin me now? Wha fire is dat?

You gon blind in de night? You doan see dat ugly smoke risin from de town?

Dat smoke it deh very black, mon. Black as my face. So why you call dat smoke ugly?

Your face ugly too, mon. I tink you go blind from lookin at dat face in de mirror…

I feel feverish. The sun sets in a bad haze of gray, and the water darkens. I'd go swimming, but the dark water frightens me. I have never been afraid of the water before, but here I am; I can't make myself dive.

In the thickening night, my own blindness frightens me. I can't see the water at all. I go below and switch on all the lights in the cabin, and then I don't know what to do.

Drink some bottled water. Slowly. Now go and lie down.

I go and lie down beside Michelle.

Michelle, listen. I know you can hear me. I'm afraid. There's no wind and I can't sleep. José Luis set fire to the bar after all, and I never let that bird out of its cage. Bad luck follows you everywhere if you kill a bird by mistake; Josephine told me that.

I'm not thinking straight.

Michelle, do you hear me? I need you here. If you're not here then I'm not here either. Please...

Leave her alone.

I rearrange her limbs to look more peaceful. I move her arms closer to her body, change the angle of her head. Her hands I can do nothing about: They remain fists and sleep will not come.

I tellin you, mon, he deh too damn choopid, dat Tollomi. Dat odda bwoy come burn down de bar, but it de Tollomi fault. Now de bad luck gon follow him round de world like his own shadow.

I might be dreaming. After so many dreamless years, I might be dreaming at last, a long terrible dream of a becalming, like the one in the story of the sailor who made the jumbies so angry that they took the wind away. In this story the jumbies bewitched the sailor's boat so that the wind would never reach it, and he drifted for months and then years in perfect stillness, never catching even a breath of wind. He had plenty to eat, the fishing was excellent, and it rained often, so he always had fresh water. But even when the rains came there was no wind. And so there was no way he could ever reach shore. At last he was so wild to feel land beneath his feet again that he could stand it no longer. He jumped overboard and found land in the only place he could, at the bottom of the sea.

Tollie, you doan believe none a dis foolishness. See Henry here, he deh tellin you all dese story an' ting an' tinkin he could sail a boat. But de truth is dat he can't nevah find de wind less it knock him right over fuh true, so he gon blame dis on a jumbie, an' say de jumbies dem what tief de wind—

Eh, what you know bout boat, Josephine? De day I see you set foot in a boat is de day I jump over de side myself.

Henry, you hush about dat—

See, Tollie, what de truth is, is dat de sailor, he jump from de boat 'cause he wan get away from his woman! Das what he doin, Josephine, he have de bad misfortune to get a woman what talk back like parrot, an' so he ain' got no choice but to—

Oh? De way you sailin dat boat, Mistah Henry—Cyaptin Henry, pahdon me—I tink you most likely mash it up on de reef an' drown your-self an' de whole damn crew. An' dat gon save you de trouble of havin to jump over de side!

You hear how she talkin, Tollomi? Josephine, you find me one mon wha can say I ain' de best damn sailor round dis whole coast—one mon, Josephine, an' I gon give him de Lilah fuh his own self. One mon wha can say dat, Josephine!

(She laughs, her gold teeth showing, slaps him on the back of the head. Closes her mouth long enough to kiss him, but as he reaches for her hips she jumps aside, still laughing, and goes out of the room.)

Dusk. There's still no wind.

Darkness again. The faint lap of water on the hull a joke against the enormous canopy of soundlessness around me.

What I want to know then, Henry, what I want to know, Josephine, if from beyond time and breath you can hear me, what I want to know is this: What was it that the sailor did to anger the jumbies so much that they took away the wind? Had he spoken ill of someone? Scorned some grave? Boasted? Let a death go unmourned?

Josephine, if I ever get the chance, if the wind ever deigns to fill these sails again, I will sail back to where your body is buried. I'll walk up the hill to the cemetery, through all the rubble left by the hurricane. I'll find the place, the piece of earth you're buried under, and I'll lie down on it and mourn you properly. If where you are is where there are jumbies, Josephine, please, intervene. Light the herbs you used to burn sometimes to stay on their side. *Ask dem not to be so vex wid me, Josephine, dat dey doan send me no wind...*

My eyes are sandpaper. It is morning again and nothing has moved. Not Michelle, not the sails. I peel an orange with shaking fingers, bits of peel like dead butterflies dropping all over the place, on my legs, on the galley floor. I eat the orange, I drink some water. I drink a little Scotch in hopes of getting drowsy. Not too much or I'll get dehydrated. I open a tin of nuts and brush the salt off each individual nut. Then I eat them one by one, sucking on them like fingers before biting down, just to give me something to concentrate on, something to do.

Noon, more or less. I can't see any shadows because of the haze. The sea is a dark and solid blue, tarnished by the dull gleam of cloudlight, the sky a pale gray unbroken mass. My eyes ache in this pale pearlescent light; there is nothing to see, nothing to break up either the desert stretch of water or the flat, oppressive canopy overhead. Nothing but the bright pearl of the sun, and I can't look at that. The air stinks of salt and the sea is empty.

It's late afternoon. I can tell by the quality of the light; even through cloud cover I know it, its choked intensity. The sea is flat and empty.

I have heard of a kind of madness that possesses sailors who have been at sea too long. When they look over the rails at the sea, the water appears to them as a rolling meadow: grasses and flowers and earth. So convincing is the illusion, and so starved are they for the weight and smell of land that they have to be restrained from jumping overboard. There are stories of men dying this way, jumping overboard and drowning in imaginary land. Does the delusion end with the shock of hitting the sea? Do they startle into truth, spitting out mouthfuls of seawater, and call to their shipmates to bring them aboard? Or does the madness persist even as they are drowning? Do they jump to their dream of land and find it? Do they die with the smell of hay and wildflowers in their lungs?

I look at the sea. It's sea. I fix my aching eyes to one spot on the water and wait.

The sun is going to set again. How can there possibly be no wind still? Look at the waves, the water. The kind of light. Late afternoon light. It makes the water shimmer. It's too bright for this haze; the shimmer is too bright and too solid, as if its source were in the water and not merely reflected on it—

The pale flash like the flash of a fish was the thing I saw first. Then a seaweed darkness appeared in the center of that brightness all at once, as if a shadow had fallen on that spot, darker than the dark blue of the water. The spot grew larger, like a pupil slowly dilating in the eye of the sea. The water trembled. On my hands and knees on deck I leaned over the toe rail. The dark flash of a deep-water fish. Scales. Seaweed. Hair—

Skin. I lay on my stomach and hung over the side of the boat and looked down into the surfacing face of my mother.

Her face came into the air. It had not changed. Her algae-green hair was plastered dark and wet along her head; below the surface of the water it streamed out in green tendrils, undulating. Her skin was pale, her dark tail lost in the depths of the water save for an occasional shimmering flash.

"Come here," my mother said to me, and without hesitation I stood up and stepped overboard. *I am dreaming,* I thought in the second it took to fall, and then I hit the water and shot down past the length of her body. Through the water I saw the cleft in her tail; then I slowed and kicked to the surface. I shook the water from my eyes and blinked: She was still there. I tread my legs in the sea and looked into my mother's blue eyes.

She took a hesitant breath of air.

"This air smells of smoke," she said.

"What do you mean?"

"It's a beautiful boat," she murmured as if she hadn't heard me. She ran her fingers along the side of the hull. Her hand had no webbing; it was a woman's hand.

"Did he push you?" I asked.

"Who?" She looked at me then.

"My father. I mean the shipping magnate. Your husband in St. Croix, did he push you overboard?"

She stretched out her hands and buried her fingers in my hair. She began to sink below the surface of the water, and I let myself sink with her, pulled down beneath the weight of her hands. We sank down, through the upper registers of greenish light that deepened imperceptibly to blue.

"Take a breath," my mother said.

"I can't," I answered. A cloud of bubbles escaped my mouth and rose to rejoin the rest of the air far above.

"Try," she insisted. Her own mouth was full of the sea.

A lifetime ago I was here in this same sea, longer than a lifetime ago it was; it was a different life entirely, the life I had as a little boy. A boy who followed a mermaid to the bottom of the sea and breathed seawater as easily as air. I had done it then, wide-awake and really: surely I could do it dreaming now. I opened my mouth to the water and exhaled. The last air in my lungs rose up in fat silver marbles and was gone.

I drew a breath, and then the sea was inside me. I choked once. A slow heaviness spread from my chest out through my limbs. My mother freed her fingers from my hair, and I sank of my own accord now, through the heavy and sweet salt water that grew bluer and darker and more solid as we sank into it, down and farther down.

"I'll show you to your father," she said.

"My father?" I echoed.

"The real one. Oh, you must have known, Bartholomew, dark as you are." There was amusement in her voice.

"Who is my father?" I asked.

"A sailor, of course." She smiled.

"From St. Croix? A Cruzan?"

"Yes."

"Is he still there? Could I see him?"

Her hand moved in the water. "Down," she said, and pointed.

"He's dead?"

"Since before you were born. I used to walk on the beach hoping he'd swim back to shore."

"He drowned?"

"A sailor's death, my love." She smiled an inscrutable mermaid smile.

"And your death? Were you pushed?"

"The husband pushed, the lover pulled," she said. "An irresistible combination. But now here *you* are: my blue-eyed boy, still suntanned like the day he was born. What would you like from the sea? Let's see if you answer like a sailor or a pirate." Her teeth flashed in a laugh.

"Treasure," I said, knowing which answer would please her.

"Pirate! Very good. You've already stolen a boat, I see. Now what will this treasure look like?"

The light was nearly gone, we had sunk so far below the water's surface. I could still see her pale face, but it was vague now through the black water, and I wondered if she could see my face as I felt my expression change.

"The treasure will look like my old life," I said. My voice was all water now. "It will look like St. Croix."

My mother stopped sinking. Her dark hair swirled. "You won't find that treasure," she said. She shook her head. "If that's what you wanted, you should have gone into the sea twenty years ago and stayed. It's too late now. The old St. Croix is gone."

"I know," I said. "I saw it start to go. And I can't forget it. I've tried and I can't—it's always there inside me. Not what I had, but the feeling of losing it."

"I know. I'm sorry."

"And now Josephine is gone too." Though we were deep in the water, I felt my eyes fill with tears.

"Who?" my mother asked.

"Josephine. *Josephine*."

"Who is Josephine?"

I stared at her, this shimmering creature with the scales of a fish below her waist and on her face the blue eyes and Caucasian nose my own face wore.

"Who is Josephine?" she asked again.

And I answered, "Josephine is my mother."

I choked with the last word. I tried to speak again and choked; I was choking. A shadow of pain passed over the pale mermaid face. "I can't breathe," I gasped. Her hair was a mane in the water.

"Drowning is hard," she said flatly. "Be patient. It will pass."

I don't want to drown—I tried to tell her this and felt only water leave my mouth. My chest was convulsing. The sea was leaking darkness, around the edges of my eyes was only darkness, a loose fist of darkness beginning to squeeze shut. My heart pounded in my temples. *I'm blacking out,* I thought. *I want to wake up*—

The fist tightened, and the last aperture of light left to me shuttered closed.

I will not wake up. I am already awake. I will not die in my sleep like Josephine.

I will drown alone in the sea.

I could still feel my body. The water that my arms and legs continued to struggle through was endless and warm.

Once upon a time there was a young girl who like all children had in her possession many valuable things. But Fate had set her down in a dangerous place, and the girl determined that it was too dangerous to keep her valuables with her. Like all children she was ingenious and resourceful when in trouble, and she locked her things in a box for safe-keeping.

She buried the box under her bed.

She thought she could get it back anytime she wanted.

Like much buried treasure, its location was forgotten.

Often she felt that a part of her was missing, but she didn't know what it was.

I'm awake. I have not yet opened my eyes. I have no idea what I will see when I open them. I do not know where I am.

Not knowing is like not being born. You could stay that way forever, but you would never live. I could stay this way forever, in this place of darkness and unknowing, this absence of experience—but it's not what I was made for. I can't stay anywhere forever. Not even here.

I take a deep breath.

What will I see? Barren desert? Dense jungle? The pockmarked landscape of the moon?

I open my eyes, and the infinite possibilities of my absent life reduce themselves to one.

I'm looking at a rug. A red rug under my feet. I recognize it at once. It used to have patterns on it, but over the years it faded until all you could see was that it was red.

I know exactly where I am.

I'm in the living room of the house I grew up in, and it looks exactly as it used to. Nothing has been moved; it's as if I never left at all. I go through the hallway and up the stairs, which creak as they always did, to the second floor. At the top of the stairs is the door to the room I used to sleep in, my bedroom. I turn the knob, and the door opens. It was never locked.

When I sit on the bed, the mattress sags the same way. The same mattress. Still here too is the long gouge in the headboard that looks like it was made by a tiger's claw.

I kneel down on the floor and push the bed out of the way. The floorboards under it are still loose, and I pry the right ones up.

I lean over the hole and look into it.

Down in the hole is a box made of dark wood. It's been there a long time, and its sides have bulged and swollen as if it's infested with termites.

I don't want to touch it.

But it's mine.

The time for choosing about such matters, if it ever existed, is long past. If there was a time for choice, I missed it. When the question was asked, I was off somewhere else. Now I am here and I will do what has to be done.

I take out the box and set it on the floor. It's not a pretty thing. I look at the key that opens it. The key is beautiful, heavy in the palm of my hand, ornate and old. The lovelier the key, the more secrets it locks up. The best place to lock your treasure is in the house of the thief.

I put the key in the lock and turn it. The lock clicks.

The top of the box springs open, and every day of my lost life comes tumbling out.

It's all here. This is the room I slept in for eighteen years, the disoriented mornings and the long and dangerous afternoons, the window I climbed out of when I was so small. The nights I used to lie in bed without sleeping, waiting for the sound of the turning doorknob. This is the room where he comes in, my grandfather, sometime after midnight and before dawn, in the thick time of darkness, the quiet time. I wake to the sound of the knob and then his feet in wool socks crossing the floor and then the touch of his hands, his beautiful hands, and what happens after that I'm there for only once. After that I blow out the candle in my mind and leave my body there in darkness, and my mind slips out, easy as curling smoke into the air, and joins the darkness and travels with the night far away.

In the mornings I'm exhausted and can barely get out bed.

That is the bed, right there. As I look at it, it begins to be underwater. My eyes are underwater. And then I can't see anymore—I am crying too hard.

I know it is me on this floor, crying as if my heart would break. I know too that this can't happen, that my heart is already broken.

His beautiful hands reached inside me and squeezed my heart until it broke like an egg or a piece of fruit, some living thing that was not done growing. It's not what he did to my body that matters so much. The body will grow anyway. It will fill and swell in the right places and be perfect, really, you would never know, it's not the body, it's the heart, it's my heart he damaged.

By touch I take things out of the box. Each memory is wrapped around a lump of grief. Each one I unwrap, it's grief I find at the center.

All the grief that was ever mine is in here, opened at last by the brilliant fuse of recognition, and the terrible nameless explosion that always follows. If that explosion did have a name, its name would be rage.

Somewhere the body of a man lies spread-eagled on a freshly-scrubbed wooden floor. He's no longer breathing. Somewhere a young girl is wiping off her thighs and hiding the rags. She's holding her breath. Somewhere, everywhere, no one notices anything at all.

I get up. My hands are shaking, but not with fear. I don't think I will ever be afraid of anything again.

What I feel now is different. This is what surged through me when I saw him bending over her as my grandfather bent over me; this is the anchor I hit him with so hard that I heard his skull crack as loud and clean as a shot; this is the spring on the box that sends its lid flying open. This is rage. It is as passionate as love. I dance through the house, breaking things.

The framed photographs on the mantel downstairs I throw into the hall one by one and listen to the smashing of glass. I turn over tables and yank out drawers, the silverware drawers, the drawers in the linen closet. It's not until I get to my parents' bedroom and pull out the drawers of the dresser and see and feel and smell my mother's clothes that I am stopped. I sit down quietly on the floor. I remember these clothes, their fabric, the smooth oldness of it, the wrinkles from being packed in a drawer instead of hung up, and the smell of her body a part of the cloth itself. It makes me cry again.

When I stop crying and look up, the room has grown darker. I am exhausted. And I have to get out of here.

I flick the light switch but the lights don't work. I go out into the hall and trip on something I've thrown and nearly fall. Where is the staircase? I turn and go the other way and find myself in a room I don't recognize, with nothing in it but a freshly-made bed. I back out and start down the hall again and wind up back in my own bedroom.

Years ago I tried to leave this house through my bedroom window, climbing along the roof. I didn't make it then and I wouldn't now, not even by jumping. I'd never make it to the next roof, it's too far.

I sit down on the bed.

I have gone so far, so far away, and I have never gone anywhere. I have gone everywhere and come back to this place, and here I sit on this same bed. Is this what I get for finally knowing?

Now that I've found my way in, will I will never get out?

If this is destiny, I want to see its face. My grandfather was too small a man to have done this all by himself, to have scratched so deeply into the map the line I have witlessly followed my whole life.

But the heart is so easily wounded. I was too young.

There's a creak on the stairs. Footsteps coming up. It's not my grandfather. He had discovered some way of walking up the stairs silently—no one else but he could do it. With him there was never any sound until the click of the latch when he opened my door.

I listen to the footsteps climbing the stairs. If it's not him, then who is it?

And then I think I know who it is. Just like in the old story, it's Death who is coming to call. Who else would find me here, in the place I have spent my whole life running from? Who else would know where to look, how to arrive?

The doorknob clicks and the door opens. The footsteps come into the room and I look up. I will meet Death eye to eye.

It takes me a moment to understand what I am looking at.

It's not Death's face I see looking down at my own.

It's Tollomi's.

I get up. I follow him. We go along the hallways of the house together, and this time I find the stairs. We go down the stairs and across the red rug, and there is the front door. I put my hand on the knob and turn.

Outside, the sky is very bright.

There was nothing. No longer any sea to drown in, nor any air to never again breathe. There was darkness, never again light or thinking, but in this darkness my body came back to me in a jarring rush of pain, and I thought, *I'm still drowning, then.* My mouth was full of a salt liquid warmer than the sea had been. I thought, *Now there's blood in my lungs.* The salty taste of blood in my throat, my mouth.

Then through the racking pain in my body a redness, sense of light, of color, sense of my eyes again. My eyes were closed; I opened them. I was in air. My head hanging down through air. The sea was inches below my head. Something hard beneath my hips, my chest hanging down, jerking in knifing spasms.

In my mouth was not blood but seawater, warmed inside me and now fighting its way out of my upside-down lungs to rejoin the water below. I was choking, on air now. I was being hit hard between my shoulder blades. Then I was pulled up and the hard thing was beneath my head too; I was lying on my stomach against hard boards. The knife-sharp pain in my chest receded a little, and I became aware of the boards against my forehead, the rattling sound of my own breaths.

A hand turning my head to the side. Someone was speaking, bending toward me.

"Josephine?" I asked.

The word seemed pulled out of another language, another lifetime. I wasn't sure I was speaking it right, but the hand touched my cheek at the sound of the name.

My eyes had closed again; been closed a long time, it seemed. When I opened them, it was to the filtered light of dusk. My lungs ached. The hard boards on which I lay were the deck of a boat. A face moved above me, paler than mine. Not Josephine's.

"Michelle?"

She was turning me onto my back, holding my head in her lap, her face bent upside-down over mine. Her eyes, her hanging hair—she was awake, she was here with me. She had pulled me out of the sea and I was alive.

Cross-legged on the deck she cradled my head and at last helped me to sit up. The taste of salt and the ache of so much water still burned my lungs. I started to speak and coughed, spat salty water. Michelle looked at me, then around at the boat, then out across the darkening water. She ran her hands slowly back and forth along my arm, and then across the deck.

"I didn't know it would be like this," she said slowly. "This is my life. I feel this wood under my hands. I feel my heart beating." Her face trembled in a mixture of pain and, I think, wonder. "It hurts," she said. And then she cried.

I found her hand and held it. Her hand shook as she wept, and I felt the shakiness of deep water in my own body, in my lungs, in my blood.

"I would never have gotten out of there," she sobbed. "I would have sat in that bar until someone came in for a drink and found the body. I remembered everything until I couldn't move. That's why I forgot for so many years—I had keep moving, to escape from there. But when I remembered I was back there again, in my old house. If you hadn't come and got me, Tollomi, I would have stayed stuck there; I would have been trapped..."

And had she not pulled me from the sea when she did, I would have become part of the sea. Me, you, me, you—who saves who on this journey? Coughing still, I held her as she cried. Her dress was dripping wet as if she had drenched it with tears only, as if the sea she had pulled me out of was the same sea falling from her eyes. The same sea my true father had drowned in. The same sea on which Henry taught me to sail. The same sea I had promised I would cross to say goodbye to Josephine, if we ever found the wind.

But there was no wind. As the earth rolled us away from the sun into darkness and we sat in our wet clothes, I grew cold. A chill began in my limbs and worked its way into my stomach. Only my lungs still burned. Michelle's body leaning against mine was cold, too. When at last we stood up, my teeth chattered. We climbed down the ladder, shed our wet things, and wrapped ourselves in sheets. I thought of shrouds. My mouth still tasted of seawater. We lay down in the bow of the dead man's boat, and both of us slept.

I wake in darkness and don't know where I am. I'm alone and tangled in panic, tangled in a sheet, I can't breathe, my pajamas are gone.

I throw my arms around and hit close walls, and a wall above me too, a coffin lid: I'm trapped—then a square of darkness I touch and find open. A hatch.

The boat. I know where I am. And I know how I got here. The anchor I hit him with—the dead man, Sam. Sonya, my grandfather, Tollomi, and now I'm here, alone in the berth of a boat, the sheet wrapped around me for sleeping, my dress drying on the deck above. But I feel as if I'm back there still, smothered inside my newfound old life. In my old room, in my old bed, trapped.

All the times my mind went off, my body stranded behind for my grandfather to play with; now it seems my mind wasn't completely away after all. My mind knows what went on after all. It's still going on now, it's never stopped: Now, here, the smell of sea and canvas changes to the breathless smell of his skin, his aftershave. And I've never been anywhere or done anything but lie frozen beneath his warm and beautiful terrible hands while he touches me in the darkness of my childhood room.

I put my head up to the hatch, gasping for different air. When I can breathe again, I slide off the mattress into the galley and climb the ladder to the deck.

Tollomi is there, sitting in the cockpit looking up at the sky. "Look," he says, "the sky—" He coughs and breaks off, coughing. Then he sees my face, and his own turns sad. "Oh, Michelle," he says.

I don't need to explain it. He can see on my face why I woke, where I've been. I sit down beside him, and he puts his arm around me. We sit like that, quiet for a long time, and I remember that not all embraces trap. Some free.

"What were you going to say?" I ask after a while.

He coughs again. "The sky is clearing," he says.

I'd forgotten about the sky. I look up and see the layer of clouds dissolving, coming apart. Behind them, in glimpses as if I'm looking through torn curtains, I see the wash of stars.

I sleep again. When I wake it is to thin daylight and a sound like the wings of many birds. In my ears a wild insistent flapping. I hear Tolomi climbing fast up the ladder to the deck where he pauses to yell down, *It's the wind.*

I get up and climb up beside him. The noise that awakened me, the flapping sound, was the sound of the sails. Tollomi is jumping back and forth with the lines in his hands, pulling.

"Michelle, we have wind!" Still holding a line, he reaches out as if to hug me, then ducks and pulls me down too as the boom goes careening over our heads. The sails fill with wind and tighten, and suddenly we're moving forward.

The stilled world on whose surface we have been floating is suddenly charged with life: wind, water, spray in motion all around us. I brace my legs against the cockpit to keep from falling, and Tollomi does the same. There is a kind of grace in this movement, like the grace of the wind itself. The grace of pure motion that even now, against the weight of our circumstances, cannot be dispelled or made small.

The wind is so strong that it's difficult to talk without shouting. We save our words for sailing: questions, instructions. Not until dusk, when the wind drops, do we speak of the situation we are in.

Side by side in the cockpit we share a tin of nuts, divide an orange.

"You know sooner or later they'll be looking for us," Tollomi says.

"Do you think they're looking already?"

"It's been three days. Sam's an American. All your faithful customers will have noticed you can't be found. There's going to be an investigation. And sooner or later they'll notice his boat is gone. We have to get off the water."

I look at the water. It's all there is to look at besides the sky. The idea of land in the midst of such water seems peculiar, absurd almost. As if land doesn't exist, really. As if we'll just go and keep going, fall off the edge of the earth after all.

"*Can* we get off the water?" I ask.

"Oh, yes," Tollomi says, his voice quiet suddenly, half-thinking of something else. "With wind we can."

"But the boat," I say.

"Yes?"

"They'll be looking for this boat. Not for us, necessarily. For this boat."

"Yes," he says, "but because the bar was burned everyone's attention will be on that. They'll be looking for Dominicans. It's possible no one has even noticed the boat is gone."

It sounds thin to me. To him too, I can tell. But he can't think of anything better, so he goes on: "And even if they find the boat after we've docked, so long as we're not on it, they'll never know who—" He stops and sucks his teeth in disgust. "Forget it," he says. "That's ridiculous. You can't sail a boat like this, a wood-hulled Sparkman & Stephens, for God's sake, into *any* harbor without everyone finding out who the skipper is. We're in an impossible situation."

"Because of the boat?" I ask.

"Yes, because of the boat. Because it belongs to a dead man who you happened to kill."

He's scared. I realize why I don't feel frightened as well: What's already happened is more frightening than what could possibly happen in the future. Or is that what everyone believes to give themselves the courage to go forward? I don't know. But we're going forward. "This boat," I say, "we'll have to sink it, then."

"Michelle, come on."

"I'm serious." I am.

"You want to try *swimming* to shore?" He grips the tiller as if I might try to pry the boat out of his hands.

"There's a dinghy," I remind him. "Tollomi, we have to sink it. You just said all the reasons why yourself."

"Michelle, it's impossible. You're suggesting that we sink this boat offshore and then what? Just row the dinghy, a *mahogany* dinghy, for God's sake, into some harbor and hope nobody notices?"

"Does it have to be a harbor?" I ask. "Isn't there some way we could just row to shore on some beach?"

"And come ashore in the midst of a gaggle of sunbathing tourists?"

"I don't mean a beach like that. Just listen to me for a sec—"

He starts coughing again, deep rattling coughs still full of seawater. I wait, and finally he raises his head and does listen—I can tell by his eyes.

"A beach where no one is," I say. "You know these islands: Think. Somewhere deserted, where no one would see us come ashore, but where we could find some way of getting to a town, a city. There must be places like that."

He looks at me for a while without saying anything. Then he gets up and goes down into the cabin. I think he's gone to get a map, a chart, but he comes back empty-handed except for an orange. We've already eaten our ration for the day, but I don't say anything.

Without speaking, he peels the orange, taking a long time. He eats half, offers the other half to me. We eat in silence; I wait. And then he begins to speak, to tell a story. He begins at the end, with a promise he made to a dead woman. He promised he would go and say goodbye to her, if only the wind would return.

"What was her name?" I ask.

He holds up the orange peel, shaped like a star. "Josephine," he says. And then in a different voice, a strange singsong voice I have never heard him use before, he repeats it.

"Jo-se-phine."

Impossible, I told her. We can't sink it. Cannot. No.

But even as I said it I knew I was wrong. It is not only possible but necessary: She's killed a man. I have stolen his highly conspicuous boat. If we are to reach a shore safely, the boat must not. The boat will have to go the way of everything that doesn't make it back to land. There is no way it can be otherwise. This boat with its mahogany and brass and hand-rubbed oak is another body whose time has come to drown.

But I don't like the idea. I don't want to be part of drownings anymore. And I don't want to let this boat go. And, more simply, I'm afraid.

Strange that we, who have spent our lives running away from places, have taken this tendency to such a wild degree. And strange too that stronger than my fear of being caught, stronger than the fear of drowning even, is my fear of going back to St. Croix.

Everything will be changed. Really everything. Even the house is gone now, even the trees, uprooted in the hurricane. Months have passed since then; new, unrecognizable buildings will be going up. Everyone I loved there is not there anymore, gone away, dead. Even the reefs will be different; I read somewhere years ago that the oil refinery broke them up.

But the wind freshens, blows hard as the moon rises. And I come about, run south through the night, through the Mona Passage. I will never again see Josephine's face. Nor walk through the rooms of the house we lived in. The house has been swallowed up by the sea. But this wind continues, pushing us on, a perfect wind, steady out of the northwest. We point toward St. Croix so easily I scarcely need to sail.

A day, a night, the day again. Save for the sun transiting slowly, the stars wheeling around Polaris at night, there is no indication time is passing. A day seems enclosed into a single elongated minute, compressed, while the sea around us in all directions expands.

Strange to sail a boat you know will soon be sinking. Strange to know the man who fathered me was a sailor too. Strange I cannot get the sea out of my lungs. I can't stop coughing. My lungs still feel heavy with water, and when I swallow it's with the taste of salt. I'm a sailor. I've nearly drowned before. But this time it seems to have stuck with me. The salt on my skin from sweating no longer seems indigenous to my body. It seems to be sea itself inside me, leaking through my pores.

I show Michelle the rudiments of night sailing. She wants to sail at night; she can't sleep at night anymore, she says. She's quiet, sleeps on deck all morning, a sheet thrown over her body to shield her from the sun. When she wakes in the early afternoon, she goes and sits in the bow, the wind hard on her face. Then she comes and sits by me, eyes streaming from the wind or from memory; she doesn't care to say. I give her the tiller and lie stretched out on deck. Night comes. I note the stars overhead, check our bearings. The stars anyway are the same.

I didn't know it could feel like this, my body. The feel of the wind on my face, the feel of darkness, the pull of the tiller against my hands. The feel of night above my head, stretching up and up, the feel of the stars. My hands around Tollomi's arms when I pulled him out of the water. My feet, my toes against this varnished wood. The feel of salt drying on my skin. The bottled water tasting of sun and plastic. My hands around the anchor I hit him with. Sam. This has turned out to be my life. I have made it, like I made the house. What my grandfather set in motion has been ridden by me up to this point, this astonishing point.

And now I am coming about, trimming the sails.

My body hurts. My skin hurts, and under the skin, my muscles. Not with the ache of work—they're too strong for that. They hurt with the ache of waking. It's as if I didn't recognize these sensations as belonging to my body, as if I didn't recognize my body itself, as if I thought it was someone else's. It was someone else's. But I can feel it now, like I can feel my own destiny. This is why I left home. It's why I built the house. This is why I raised that anchor and brought it crashing down on the head of a man whose touch on that girl's body I knew as if her body were my own. This is why I lay motionless through years of darkness under my grandfather's beautiful hands, the same hands that signed bogus land deals, carried suitcases, lifted highballs to his lips again and again and again. To arrive at this astonishing place. To discover my body. Like any discovery, it's a surprise to the discoverer only. It's been known to itself all along.

The history of travel is the history of mistakes. I didn't mean to kill him.

But am I sorry?

No.

The cloud mass is visible before the island is. Drawn by the heat of earth, fat cumuli gather like gulls do above a fishing boat, white, rolling, waiting to descend. The land itself seems a cloud at first, something humped low on the horizon, a mist mound, peaks swollen with rain. But no, there's the gray-green of foliage as we draw nearer, the outline of rock suddenly sharp in the brilliant light of almost dusk that makes everything look slightly surreal. *Mirage,* I think for a moment, relieved at the idea: Perhaps there is nothing there, we're off course completely, we'll sail until we drown. I am afraid of this island. I am afraid that despite all its changes it still exists, is still real. And it is: The sun sets, the light shifts and changes, and though the island fades into darkness even as we approach it, no stars appear to falsify the space it occupies.

I sail another hour only. We have to stay well outside the reefs. We're still too deep to drop anchor, but I remember the currents out here. I remember the drift. We're on the southern approach, offshore from the east end, the deserted part of the island where no houses are, no people, no dock, nothing. Just coastline and cliffs and birds. Assuming the land here is the same as it was twenty years ago. Perhaps a big assumption— I don't know anymore. I know we've crossed the line beyond which other courses of action become impossible. We've charted our approach in indelible pen.

Neither of us slept that night. We stayed on deck watching the stars shift as the world rotated on its puny axis, the sea with it. In the half-light before dawn the island grew visible again, dark while the sky behind it lightened, a suggestion of solidarity, no more. We were too far offshore for safe rowing, but to go closer would have meant trapping the boat inside the reefs. There was no choice but to do it where we were. So we did it. Into the dinghy we put the last gallon of water and the remaining tin of nuts—we had finished the oranges. As the sun was coming up we took the boat's axe and together chopped a hole in the beautiful mahogany hull on the lee side of the stern.

I wasn't sure how long it would take to sink. In the minutes when I could hear water rushing but we still floated well, the panic of drowning surged back into my lungs in stabs of pain. The suck of the sea all around us, pulling at the hull, waiting to pull us down. Suppose I had misjudged the distance and we were still too far offshore? Suppose the dinghy leaked? I began coughing again and couldn't stop. Michelle was already seated at the oars, waiting. Beneath my feet the boat shifted almost imperceptibly, but with a sickening in the timber that I felt shoot through me, and I knew then what rats feel that warns them that a sinking is at hand.

Coughing again, I climbed down into the rocking dinghy and put my head between my knees, willing the spasms in my chest to ease, subside. I felt Michelle begin to row. When I sat up again, I looked past her head bent over the oars. I could see color on the horizon, a distant green and brown, vague in the morning light. And in this blurred and partial glimpse of land, even from so far away, I recognized for the first time its outline as familiar, the way you recognize a beloved face still too distant to really see. So I recognized the island; the same rocky earth, the same shape rising above the water. I knew the color of the water at this hour of the morning, I knew the look of the land, the earth in which Josephine lay buried. Even after so much time and at such a distance, I knew it. These things, and perhaps only these things, were the same. I could see that they were, even blinded as I was by sunlight and tears.

My arms rowing, the pull of the water around the oars as I pull them again and again through the weight of the sea. The sun climbs. *Rest. I'll row now,* Tollomi says. But I don't want to rest. Not because I can't stop, not because I'm afraid of what will happen if I hold still. It's already happened. And my heart hurts now in a way that nothing has ever hurt in me before. But it's my heart. Mine.

I don't want to rest because my body is strong enough now that I don't have to. Because I built a house. Because I've killed a man. Because I like the feel of pushing backward through the water. Because I like the shifting in the muscles of my back. Because I can.

No shadows. Skimming over the reefs. Blue water changes to green. Across the water, the line of the cliffs comes suddenly into focus. And down through the green water, the sight of sand.

We're almost there. The groves on shore are visible now, the great manchineel trees clustered together, the shimmering heat held within. Here we stop rowing. We go over the side of the dinghy, first one and then the other, and capsize it, nothing between the water and our bodies now. We will swim the last of the way, come ashore with no sign of what brought us here, meet the land with our bodies and nothing more.

Salt water all around. The land smell of the cliffs. No sounds but the wind and the water and our limbs moving through them. Then the sound of birdsong, birds calling. On shore the trees are filled with birds.

Inside the last reef, the surf quiets. A pale beach, empty save for one silvery dead tree trunk and masses of black seaweed strewn along the waterline. We swim through the moving water. In a moment our feet will hit sand.

Rising up, the backward slap of waves. One step, then another. Blinking in the sting of salt and brightness, at the strangeness of after so much sea, the land. The shift and turn of sand beneath our feet. Here we are. We have reached this place at last. This is the place beyond the edge that looked like the end of the world.

ACKNOWLEDGMENTS

I am grateful to Dina Ciraulo and Heidi Ehle for the patient attention and wise words they gave to the shaping of this book. My sincere thanks also to Jeannie Simms, Erik Gleibermann, Terri Winston, Michael Gabriel, Debra Griffin Greene, and Martha Steele for critical feedback, encouragement, and typing—over a very long period of time. I was fortunate to be part of the Caribbean Writers Summer Institute and the Shoeless Writing Group, both of which provided much-needed community and insight. Angela Brown and Karen Nazor made excellent editorial suggestions during the process of bringing this book to publication.

The transliteration of the Taino language in the story of Cotubanama follows Joaquin Priego's retelling of this legend in *Cultura Taina*.

My family—all of it—provided key inspiration; special thanks to Pinky Hart for laying the foundation.

To Jaem Heath O'Ryan and Victor Vásquez y Vásquez, enormous gratitude. Without your presence in my life, this story would not be.

Sarah Pemberton Strong was born in California in 1967. She now lives outside of Boston. *Burning the Sea* is her first novel.